Scarlett Says

Other books by Julie L. Cannon

Twang

Truelove & Homegrown Tomatoes

'Mater Biscuit

Those Pearly Gates

The Romance Readers' Book Club

I'll Be Home for Christmas

Scarlett Says

Julie L. Cannon

Abingdon fiction
a novel approach to faith

Scarlett Says

Published by Abingdon Press, P.O. Box 801, Nashville, TN 37202

www.abingdonpress.com

Published in association with the MacGregor Literary Agency.

Library of Congress Cataloging-in-Publication Data

Cannon, Julie, 1962-
Scarlett Says / Julie L. Cannon.
    pages cm
ISBN 978-1-4267-5357-2 (binding: soft back; pbk./trade pbk. : alk. paper) 1. Self-realization in women—Fiction. 2. Identity (Philosophical concept)—Fiction. I. Title.
PS3603.A55S33 2014
813'.6—dc23

2014002087

Printed in the United States of America

1 2 3 4 5 6 7 8 9 10 / 18 17 16 15 14

F
Can

1

It's Friday, and Siegfried's being particularly annoying as he walks back and forth through the front office, emptying all the wastebaskets and saying things like "It grieves my heart to see you missing out on life, Miss Joan. Spending all your time on that computer."

He thinks I should get out more. But he knows that's not really gonna happen. And he knows all too well why. That I *can't*. Still . . .

"You gonna retire one day, and you won't have no children or grandbabies to come by and see you and light up your life."

I try to ignore him. Not easy. His tone is light, but his voice booms around the cubicles. He knows I don't worry about the future and being lonely, so I say nothing. Unfortunately, Siegfried really gets bent out of shape if you ignore him. Believe you me, I've tried numerous times over the past three years to wait him out, and it never works.

But I'm just impatient and irritable enough today to try one more time. I noisily shuffle some papers and try to exude invisible waves of unapproachableness as I check my watch. Not quite 4:00 yet. Siegfried's early with the trash. He usually is on Friday because he knows everybody at Giffin & Burke beats an early retreat for the weekend. Except me. I'm basically through with work, but I have to man the phones until 5:00, so I'll have a good hour to respond to Laverna in Alabama's comment about my latest post on my *Scarlett Says* blog.

"Tomorrow Is Another Day: The Beauty of Putting Things Off" had generated some serious feedback.

"You deaf?" Siegfried finally stops in front of my desk, one arm around the breakroom wastebasket. Picture a tall, bone-thin, very dignified, elderly gentleman with dark skin and fuzzy gray hair who wears half-lens reading glasses so low on his nose they look like they're fixing to slip off any second.

"I'm not missing out on life! And you don't exactly have a passel of grandkids running around." I let out a long breath, trying to show how tired I am of this. "I do socialize!"

"But I've got a big family. And my church. You just got a mama you don't talk to much, and that computer—"

"You know why I don't talk to Bitsy. You even encourage me not to."

He won't be discouraged. "—and a computer is . . . that's *anti*social!"

"Okay, Mr. Brilliant. So that's the reason they call it 'social media' and 'social networking'?"

He puts one hand on his chest. "My opinion, virtual and reality do not even belong in the same phrase."

"Would you kindly just let me finish my work, Siegfried?"

"I can tell you're already done, the way you keep shuffling things around. And I *am* your work," he says. "I'm employed by Giffin & Burke, and that makes you *my* administrative assistant, too." He stops, grinning at me.

This is actually true—occasionally I make calls and place orders online for the cleaning products, toilet paper, and paper towels Siegfried requests. I process payments and receipts for businesses he contracts with, folks like carpet shampooers and window washers. I sigh again, looking up at his beautiful smile. "Okay. What do you need?"

He sets the wastebasket down, puts his hands on my desk, and leans in to whisper, "I need you to type a e-mail to one of my favorite women in this world. In the universe! Ask her if she would be willing to meet a tall, dark, and handsome gentleman at the V for supper tomorrow."

I intend to say quit harassing me, but I can't. Despite our age difference, Siegfried is one of the few friends I have who is not on the other side of a screen. And his eyes are so sincere and kind, so touching. "Thanks, Siegfried. That's really sweet. But I can't. I'm busy."

"Then get unbusy. Let a friend buy a couple dogs, some crispy rings, two tall frosty FOs." His eyebrows are way up high, his glasses literally trembling on the tip of his nose. He definitely knows my biggest weakness. Just thinking of the smell of fried onions and hotdogs on the grill at the Varsity, washed down with a delectable Frosted Orange, is making me salivate.

But I shake my head. "You know I'm a takeout kinda girl."

"Come on. Be fun. I know you ain't busy *all* the livelong day. We could meet for a late breakfast or lunch or an afternoon snack of chili-cheese fries and Co-Colas with crushed ice!" He closes his eyes, shakes his head in ecstasy to hum three beats—"Mmmmm mmmm mmmm."

"Oh, Siegfried, you act like . . ."

"Like what?"

Like I'd be able to just up and do something like that, especially on such short notice. Like I'm some kind of confident social butterfly who can decide to alter her usual Saturday routine and flit off to downtown Atlanta with calmness and confidence. Like I don't have an actual diagnosis for my anxiety . . .

7

"Like I'm lying. I really *am* busy all the livelong day."

This is true. On weekends, besides eating, sleeping, reading an occasional novel, reading or watching *Gone with the Wind*, and doing household duties I absolutely cannot avoid, I work on my blog for the coming week.

I love my blog. And my followers. The thing is, I cannot force the posts. They almost always come as a surprise, but that said, I do have to be available to the inspiration, and before I discover it, there's this huge pressure in my chest and stomach, an incredible frustration mixed with insane hunger. I'm a complete mess, at least before I get the topic. And I don't get soothed, feel anywhere near human, until I'm sitting at my computer, typing away like crazy. My search for, and the writing of, my blog posts involve a concentration that is totally encompassing.

And I do this at least three times a week. I need Saturday to write one . . . and recover.

But I love it. Because no matter how difficult or frustrating, it's a blissful state. A mental zone. Being focused like that is satisfying. It's why I'm so happy to seclude myself. Why I feel grouchy when I have to deal with other people's unreasonable expectations. Like my mother's. And Siegfried's.

Expectations that make me break out in a cold sweat.

" 'Hast thou found honey?' " Siegfried quotes. " 'Eat so much as is sufficient for thee, lest thou be filled therewith, and vomit it.' "

"Okay." I sigh. "Tell me what verse and its practical application for life today." I say this dutifully, though I know he will anyway. Another annoying thing about Siegfried is that he has memorized the entire book of Proverbs in the King James Bible, and like a Hallmark greeting card, he has one for every occasion.

"Chapter 25, verse 16. Means a person's got to have moderation in all things of life—in food, work, enjoyments, et cetera." He turns serious. "Everybody needs some downtime, Joan." He looks pleadingly into my face.

I'm struck a little mute by his comment about food because I'm a big woman—five feet, three inches, and size 16. Bitsy calls me stout, disapproval in her voice. One reason, of many, we don't talk much.

But just as quick, I know Siegfried doesn't mean anything negative by it. Not like my mother. Siegfried may be a string bean, skinny enough that he has to run around in the shower to get wet, but I'm certain he's not getting down my throat about weight. I'm sure, because he's constantly bringing me calorie-laden treats, and here he is, trying to get me to meet him at the Varsity, no less, where I'm sure you could get fried Coke if you only asked.

"Yes, that's true," I finally say. "But we all have different kinds of ways of getting our downtime."

"Don't nothing substitute for the heartfelt, personal connection." Siegfried speaks in a solemn tone. "Plus, I can't believe you turning down a friend who wants to celebrate the day of your birth. And, after our sumptuous repast, I plan to carry you down to the Margaret Mitchell House on Peachtree Street for a little tour, because I ask myself, I said, 'Siegfried, my man, what would delight Miss Joan's heart the most on her special day?'"

I feel myself stop breathing. How in the world does he know it's my birthday tomorrow? My birthday plans, besides avoiding phone calls and drive-bys from Bitsy, are to pick up a Murphy's Burger—avocado, mayonnaise, Swiss cheese, smoked bacon—and a side of fries from my favorite neighborhood restaurant, Murphy's, on Virginia Avenue, and then run into Kroger for a container of Ben & Jerry's Heath Bar Crunch ice cream. The perfect feast to enjoy while perusing the pages of a Doubleday Book Club catalog for a gift to myself.

Suddenly, I'm ashamed at the self-centeredness of it all. I feel like the biggest heel on this earth as Siegfried stands there, waiting for my reply.

I look up at him, flustered, my heart beating out *No, no, no, no, Joan. You must avoid saying yes to him at all costs*, and then I shock myself silly by saying, "All right."

2

Just *thinking* about tomorrow, about the Varsity, makes my palms sweat so much that I rub them on the sheets repeatedly. How did Siegfried get me to consent to meeting him? I may be outspoken on my blog, but I don't handle the outside world with its demands and expectations very well. I'm an absolutely awful dinner companion, the worst party guest you can imagine. Bitsy has reminded me of this many times.

I roll over onto my back, then to my stomach, my side, curl into a fetal ball while clutching the extra pillow for a while, then back to my stomach. I squeeze the pillow hard, fervently willing it to have been a dream, er, a nightmare. But no, this is real. I look at the glowing red numerals of my digital clock—1:43 a.m. I should cancel, just call him and cancel. But I like Siegfried. Not "like" like, I mean, he's way too old for me. But he *is* a friend. I don't want to disappoint him.

I press the pillow over my face, have one of those very brief and not truly heartfelt fantasies about dying, thinking, *This'll show Siegfried—when he finds me dead!*

Then it hits me—what my salvation will be! Must be! I need some of Scarlett's boldness, her defiant demeanor that says *Forget the world. I'll do whatever I darn well please.* Snaking my hand out through the dark, I turn on the bedside lamp, maneuver onto my side, and pick up the weighty copy of *Gone with the Wind* from my nightstand. There's a small, sweet meditative silence as I prepare to channel some inspiration, some wisdom from the thousand-plus pages that transformed my life long ago.

With a deep breath I bow my head, close my eyes, open the novel at random, and plunk my pointer finger down on the page. My "literary roulette."

The place I land is smack in the middle of chapter 22, right after Prissy has delivered Melanie's baby. I could quote it by heart, but I read every syllable about how Scarlett thinks Prissy's bragging, how she gets jealous, and then how she muses that if the Yankees wanted to free them, they could have them.

I stop, scowling, and Siegfried's face comes to mind. He's certainly not the first black person I've ever known, but he's the first one I've ever had as a friend. Not that I've had all that many friends. But for the first time, in all the times I've read the book, when I read the words, I see a friend's face in them.

All of a sudden, my stomach lurches, and I feel the blood fly out of my head with shock. I lie there numb, light-headed, my mind whirling. *This is awful! It's offensive! How've I not seen this before?* But as if of their own volition, my eyes read on—to the part where Scarlett pushes Prissy down the stairs and threatens to sell her.

I slam the book shut and hurl it across the room. I've read this novel, and thus this scene, more than twenty times prior to this, but never have I felt like I want to climb into the pages and slap Scarlett senseless. Scarlett! The person I love more than anyone else in the world. On second thought, it would be more gratifying to watch *Prissy* slap Scarlett while I cheer her on from the sidelines! Why have I never noticed this ugly side of Scarlett?

Is it because of Siegfried? Or have I just been blind to this side of Scarlett because I love the rest of her so much?

After several minutes, I turn over on my stomach and cry for a long time. I'd been so caught up, lost actually, in Scarlett's beguiling nature, her charisma, as well as her stormy relationship with the debonair Rhett Butler, that I failed to see the principles that guide her life. I consider this and finally tell myself I obviously did not start my *Scarlett Says* blog with a surplus of wisdom. It wasn't like I said: "Man, Joan Meeler, you need an outlet for this brilliance running around in your head!"

When I began my illustrious blog, I was just trying to repay a debt I owe to Scarlett. I needed a way to make my voice heard despite my affliction.

Saturday morning my eyes pop open at 6:00 on the dot. I lie in bed, desperately wishing I hadn't agreed to go to the Varsity, thinking, *If I'm meeting Siegfried at noon, I've got four hours to write my blog with two hours left to get ready and make my way to downtown Atlanta.* There's a tightness at my center, and I know I need to sit down and start typing. I need to feel that release. But the problem is I'm not a robot. I'm an artist, and I can't push myself into creativity. There's a certain element of surrender involved in writing my blog, and even after two years, I still have to work hard to let go of my crippling self-consciousness so my muse can swoop into action.

I go into the kitchen and make coffee double strong. Looking out the kitchen window as dawn breaks over Virginia Highlands, I fancy I see the shape of Bitsy's gray Escalade gliding along Ponce de Leon Avenue. My stomach pulls into a knot. There's no way I'm answering the door today, I think, struck anew at how close I live to my mother and simultaneously wondering for the zillionth time if I'm not just some glutton for punishment.

After graduation, I stayed here in Atlanta, less than half an hour from where I grew up in Brookhaven. I picked this area because it's an old, historic neighborhood in the city, with charming twentieth-century bungalows and tree-lined streets. I rent a one-bedroom, one-bath apartment in a complex modeled after those homes—but not really anything like them. It would take an inheritance for me to be able to afford to buy one of the cute homes I long for.

I wonder briefly if I'm one of those subconsciously graspy children wishing for a parent's demise. I close that thought down by acknowledging that in the natural order of things, parents do precede their children in death.

Anyway, due to our proximity to each other, every now and again Bitsy drops by unexpectedly. If I'm not on guard, she'll pop right in, stand there inside the door—tall, slender, and elegant, her frosted hair perfectly coiffed, stylish earrings dangling on either side of her still-pretty face with the perfect bone structure. She wears the latest fashions and coordinating Manolo Blahniks on her feet. We're like two negatively polarized magnets being pushed apart by some invisible force—she with her shopping and ladies' luncheons and cocktail partying and decorating, and me with my hermit self, content in an apartment with nothing but the 1980s neutral-colored furniture I bought at a thrift store the day I moved in, in exactly the same arrangement I put it in that day.

Except for the red sofa. I love that sofa, with its high back and winged sides. Siegfried helped me pick that one out during one disastrous afternoon—that's when he got to see the "social anxiety" (that's what my therapist calls it) in high form. A complete meltdown when the salesmen kept hovering, kept pressuring. Siegfried shooed them away, got me to admit I loved the sofa, took my credit card, and made it all happen. He even drove me home and waited for them to deliver it.

Bitsy's always hated it. Calls it old-fashioned and out of style. Like me. Yep, I do love that sofa.

The last time she dropped by, unannounced as usual, was a rainy Saturday afternoon two weeks ago. I stood, surprised and clutching a half-empty bag of mini powdered doughnuts as I spied her head through my door's peephole. I had to fight the urge to crawl under the table and hide. I stashed the doughnuts behind the telephone shelf near the door and let her in. She looked remarkable in a shrimp-colored cotton sweater, short black skirt, and flirty sandals with ankle straps. I was in my blogging clothes, with no makeup and lank hair. She wore a tight smile, and I could see disapproval in her green eyes, but out came her lilting cocktail-party voice.

"Joan, darling, how nice to see you! I called and called but couldn't get you, and so I thought I'd just drop by with this lovely dress I found for you at Betsey Johnson." She paused and held up a black sheath. "I know it will be so slimming. Now, go get cleaned up and I'll treat you to dinner at the Capital City Club. You've got two hours to get your shower, do your hair and makeup. I brought a novel along to entertain myself while I wait." She dug in her giant leather handbag and produced a battered paperback of Judith Krantz's *Scruples*. "Be a great way to meet lots of eligible hunks, I'm certain of that." She lifted her finger holding the dress and waggled it so that the plastic bag rustled, as though it were some juicy bone, and I was a starving dog.

I shook my head. "No. But thanks."

"What?" Her voice crescendoed to a shrill note. "Whyever not?"

"I'm working on something."

"On what?"

"Something."

"Oh, Joan," she said with an exasperated sigh. "What is *wrong* with you?"

When she was gone, a hollow ache tugged at my heart as I sat at my desk finishing my doughnuts. I didn't *want* to feel happy that I'd evaded her yet again. Having such an unattractive hermit for a daughter must be a hard cross for Elizabeth Hargrove Meeler to bear. That's why she sent me to the therapist when I was a teenager. She was convinced the right drugs, the right "talk therapy," would turn me into her.

It's been a splendid success so far.

Well . . . okay, I can keep a job now. I can deal with familiar people and situations. But it's always going to take a major effort of will to get me out of the house every day, and nothing short of a personality transplant will ever turn me into another Bitsy.

Even if I wanted that.

The coffeemaker gurgled. Removing the half-and-half from my refrigerator, I spy a luscious-looking ruby red quarter of a watermelon purchased on my last grocery trip. It makes me think of this news story I read several years back about a black salesman who worked at a car dealership in Kentucky. He was suing them for racial harassment, alleging that two supervisors insulted him by giving him pictures of gorillas eating watermelon. I contemplate hunting that story down, posting it on my blog, then getting an ongoing dialogue on whether that's racism or not. Just as quickly, I discard the notion.

I'm not so quick to jump on a topic these days. I've come to realize that when I'm incubating ideas for my blog, every single activity becomes imbued with deep significance. I find merit in almost everything I encounter. And I don't want to jump into this because I know race can be a volatile subject. Out of respect for its importance, I want to use some time to take stock of my own attitudes, as well as Scarlett's.

This topic would be a lot more difficult than one that comes up every so often—that ever-popular question: *Did Scarlett ever get Rhett back?*

And I never know what'll set readers off. Toward the end of March I was driving down Briarcliff Road, and I got behind one of those huge monster trucks about twice as tall as my little Toyota. The back windshield was a see-through decal of the Confederate flag. That was on a Thursday, and come the weekend, I'd formulated a blog about the history of the Confederate flag, including that it's based on Saint Andrew's cross, as many other national flags are. Pretty much just the facts.

But this led to one of my more controversial blogs ever. My fan comments went into overdrive. One man said the flag should be banned in the twenty-first-century South because it was a shameful reminder of slavery and segregation. Another follower started arguing with him and said it was a proud emblem of Southern heritage. One fan, a historian, said that a large degree of the Southern population was of Scottish and Scotch-Irish ancestry, and thus beholden to Saint Andrew, the patron saint of Scotland who was martyred by being crucified upside-down on an X-shaped cross. He was all for displaying it with pride.

My angriest, most vocal responder was a man from Boston, who was furious that people still displayed the Confederate flag at all. He said that had it been appropriated not only by the Ku Klux Klan but also by more than five hundred extremist hate groups. What astonished me most was when he said he wished he had the real names and addresses of several pro responders to my post so he could "personally come and blow their heads off!" An awful reaction for someone preaching against hate.

I carry my coffee and two Cinnabon cinnamon rolls to my desk and turn on my ancient laptop. I contemplate opening lines while waiting for it to warm up. Generally, it's Scarlett's "spirit" I try to channel when I sit down to blog. But this morning, the scene with Prissy continues to haunt me, so I'm trying hard to ignore Scarlett and choose my own thoughts to begin.

I type: *Is racism more deeply ingrained in the South, the states of the old Confederacy, than in other areas? After all, it was the issue of slave labor from Africa that separated the Southern states from the rest of the American union.* Just as quickly, I highlight this and hit delete. Too in-your-face. My job is to lure my readers in gently, make them understand something important that they need to see. I know that to rattle, to confront too soon is to drive them away.

I begin again: *My favorite quotation in the entire world is what Martin Luther King Jr. said about prizing the content of a person's character over a person's race.* I delete that, too, finish my cinnamon rolls and lick the saucer. My mind races back to history class and Lincoln's Emancipation Proclamation of September 1863, and the black abolitionist Frederick Douglass's shouts of joy. No, this isn't a history lesson. I go make more coffee and return, shaking with the overdose of caffeine and the agony of writer's block. This blog's a real bear. I'm scared I'll never get it right.

Two hours pass and I decide to call Siegfried and tell him I can't come. Just as I'm dialing him, my phone rings and Bitsy's number appears on the screen. On impulse, I fling my phone out of sight. I rest my head on my desk until I calm down enough to try again. By 10:45 a.m. I've done six different beginnings, one major write on two, a sort of rewrite on one of those, deleting them all with an exasperated press of my index finger. At eleven, time to stop and get ready to meet Siegfried, I know without a doubt this entry's never, ever going to come together. There are holes a mile wide in everything I've attempted to say. Even my thoughts about racism have sizeable gaps. Just as I'm turning my computer off, this lilting cocktail-party voice chimes in my brain, and it's not Scarlett's. It's Bitsy's, saying how incredibly improper it is that I'm meeting a black man for lunch.

3

My apartment is less than two miles from the Varsity, and because traffic is light, I pull into the parking lot with ten minutes to spare. I sit in my car, short of breath, nauseated, and feeling faint. I talk to myself, just the way my therapist coached me to. "Breathe slowly, Joan. Relax your muscles. Deep breaths. Siegfried will be here soon. You know him. He'll be an anchor. He'll make it okay."

I went to a focus group on social anxiety one time, although my therapist suggested I wasn't ready. The leader gave us this sentence to memorize, and I taped it to my bathroom mirror when I got home. It said, "Our thoughts trigger our emotions, which drive our actions, which then create our circumstances." He said all I had to do was think different thoughts, and a beautiful life would fall into place. I believed him, and so that Friday night I put on an orange sundress I'd never worn before and walked to Blind Willie's on West Highland Avenue. Blind Willie's is a blues bar with live music, and the whole way there, I was saying to myself, *You're a social butterfly, and you're gonna have so much fun. You'll meet lots of people, and it'll be great.*

When I got there, I was sweating all over, but I walked right in. The house band, The Shadows, was performing, and as I stood there in the crowd of people dancing and laughing, I really tried to move my hips and laugh, but I got dizzy and confused, and my heart started going like a jackhammer. Even though inside I was saying, "Joanie, you're calm. You're good," my body just had a mind of its own and I got a bit frantic. I ran outside and squatted behind some camellia bushes until I got myself back together enough to get home.

No more focus groups with promises of quick fixes.

My Toyota is getting to be a sauna. It's four minutes past noon, and I'm sweating profusely. I straighten the stack of fast-food napkins on the passenger seat while I try out my excuses. "Well, you were late, Siegfried, and I figured you were sick. I didn't notice my cell phone was turned off until I got home." I dig through my handbag and turn my cell phone off. "I wasn't feeling well, Siegfried! You know about my acid reflux." This is sort of true. I'm not feeling well, and he does know about my acid reflux, though I'm not experiencing it at the moment.

I try a relaxation technique I learned online: breathing to a slow rhythm while visualizing myself in a field of flowers beneath a blue sky. But what I see instead is a swarm of bees that are there to pollinate, and then I imagine myself passing out as Siegfried introduces me to several people he knows who're having lunch inside the Varsity. Generally, in a one-on-one situation with someone I know and trust, I can make it. But the thing about Siegfried is, besides knowing 99 percent of the population in Atlanta, the man never meets a stranger. He'd strike up a conversation with a telephone pole if it would answer. It's going to be the furniture store all over again. Meltdown.

Although I did get my red sofa out of that one.

No. I can't do this. I'm reaching for the ignition when I see Siegfried's emerald green Buick LeSabre pulling into the parking lot. He parks and climbs out, dressed in a black suit, white socks, and shiny black wing tips. I swear he looks like an exclamation point. He walks around to the passenger side of the backseat and bends over to get something—a large pasteboard box with a pink bow on top. He spies my little Toyota, and as he gets closer, I see glitter in the bow catching the sun and shooting sparkles.

My sweaty hands are slick on the steering wheel as I see him mouth "Hi" at the window on the driver's side. "Miss Joan!" he says, opening my door.

I turn to him and squeak out, "Hi, Siggy."

"Happy Birthday! You sure are a sight for sore eyes. Don't look a day over thirty!" Siegfried cracks himself up with this joke.

"Thanks. But I . . . I'm not feeling so great."

"Well, I know the cure!" He holds the box with his left arm, grabs my elbow with his right hand, and practically lifts me up and out, then closes my car's door with his foot. The words I put to the rhythm of our steps are, *What am I doing? Oh, get me home, please.*

When we get inside, Siegfried seats me at a window booth and places the box on the bench across from me, asks for my order, and goes to the counter. The Varsity is huge, all chrome and Formica and windows. The counter stretches the width of the restaurant, and behind it you see a dozen cooks flipping food on a sizzling grill. At the counter, a dozen employees are shouting out the infamous line "What'll ya have?" to endless lines of people waiting to order. The menu features your all-American favorites: hamburgers, hotdogs, grilled cheeses, French fries, onion rings, milkshakes, sodas, various fried pies, ice cream, and their famous concoction: the Frosted Orange, a blend of tart frozen orange juice and vanilla ice cream.

I sit motionless, avoiding eye contact with anyone, the hairs on the back of my neck standing alert.

A flash of memory shoots through my head, of being at a Junior League mother-daughter luncheon in Buckhead when I was sixteen. Bitsy kept prodding my knee beneath the white linen tablecloth, hissing in my ear, "Why didn't you answer Mrs. Kirsch?" and

"Sit up, Joan Marie! Smile! Compliment the food, the flowers, the room! Be sociable! Or you won't be invited back!"

Good, I thought.

Then there's the birthday card from her I got in yesterday's mail, lying unopened on the table in my kitchen. The recent string of messages on my phone about a thrice-divorced son of a friend of hers she wants to fix me up with. *Bitsy, please leave me alone.*

The box across from me moves a little bit and I jump, coming back to the present. I sit staring at it like it's a bomb.

Siegfried is back, bearing a red plastic tray laden with food and drinks. His presence, and the nearness of a hotdog running over with chili and a red-and-white checkered cardboard boat full of crispy golden onion rings, make me feel more relaxed. The smell of the onions mixed with the grease is heavenly. Beads of condensation run down the outside of my Frosted Orange.

My jaws are literally aching to eat, but Siegfried reaches across the table and grabs my hands. He closes his eyes, bows his head, and says in a singsong voice, "Dear Lord, thank you for knitting this child together in her mother's womb nine months and thirty years ago. Please give her a good year ahead, and thank you for this delicious food you bless us with. Nourish our bodies as we celebrate your gift of life to us. Amen."

There is a moment of silence, and I just sit there, looking down at my food, still aching to take a bite, but aware that Siegfried's waiting for my response. "Amen," I say, though I am not the praying sort.

He smiles and lifts his cheeseburger for a huge bite.

I take a slurp of Frosted Orange, a bite of my overflowing all-the-way dog. Delicious. I'm feeling pretty good right now. "Thank you, Siggy," I say, after blotting my chin with a napkin when I'm a quarter of the way through.

"You're absolutely welcome. It's my pleasure."

Just then the pasteboard box moves again. A scratching noise comes from inside. I try to ignore it because I'm about to begin my onion rings. Siegfried looks over at it and says, "Hold your horses in there. It ain't time for the gifting yet!"

I stuff a bunch of onion rings into my mouth, thinking of saying, *Siegfried, I'm allergic to animals* or *It would be cruel for me to have a pet as I'm gone so much.* Or, better yet, the truth, that when I was a child, my mother strictly forbade any "nasty, dirty, messy, disease-carrying animals" in our home, clucking her tongue, saying, "Shoo! Scat!" with fierce eyes, if I ever brought home a stray puppy or kitten or a wounded bird. It was as though the seeds of aversion that had been planted in me long ago were now giant oaks. I regarded house pets as most people regard opossums and armadillos— something okay to look at but not to touch.

Siegfried finishes his burger and dips his French fries one by one into a little cup of bleu cheese dressing. When he's all done with them, he slides a fried apple pie in front of me and another in front of himself. "Okay," he says, "time for a song."

I like our little insulated table, and I don't want to be gawked at. My heart begins pounding, and I can't get a breath as he reaches into his coat pocket and pulls out a tiny blue candle and a lighter. He sticks the candle into my pie and lights it.

Thankfully the Varsity's so packed and loud, and everybody's paying attention to their own food and people, that we get through Siegfried singing "Happy Birthday" without any foreign eyes on us.

I bite through the warm, flaky crust into a perfect tart-sweet blend of apples, cinnamon, and sugar. "This is delicious," I say, and I mean it, savoring my pie oh so slowly.

When we're done, Siegfried moves all our trash aside, lifts the box, and slides it across the table. Clearly he's excited, enjoying the anticipation. I'm not excited. My stomach wants to heave up everything I just enjoyed.

I clear my throat. "Really," I say. "You shouldn't have." I mean it with all my heart.

"I wanted to. Go on, now, open it up!"

My hands reach out and unfold the box flaps. Inside is a teeny little gray-and-white ball of kitten fluff, shaking and so skinny I can count every rib but with the most lavish tail I've ever seen. I mean, that tail must be two inches in diameter. "Thank you," I say. "But I really can't keep it."

"Yes, you can. It's a she, and I called your landlord before I went down to the shelter, and they allow pets."

"I meant the food and the litter box and the veterinary bills. I can't afford it." I tried not to look at the needy little creature who was now standing on tiptoe, her front paws on the edge of the box. She mewed up at me. *Stop being so cute!*

Siegfried laughs, slides his fingers back into that bottomless pocket of his suit coat, and pulls out an envelope. "Don't got to worry about that neither." His voice is warm and slow. "I went to the PetSmart and purchased a gift certificate."

I look away from him and say nothing. Since the first day I met him, Siegfried has pushed and pushed. Sometimes, since that day at the furniture store, it's gotten worse. Like he wants to cure me or something.

He lifts her from the box and presents her to me by stretching out his arms. The kitten rubs her cheek insistently against my wrist, and I feel an unexpected urge to hold the tiny creature. I take her slowly. She doesn't even weigh two pounds, and her bones are so sharp it feels like I'm holding a bird's nest. She curls into me and starts to purr so loud it sounds like a miniature jackhammer. All of a sudden, an unnameable feeling comes over me as I peer down at that pink nose, the spindly whiskers, and beseeching green eyes.

It's a little overwhelming.

Siegfried laughs. "I know you think she'll just be a bother. But this little girl will give back much more than the time it takes you to freshen her box and sprinkle chow into her bowl. She'll be waiting to greet you when you come home from work, she'll warm your feet on cold winter nights, and she will love you more than life itself."

Somewhere inside me, I think he might, I said *might*, be right. This shocks me even more than the fact that Siegfried is getting away with having a *live* animal inside the restaurant! Granted, there's no sign saying "No Pets Allowed" like there is one about "No Shirt, No Shoes, No Service," but knowing Siegfried, he'd get away with wearing only his swimsuit.

"What you gonna name her?"

I don't respond. Giving a name to this kitten will surely seal the deal. I put her back into the box and push it toward Siegfried. "Well," I say, "it would be unfair of me to take her. I might start traveling, and it would be terrible to leave her like that."

"Better watch out, your nose is growing." Siegfried chuckles. He pushes the box back toward me. "How 'bout call her Scarlett?"

Indignation shoots through me like a current. "No!"

"Whoa, now!" He flinches, tilts his head back, and looks hard at me through his half-lens glasses. "What's eating at you?"

I don't know how to say it.

"You look mad. You mad?"

I nod.

He reaches over, takes one of my hands between his own. "What's got your dander up?"

I don't want to say it. But as I sit, trying not to look at the kitten, trying not to feel these rough, warm hands, willing myself not to cry, everything comes spilling out of me. The whole story about my fury at Scarlett O'Hara's racism, how I feel guilty, betrayed, and frustrated that I cannot for the life of me get my blog written now that my muse is on my "bad" list.

"So, what I've decided is this," I say in a resolute tone that shocks me. "I'm going to quit *Scarlett Says*. I can't continue to promote her and have a clear conscience." *Where did that come from?* I don't know. But now that it's out, I'm certain it's the only solution to the growing turbulence inside me.

Siegfried's mouth falls open. "You're kidding!"

His response shows that you never really know anyone. "I thought you'd be happy, Siggy. I thought you were against 'social networking.'"

"I am. If that's *all* a person does. But you got a gift, Miss Joan. That blog you did on Scarlett's last line in the book was brilliant."

I smile, feel the heat of a blush warm my cheeks. Actually, Siegfried already said as much when he left a comment on my blog. He also included a proverb, something about not boasting about tomorrow because you don't know what a day may bring forth.

"If you quit blogging, what are all your virtual friends gonna do?" Siegfried is truly worried. "How many followers you up to now?"

In an intentionally blasé voice, I say "4,277," while millions of tiny bubbles dance around inside me. This feeling is a good one, and I wouldn't mind nurturing it, even if it is pride. But I can't let Siegfried see it, or else he'll find some Proverb to douse it with. Just saying this number aloud makes me miss my fans. Already, I feel a sense of bereavement for my online community. Before yesterday's, well, actually, this morning's revelation, it was my goal to reach five thousand.

"So, you planning to leave those loyal followers hanging?" Siegfried picks up some bits of leftover hamburger bun and feeds them to the kitten. She even looks cute chewing. "After they done put so much time and emotion into you?"

I sit there looking at him for a while, thinking of the myriad responses to "Tomorrow Is Another Day: The Beauty of Putting Things Off," especially one from a faithful Manhattan follower named Charles that went back and forth between us a dozen times at least. In fact, I'm still waiting on his response to my latest rebuttal. Charles was one of my very first followers, and sometimes at night, in bed, in the dark, I try to picture what he looks like, and sometimes I imagine how it might feel to have him in bed beside me. The first "marriage" fantasy I've had since I was nine. Charles has said before that he likes a "generous woman," which I interpret as large, and I like how we think so much alike, how we both enjoy a good argument. He calls me his feisty Scarlett.

Thinking of this, I feel a flower blooming inside, a warm blush in my cheeks. I can't do this right now. Instead, I turn my thoughts back to this dear man sitting across from me, this man who surely went through the thick of the civil rights movement. Funny, but I realize that I've never heard Siegfried complain a bit about the prejudice he must have encountered before, during, and even now. But here he is just sitting, perfectly at ease with himself, with the world.

How old would Siegfried have been when the civil rights movement began? The church bombing where the four girls died was in 1963, but I know it all started in the early '50s. "Um, well, I . . . I just don't know if I . . . well, I mean . . . Siegfried! Aren't you offended by the way black characters are treated in *Gone with the Wind*?"

Siegfried's eyebrows form an inverted V. "Okay," he says, slow and thoughtful. "Let me say this. I know lots of folks don't like the way Margaret Mitchell depicts black characters in her book. Claim her novel is hurtful and racist. But you got to remember, she is telling the story of the American Civil War and Reconstruction from a *Southern* point of view. Some folks say it's her personal hymn to the Lost Cause."

I cannot believe this! Betraying his own! "So?"

"So you can't escape history. Can't gloss over reality. I see it as her simply showing the way things were. I mean, let's face it, it definitely weren't no pretty time in our history!"

I sit quietly for maybe five seconds. I'm not so naive as to believe racism didn't exist then, or that it will ever be totally gone from the Deep South, but I'm shocked to hear this, and I say, rather loudly for me, "Siegfried Obadiah Smith! Scarlett treats Prissy like a dog! She even threatens to *sell* her!"

"Hey, hey, now. Calm down. I read the book. Seen the movie, too—couple of times—and I know personal liberty is many people's most precious possession. But you ought to know by now that I do not advocate censorship. Lots of things I read in my *Holy Bible* every morning, my *Atlanta Journal* every evening, see on the news, hear on the radio, lots of issues come up that seem—by my standards anyway—shocking, disrespectful, unkind, unfair, lewd, even prejudiced. Now, you know I personally do not condone exploiting or treating with disrespect even an imaginary person like Prissy, but at the same time, I realize I got to keep my personal reaction at bay. Yes, it is wrong to own another person. It is wrong to treat somebody the way slaves was treated. But I can't universalize my moral standards. I feel it's important to let people tell their stories without censorious interference." Siegfried rubs his chin. "Well, except in very extreme cases."

I sit there, a little stunned, taking it all in. He's right about some of it. Siegfried doesn't universalize his moral standards. He does make them known, however. Every single chance he gets. Funny, while I'm fairly certain Siegfried does not approve of the way I answer my blog followers while I'm on the clock, well, on the salary, at Giffin & Burke, neither do I think he judges me for it. "Aren't you mad?" I ask him. "Don't you have lingering wounds, hurts from before integration? Memories that haunt you from the civil rights movement?"

He sits quiet a minute, pulls a hanky from his trouser pocket, and pats his forehead before saying, "Got plenty of memories about growing up."

His gaze turns distant, and he wipes his eyes before tucking away the handkerchief.

I nod. "Tell me?"

He lowers his voice. "I lived with my auntie in Birmingham, and one night I remember we had to hide in the back of her house because of death threats. I remember the two of us listening to insults from whites on a long bus ride from Birmingham to Atlanta. I remember not being able to eat hotdogs at the lunch counter at the Woolworth's. Had to go to a back window. I wasn't allowed to go to the big public library, either. Had to go to the library for colored children. We drank out the water fountains with a sign that said 'Colored' fastened to the wall above it. I remember segregated schools and churches, my people not being allowed to participate in politics, not being covered by the law's protection."

My eyes stung. "Wow."

"But you know what?" He smiles such a big, genuine smile that my tears absorb back into the ducts. "Now I can enjoy all those things. And you want to know something funny?"

I'm afraid to ask. "What?"

"Mount Carmel Baptist is *still* segregated!" He laughs. "Not by law. We welcome peoples of all colors, but it is rare for a white man to darken our door. I'll tell you this, Joan, race relations may not be perfect, but they are dramatically better today than when I was growing up. Now we even got a *black* president!" He laughs and reaches in the box for the kitten, lays her gently against his shoulder like an infant.

This conversation is not going the way I imagined it would. I thought he would *want* me to quit, to return Scarlett to the past where she belonged. And I haven't read much of the Bible Siegfried likes to call his favorite book, but surely this Being called God doesn't condone slavery.

"So, what does *God* say about slavery?" I ask, my voice sounding screechy to my own ears.

A beautiful smile floods Siegfried's face. "Well, He is against it. He despised it when His peoples were slaves for the Egyptians for four hundred years! He sees oppression down here. He hears folks' groaning. And He moves to deliver in *His* time."

The man is so serene, completely peaceful, I'm almost afraid Siegfried may not be dealing with a whole deck. I'm confused about what to say to this last comment. *His* time?

I sit a minute, then look him right in the eye to say, "Well, I do not believe in slavery at any time, and I think we should do all we can in the fight against it."

"I like your passion, your ideals, but they don't change the past. I don't believe in censorious interference. What was, was."

The kitten is sound asleep, and we all sit quietly another few minutes until suddenly Siggy's eyes pop open wide. "How about Dandelion? She feels just like a dandelion puff!" He rubs the kitten behind her ears that are so big in proportion to her face that they put me in mind of a bat.

I shrug, my throat aching as I line up the salt and pepper shakers beside the napkin holder.

Siegfried is quiet for a moment. Then he says, "So . . . what made you pick Scarlett as your best friend in the first place?"

Every cell in my body tightens. I feel fear rising like a tidal wave. I will not tell him about my greatest shame, the fiasco in high school that started my love affair with Scarlett and *Gone with the Wind*. I say, "Well, she's fiery. She's strong and gutsy, and I appreci-ate—*used* to appreciate—Scarlett's ambition and the way she chal-lenges authority. My high school English teacher called her a rebel. I remember a line Mrs. Darnell wrote on the chalkboard that we had to copy down. 'Scarlett rebels against the restraints of a code of behavior that relentlessly attempts to mold her into a form to which she's not naturally suited.'"

Siegfried smiles. "Ain't that the truth! Scarlett sure ain't no sweet, ladylike Southern belle. She's gutsy, stronger than the men in the book, 'cept Rhett Butler. But being a rebel is how she man-aged to survive. Why she was able to rebuild Tara. She couldn't have done that if she was a simpering, faint-hearted female. Can't help but admire that."

"No! She's the pampered, spoiled daughter of a well-to-do plantation owner, born to privilege, arrogant and *mean*!"

"Scarlett ain't perfect, that's true. But like I said, racism and slavery were real things at the time *Gone with the Wind* took place. If she hadn't behaved the way she did, it wouldn't be real. Be a good thing for you to talk about in your blog."

I believe blogging about racism would be a very worthy subject, something people really need to think about, but I don't feel very confident about approaching it, about writing a compelling piece, and plus, my muse *is* a racist of the highest degree.

Siegfried strokes Dandelion's back while quiet moments pass between us. I can tell he's thinking hard, and now I'm starting to think about how much I'll miss Charles and our repartee. Also, I'll have a lot of empty hours to fill.

"I know!" Siegfried says suddenly, so excited that Dandelion pulls her head in and lays her ears back. "You could write about how Margaret Mitchell is the exact opposite of her character Scarlett! I read one time how she denied any similarities to Scarlett in her personal life. Say she favor Miss Melanie more than any of her characters. In fact, Ms. Mitchell secretly sent donations to Morehouse College, funding the education of dozens of African American medical students."

"Really?" I have to admit I'm shocked. "Why did she do it secretly?"

"Well, she could have gotten herself killed if word of something like that got out. At the time, there was a resurgence of the KKK, and there was lynchings going on, and a lot of racial violence in the South. Ms. Mitchell had to go underground after all her fame following the book. She couldn't say what she wanted to say in public. But, she kept doing what was in her heart. What she thought was right."

I am speechless. "How do you know this? Why do you know this?"

He laughed. "After I started reading your blog, I got curious. I hadn't exactly spent a lot of time with that book before. You were telling us everything about Scarlett, who ain't real. I wanted to know more about the real girl."

"You looked her up?" I'm annoyed that I'm so surprised.

"Yep. It ain't that hard. Ms. Mitchell created one of the most amazing books ever published, won herself a Pulitzer for it, and yet, the woman didn't take herself too seriously. She cared about people." He ruffled the fur underneath Dandelion's chin, laid her flat on her back in the crook of his arm and gazed tenderly at her. "But I believe there might've been a little bit of Margaret Mitchell in Scarlett. You ever hear about what got Ms. Mitchell shunned by the Junior League?"

This is right down my alley! "Tell me."

"Okay. There was a debutante ball, and Margaret Mitchell performed this dance with 'Apache' moves she learned watching Rudolph Valentino in a movie. We'd just passed the Nineteenth Amendment giving women the right to vote, and Ms. Mitchell and her partner were throwing each other around like savages. I heard it even caused some of the onlookers to faint." Siegfried chuckled. "Anyhow, it was a huge story. The *Atlanta Journal* had articles two days running. So Ms. Mitchell wasn't invited to join the Junior League. Wasn't but a little more than a decade later when she created Miss Scarlett, one of the strongest female figures in literature."

I say nothing. Just sit there taking all this in, gazing at Dandelion as she stretches luxuriously and yawns, the inside of her mouth such a tender shell-pink. I start thinking, *Okay, Joan, you've got your new plan. You need to be a sponge when we get to the Margaret Mitchell House. You'll step into that apartment where Margaret Mitchell wrote her masterpiece, and like osmosis, you'll just soak her spirit in. She can be your muse.*

Siegfried interrupts my daydream. "Let me add this, Miss Joan. I appreciate where you coming from about hating slavery and all, but lots of folks still get real worked up about how the South lost the war, and about the different races. I believe that you, being smart as you are, can use your fury over Scarlett and her treatment of blacks to write an honest discussion about slavery and racism in today's world. But you listen to me, you gonna make some enemies for sure if you start writing about those things, getting into discussions."

"Um, yeah, sure," I reply, only halfway tuned in.

Siegfried leans forward and pats my hand. "You hearing me?" His glasses tremble at the tip of his nose. "I want you to keep this in mind when you start getting into arguments with folks online, 'A soft answer turneth away wrath.'"

I don't give him the pleasure of asking about his proverb. "I'll be fine," I say. "Why would I be afraid of virtual enemies?"

"Because if the police use digital technology to find criminals on social media websites, I know regular peoples out there can, too. Plenty regular folks know the Internet backward and forward, and you sure don't want to make the wrong person mad. You gonna have to be careful what you say about some topics. Promise?"

I'm not scared, but I whisper, "Hush! You worry too much! Isn't there some proverb against worrying?" I pause dramatically, speak even softer. "Siegfried, nobody knows I'm hostessing this blog but you. I've got a fake profile. I'm absolutely safe."

I rarely even think about how it felt when I read the angry comments from the furious historian after my blog on the Confederate flag. I admit, I was scared to read my responses for a few weeks, and yes, it did make me tighten up my Internet identity, my security, but it eventually passed, and as far as I'm concerned, I created this virtual identity so I can do and say exactly what I want, when I want, with no fear. I've invested a lot in this blog, in finding a place I can feel safe in this life, and I definitely am not going to let anything ruin it for me.

"Law enforcement officials found a pedophile who was using a fake profile! Cop said advances in technology helped him snag that bad man."

I will Siegfried to hush. There are only a few places where I know I'm safe, and one of them is behind my keyboard. Virtual reality is enough! Plenty! It's not like I'm back in ninth grade—so shy and insecure I hooked up with the gorgeous Cynthia LaForgue, head cheerleader, captain of the girl's tennis team, and editor of the Pace Academy yearbook. Not to mention the evilest girl on this planet. I was such a dumb phony back then—false eyelashes, bust enhancer, bleached hair—I almost went nuts before that was over. I do not want to think of all the ways Cynthia influenced my life. Bitsy was the only person who did not recognize what a pathetic person Cynthia was. I hate that my mind is zipping over to that unbearably depressing time.

"Bless your heart," Siegfried says. "Everything's gonna be okay." He leans forward and pats my shoulder. He thinks I'm crying because I'm scared.

4

We pull up side by side at my apartment to drop off Dandelion and my Toyota, and Siegfried gets yet another gift for me off the backseat of his Buick—a small rectangular plastic tray holding a glossy yellow bag. "Highly absorbent and odor masking," he reads, holding everything aloft. "Ain't that great?"

"Yeah, just great," I say. He sure is assuming a lot. I'll have to look up on the Internet about cat care.

A minute later we're standing in the middle of my den/office, and Siegfried is looking around for the longest time. He eyes my old behemoth of a television and the VHS player beside it, along with my well-worn cassette of *Gone with the Wind*. I see him tilt his head back, straining through the lens of his glasses into my kitchen at the small table pushed against the wall, one chair tucked in along its outer edge. He draws his gaze back closer and smiles at my red sofa and my laptop. Finally, he pivots and fixates on the center-piece, the masterpiece, actually, of my entire apartment—a seven-foot-tall, four-and-a-half-foot-wide, six-shelved bookcase made out of knotty pine. But it's not the disapproving look Bitsy uses when she comes by with a gilt-framed picture, a colorful throw, or a piece of decorative bric-a-brac—things I just stuff into the linen closet

35

the minute she's gone. I can tell Siegfried is appreciative, sincerely admiring the precise, dust-free rows of books, arranged alphabetically by author. "So this is where the famous hostess of *Scarlett Says* lives, breathes, and writes?"

"Yes," I say, nestling Dandelion's box in the corner.

"Streamlined."

"Yes. People who are too attached to their surroundings are not as effective as they could be. That's why I'm not into home decorating. Or decorating myself either. If I were, it would be counterproductive."

Siegfried looks at me with one eyebrow raised, nods at last. "Okay. Let's get this little girl set up with some food and water and a toilet before we head out. I got some cat food samples at the PetSmart, which I believe ought to hold her." He digs in that coat pocket and pulls out yet another surprise—two small pouches of tuna-flavored kibbles in the shape of Xs. "Got a couple of bowls? We need one for water, too."

I definitely don't want the cat eating out of the same bowls I do. After I open and shut all my cabinet doors, I recall the stash of jar lids from the Tomato & Basil Classico pasta sauce I'm crazy about. I pull two of these from the jumble drawer and set them inside her box. Siegfried leans over and sprinkles food into one, then lifts the other and carries it toward my sink, but right before he gets there, I see him double over and wince. The lid slips from his hand and rolls under the table. "Oof! Ohhh, owww," he moans under his breath, staying bent like that for what seems forever.

I stare at the stringy chords in the back of his neck, silently freaking out, wondering if he's having a heart attack. I've seen plenty of television scenarios of people having heart attacks, and I think possibly I could manage to do chest compressions. But I recall that many times this is not enough. They have to use a device called a defibrillator that shocks the victim into responsiveness. I'm sweating and thinking I'm about to pass out, until at last, somewhere in my brain is a rational voice saying, *Call 9-1-1!* But right as I'm dialing, Siggy turns his head to give me a weak smile and shuffles those long feet over to my couch. He literally falls onto the cushions, his arms hugging himself, saying, "Whew. You gonna have to forgive me, Miss Joan. I'm sorry. I shore didn't feel that crisis coming on. You mind if I lay down?"

"Of course not." I end the call, feeling like an actor in a play. I've never had a guest here, besides Mother, and it hits me that she's never even sat down, and now here's someone lying on my sofa. I decide I better keep him talking, so I kneel at his side. "Siggy," I say softly, "you don't look so good." It's true, his nail beds are so pale it looks like he's got on pearlescent polish, and there's a yellow tint to his skin. The whites of his eyes are yellow, too. "Should I call a doctor?"

"No, no. If I got to, I can call Olie."

It takes me a while to remember that the aunt who raised Siegfried is named Oletha. "What? Is Olie a nurse?"

"She's a seamstress."

My heart is racing and I clench my fists, try to slow my breathing, and just wait out the inevitable. There's a long moment, the butterflies are having a heyday in my stomach while I hear the refrigerator ice maker dropping cubes into the bin, then the sound of what I guess is Dandelion crunching a kibble, my neighbor slamming his front door. It's scary to be kneeling here, beside another human being who is clearly ill, but mildly irritating, too, as Siegfried has just dropped this crisis, or whatever it is, on me with no warning. *Crisis* is a good word for this, I think. I did not sign up to play nurse when I agreed to a birthday celebration at the Varsity. Do I have any medical skills at all? No. I fainted in tenth-grade science when we were dissecting fetal pigs. I want Siggy to get up from there and return to his usual bossy, stubborn, *healthy* self. I'm not really mad. It's just that I'm scared. Scared I'll fail Siggy.

A few trembly minutes later I touch his arm gently. "Siegfried? Are you feeling any better?"

He shakes his head. "I'm just . . . pains in my chest and in my bones. I mean, I didn't have no forewarning for this crisis. Give me a bit, and Lord willing, it will pass. In fact, I believe I need to talk to my Lord now, if you don't mind."

I feel sweat beads pop up on my forehead, but I nod.

Siegfried closes his eyes, and I believe he is saying, "I plead the blood, I plead the blood," over and over, but it is hard to tell—his lips are moving but the words are silent. I'm not sure what to do, so I wring my hands, thinking I'll just let time pass, that I'll definitely do like Siggy said and not worry. I recall something about how pets can calm blood pressure, so I rise carefully and tiptoe over to scoop up Dandelion. Before I get her to Siegfried, I hear a knock on the door: *shave and a haircut, two bits.* I'd know that knock anywhere, but I tiptoe over to squint through the peephole.

"Joan? Joan? Happy birthday to you, happy birthday to you . . ."

I hear Bitsy's lilting cocktail-party voice singing through the door at the same time I see a crazy, distorted fun-house version of her perfectly made-up face. Just when I thought things couldn't get any worse. My stomach tightens even more when her voice changes to shrill.

"Open the door this minute, Joan Marie Meeler! I know you're home. I saw your car!" I realize I didn't lock the door as I figured Siggy and I were just making a quick drop off, so I attempt to stealthily lock it. Oh, but it is too late because she's stepping over the threshold, pushing the door open, smiling with coral lips around clenched too-white teeth. And I am speechless.

"I knew you were home, and I was just saying to myself that I am going to wring your neck if you ignore your mother on the day she gave you birth! I ruined my figure for you, and I deserve some respect! Now, I came to tell you that they're saying thirty is the new twenty, and it's not too old for finding . . ."

The words die in Bitsy's throat as she focuses in on Dandelion, while behind me I hear Siegfried hefting himself over onto his side out of respect. I hate to admit it is satisfying to see Bitsy genuinely paralyzed, like a big hand has removed the batteries from her back. With an open mouth, bulging eyes, dangling arms, and her black leather Gucci bag in a limp heap on the floor, her eyes look past me at Siegfried, then return to Dandelion, and she makes a muffled, agonized sound like "Ayeeeep."

I take in a breath, say so cheerfully it convinces even me, "Hi, Bitsy! Thank you for giving me birth! Speaking of birthdays, look at this darling kitten Siggy gave me for a present. This is Dandelion." I lift the collection of bones and fur. "Dandelion, say hi to your grandmother Bitsy."

Dandelion mews. Probably more from being suddenly hoisted into the air and stuck in Bitsy's face than my words, but still . . .

"Wha—!" Bitsy wobbles on her Prada heels, sways, clutches the air, and I fear I may have two prostrate people on my hands. But she manages to gather herself together, breathes in deeply, and screeches, "Get—that— filthy—rodent—away—from—me!"

"She's not a rodent. She's a cat. She's perfectly clean. She bathes constantly." I don't know if the perfectly clean part is true, but Dandelion has hardly stopped licking a tiny paw, swiping at her ears, her side, wherever she can reach.

"Let me also introduce you to my friend," I say, pivoting to nod toward Siegfried. "Siegfried Smith, this is my mother, Elizabeth Meeler. Everyone calls her Bitsy. Even me. She prefers it that way." Siegfried gets up to a sitting position, winces, says, "Good afternoon, Ms. Bitsy. It's a pleasure to meet you," and he puts one hand on the arm of the sofa and pushes himself up, then shuffles over to offer her his long pink-palmed hand.

Sparks fly from Bitsy's eyes, her highlighted hair trembles along with her clenched hands, which are still hanging at her side. "A . . . a *black* man, Joan Marie?!"

"I'm not actually black," Siegfried says playfully. "More like pecan colored."

"Oh, good Lord." She sighs from the depths of her soul. "Oh, my God."

"Please, ma'am"—Siegfried draws himself up tall—"I must ask you to respectfully refrain from using the Lord's name in an irreverent manner in my presence."

Well, that was the straw that broke the camel's back, as they say. Bitsy gathers herself together enough to yank her handbag off the floor, pivot on her heel, and clip-clop right out of my apartment.

I close the door and gently place Dandelion back in her box while Siegfried lies down again, groaning as he settles in. I hardly know what to say. I feel like wringing my hands. At least she didn't call Siggy a darkie, or heaven forbid, the N-word, which I have heard her say plenty of times. After a moment of what I think of as stunned silence, I ask, "How are you feeling now? Can I get you anything?"

He shakes his head.

"I've got some chicken noodle soup. Saltines."

He doesn't respond.

"You sure you're okay?"

He nods. I go in the kitchen and make a big production of filling the jar lid with water for Dandelion. When I look over at Siegfried, his teeth are bared like he's really hurting. I go into the kitchen and start a pot of coffee and nibble on a coconut macaroon. By the time the coffee's done, I've had six macaroons. I call, "Coffee, Siggy?"

"No, thank you. I appreciate it. But you go ahead."

I pour a cup, add lots of half-and-half, and mindlessly finish off the package of macaroons, thinking, *Oh please, just let him get better.* I feel like a stranger in my own apartment, awkward and uncertain. I'm not sure what to do. Should I stay in here, watching Siegfried but acting like I'm not? Go sit near him? There's an ottoman I could pull up beside him, but that feels wrong. I fix another cup of coffee, figure I might as well go sit at my desk. It's close, yet not hovering. "Feeling any better?" I say after a minute of staring at this man who seems to be nothing but hollows and joints.

"Not yet."

"Do you want me to call Olie?"

"Not yet." His voice is still pinched.

I reach for the edge of my desk to steady myself. I think of the scene if Siegfried passes while in my apartment. To anyone, it would be a horrible experience, but for me in particular, it would require a cool-headedness, a rationality with strangers, an ability that I will never have, no matter if I live to be a hundred. My heart races even more. I try to think of some way to calm myself.

I don't know what to do! Siggy, tell me!

He's silent. My heart pounds. *I need to calm down! What would calm me down?*

"Um, Siggy?" I say after a minute. "Would you mind if I check my responses? Would that bother you?"

Siegfried shakes his head. The yellow skin on his prominent cheekbones looks almost translucent in the overhead light. It feels heartless, even to me, but when my computer's on, an immense relief settles over me. "I'm sorry," I say after a minute, sliding my mouse over to click on my blog. "About my mother. I think she thought we were together. You know what I mean, *together*? And she's not real modern when it comes to interracial couples."

He shrugs. I appreciate the fact that Siegfried didn't get all flustered in the presence of Elizabeth Hargrove Meeler like some men do or mention her modelesque beauty or especially say something to the effect that I don't favor her at all.

Yeah, that. That was one constant comment I heard growing up, particularly in high school when she loved to come flaunt her size-two self every time she hung out with the cheerleading squad as their sponsor. She even ordered herself a cheerleading uniform and got such a kick out of it when people would say she looked just like she was still in high school! On the squad herself! My doughy midriff seemed even bigger whenever she was around.

I feel compelled to elaborate. "You know what, Siegfried? Bitsy and I aren't actually very close. In fact, I try my best to keep away from her, and after this today, I honestly wouldn't care if I never see the woman again."

"You think?" Siegfried opens one eye, rolls his iris to look at me. "I *know*."

"My daddy died before I was born, and my mother passed when I was two. I don't remember either one of them. Let me say this. Watch out—you might get what you ask for."

"My father's dead." I nod, like I'm agreeing with Siegfried, although what I'm thinking is it would be very freeing on many levels if Bitsy were to pass on. I realized early on that Bitsy and I had nothing in common. Besides the fact that I'm not beautiful nor thin, which grieves her, I think what hurts Bitsy the most is the fact that I'm totally deficient in the area of schmoozing.

My mother raised me in a very deliberate manner. She believes that looking beautiful, having money, and being in the right strata of society are the only worthy pursuits. She did not believe in allowing her child to march to the beat of a different drummer, particularly if it meant sitting in a beanbag chair with her nose in a book while eating Doritos. She constantly hid my *Little House on the Prairie* and *Nancy Drew* books and insisted on dragging me to the country club, to meetings of the Junior League, to the right salons to have my hair and nails done. She even pushed me toward Mr. Carlton, a tall, skinny man with smooth hands and a lisp who coached young ladies in etiquette and poise.

I call her Bitsy because my mother would never allow me to address her as Mother. She felt that was some sort of conspiracy by men to take away a woman's sex appeal. She told me it was a deliberate label to age women, to make them workhorses. I lost count of the times I heard her say, "I don't know why people call the person who happened to give them birth Mother or Mama or disgusting things like that. Do not refer to me as your mother, Joan. If Bitsy is good enough for my friends to use, it's good enough for you. I am Bitsy."

She can be very convincing, and I called her Bitsy. I remember that when my classmates remarked how odd this was, I was Bitsy's firm defender. I stood with my arms crossed, and I said with absolute conviction, "No one owns Bitsy. She's young and beautiful! Just because she gave birth doesn't mean she has to be called some boring, utilitarian name that five hundred million other females are called!"

Yeah, I was never Miss Popularity, but I went along, fairly unremarkably, all the way to ninth grade. Every high school has a Cynthia LaForgue. The queen bee. Every boy's fantasy. The well-built, confident, sassy cheerleader who engenders awe in even the teachers. One evening I'd been watching *Frasier* on television, and Bitsy came bringing the phone to me like it was a brick of gold.

"Joan Meeler? This is Cynthia LaForgue," a familiar voice came out of the receiver and made my skin tighten. I'd never gotten so much as a "Hi" in the hallway from Cynthia in ten years of school together.

"Hello," I managed, while Bitsy hovered beside the sofa.

"I want you to meet me in the locker forum at eight tomorrow morning." Cynthia didn't ask, she commanded.

I gasped. The locker forum was where the cool, popular girls convened. That exclusive group of girls who knew how to dress, who talked to boys, and who got invited to all the dances. The ones who went to movies, parties, and shopping together. "Okay," I said.

After we hung up, I sat there staring at those holes Cynthia's voice came through. Like the Queen of England had just called me. My shame is that I was so gullible I became a sponge, eager to absorb everything Cynthia knew instinctively about keeping at the pinnacle of the high-school social structure.

When the inevitable happened, it was not my mother I turned to, it was to that which I deeply love—books. Books, which had been before that brief foray into high school culture—and have remained since—my only friends. In fact, it was the moment my English teacher, Mrs. Darnell, introduced me to Scarlett in *Gone with the Wind* that I finally felt the beginnings of a kind of healing after the foolishness that went too far. That episode in real life that I couldn't make unhappen no matter what I did. I know for certain that time does not heal all wounds. Not everything is lost or forgotten in time. I know without a doubt that the past, the details of the past, in a terrible way, matters still.

I realize now it's time to get my brain off this track. Now is the perfect time to go make a connection at the museum on Peachtree Street—with the woman who penned my salvation.

As though sensing my thoughts, Siegfried shifts his shoulders painfully, turns his face to me. "Miss Joan? I hate I can't honor my word, but I don't believe I better go to the Margaret Mitchell House today. This crisis is laying me low big time."

I feel my heart sink for two reasons. My hopes are dashed, and he looks worse—an awful sunkenness to him. I get up, start walking, to obey my reflex to kneel at his side again.

"Keep your seat. I'll be okay, given time."

"What's going on, Siggy?" I ask, sinking back down behind my desk. "Are you diabetic?"

"Naw. Ain't afflicted with the sugar diabetes." He pronounces the disease with the second *e* short, a hissing *s* at the end.

"Heart problems?"

"Naw."

I clench my hands, swallow hard. "Well, should I call Olie?"

"I believe I'll be able to get myself home in a bit."

I look at him, and let out a huge blast of air I didn't realize I was holding in for so long.

"But, now, you listen to me." Siegfried settles back, crosses his arms over his chest. "I may not can go to the Margaret Mitchell House, but I want you to go on by yourself."

My stomach pulls into an even tighter knot, my heart hammers, and my breath gets short as I picture myself going to the Margaret Mitchell house by myself.

"Joan?" Siggy's voice is echoing in my head. He reaches for my hand. "Joan, you can do this."

I look down at our intertwined fingers and shake my head. "I get anxious thoughts . . . and it's . . . I don't want to go by myself."

"I know," he murmurs. "But you can do this."

He's pushing again, and I fight the urge to be angry at him. He's sick. It's not his fault I allowed myself to hope. Words always seem inadequate to convey something like my anxiety. Even though part of me realizes my fear is at least somewhat irrational and over-blown, I can't just tell myself to be calm. Social-type interactions are always bad, but even worse can be an outing that's not in my usual routine. When I'm somewhere unfamiliar, it feels like any moment I'm going to say or do the wrong thing, like I'm this giant mistake just waiting to happen, like public humiliation is right around the corner.

I turn to my computer's screen and stare at the latest response to my most recent entry on *Scarlett Says*, reminding myself that here is where I shine. Virtual reality is my forte. Siegfried is silent a good long time, and finally I think things are okay enough for me to begin to read Laverna in Alabama's comment. I'm cruising along, feeling better and better until I reach a certain question she asks of me, and I make an involuntary noise, a stupefied grunt—"Huh!"

"What?" Siggy turns to me, his eyes bugging out.

"I . . . I don't know what to say to this follower."

"You want to tell it to me? I'll tell you what I'd say."

I don't, really. But it's not like Siegfried will let me alone if I don't. Anyway, when he gets home he can hop right on his computer and read it, along with my reply. Second after second ticks by. There's no way out of this one. Maybe if I read it to him, by that time he'll feel strong enough to go home.

"Okay," I say, feeling my stomach lurch. "Here we go":

> Scarlett, this post about procrastination is awesome! I totally agree with the last words in the novel, "I'll think of it all tomorrow. After all, tomorrow is another day." Sometimes the best course of action is truly not to act! To do nothing and just ignore whatever it is. Definitely days when pulling the covers over my head and watching a hundred episodes of *Sex and the City* works better than anything. I've always been a procrastinator, and tons of times it has served me well. Like, if I hold off too long raising my hand at a PTA meeting, somebody else will head up the fundraiser, and ditto for doing laundry and cooking. I just wait and wait, and there'll come that moment when Ronnie will succumb and do it. Yes, I adore putting things off! Except, and this is why I'm writing you again, there's one time procrastinating backfired on me. I should have said yes to Wallace Dean the split second he asked me to run off to Gatlinburg for a quickie ceremony, but I put him off till it was too late. All because my girlfriends warned, "Oh, Wally's such a bad boy, Laverna!" But I've always preferred the more dangerous men. I mean, I totally agree with you that Rhett Butler is way better than Ashley Wilkes! It's the honest-to-goodness truth. I like me some danger, a rogue, when it comes to my men! And here's the thing, Scarlett, after eight years I've just gotten bored to tears with my sweet, considerate husband. Dull Ronnie is faithful, he says nice things and gives me whatever I ask for and all that, but he's just too darn nice. Is there such a thing? I'm thirty-five years

old, and I'm bored out of my mind. Don't I deserve excitement? Fulfillment? I'm feeling like I should run out and have me an affair. Because what if I wait too late and I've gotten too old and nobody wants me? I don't want to squander all my youth and beauty on Ronnie. Shouldn't I just go ahead and tell Dull Ronnie good-bye while I'm still young and good-looking enough to get me another man? I sure do appreciate your willingness to give us such great advice for free, Scarlett! I rely on you, and you're a dear!

Siegfried is sitting up halfway, shaking his head, grunting in a three-part rhythm, "Uh uh uh!" He looks at me with narrowed eyes. "That sure is a loaded question, isn't it?"

"Mm-hmm." It does give me a pang to think about nice, vulnerable Ronnie getting the rug pulled out from under him. In my personal life, there's not much experience I can draw from to advise Laverna, but Scarlett faced this delicious contradiction, longing for the sure, solid comfort of Ashley, while the great love of her life was Rhett, a rogue to the core. I make a nervous, shrugging gesture and raise my eyebrows.

"These are *real* people, Joan. If she leaves Ronnie, you gonna feel responsible."

I nod.

"You could remind her that at the end of the book, Scarlett lost *both* Rhett and Ashley."

I think about Rhett saying to Scarlett, "My dear. I don't give a damn," and the line not too far after that which says, "She had never understood either of the men she had loved and so she had lost them both."

Siegfried gets that look on his face, gazing upward as if my ceiling is heaven. "'Who can find a virtuous woman? for her price is far above rubies. The heart of her husband doth safely trust in her, so that he shall have no need of spoil. She will do him good and not evil all the days of her life.' "

He looks hard at me. Encouraged to see his color is better, I squelch my temptation to sigh. I dutifully ask, "What Proverb is that, and what's its application to life today?"

"That is Proverbs chapter 31, verses 10 through 12, and I'm sure you know the question is rhetorical, assuming you know the answer is not very many! What it means is that a virtuous woman is rare, more valuable than a precious gem. Means people are generally so morally weak and anemic in character that when a woman of virtue shows up, even in Bible times, it is a marvel! One reason is they got all these dubious role models on the television and the Internet. In books, too." Siegfried looks pointedly at me, and I cannot stifle my groan.

"Joan," Siegfried continues, "the term *virtuous* means that a woman has a moral firmness most women don't. But sounds like, in addition to having no moral strength, Laverna got her a discontented heart, and you know what that leads to?"

I shake my head.

"A frustrated life. What she's got to realize is that all married folks gonna get bored at some point if they stay together long enough. No matter how much they love each other, there's going to come a day when it ain't exciting no more. They think they'd be happier with someone else. Someone new. The grass looking greener on the other side of the fence and all that. But they get going on a new relationship, and after a while, that get boring, too. What I think is Laverna made a marriage vow, and long as he ain't abusing her—emotionally or physically—she need to honor that vow. Otherwise ain't no man gonna trust her. You tell Laverna to hang in there and she will get herself a deeper intimacy. That excitement she wants will come back in a different way."

I'm not in the mood to argue, but I think Siegfried belongs back in the first century.

"You know what I mean? What I'm saying?"

"Sure," I say, then quickly add, "You're looking better." He is, too.

"But I know it's hard to light right into advice like that."

"Sure. Can I get you something now? Tea? Coffee? A Dr Pepper?"

"Naw. I'm good. I suggest first you empathize with Laverna. Get her ears open to you by saying something like, 'I know it must be hard for you, how Ronnie falls short of your expectations. How he ain't exciting.' Then, you could say something like, 'But I don't believe you ought to do nothing before you think this through real good. Procrastinate a bit, 'cause I know lots of folks who lived to regret a rash decision about leaving the marriage, about not taking the time to think about the best course of action.' You could tell Laverna she needs to at least try having a honest talk with Ronnie."

"Okay, Siggy," I say. "Thanks."

There's nothing worse than getting a bunch of advice you didn't want in the first place.

"You ain't with me on this, Miss Joan. I can tell. But I'm a man who attracts stories. I don't know why, seems people come to me to pour out their hearts, and I don't know, just seems . . . I have to say I'm surprised a lot of times at the things I hear. But from all the stories, I've figured out a lot over the years, and one thing is that we humans teach other humans how to treat us by how we act and respond to them. So maybe in addition to talking honest with Ronnie, Laverna need to start dressing up to go out. When he walks through the door on a Friday night, she need to be all fixed up, kicking up her heels, squealing, and saying, 'Let's party tonight, Ba-by!' and Ronnie will understand the dynamic of their relationship has changed. She may get a nice surprise her own self!"

"You should start your own blog, giving wise advice, and call it *Siegfried Says*."

He laughs, immediately winces and clutches at his rib cage.

"Oh no! I'm sorry." I lurch forward and pat his wrist awkwardly. "You all right?"

He nods, eyes closed tight. After a spell, he says, "Ain't *my* wisdom I'm spouting. All I am is the conduit."

"Okay." I move back to my desk, gulp the last of my cold coffee, and decide to answer Laverna later. I move my eyes down to my next response, number 27. It's Charles in Manhattan, and when I see the little signature smiley face he puts on every response, I smile.

> My feisty Scarlett! I am humbled in your presence, and I echo previous commenters—this post is totally awesome! I adore the way you explain procrastination, and I especially agree with your point that putting things off gives a person some time to think, to not just respond to stimuli, which leads to mistakes. Speaking of procrastinating, I've been putting something off, and I believe the time is ripe now, and so before I sign off, I'm going to reveal to you and your followers my most passionate hobby.

I stop reading, close my eyes, breathe in slowly, deeply through my nostrils. I don't know what to do with all Charles's adoration sometimes. He gushes over every single thing I say, every week. I bet he'd switch his favorite ice cream or his political allegiance if I said I was. What makes me most uncomfortable is that it feels like he's giving me the power to crush him. And honestly, I never encourage him. I just thank him for his comment and leave it at that.

I have a strict policy to never, ever, for any reason, get involved on a personal level with any of my fans, even my favorite ones like Charles. I've had enough male followers through the postings of *Scarlett Says* develop a crush on me, which is flattering, but I finally realized that they were only in love with the forcefulness, the sureness of who I am as Scarlett.

There's a particular way they reply to my entries, praising and agreeing with me unreservedly. In awe, even. I think I've always understood that their adoration would die if they actually met me, that really, it's limited solely to virtual titillation. When they ask me to meet them live and in person, I always tell them it's nothing personal, only that I'm unwilling to commit myself to anyone. I say, "I'm an independent type of woman," which is a vast understatement.

I love each and every one of my followers. But if a week or two goes by, even a month, and I don't hear from most of them, I'm okay. Charles is different, and right now I can't explain it. I can't handle it when even a single day passes and I'm not talking back and forth with Charles on the responses for *Scarlett Says*. It's like I'm addicted to that contact with him. Usually I can't stop myself from reading his response. But since I generally feel short of breath and shaky whenever I read words from him and because he wants to reveal something personal, I am trying to postpone it today until Siegfried has left. He never misses a thing.

Namely, I like Charles thinking of me as his feisty Scarlett. I bet he pictures a raven-haired beauty with bewitching green eyes, like Vivien Leigh. He doesn't picture me with a seventeen-inch waist, however, because on a blog about barbecue, I totally debunked that idea. I was so honest it scared me when I went on about how I love food. I wrote "I'm built like a linebacker, I eat like a fieldhand, and I am proud of it." I remember being a nervous wreck right after I posted that blog. I curled up in my armadillo pose in my bed for three hours, worried it would put Charles off. But then after supper, I was brave enough to read his response, and that's when he said he actually preferred "generous women" to scrawny little dried up prunes who were scared to throw down!

I didn't say, however, that I favor Eleanor Roosevelt, that from age five or so, people have compared me to her constantly. I know Eleanor was an influential woman, but she was not lauded for her beauty. In fact, I've seen her name on lists for the World's Ugliest Women.

As I just glance at the words "my most passionate hobby" in Charles's response, I can feel warning signals going off in me like millions of tiny flashbulbs. I pull my eyes away and decide it's just warm in here and that I'm overdosing on caffeine. I check my watch—2:13 p.m.—look up, over at my bookcase.

Siegfried notices. "I sure am sorry, Miss Joan. For letting you down. Forgive me?"

"It's all right! I just want you to lie there and feel better."

"I like to be a man of my word."

I'm quiet a moment, then I say, "This is better anyway, Siegfried, because I still haven't got my blog figured out. I'm gonna wait and tackle slavery and racism later but not because you said it's dangerous. I just don't want to do it till I've thought it through enough, done my homework, and gotten ready. I don't want to insult or offend *anybody*! I see certain things in *Gone with the Wind* that are reprehensible, and I can't believe it never hit me before."

"I can. You're growing up, wising up," he says. "Thirty years old ain't a child no more."

"Thanks," I say, flattered.

"You're welcome. Some folks don't wise up on the subject of race until they're twice your age. Some don't ever wise up. Like your mama." Siegfried shakes his head in a disbelieving way. "I'm glad you're going on with the blog, Joan. For sure racism is a sensitive issue in *Gone with the Wind*. But that said, a person can't insist we not read Margaret Mitchell's masterpiece just because they don't happen to agree with the social conventions of that time."

"Yeah."

"Come on, say it a little stronger now." Siggy is smiling playfully, not wincing a bit. "You love that book. Carry it with you to the breakroom every lunch hour. Or maybe you're just trying to avoid me."

I feel hot spots rise in my cheeks. Siegfried is perceptive. He brings books to the breakroom, too. Lately it's been Whitman's

Leaves of Grass. For the whole first year I knew him, he was poring over this tome on John Calvin and the Protestant Reformation. The difference between us, though, is that Siggy will close his books at a moment's notice if someone else comes into the break-room. Unlike me, who will hold my book closer, higher.

Siegfried knows why. When I started at Giffin & Burke, I still saw my therapist once a week. The therapist saw my ability to get and hold a job as progress, and I guess it was. I made it through the interviews without throwing up on anyone. I tried to keep the appointments private, but then I got mad at him once and blurted out to Siggy why I was out of sorts. When Bitsy realized therapy was never going to make me thin or more likely to go to the club with her, she stopped paying for it. I can't afford it. Siggy told me God could make more of a difference than therapy could.

Right. That's why being alone is, for me, pure bliss. I could go for days without hearing another human voice, touching another person, and never even notice it! Books are by far the best company. Nothing's better, more human, than a book!

"Hey, Siggy, care for a book to read?" I do a Vanna White gesture toward the Emily Dickinson, F. Scott Fitzgerald area.

Siegfried tilts his head and does a cartoonish blink-blink. "Well, I dee-clare! I don't see that famous book by Miss Mitchell, do I?"

"Seriously?" Cartoonlike, I let my mouth drop open, then I jump to my feet and go retrieve my precious copy of *Gone with the Wind* from its ignoble spot among the dust bunnies on my bedroom floor. Back in the den, I sit sideways on my desk chair, facing Siegfried, the novel balanced on my knees like a prized infant.

He leans forward, peers hard at it, looks up at me, and shakes his head. "Now that is what I call one well-loved book."

I try to see it as a person who's never seen it before, through impartial, fresh eyes. It's scuffed and worn all right—dog-eared, peppered with sticky notes, and generally swollen with oil from my hands and sweat from my brow. I open it at random and have a sudden urge to place my palms over the pages, to hide the notes scribbled all which-a-way in the margins, the phrases highlighted with luminous yellow. My eyes fall on a twice-underlined and circled passage from Scarlett: " 'I won't think of that now,' she said firmly. 'If I think of it now, it will upset me.' " And my name with an arrow, and the words, "Look, Joan!" in the margin beside it. The spine is cracked so that the pages lie open flat, and I'm scared one of these days the stitching's going to give up the ghost and the pages will spill out, and I'll have to use a heavy-duty rubber band to hold it all together.

I remember the afternoon I lugged the heavy volume of *Gone with the Wind* home from Mrs. Darnell's class into my bedroom and locked the door. I made a comfy pit in my beanbag chair, and while mother engaged in one of her endless phone conversations with a girlfriend and my father camped out in his study, smoking his cigar and drinking his brandy, Scarlett's voice rose from the pages and into my heart like blood. I shut off the rest of the world along with my pain, getting my infusion, my transfusion, being filled with her strength, her ability to make it through things like hunger and war and death. I knew from that day forward that Scarlett's spirit was what I needed to guide me through the wilderness of life.

I was relieved, but I also carried around this great sense of indebtedness until that cool October morning twenty-six months ago. I sat sipping a gingerbread latte with extra whipped cream and chocolate shavings on top when I had a sudden realization: I was nothing but a self-centered hedonist who ate, slept, worked, came home, read books, and watched movies, and I'd just fall into my grave without ever finding any real sense of fulfillment unless I made a change. And with that, I decided to begin a blog dedicated to helping other people find the strength and wisdom that had rescued me. Scarlett's strength.

And *Scarlett Says* was born.

Siegfried gingerly touches the page, whistles through his teeth, exclaims, "Looks like you've been studying for a final exam!"

He's right. But there's only kindness in his words. After a profound silence, Siegfried looks into my eyes. "Talk about studying. You ought to see Olie's Bible. It's marked up worse than this!"

"Are you serious?" I ask, for want of anything else to say. I couldn't imagine anyone marking up a Bible the way I had *Gone with the Wind.*

"Mm-hmm. That woman has had her a pretty hard life, and she says the Holy Bible is her road map—shows both where she's been and where she's going. In the margins, she lists her mountains and valleys. Mountaintops are happy things, like marriage and babies; the valleys are where folks have done her wrong or loved ones dying. The deep holes are where it took awhile for the Lord to lift her out."

I smile, say nothing. Now that Siegfried is feeling better, I'm totally distracted. I really need to get going on my blog. I'm starting to feel nervous about the time slipping away, and I don't think I can do it with someone else in the room. That would be worse than writer's block.

Siegfried continues. "Gives Olie comfort because she knows where she's gonna end up and that finally, eventually, in the end everything's gonna be all right. Only crying will be happy tears."

I'm supposed to say something here, but I can't think what. For me, platitudes of possibility are not enough. I don't want some "pie in the sky, on high, by and by, when I die" kind of promise. I like a practical, concise, rubber-meets-the-road type of guidebook that will get me there with no questions asked, no requirement of something as esoteric as faith.

"Guess we all got a lot of questions on this journey down here, hmm?" Siegfried asks after a minute. "Questions, questions, questions."

"Sure," I murmur in an unguarded moment. I've got volumes of unanswered questions. A lot of them probably dumb and very different from Olie's. I think about what an awful, insatiable thing the desire for popularity can be, turning you into a spineless, heartless blob of no resistance. I wonder if maybe Siegfried could offer me some wisdom, some peace about certain matters, but just as quick I know the reality is that I'll never be ready to reveal what happened back then.

"Listen, Siegfried. I . . . there's something . . . well, I can't talk about it . . . but just trust me when I tell you that this novel"—I pause and hug *Gone with the Wind* to my chest—"it literally saved my life. I wouldn't even be here today if it weren't for the words in this book." This is truer than anything.

He gives me a long, steady look as particles of what I mentally refer to as my Day of Shame begin to materialize in my consciousness. The morning began with Cynthia LaForgue, me, and a collection of other popular girls standing around in the bathroom, passing a cigarette around as we gossiped and made snide remarks about our teachers. Bright fluorescent lights crackled and popped overhead, and there was the sharp smell of Pine-Sol mixed with smoke as Lydia Lydelle lumbered into the bathroom, breathing heavily. She had rolls and rolls of fat encased in a cheap, baby-blue polyester sweatsuit, rings of white salt from her profuse sweating at the crotch and the armpits. Stringy, lank brown hair hung down around her shiny pink-splotched complexion—what we called "pizza face" because it was covered with so many zits.

Lydia went into a stall, came out to wash her hands, then leaned into the mirror to apply some Bonne Belle lip gloss when Cynthia laughed meanly. "Don't bother, Lydia. Won't make any difference to a fat, ugly heifer like you." I felt shocked that she'd said anything that ugly, but I was still walking on eggshells with the wonder that Cynthia LaForgue had drawn me into her inner circle. Lydia Lydelle was on an even lower rung of high-school social strata than me, if that were possible. She was an outcast, a pariah. The type who sat alone at lunch, hunched over her sectioned tray full of meatloaf, tater tots, and waxy green beans. But I was spineless, just desperate enough to agree with Cynthia. "Yeah!" I laughed. "She's right. It's a waste of time. Nothing'll help you. You're hopeless."

By sheer force of will I dismantle the scene. Siegfried's a pretty cool guy, but how could he not judge me if he heard what happened to Lydia Lydelle after that? My stomach is feeling really nervous, and I need to bury myself in my blog. As though sensing my thoughts, Siegfried shifts his long torso up onto his elbows, gripping the sofa cushions with trembling fingers. After a moment, he says, "You know, I believe I can get myself on home now."

"Great!" I hop up so fast I get dizzy. "I'll walk you out."

"No, keep your seat. I can manage."

"But I want to." And this is true.

"Well, you put it that way, I accept, beautiful lady." He tips his head in a chivalrous gesture that makes me exquisitely sad for some reason.

Except I laugh.

"What? It's *true*, Joan! You are one beautiful lady."

"I'm not." My throat aches. "Don't lie to me, Siggy."

He reaches out, cups my cheek in his palm, says softly, "One thing I don't do, and that is *lie*."

I meditate on this as I walk behind Siegfried out of the apartment, watching him amble along toward his boat of a Buick. He's humped over, and his suitcoat is cattywampus, half up, half down. His ears are catching the fading sunlight, and they glow red.

"Lord willing, I'll see you Monday morning," Siegfried says, opening the driver's door to lower himself painfully in.

"Yeah," I say, trying to lean casually against the side of the hood. "So, thanks for lunch. For the, um, the cat." I feel a little embarrassed for him and this weakness, whatever it is. I want to ask him what's wrong, I almost touch his wrist, reassure him that *of course* he'll be at work Monday, but I draw back at the last instant and think, *Oh, what am I doing?* I don't like it that I'm feeling a little surge of protection for this man. It's a reflex I've simply got to squelch. I never let anyone get close to me, not to the real me.

Anyway, didn't he say to me not to worry? I won't. I can't afford to.

With an image of Siegfried's face burned into my brain, I stand listening to the locusts. At last I turn and head back toward my apartment. The air so sticky hot I can hardly breathe as I climb the steps, my sweaty thighs chafing against each other, burning. For the millionth time, I tell myself I really ought to lose this forty, or maybe it's fifty pounds by now, then just as quick I think, *Tomorrow. I'll think about it tomorrow.* Today's my birthday, and I'm supposed to indulge myself. Plus, dieting works best on the first day of the month.

Back inside, I head straight for the kitchen. When I've decided on ranch-flavored Lay's potato chips as my salty and a giant frozen Snickers bar as my sweet, I place them on a black lacquered tray with an icy cold Mountain Dew and a folded cloth napkin and carry it aloft on my palm, like a waitress, to my desk. I type in the address for Amazon.com, type in "Margaret Mitchell biography" in the search bar, then tap Go.

I hear a mew, and I look down to find Dandelion nuzzling my ankle. "How did you get out of the box?" I pick her up, intending to put her back in the box, but Amazon delivered a list for me, and I sat back down, setting Dandelion on a stack of bills. She pawed through them a moment, then curled up with one foot outstretched, resting against the edge of the laptop.

There are quite a few choices for me to ponder while I alternate bites of Snickers and potato chips with gulps of Mountain Dew. Finally I decide on one called *Road to Tara* by Anne Edwards and also one called *Southern Daughter* by Darden Asbury Pyron.

"Well, happy birthday to me," I say softly, then click over to *Scarlett Says.*

5

That night at ten, I scroll down to Laverna's response, stare blankly as I take in a deep breath, slowly let it out, breathe in again. Do I even want to *try* to channel Scarlett's guts, her fire, to answer this one? Without a doubt, if only for the sheer carnal joy of being self-centered, Scarlett would say, "Gather up your gumption and go for it, girl! Leave that boring Ronnie in your dust." But after I heard what Siggy had to say, I am conflicted. There's no way I'm quoting his proverb, but the rest of the stuff he said sounded pretty good. Basic common sense. And the point of my blog is to make people think, isn't it? To look at all the sides of things so they'll experience life more broadly. Still and all, monogamy is kind of outdated and old-fashioned. It's one of those large, extremely con- troversial themes, sort of like premarital sex, poverty, alcohol, and drug abuse. And racism.

I ponder for a good twenty minutes. If I tell Laverna to go for greener pastures and it backfires on her, it'll be hard to watch one of my followers suffer, especially if I know it was my advice that led her astray. Siegfried says he counsels couples at his church, which is funny since he's never been married. You'd think they'd want someone with firsthand knowledge. But before I can follow that train of thought too far down the tracks, I start typing:

> Dear Laverna, don't do anything rash. You need to think this through real good. You were in love with Ronnie once, weren't you? I know you've heard that old saying "The grass is always greener on the other side of the fence." Even if you do find a new relationship, and that's a big *if*, after a while that'll get boring, too, and you'll start looking through the boards of that fence at the greenness of other pastures. I know it must be hard for you, how Ronnie falls short of your expectations and all, but if he's not abusing you, you ought to be a strong woman and honor your marriage vow. Plus it's not even guaranteed you'll find somebody else. What if you throw away your one chance at love? What if you end up all alone with nobody loving you? Have you ever thought that Ronnie might be totally unaware of how unhappy you are? My advice is that you try some honest communication. Talk to him about how you feel. Use body language, too. What I mean is, fix yourself up to go out on the town, and when Ronnie comes in from work on Friday night, jump into his arms, squeal, and say, "Let's party tonight, baby!" Try that and see what happens.

Before I chicken out, I make my index finger hit Post. I sit back in my chair, stunned, dazed to some degree, until Dandelion mews again. I blink at her; I'd forgotten she was there. I offer her a potato chip, which she sniffs at, then ignores, looking at me instead.

Stop that. I don't intend to get involved with this feline, to do anything beyond feeding her and scooping her litter once a week. Her saving grace is that she's an excellent Bitsy repellant, and therefore fully worthy of food and water. But that's the extent of my involvement.

I pad over to her box and drop her back in, then sprinkle some Xs that smell worse than the fish department at Publix into her food bowl, then fold the box flaps in on themselves to make a secure top that still allows her to breathe.

I return to my desk, swallow, and mentally prepare myself to read Charles's revelation of his most passionate hobby. When I see his signature, my heart leaps and I close my eyes, grinding my teeth to stop the palpitations. One good thing about getting older is that your brain can do amazing things. I picture my arms hefting up a gigantic grain of salt before I reopen my eyes and allow them to drift back to Charles's words.

> Okay, my feisty Scarlett, and peeps who follow this illustrious blog. I've been procrastinating admission of this because some people are rude. They say people like me are just silly men in costumes playing grown-up versions of cowboys and Indians. I absolutely *hated* my childhood. School days were torturous. What I remember is that from the beginning I just didn't fit in. Like I was wearing this neon sign that said "Pick on me!" Of course, my natural reaction was to pull away from other kids. Grown-ups said, "We cannot change what other people think or say about us, but we can change how we react." It didn't soak in till this one day when I was in my mid-twenties. I'd been sitting in the basement all day watching reruns of *Battlestar Galactica*, and I started flipping channels and came across this PBS show on the Civil War, and it was like I *knew*! I knew I'd been born in the wrong time, and so I became a Union soldier.
>
> I'm a Civil War reenactor. I assure you it's not fun and games. I don't even have to summon up what is called a "willful suspension of disbelief" for it to be a totally authentic experience. The sheer scale

of a major Civil War reenactment creates an inescapable atmosphere of reality! When I'm in battle, all my senses are engaged; I'm carrying my heavy rifle, one man among many in the masses of troops moving across landscape at the shouts of officers' commands, thundering cannons, the smell of gunpowder following the crack of thousands of guns, smoke, and sweat. It's an immersive experience, to say the least. We spend our evenings in camp sitting around the fire, singing, telling jokes and stories, drinking plentiful libations. I'm telling you, sometimes it's an effort to remember that it's NOT real ☺. One reenactment I did had 15,000 soldiers, if you combined Union and Confederate soldiers along with several thousand civilian reenactors. In September 1997, I stood with 7,000 other Union reenactors during a review at Antietam while bands played, men cheered, dozens of regimental colors were paraded, and mounted officers and their staffs galloped to and fro. The Antietam battle reenactments, including a massive dawn assault by Union forces through a cornfield in a dense morning fog, was so very real! Then, in September 2012, I participated in the 150th anniversary of the Battle of Antietam in Maryland. It was incredible. An authentic Civil War experience. You know, don't you, that Antietam was THE bloodiest single-day battle in American history? With 22,720 casualties? The Civil War really does come alive again.

By the way, I'll be participating in a battle reenactment the first weekend in August in Galesburg, Illinois. It's a festival called Galesburg Heritage Days, and I would like to invite all followers of *Scarlett Says* to come and see, as I am confident such a true Civil War experience will interest each and every one of us. Especially you, my feisty Scarlett! As always, you're so generous with your wisdom. And so brilliant. Whenever I sit down here to read your words, I'm constantly amazed at the way you're helping so many people by taking your time to dissect such intangible subjects. You always make me feel hopeful. Please come see me in Galesburg, Illinois! I'll be waiting to hear. RSVP to Charles, Company H, 28th Massachusetts Volunteer Infantry Regiment.

Fondly, Charles in Manhattan. ☺

I don't even consider it. Avoiding eye contact with his smiley face, I type fast, "Well, thank you very much, Charles in Manhattan. Regretfully, I am busy on the first weekend in August. Your feisty Scarlett."

I jump up from my desk so fast the room starts spinning, walk four steps, collapse onto the couch, and spend the rest of the afternoon and the early evening curled in my armadillo pose as I watch *Gone with the Wind*. When the credits start rolling, I slowly stretch and go preheat the oven to 425 and pour an entire pound bag of frozen battered onion rings onto a cookie sheet. While those are crisping, I eat a pint of Heath Bar Crunch ice cream standing at the sink. I sit down to feast on my onion rings, but they are very disappointing compared to the Varsity's. The ones they fry at the Varsity are not pressed and chopped into unnatural mushy circles that your teeth slide right through. I have a fleeting impulse to call and check on Siegfried but squelch it because I'm not going to worry.

No getting involved. No accounting to anyone else on this planet. I stand at the sink looking out the window at the sky, a soft pastel summer blue about to be overtaken with the dramatic colors of dusk. And I suddenly wonder what Charles looks like.

No! I clean up the kitchen, turn out the lights, walk through the den to the bathroom to wash my face and brush my teeth. I get into my soft cotton pajamas, slide under my covers, check my clock. I've got a good lucid half hour to read, and I open *Gone with the Wind*.

I crawl into Scarlett's skin, and when I start to drift off, I'm in Atlanta on a cold January day in 1866, writing a letter to Aunt Pitty, explaining why I can't come back to Atlanta to live with her. The sound of frantic shuffling followed by a yowl makes my heart race. I stiffen, fully awake. *Let it be a dream.* But then I remember, I totally forgot about my kitten.

I tiptoe into the den, flip on the light, unlace the box lid, and stand there, mesmerized at the sight of Dandelion. I haven't had the chance to look at too many animals up close, and I notice the exquisite details: how all her paws look like they've been dipped into milk and her body fur is this really interesting stripey mix of light and dark gray. She's got a salmon-pink spot at the end of her nose and teeny lips and white tufts of fur inside her ears. There's a distinctive M traced on her forehead, and her oversized tail looks like a bottle brush. And her eyes. They're olive green and outlined in black like Cleopatra's, huge black pupils focused on me like I'm the answer to all her prayers.

She is beautiful, so exquisitely wrought, and I can tell she's longing for me to cuddle her, feel our hearts beating together in unison. Briefly, I consider how it would feel if Dandelion slept in the bed with me. It wouldn't actually be breaking my rule, because letting a four-footed feline who can't even speak English into my life doesn't break my vow of no three-dimensional engaging beyond what is necessary.

I take in a deep breath, about to lift Dandelion—but then with hands in midair I stop. "You've still got Xs," I tell her firmly. "You've got water, too. You're fine." I pull off my pajama top, fold it, and put it in the corner of her box. After a resigned moment, she steps into the center, turns around several times and curls into a tiny puff. She looks up at me before she tucks her head in, and I swear she smiles.

I grab a T-shirt, go back to my bed, and lie in the dark, listening to the deep quiet. You never really know what a day might bring. When I woke up this morning, I fully expected the worst to be getting myself to the Varsity to meet Siegfried. I sigh.

Oh, it does hurt, thinking of poor Siggy in pain, but I can't get involved. I'm not even sure Siegfried would want me to. Not really. Would he?

I tell myself to stop thinking about that, and all of a sudden my train of thought jumps track, and I recall Charles's latest note and an unfamiliar little *ziiiip* runs up my spine.

"Wow," I say aloud, and I giggle. I, Joan Marie Meeler, *giggle*! I don't believe I've ever giggled in my entire life. I've never been in love, so I'm not exactly sure of the signals. What happened with Lydia and Cynthia shut all that down, and I swore I'd never let this happen. I am sure that what Charles and I have together is solely mental. Just similar beliefs about life and a satisfying back-and-forth repartee of two souls in tune on certain issues.

It's definitely not going any further. No use even fantasizing about that because the idea of us ever being in a three-dimensional relationship is laughable. I grab my spare pillow, clutch a fistful of polyfiber foam, and twist till it hurts my wrist, forcing myself to focus on the good things about being a single woman.

In my free time, I get to do whatever I want, when I want. If I want to lie on the carpet and eat an entire bag of Nacho Cheese Doritos while listening to an album by Nine Inch Nails I bought myself for my sixteenth birthday, I can. I can watch *Gone with the Wind* every Saturday night if I so desire. There is a beauty in being alone and doing what I want, when I want. No partner who wants the lights out at a certain time. I could never handle someone saying to me, "Are you reading that book *again*?"

On Monday, a few minutes till eight, I sit down in my desk chair, feeling pretty anxious. Giffin & Burke is a full-service marketing communications firm that does branding, design, advertising, Web development, multimedia services, and media planning for some of Atlanta's biggest companies. It took a lot of therapy to get me this far, but Monday mornings still take a little extra adjustment, coming off a weekend, and this one's especially hard. I stopped at Dunkin' Donuts and bought two Long Johns filled with custard, a half-dozen Munchkins coated with powdered sugar, and a large scaldingly hot coffee. I'm discreet and put the box of pastries in an empty file drawer.

I nod an innocent good morning at Philip Giffin and John Burke as they walk into the office hip to hip, carrying identical leather briefcases. As my computer boots, I tidy the paperclips, the pen cup, and make sure everything's in order before I eat. I don't know a thing better than a bite of sweet dough chased by a gulp of rich coffee. When I finish, I sink into the familiar routine of checking company e-mails and the online calendar for the week, which gives me a measure of comfort.

Friday will be July fourth, but I see no company celebrations planned, and I let out a relieved sigh. When I first started at Giffin & Burke, the element that made my anxiety flare up the most was all the social functions employees had to attend. They expected all of us to go to happy hours, lunches, and clients' functions, as well as birthday parties and anniversaries of bosses and certain employees around here. It seemed like every other week was a cause for some big social event. Completely maddening.

Fear would consume me every time I got word of one of those. My stomach would be churning, and I'd start thinking how I could get out of it. I had a kazillion excuses, and I must have used every single one. It was agony until eventually everyone learned just not to ask me. I keep to myself. I keep up a wall, a very courteous wall, but still a wall. No one knows me well, and I prefer it that way.

They like me because I'm responsible, conscientious, a perfection-
ist about my reports, mild mannered, and punctual as the sun. I'm
discreet. I keep out of everyone's private business.

After I refill the clear acrylic business-card holder and sprinkle signature mints with our website printed on the wrappers into
a cut-glass bowl, I sit watching the front door, thinking of what
I'll say to Siegfried. *Good morning. Dandelion's fine—I sprinkled
extra Xs in her box before I left. You sure look like you're feeling better.
Anything I need to order for you this week? Ammonia? Paper towels?*

I hate to, but I have to admit, there's a comfort to having
Siegfried here at work, as if he is my sentry, some line of defense.
Even if I hate to admit it, I miss him. Now it's a quarter after, and if
there's anybody more dependable and punctual than me at Giffin
& Burke, it's Siggy. He even has his own key. I know if he's not here
by now, he's not going to be.

I sigh and stuff two more soft, powdery donut holes into my
mouth. It's going to be a long day without Siggy. I recall his face
contorted in pain from his "crisis" at my apartment, and then I
remember my plan to check his application on file. Since he's been
here almost twenty years, his application was not on the computer.
I recall a tattered manila folder marked "Employees" at the back of
a metal behemoth filing cabinet in the storage closet.

When I get the folder back to my desk and start rifling through
it, I get that feeling of prying into something I shouldn't. But I take
all incoming applications. I've had access to everyone's info for
years, and Mr. Burke sometimes asks me to look up an employee's
address if we need to send flowers or something. I flip through,
finally finding Siegfried Obadiah Smith's application.

In his thin precise handwriting, it's dated February 10, 1992.
He's been here *more than* twenty years! Nobody gave him a party,
nobody even mentioned it. Maybe that's the job of the administrative assistant! I cringe at this thought, skim the contact information, glance down to birthdate and education.

He was born in April 1957, so that makes him fifty-seven years old. Down on the line for Position Sought, he's written Sanitation Engineer, and where it says Desired Pay Range, he put $4.25 per hour. Apparently he's had no trouble with the law. For Education, it says he completed the eighth grade but has no high school or college. Under Other Education he's written something about a class on Ancient Greek at the community college. I think about how I hear him having passionate discussions with John Burke about everything from public policy to matters of theology and philosophy. Siggy holds his own, too. He can render John Burke absolutely speechless, even though John's got a doctorate from an Ivy League school.

Most interesting of all is near the bottom where it says "Please list your areas of highest proficiency, special skills, or other items that may contribute to your abilities in performing the above-mentioned position." Siggy wrote, "From 1970 until 1972, I was a houseboy at the Peters residence in Birmingham, Alabama. Part of my duties included being a janitor."

If he was born in 1957, he was only thirteen in 1970! No wonder he didn't go to high school. That means Siggy was six years old in 1963, the year of the bombing in Birmingham, Alabama. I'm surprised, because though I know that the shape of a person's life is determined by a lot of things combined—background, childhood, an individual's mind and education, a conscience, the desires of a heart, and so on—it just seems Siggy has such an unentitled sense of living. A purity of intention that's hard to describe.

For the next couple of hours, I work on tidying up online files because I don't want to think about any of this. The most exhausting thing in life is *caring* about people!

My followers are a different story. I can easily turn my brain off when it comes to people I don't interact with in the flesh. With mere headshots—and avatars of cartoon people or pictures of their pets—I'm not vulnerable. Right before lunch I sneak a quick peek at the responses on my latest *Scarlett Says* entry. Twenty-two so far, and I didn't post until really late last night. There's bound to be a lot more coming, and they'll definitely take some time to answer. I imagine myself lunching at my desk, one hand typing away while I eat with the other. Mondays are Dairy Queen, and I don't think a hamburger, fries, and a Blizzard will be too hard to manage.

I always answer my followers in a timely fashion. It's not necessary to answer each one. Oftentimes, they're just things like "Love this!" "I totally agree." "Intriguing, brilliantly written." "So true." "Hear, hear, Scarlett!" "Fantastic post!" "This is such a valuable perspective." But some demand a great deal of pondering before I'm comfortable responding.

I've had a number of commenters who took longer to answer than I did in writing the actual blog. An image of Charles's signature smiley face pops into my head, because his are often in that category. His are never mean or nasty; he just likes a lively argument. I have a feeling this entry is going to bring out the trolls even more than my post on the Confederate flag did. Yes, *Gone with the Wind* is a beautifully constructed, magnificent novel, a work of art, and to this day, still one of the most successful novels ever published in the United States. And I owe a huge personal debt to this novel. However, I'm not sticking my head in the sand about its flaws any longer.

From the beginning I'd heard people saying it's a highly controversial book, and I knew there were legions of extremely vocal critics who despise it. I guess I just ignored all that. But like Siggy said, it's a worshipful hymn, and it's sung in praise of a society that enslaved people! But here's the thing, after I talked with Siggy and he wasn't offended by it one teeny bit, it gave me the confidence to keep writing *Scarlett Says*. I pictured his face as I wrote my blog post yesterday—"Pondering the Pros and Cons of *Gone with the Wind*."

So, Siggy gets the credit for making me look through a new filter. Now I see the book that answered some odd hunger in me, that restored me, especially the heroine I modeled myself after, that privileged Southern daughter who rose to meet challenge after challenge, as solely the creation of one artist's imagination.

Sure, Scarlett has flaws, *Gone with the Wind* has flaws, but if Siggy's okay with it, so am I!

Nonetheless, I was petrified about getting it right. Lots of first drafts, heavy construction, and major revisions. It really tried my patience, but it was very much worth it when I realized I finally had something in that alchemical way, like when you're experimenting in the kitchen and you know you've tossed ingredients around in a combination that works like magic! My new recipe has the sweetness of romance, gallantry; spicy bits of demeaning dialect; hints of Confederate pride and secession; a dollop of self-centered, manipulative, and charming heroine; scalding portions of war and hotblooded Southern men; crushing defeat; and Sherman burning Atlanta. It's got a sweetly passionate defense of the Confederacy, bitter hints of slavery, and deep flavors of Yankees and secession, blood-drenched battlefields, the smoothness of hoop skirts, and a chewy satisfying bread of allegiance to the land.

At two minutes till midnight, I clicked Post. I sat there, a lot relieved and a little dazed, and I tried to pull up that fury toward Scarlett. I could not find it! I couldn't remember how mad Scarlett's treatment of Prissy had made me. In a way, it was an immense relief to know that my seething rage toward my savior was no longer there, that some emotions are temporary and can slip away like mosquitoes when the citronella candles are lit.

Other feelings, however, seem to grab hold like vice grips, and I can't hide from the fact that I've developed a crush on Charles.

My plan is to ignore this and respond to Charles in a very appreciative, professional, and businesslike way that will preserve our online relationship yet prevent anything more. I don't need face-to-face interaction. It really shocked me last night when Charles requested I post a photograph of myself. I found a picture of Vivien Leigh online, in a photo archive, taken when she was in Atlanta at the Loew's Grand Theatre the night the movie *Gone with the Wind* premiered in Atlanta on December 15, 1939. I posted that.

⎯⎯⎯⎯

Dandelion is going crazy when I get home, meowing and scratching on the sides of her box. I can't imagine she's run out of her stinky Xs, because I sprinkled more than her weight of them into the jar lid before I left this morning. After I set my bag down and slip out of my pumps, I go unfold the flaps. Yep, still got plenty of kitty chow. She locks eyes with me, and I get a whiff of cat poop that makes me gag. It comes to me that it might be okay to let her walk around outside of the box for a short time and clear her lungs.

"There you go," I say, setting her featherweight body onto the floor. She streaks off, and I stand there tense, holding my breath, watching her tearing around, exploring. I'm using a doubled-up plastic grocery bag when the old phone rings. It's my landline, and I never get calls on it. Bitsy insists I keep it for emergencies. I don't recognize the name on the little screen, but I'm still so discombobulated that I answer it. An older woman's voice says, "May I please speak to Miss Joan Meeler?"

"May I ask who's calling?" I'm squeezing the receiver hard with one hand and holding the poop away with the other.

"Oletha," she says. "Oletha Evonne Lattimore."

"Um, okay." Something in that name, that voice, is familiar, and also very serious. I feel fear rising in me like a wave. I wrap the cat poop up in the bag and set it on the desk.

"This Joan Meeler?" the voice prompts.

"Yes." I swallow hard, glance at Dandelion leaping up onto the back of the couch, prissing along like the belle of the ball. Instinctively, I lunge toward her, reach out, get yanked back, and realize I'm tethered by the phone cord. I stand there feeling like I'm in one of those dreams where you're paralyzed. After a moment, I hear the sound of a throat clearing and the voice says, "I need to talk with you about my nephew, Siegfried Obadiah Smith."

Gulp. "You do?"

"Mm-hmm. I'm sorry to bother you, but I'm worried about Siegfried and I need somebody I can trust, and he seems to think a lot of you. He's all the time talking about his friend Joan Meeler at work and how he respects you. And if he feels that way about you, I know you a good person. Person I can trust."

I stop breathing.

"So, I decided to call you and see can I set up a meeting for us to talk confidentially."

"Um, I'm not sure I understand."

"The fact is, I don't want Siegfried to know I'm telling you about some things. He don't want to bother nobody. He a private man about some things."

"Then you shouldn't!" I practically shout. Ahh, I think, that ought to be the end of that.

"Honey," she says in a powerful, quiet voice, "some things a body just knows. And I know I got to talk with you. Siegfried and me, we were enjoying a quiet afternoon yesterday when we got home from Mount Carmel Baptist. And before I knew it, he was having one of his crises. Last a good, long while. First I was okay about it, didn't think nothing too bad about it, but then he tell me he had one at your house the day before!"

"Um, yes. He did." *I don't want to hear anymore.*

"So, I say to myself, Siegfried needs to go see his doctor. But he tells me he won't." I hear tears in her voice.

"I'm sorry," I say when it gets uncomfortable.

"Thank you, honey." She blows her nose. "What time be good for you to meet with me? I got my ladies' meeting at five tomorrow evening, but I be done by six, and we could get together after that."

I say nothing.

"I don't expect we better meet at my house," she says finally.

"Well, I guess you ought to come here, then," I say and give her directions to my apartment.

I hang up and think, *What I have just done? Why did I agree to this intimate act?* My heart is knocking in my chest, and I break out in a sweat, imagining already what it will be like to have a stranger standing mere feet away from me in my apartment.

My anxiety grows to such enormous proportions that it muscles reason right out. I was planning to have a salad and low-fat yogurt for dinner, but I open the refrigerator and root around till I find three slices of double-cheese pepperoni pizza from four nights ago. I dip them into cold, congealed garlic-butter sauce and eat them standing there, with Dandelion twining herself around my ankles. Then I pull a half gallon of Edy's Rocky Road ice cream from the freezer and sit down at the table to eat it with a fork so I can dig out the almonds and mini marshmallows. When Dandelion puts her front paws on my leg, I use my free hand to scoop her up beneath her fluffy belly and set her on the couch. She curls up against my leg, and I stare at her as I eat. How much more am I going to let into my life?

After I finish the ice cream, I go through my mail. Among the junk is an elegant ivory linen envelope with a distinctive gilt-embossed return address label that says Elizabeth Hargrove Meeler above her Brookhaven address. After I put the junk mail in the paper-recycling bin in the laundry room, I shove the envelope beneath some dusty boxes of lightbulbs on a shelf.

Beckoning to me like a warm silky bubble bath is my laptop. My insides have felt raw all day, and I didn't get one single fan answered. When I checked just before I shut the Giffin & Burke computer down, the number of responses was up to 242. A record. I could see at a glance that most were just a couple of words of affirmation. But I couldn't help noticing that what I'd said stirred Charles up even more than usual. There were at least six more responses from him. I wasn't sure whether to be happy or sad. I love my sparring with him, being his feisty Scarlett, but I don't like the way his responses are heading, like he's slowly unzipping this storage bag that's hiding his real self. I don't want him to open himself up so completely to me. I need everything to be the way it used to be, and this is what I'm willing with all my might to make happen as I read his second response.

> Oh, my feisty Scarlett, when I sat down here and read this awesome blog and then added to that the fact you're busy on the first weekend in August, I fell into a state of despondency. I'm crushed that you cannot make it to my reenactment! Also, the photo of Vivien Leigh is fetching, but I meant one of you, in the flesh. Please post a photograph for your loyal followers! Speaking of states, I'm often in a state of unrest until I sit down here and find an answer. Answers that you give us here! Fantastic posts. You are really helping out a lot of people by taking the time to dissect such a subject as the ugly side of *Gone with the Wind.* Or shall we call it the dark side of Scarlett? As always, you're truly brilliant. I'm beyond thankful to have you in my life. I loved it when you said you also hated high school! So many define themselves by their high-school experience, and I could not wait for that heinous time of my life to be over! I've never attended a reunion either. How about we put our brains and calendars together and come up with a mutually agreeable time and place to get together? Charles in Manhattan. ☺

His signature smiley face leers at me as I plant my elbows on my desk, bury my face in my hands, and whisper, "There's no safe place to fall anymore."

It really isn't so peculiar, is it? Didn't I used to will myself back into the 1800s? This runs through my mind as I make sure there's toilet paper and hand towels in the bathroom at Giffin & Burke since Siggy's out again. Yes, I pined to be back in Civil War times, except not on a bloody battlefield of Gettysburg or Vicksburg. I literally lived inside the fictional world of Tara and Twelve Oaks. I fell asleep dreaming of parties where hoopskirts swished and Mammy stood beaming in the wings. Gentility and chivalry wrapped me in their arms, and every time I finished reading *Gone with the Wind,* I let less time elapse before I began it again. When I was not in the thick of it, I missed the characters terribly, felt bereaved in an odd way. I even loved the scenes of desolate loss and starvation, places where the hard truths of war rendered Scarlett and her sisters poor and defeated. Living in that fictive dream was the only thing that quelled my anxiety. I felt emboldened when I was living vicariously through Scarlett. I learned how to direct my mental energy so I would not be overwhelmed by negativity, by self-criticism and anxiety. I was in control during the time I consumed that book and sometimes for days afterward as I lingered in the fictive dream.

I knew it was peculiar, rare for a person to crave living in the past that way. But I never considered myself mentally off or untouchable because of it, and it might not be a bad thing as far as two people bonding, as part of the courtship process. Emotional attachment, connecting on a deep level. As far as relationships go, Charles and I have a good deal in common. I've heard of folks bonding over a season of *Friday Night Lights* or *West Wing* or, hey, even *Battlestar Galactica.*

After I clean the front door, I go to my desk and make a few notes for Philip Giffin. "Meeting at noon with Alan Goldman at Imperial Fez at 2285 Peachtree Street in South Buckhead," I write. And then, "New intern needs to talk with you about the marketing plan for Delta Airlines."

Thinking about how Charles thinks I'm so wonderful brings a smile to my face. To put it simply, I'm attracted to him and part of me doesn't want to stop it. It might be an online, virtual flirtation, but I am enjoying it.

Until I stop and really think about it, that is. Then I scare myself. This emotion, has grown stealthily, and it is not welcome here.

6

Tuesday night at 5:23 p.m. I sit on the sofa, waiting, feeling my heart beat way too fast. A bag of Lay's Sour Cream & Onion potato chips is beside me, and a twenty-ounce Mountain Dew. I'm anxious, but also I am curious. I've been picturing Oletha Evonne Lattimore as a female version of Siggy—tall, skinny, a long striated neck with an Adam's apple that moves up and down comically like his does.

I'm also feeling a bit indignant. I don't think strangers should just call up and invite you to meet them. And if she's a Bible thumper like he is, I've got one for her. I spent my lunch hour combing through Proverbs online, and I've got the perfect verse to hush her up.

Work today was just as bad as Monday. Oh, it wasn't that Siegfried was out and I had to continually freshen up the lobby. In fact, it was kind of fun to spritz smudges off the black lacquer trim and pick up bits of trash in the lobby. And it's not that I miss him per se, I just miss the presence of another person who's not one of the marketing and public relations gurus on their way to or from a power lunch. I miss another person who loses track of time when he falls into a book. That's all. And he makes good coffee. I can't figure out the right ratio of coffee to water in the huge office machine.

I bet Siggy'll be back tomorrow. *Hey beautiful*, he'll say, *you're a sight for sore eyes*. What he says every Monday morning. Oh, it will be nice to get back into our routine. I am not good at adjusting to change.

I close my eyes, feel the butterflies fluttering in my stomach, my breath catching in my throat. I can't face this Oletha person. I don't want to have the confrontation required to get her out of my life. Mentally I rehearse my proverb, then drain the Mountain Dew. I wonder if it'll matter that the translation I memorized said NIV instead of King James, which is Siegfried's personal favorite. I look at my watch, stare anxiously at the door. Dandelion lets out a pitiful meow, and I realize I forgot to feed her. I go to her box and sprinkle in fresh Xs. Suddenly, I get an encouraging thought. What if Siggy's aunt is allergic to cats? Lots of people are.

I lift Dandelion and her food bowl from the box and say, "Now, I'm not wishing Oletha to be allergic; I'm just saying *if*, if she is, then, well, she'll leave faster." *Oh, what am I doing?* I think. *Talking to a cat!* I take the chips to the kitchen, roll down the top, and fasten it with a clothespin to keep them crispy. I'm shocked that I didn't eat them all. I return to the couch and sit down to wait, Dandelion twining around my ankles. And then I realize I'm still in my blogging clothes, and there are grease splotches from the chips on my thighs, a rip in the neck. *Oh, why do I even care what I look like for her?* I think as I head for my bedroom to change. But before I can, the doorbell buzzes, and I breathe in deeply and go look out the peephole. It's a wide, older black woman, holding a little terra-cotta pot with an African violet shooting up.

I open the door and Dandelion zips out past my guest, does a U-turn, then prances back and stops at her feet, looking up expectantly. I see bubble-gum pillows of flesh oozing over shiny wedge sandals as Oletha squats a bit to pet Dandelion's head, using baby talk to say, "Well, ain't you a purty lil' ole puddy tat." She stands tall, looks up at me, and says, "That is a fine welcome, sure enough!" and I see a pleasant face with genuine delight in the smile.

"This is Dandelion, and I'm Joan Meeler. You must be Mrs. Lattimore. Please won't you come in out of this heat." I'm amazed at the words pouring forth from me. I cringe, feeling as if I've suddenly turned into Bitsy.

"Thank you, honey," she says, stepping inside. "Just call me Olie."

Where Siggy is tall, skinny, and "pecan colored," as he told Bitsy, Olie is no more than five feet, caramel brown, with ample everything: ample bosom, ample rear end, ample arms, ample cheeks. She has curves everywhere. But she doesn't camouflage them. She's dressed in a form-fitting bright-orange terrycloth dress. Big luminous pearl earrings. A necklace with a matching pearl nestled in her cleavage. Her hair is styled into a Jackie O bouffant-flip from the 1960s. If she was an adult when Siggy was little, say she was eighteen, then she has to be in her seventies. But her skin is so smooth, I'd be hard pressed to think she was out of her fifties.

We go into the den, and I sit in the armchair and she sits across from me on the couch. "Thank you for inviting me," she says, and I only nod because now the cat's got my tongue. I cannot swallow and I feel my hands trembling, so I put my palms together and mash them between my thighs.

"This a real honor," she continues, "to meet the great Joan Meeler in the flesh."

"Thank you," I manage, fascinated by the shiny beads of perspiration on her forehead and upper lip. She is radiant. "Want some water?"

"That would be nice. It is hotter than the fourth of July!" she says, and chuckles.

I go into the kitchen and get a glass, fill it with ice and water. When I get back, Dandelion has squeezed between Olie's feet and the couch and promptly dozed off.

"Thank you, honey," Olie says when I put it in her hand. She swills it down with her eyes closed.

"You're welcome."

"I bet you wondering what I came here to say."

"I am kind of . . . curious, I guess. But here's the thing, I'm not really . . . I don't usually . . ." I laugh and it sounds so awkward I'm embarrassed for myself.

"I know," Olie says, and I see the same genuine kindness in her face I saw earlier. She clasps her hands together, tilts her head, and we sit quietly for a while. At last she leans forward and says, "Siegfried tell me you ain't the social type, that you have a problem with people, but that you so smart, with so much to offer, and so I decided I need to take the chance and come tell you something. On account of we might not have much time."

I feel my cheek and eye muscles twitch. "What?"

She reaches for my hand, and for the first time that I can remember, I don't pull away. Her hand feels silky and strong at the same time.

She swallows meaningfully and says, "Siegfried got the sickle cell."

I try to speak, but cannot. Sickle-cell anemia? Wasn't that wiped out years ago, along with polio and scarlet-fever epidemics? I feel faint and my face is hot. I want to scream and say, *Tell me you're lying!* Finally, I look down at my watch, squeak out, "I am so sorry to hear that, but it's late and I've really got to tend to some things."

Olie looks into my face with this pleading look like nothing I've ever seen before. And then she says, "I hate to inconvenience you, but I promise I be quick."

Something makes me nod.

"Against his will, Siegfried has been staying at home to elevate his leg. And I believe he's past the danger point with that and I will allow him to go back to work tomorrow. But he needs somebody at Giffin and Burke to look out for him."

"Huh?" My voice is thin, strained.

"Siegfried has an ulcer on his leg, and it wasn't healing quick enough, so I tole him he had to stay home and elevate it. Infection the most common cause of death in peoples with sickle cell, no matter what their age. He been taking his folic acid to help his bone marrow make new red blood cells, and he been drinking water throughout the day. The doctor says getting dehydrated be risky, it increase the risk of taking a crisis. He done had two big crises lately, as you know, and the doctor say they probably done brought on by him having a little virus a few weeks back. Doctor done put him on pain medication and say to increase his fluid intake so he don't have to go to the hospital for intravenous fluids."

I sit there, swallowing hard as I listen to what sounds like a garbage truck's engine slowing down out on Ponce de Leon Avenue. Sweat beads feel cool on my temples.

Olie looks at me for a long moment, and she says, "Joan Meeler, I want you to keep a eye on him. Make sure he drinks plenty of water and don't stress hisself out too much. Stress can bring on a crisis, too."

There is a long silence. I summon up that proverb I memorized and go over it in my mind. I'm ready to fire it out, but before I do, I need to lead her into the confrontation. "Don't Philip Giffin and John Burke know about Siggy's disease?"

"No!" Olie leans forward and holds up her hands. I notice how pretty and pink the palms are. "Don't nobody know but me and Siegfried and his doctor, of course. And now you. But don't you be telling nobody. Don't let Siegfried know I told you, neither."

"Why not?" I ask sharply.

"He don't want people to know."

Here's my entrance! I clear my throat, look piercingly into Olie's eyes, and say with perfect elocution, "A gossip betrays a confidence, but a trustworthy person keeps a secret. Proverbs 11:13." I sit quietly, waiting and watching as Dandelion suddenly stretches and eases from behind Olie's feet. She stares at me.

Olie blinks, clears her throat, smooths the fabric over her thighs, and in a wink Dandelion hops up onto her lap, curls herself into a contented ball, and there is the rich sound of her purring. Over this background music, Olie laughs in a nervous way. Aha! I think. Got you with one of those double-edged swords Siggy likes to talk about.

Then she says, "Withhold not good from them to whom it is due, when it is in the power of thine hand to do it. Proverbs 3, verse 27."

"Um, well, let's be realistic here . . ."

"I know, Miss Joan, it is the thing for me to do, to tell you about his condition. The only thing. It's hard when somebody like Siegfried is so proud, or maybe closed up is what it is, and you can't persuade him to do what he need to. Imagine if it was your nephew. I know he won't be cured, but he already beat the odds, and I'm certain he can get him some more time on this earth if he has people looking out for him. And really, that all we got down here, ain't it? Our love and our time? Who know what he can accomplish if he only get one more year than he would? I'm hoping you might keep an eye on my boy and encourage him to drink lots of water. I believe the fact that Siegfried speaks so highly of you says something about the fact that he will *listen* to you."

I feel a knife twisting in my gut. How can I argue?

Olie gently sets Dandelion on the floor, hefts herself up, tugs her dress down to right above her knees. "Okay, sugar, I will leave you be now. I appreciate your time. I just had to make sure somebody at Giffin & Burke know about my boy's condition so they can help me keep an eye on him, and you have eased the burden on my heart and mind. I will sleep easier tonight, thanks to you."

Nodding like a zombie, I follow her to the door.

After she leaves, I'm hungry again, so I throw a pizza in the oven. But I just stare wearily at it on the kitchen table, at the way the late sunlight slanting through the window makes the little puddles of grease on the discs of pepperoni shine, like a small universe. Dandelion springs up and tiptoes on her little white feet to get as close to the hot pizza as she dares. Her nose quivers along with her whiskers. I don't even shoo her away.

While I'm waiting on it to cool, I go to my laptop and do a search on sickle-cell anemia. Fourteen sites pop up. I click on one and read that more than 90,000 Americans have this inherited blood disorder, and it mostly affects people of African ancestry. Normal red blood cells usually live for about 120 days, but the sickle-shaped cells of people with this type of anemia are fragile and break apart easily. They die after only about ten to twenty days, leaving the person chronically short on red blood cells. Episodes of pain called "crises" are a major symptom. Pain in the chest, abdomen, joints, and bones that can be so severe, the person may need to be hospitalized. Sickle cell adversely affects the spleen, affects vision, causes fatigue, makes hands and feet swell, but pneumonia is to be really feared. Life expectancy is about forty-five years. That's younger than Siegfried. More than a decade younger. This is scary stuff. I don't want to know all this. I don't want to feel responsible. I want everything back the way it was.

"Mornin', beautiful," Siggy says, tilting his head back to look at me through those glasses on the end of his nose. "You a sight for sore eyes, and now I know it's true what they say about absence making the heart grow fonder." In what I think of as a "Broadway flourish," he places a cellophane-wrapped package on my desk. It's two pecan spins I recognize from the vending machine on the first floor.

I feel the knot inside me untighten a little, and I say, "Good morning, Siegfried. It's nice to have you back," then finish typing the last part of a memo.

"Looks like you kept the place fairly tidy while I was out," he says, walking around the lobby, nodding and smiling, inspecting things like he's wearing white gloves. He pauses at my desk. "Mr. Burke tell me you did double duty, administrating and scrubbing, too, and I want to carry you out for lunch to show my appreciation."

Not again. I bite my bottom lip, look up at him, and for the first time, I notice a yellow tint in the whites of his eyes, a symptom of sickle-cell anemia. "Don't worry about it," I say, acting as nonchalant as I can. "It was nothing. My pleasure."

"It was somethin' sure enough." He tucks in his shirt, pats the cluster of keys on his belt.

The anxiety is tuning up, and so discreetly I reach a hand down into the special file drawer for my chicken biscuit. It's nice and warm, and the grease has made the wax paper slick. I'll wait to take a bite when Siegfried has moved on, but he stands there, waiting. "I'm afraid I can't," I say, at the same time that Siggy says, "I want to carry you on a picnic and then to the Margaret Mitchell House. Got us pimiento cheese on rye, fresh peaches, and Olie done packed up some of her sour cream pound cake."

I settle my biscuit back down in the file drawer with impatience I try hard not to show. "Today just won't work. Okay, Siegfried? Now please let me get back to what they pay me to do around here. I need to print a letter for Philip." What I don't add is the end of that sentence, "before I let myself take a peek at my blog."

Siggy's face clouds. "But I been feeling so bad about letting you down on your birthday, and the whole time I was laid up, the only way I encourage myself to get better was by saying, 'Siegfried, my man, you and Miss Joan can *walk* to the Margaret Mitchell House during lunch when you get back to your employment at Giffin & Burke.' I called and they got tours every day of the week, Monday through Saturday, beginning every half hour starting at 10:00 a.m. and going till 5:30 p.m."

I feel a doll-size Olie sitting on my shoulder, whispering something about not withholding good from someone when you got the power to do it. I picture me and Siggy walking the quarter mile down Peachtree Street to the Margaret Mitchell House with a picnic basket between us. *Maybe it's doable,* I think. Maybe. But just as sudden I feel heat rushing to my face. Like I'm getting a fever. My hands start trembling. What I really want, need, is to just sit in the break room today and read. I want to eat my solo lunch of a Philly cheese steak sub, Nacho Cheese Doritos, and two oatmeal creme pies all by myself. Might work on answering my followers, might not, as I am avoiding Charles. I was counting on Siegfried doing his usual thing and me doing my usual thing. Will he understand that it's not because of him I'm saying no? Will it stress him out if I flat-out refuse?

Siggy clears his throat. "Well?"

I shift in my chair.

"I saw your lunch in the break room. It'll keep. You can eat it for supper tonight."

"But, Siegfried, you know July in Atlanta is so dang hot we'll sweat like pigs." I sit still, hoping he'll connect the sweating with dehydration.

"Don't you worry. I got plenty of Olie's sweet tea in a two-quart jar."

I don't answer. My heart's pounding. In my mind's-eye I see me standing out on Peachtree Street, freaking out with one of my panic attacks. Siggy is holding me up as my body twitches, as I struggle to swallow. "Here, take a swig of tea," he's saying. "You gonna be all right." His face is beaming. There's not a drop of sweat on him, however.

"Um, maybe. I think I . . . what I mean is—"

"Okay, then! Let's say noon." Siegfried looks at me, beaming, then turns on his heel.

How am I all the time getting involved in these forays with Siegfried when what I really want to do is just stay to myself and do my own thing? I hate concerned aunts asking me to keep an eye on their nephews. I hate it when one of my followers is unrelenting about asking to get together. I feel like standing up and screaming, "EVERYBODY JUST LEAVE ME ALONE!"

I stuff my chicken biscuit in my mouth surreptitiously as I watch Meghan, John Burke's new college-age intern, prance through the glass doors in a dress barely covering her panties. Her slender legs are wobbling on red, two-inch heels. *Won't that distract him?* I think as he beckons her into his office and shuts the door. I get a cup of Siggy's good coffee from the breakroom, then add half-and-half from my own personal container. The office has only powdered nondairy creamer and one plastic spoon for stirring.

Back at my desk, it's a relatively quiet Wednesday morning at the office, me trying to hold myself together. You'd think I'd be feeling happy because I hit 5,542 followers today, well over my original goal! Which, of course, I immediately revised to a goal of ten thousand. But it's harder than you think to keep yourself in the present while your heart is up in your throat. I vow to the powers that be that if I can just get to that apartment where Margaret Mitchell wrote *Gone with the Wind*, and back here without incident, I'll open Bitsy's birthday card tonight.

Siggy is at my desk at two minutes till noon. He's got the straps to an ancient beach bag in an aqua blue starfish print over his forearm. I'm not mentally ready, but I try hard not to sigh as I shut my computer down, lock my treat drawer, and slide my feet into their loafers.

The sun is directly overhead when we step outside. It is absolutely burning up, and the humidity's so thick we've barely gotten down the steps of the building before I'm sweating like a hog. Siggy has changed into white sneakers, and he has this Panama sun hat with a clear green brim in the front that makes him look sporty.

I turn, head in the direction of the Margaret Mitchell House, but Siggy grabs my arm. "How about we eat here?" I nod and follow him to the grassy courtyard between the back of our building and two others facing a parallel street. It's not big, but it is in the shade and it does have a cement table with two benches. Graciously, Siggy waits till I'm seated before he proceeds to unpack the beach bag. I feel exposed because of the three sets of windows aimed at us, and so I try to focus on pots full of bright red geraniums lining one edge of the courtyard.

"Tell me all I missed while I was out," he says, placing a napkin, a plastic fork, and a red Solo cup at each place. Next he pulls sandwiches wrapped like letters in neat wax-paper envelopes, and two Promise butter tubs. "Peaches," he says, patting the tubs.

At least it's not a personal question, I think, as I awkwardly hold my cup for him to fill with tea. "Well, let's see . . . it's been the usual. Fairly calm. Oh! Philip Burke has almost gotten that big car dealership to sign with us."

Siggy nods. "That's good. He's been working on that since Christmas."

I take a bite of my sandwich. Pimento cheese and rye is a very interesting combination. Exotic. I think of Olie's hands making and wrapping our sandwiches and the fact that Siggy doesn't know I know his aunt. I finish the first triangle and fork up a wedge of the juiciest, sweetest peach I've ever eaten. And the tea—a hint of mint and lemon and just the right amount of sugar. It's got to be the best tea I've ever tasted. "Tell Olie that everything is delicious!"

"I will. I sure will," he says. "You let me know when you ready for dessert, 'cause her pound cake gonna make your teeth dance!"

I laugh, close my eyes to taste the second half of my sandwich better. Then, recalling people inside the buildings who are probably watching me, I slow down, open my eyes, try to eat more ladylike.

It's over dessert that Siegfried brings up *Scarlett Says.* "I see Laverna is throwin' in the towel on her marriage. Her last comment says she's leaving boring Ronnie."

"Yeah," I say, feeling a little sad before I take a bite of the sour cream pound cake that Siggy has placed on a napkin before me. It's so good I'm practically weeping. I really actually do believe my teeth might be tap dancing with sheer delight. I take another bite, savor the chewy, burnt sugar taste of the crust and the moist, silky-smooth inside. I could eat the entire cake with no trouble. I should get the recipe and make one every Friday night for the weekend. This is living. Everything in life really is better when things taste like this.

After a moment, Siggy says, "Don't you get your feelings hurt when fans ignore your advice like that?"

I do, but I don't really want to talk about it. My followers are close to my heart, but here's the thing—there's absolutely no reason in this world to let my virtual relationships spill over into my 3-D world. I gasp when I taste Olie's pound cake again. "You know, Siegfried," I say when I've swallowed, "my teeth really are dancing! This cake's just about the best thing I've ever put into my mouth. I'm going to get your aunt's recipe."

"Good luck with that!" He laughs and slaps his skinny thigh. "You'd have a better chance of getting hell to freeze over. This cake is a secret family recipe. Olie won't even share it with the *preacher's wife!*"

Well, *somehow* I will get that recipe. It's a sin to keep something this good to yourself! Maybe I'll call Olie and tell her I won't keep an eye on her nephew if she won't share this recipe with me. Of course I know I won't. I would never instigate any kind of personal interaction like that.

"I always get my feelings hurt when people ignore my advice."
Siegfried is looking at me with those penetrating eyes.

I shrug.

"Yes, it's *agony* to watch people make mistakes, especially when
I done told them how to avoid it, and I *know* I'm gonna have to
watch them suffer the consequences."

"Oh, well, I don't usually—"

"You remember how I told you I've been counseling couples at
my church?"

I sit still as stone.

"Well, last year, it was February, I believe, I almost got fed up,
almost quit. I figure folks gonna do what they gonna do anyhow, so
I might as well just save my breath. Lost my patience, sure enough."
Siggy shakes his head in exasperation. "But then, one Sunday I
wandered into the library at Mount Carmel, and even though we're
Baptist, we got us a equal opportunity library." He laughs. "So, I get
a Catholic Encyclopedia and I read about Saint Monica. How she
watch her son, Augustine, make mistake after mistake. He a lazy
boy, a grievous sinner, and she spend seventeen years pursuing her
wayward son and pleading with God for her boy's soul. Call him a
child of tears."

I realize I'm staring at Siggy with my mouth open, that my hands
are clutching each other in a vice grip. I want to say, *Let's be realistic
here*, but I don't want to offend him, so what I say is, "Wasn't that
like *two thousand years ago?*"

He reaches across the cement table top, pries my hands apart
and holds one so meaningfully I stop breathing. "Some wisdom be
timeless, Miss Joan, and Saint Monica's devotion, her persistence,
inspired me to keep on offering the true wisdom. She didn't give
up, and finally her child of tears got baptized in no less than the
church of Saint John the Baptist. After all that resistance, those
rivers of tears she cried, St. Monica got to taste true peace and joy."

I'm not in the mood to talk about this. "Any more of that pound cake?" I ask.

Siggy slides his piece, untouched, across the table. I don't want to take his cake, but I do want to take it. "You need it," I say.

He shakes his head, and I feel happy all over.

After a while he says, "Miss Joan, I believe humans got two fundamental emotional needs—we need to be connected to other peoples, you know. I'm talking close personal relationships, and we need to know that what we doing with our time matters. That we making a contribution to this planet that outlasts our stay on it. I don't believe a person can be happy without these two things. We are born to belong."

"Knock it off, Siegfried, please. Let's go to the Margaret Mitchell House."

"Aww, now, just answer me one question, what they call straight from the hip, which means don't think about it too hard. Are you happy?"

I wish I were sitting in the break room with my sub sandwich in one hand and a book in the other. Why in the world is Siegfried so fixated on me and my social life anyway? I really don't think it's any of his business, because, I mean, who is anybody to say what makes each particular person happy? I'm going to answer his question honestly. "Sure," I say in my strong voice, "I'm deliriously happy. I'm content. I like being a recluse outside of going to my job at Giffin & Burke. I don't think I'm abnormal in any way. For some of us, close personal relationships, that type of thing is . . . well, for lack of a better adjective, it's agonizing."

"Agonizing, hmm?" His voice is soft as the fur at Dandelion's neck.

"Yeah. Years ago I used to dream that one day I'd emerge from this cocoon of anxiety and I'd be a social butterfly. Now I realize that the odds of me changing are basically nil. I'm thirty and I'm still as insecure as they come. But here's the thing, Siggy—I no longer care! It gets exhausting pushing a rope, and there's a ton of freedom, of joy, in *acceptance*. A lot of peace to be had when you finally figure out your lot in life."

He is silent so long I think I've finally shown him the light. I'm crumpling up my wax paper and stuffing it in the beach bag when he says, "Don't you ever yearn for some man to hold you? Don't you ever have physical longings when you laying in your bed at night?"

I cannot believe what this man sitting across me is referring to! I will not sit here and take this. I won't. "Don't you dare pry into my personal life!"

"Awww, don't get mad. I just want you to embrace life and live each day to the fullest."

"Siegfried Obadiah Smith! We're not all alike. You need to respect my solitude. Just think back to your high-school days, um your junior-high-school days. There were the jocks, the preppies, the brains, the nerds, the artists, the outsiders. There were the socialites and the loners. Well, I was a loner. And it's no different when you graduate. The fact of the matter is, I prefer to keep to myself. I accept myself, and I wish you'd accept me too!"

He picks up his tea, takes a drink. "I'm just trying to figure out why you got so much fear 'bout connecting with real live human beings, Joan. I hate thinking of you getting old and being alone."

"I've never been a socialite. I don't need other people. I am an island. A happy island."

We sit in silence. I hear traffic on Peachtree Street, the roar of a jet overhead. I realize what I just said makes me sound selfish. But I am making a difference in this world. I'm not patting myself on the back or anything, but I participate in the instruction, the care of thousands. More than five thousand if you go by today's tally.

Siegfried puts his elbows on the table, rests his chin in his palms, and looks at me for a long moment. "You don't dream of Prince Charming? Finding a Mr. Right who's gonna make you happy?"

"Sure don't."

"You attracted to the women?"

"No." I have to laugh at the expression on Siggy's face. "If I was religious, I'd make a great nun, wouldn't I?"

"Well, then," Siegfried says, glancing at his thick gold wristwatch. He stands, stuffs the rest of our lunch debris into the beach bag. "Reckon we better get on to the Margaret Mitchell House."

It's not an admission of defeat, or a truce. Siegfried and I are like two defensive dogs, circling each other, around and around, the bristling fur, the bared teeth, the tension between us palpable as we head toward the Margaret Mitchell House.

I'm drenched as we arrive at the corner of Peachtree and Tenth Streets in the heart of Midtown Atlanta. Big sweat gophers run from my underarms to my waistband. Glancing over at Siggy, I see he has remained cool as a cucumber.

Number 990 is a turn-of-the-century, three-story Tudor Revival I've driven by a million times. When we get close, I read the plaque out front that says "Birthplace of *Gone with the Wind*" and that it's listed on the National Register of Historic Places.

Siggy smiles wide at me, says, "Bet there weren't no busy, loud Midtown MARTA bus station across the road in the 1920s."

I nod and follow him down a side street, through a small parking lot and then through what seems like a back door. We walk past an old-timey elevator, a copier nestled into one corner, and then right into the midst of a small gift shop bulging with copies of *Gone with the Wind*, figurines of Scarlett, Melanie, Rhett, and Ashley, refrigerator magnets of Mammy's wide black face, collectible coffee mugs, keychains, lunchboxes, wall plaques, and something that draws me like a magnet—a salt and pepper shaker set in the shape of Scarlett's vanity and stool. No one else is here, thank goodness, and I'm about to lift the vanity to check the price when I hear, "Welcome to the Margaret Mitchell House and Museum." I jump, turn, see it's coming from a tiny Asian woman standing behind the counter. "Are you here for the tour?"

"We sure are," Siegfried says.

"You are all I have for the 12:30 tour," she says. "I am Abhati, and I will be your docent. That will be thirteen dollars for each adult, please."

I walk up to the register, reach into my purse, but Siggy flies over and says, "Uh uh. This my treat!" and pulls an ancient wallet out of his back pocket. His yellow-tinted fingers with their pale nail beds make my heart wrench in a funny way as they pull a twenty and a ten out.

"Thanks," I say. Maybe after our tour I'll buy him one of the plates with a picture of the party at Twelve Oaks painted on the center.

"Come," says Abhati, and we follow. She is graceful, moving precisely in a neatly pressed black pantsuit and spotless white Nikes that are noiseless on the wooden floor. "This house was built in 1899 and converted into an apartment building in 1919. Margaret "Peggy" Mitchell and her husband, John Marsh, moved into apartment number one on the ground floor in 1925. She called their apartment The Dump, and she never invited anyone over for dinner. Their apartment is the only interior space of the restored house that is preserved as an apartment and maintains the original architectural features—including this famous leaded glass window Peggy looked out while writing her famous Pulitzer Prize–winning book. The best-selling book in American history!" Abhati's voice is laced with pride and affection as she points at the window.

Margaret Mitchell's apartment is so small that the kitchen table is in the bedroom. I will call her Peggy now, too, I decide, right as it hits me with the fierceness of a locomotive that this tiny, cramped three-room apartment is where my salvation was born. Only vaguely do I hear our guide talking about Peggy's slight frame of 4 feet, 11 inches, her disastrous first marriage, her philanthropic work, her job as a young newspaper reporter, the lifestyle of 1920s Atlanta, and her motives for writing *Gone with the Wind*.

I move wholly into my own world as I imagine Peggy between these very walls, right here where I'm standing, bringing to life the powerful heroine of her epic novel. It's nothing short of a miracle, because Scarlett O'Hara springs alive in the very first sentence of *Gone with the Wind* and does not speak a boring word for the entire sixty-three chapters. For more than a thousand pages. Scarlett O'Hara who literally saved my life. This realization picks up my insides and whirls them around like a cyclone. I start laughing.

Siggy looks over at me. "What?"

I take in a deep breath, close my eyes, shake my head. "Nothing." It would be impossible to explain. How I have lost myself in the story that glows and quivers with a life all its own. A book that saved fifteen-year-old Joan Marie Meeler, a story that moves with such bright inexorable power that I not only lost myself in it, I also found myself.

For the next few minutes, I follow Siggy and Abhati from one tiny room to the next, listening without really hearing. Siggy asks polite questions to which Abhati gushes her answers. I feel like kneeling here in the presence of my muse, in this holy shrine to the woman whose work of art carried away the hurt places in me, restored my damaged sense of self. How did Mrs. Darnell sense that the troubled countryside of my teenage brain needed to attach itself to a survivor like Scarlett? Scarlett has gumption, and when I read for the first time that scene where she affirms to Pork in chapter 28 that SHE WILL RISE AGAIN, she gave courage to a girl who trembled constantly. Her words soothed me after that nightmarish incident at Pace Academy. I was able to win back some small part of me only by my obsessive identification with Scarlett O'Hara. Her story still possesses me. I am my happiest whenever I'm in the middle of the book that makes me forget I'm reading.

I'm looking without seeing as Abhati continues. "Peggy Mitchell had a passion for character. Rhett Butler was based on her first husband, and Doc Holliday, a distant cousin by marriage, was said to be the inspiration for Ashley Wilkes." Abhati ushers us along with a flourish of her tiny hand.

We linger at an oak table by the window in a corner of the living room. It holds an old portable Remington typewriter. "Peggy spent ten years here writing her book, and the backspace key on her typewriter did not function," Abhati says, and Siggy makes a noise of disbelief in his throat.

Minutes later, we're in a small theatre-like room next to the gift shop, and Abhati says we may watch a documentary called *The Making of a Film Legend: Gone with the Wind.*

"It's a Hollywood classic," she adds reverently.

I look at Siegfried.

"How long is it?" he asks.

"Two hours."

He looks at me, contrite, says, "Next time."

I wander over to peer at an exhibit featuring the front door from the movie set of Tara. I wish I could touch it, put my fingers right where Vivien Leigh's were. I wander back in the gift shop to turn over the china plate. It's $23 and all I've got is $11.47.

We step back outside and I feel the heat wrap around me. Siegfried doesn't seem to have much of a bounce in his step now. I see his slumped shoulders out of the corner of my eye as I ponder a placard we just passed that said Margaret Mitchell died in 1949, at age forty-eight, after being struck by a cab. On Peachtree Street, no less, without having written another novel. Now I feel a palpable pall hanging over the building and Peachtree Street. I knew this fact, had heard it many times, but it wasn't really real to me until I stepped into the Margaret Mitchell House.

I don't like how Siggy is lifting his feet, like they're made of cement, but there is one thing that's got me almost elated, and that is the fact that I didn't have a panic attack on the way to or at the Margaret Mitchell House. I hardly felt anxious. That's heady, but on the flip side, I promised to open Bitsy's birthday card if this trip was without incident. I feel like an emotional yo-yo.

Something in my neck tightens when I see Siegfried wince. "Mind if we stop and have us some of that good iced tea?" I call to him. "It's hot as get-out today."

I am just turning onto Juniper Street to head home after work when I see a new business. Open-mouthed I stomp on the brake. I have this terrible feeling like I just stepped off a cliff into thin air when I wasn't expecting it. The sign says "Dr. Cynthia LaForgue, DVM" in big bold black letters, and in red script underneath, "I treat your pets like family!" It's a good thing nobody is behind me, because I experience a visitation of undiluted terror that lifts my foot from the gas pedal. I hover there, screaming silently for probably fifteen seconds, thinking, *It can't be. There's no way it's the same Cynthia LaForgue! No way she'd ever be smart enough to be a veterinarian! Plus, she wouldn't still be a LaForgue! Knowing how boy crazy and how shallow and how manipulative Cynthia was, there's no way she hasn't been through three or four marriages and wouldn't currently be married to some rich moron who pampers her. Anyway, in a town the size of Atlanta, there's probably a dozen Cynthia LaForgues.*

I avoid looking in the rearview mirror as I speed away. Unbelievable. I will never go this way ever again. I'm definitely changing my route home, even if it's an extra five miles. Feeling those fingers of shame from my ninth-grade debacle at Pace Academy is definitely not worth what I'd save in gas or time. I know it's not *the* Cynthia LaForgue, I'm 100 percent positive of that fact, but still, it's not worth seeing a name that has the potential to shatter me.

7

Dandelion is scratching on the sides of her box like crazy when I walk in. I unlace the box flaps with such force, one panel rips off in my hand, and she stares up at me like I'm God, letting loose a "Mee-owww" that pierces my eyeballs. I reach in, slip my hands underneath her silky front legs, lift her out, and hug her hard. Her little paws scramble to be free, and I set her on the floor and watch her jet off to the red sofa. She's figured out how to jump from the cushion to the arm to the high back and then to make this gigantic leap up onto the highest shelf of the bookshelf, which is her favorite place in the entire apartment when I let her out of her box. She'll perch up there for hours, for as long as I'll let her.

I feel her eyes on me as I sit down at my desk and type in *Scarlett Says*. Usually by Wednesday evenings, I'm closing in on being done with answering all my comments for the week, but because of the extra distraction of Siggy's absence from work, and the huge response to this particular post, I'm not even a quarter of the way through. I decide to eat supper at my desk and just submerge myself in the comments until I'm done. If I have to miss one night of sleep, it's a small sacrifice to tend to my loyal followers. The number of responses is up to 122, and I count five smiley faces.

I'm intentionally avoiding all of Charles's comments until I'm done with the rest. I have to mentally steel myself to read them. Someday I hope I can get back to communicating with the man without any emotion. But right now I can't. My brain has decided to betray me, just waiting for a weak moment, a little crack big enough for the desire to weasel in, and there is nothing for it. I'm not going to buckle. I'm far too happy alone.

Cautiously, I let my mouse and my eyes drift up to my blog entry. It's funny, but after the interminable agony of coming up with the idea this week, it's almost like it wrote itself once I got the title and the first sentence on the screen. I haven't looked at it since and now it feels like I'm reading someone else's work. Also, I didn't notice the irony in the title till now.

The Dark Side of Scarlett O'Hara
and *Gone with the Wind*

When I started sharing my blogs, I never thought that one day I might have to deal with topics that are as uncomfortable as slavery and racism. If I had, I might have been too much of a wimp to begin. But here's the thing, now I firmly believe I cannot let my own little furies (and fears) quench my creative mission here on *Scarlett Says*. I realize, and I want all y'all to realize, too, that *Gone with the Wind* is fiction, for crying out loud! *Gone with the Wind* is the creation of one artist's imagination, and the beauty of fiction is that you can explore large, dark, extremely powerful and hurtful themes without anyone getting hurt for real! Margaret Mitchell was a talented author who took a lot of risks. She didn't play it safe, and I bet she found it really frustrating when readers were unable to separate her from her characters. She absolutely was NOT Scarlett!

I want to let you know that I absolutely, unequivocally love *Gone with the Wind*! And I think that every character in this novel, even those who have tons of warts, has them for a reason. Every ugly thing that happens, happens for a reason. Yes, some things are offensive, but chances are, no matter what you write, somebody somewhere is going to be offended.

Scarlett O'Hara may be one of the most arrogant, manipulative, unscrupulous, self-centered, and conniving (did I even cover all the appropriate negative adjectives?) heroines, but I choose to look beyond her flaws and focus on her spunk. I appreciate what she calls her gumption. Her ability to change and grow strong. I admire her ambition. That girl rises to meet challenge after challenge!

Not to let her off the hook, but in a way I think she's a pawn, a product of her privileged upbringing. Of course she's furious about the war destroying the only world she's ever known! She was born a plantation owner's daughter, in the white South where slavery was an accepted and essential part of the harmony of plantation life. The way she shakes her fist at hard times is enough to let me keep loving her despite the fact that she acts superior to and treats blacks like animals.

People tend to avoid contemplating uncomfortable issues like slavery. We are frightened of ourselves, I guess. I know I was when I first realized I did not hold with Scarlett's attitude toward blacks. I mean, I actually started hating her! The woman who saved my life! But after a long conversation with a black

friend of mine, who by the way, doesn't have ill feelings toward *Gone with the Wind*, Margaret Mitchell,
or Scarlett, I've come to the conclusion we're not
meant to live luxuriously wrapped in cotton, insulated
from the pain and injustice in this world. Humans are
not supposed to be unconscious. The human experience is by definition difficult, painful, full of doubt
and sorrow and unfairness, and I believe you deprive
yourself if you don't experience things like disgust
and outrage over someone else's attitudes.

Books are important to me. Not only as intellectual
exercises but as something tangible that guides me
in my life. There are certain characters that go with
me wherever I go. I never did take to Pollyana, that
character created by novelist Eleanor Porter in the
early twentieth century. Pollyana, an orphan, always
managed to find something good, even in terrible situations. Not that I believe in succumbing to despair,
but that girl's optimism was so excessive, it was
totally illogical. Atticus Finch and Huckleberry Finn
are my welcome companions. But, Scarlett, I've got
to admit, is my favorite. Picasso said we use art to
explain the world to ourselves, and intentionally or
not, stories do that. You can't have a story without
characters, at minimum a hero and a villain. Some,
like Scarlett, can be both and can become larger
than life, taking up residence deep in your psyche.

In high school, I discovered *Gone with the Wind*.
I'd been so lonesome and wounded and so needy
to hear from someone who wasn't a wimp like I
was, and Scarlett's voice, in full volume and in full
color, floated up from the pages right into my soul.
It ran down my parched throat like water. I'd closed
myself off to all relationships in the physical realm.

Mean teenage girls, including myself, had me so depressed and anxious I didn't even want to live. All I needed was Scarlett's bold, brassy, devil-may-care words to guide me out of the darkness.

I think stories are important to all of us. They work subliminally. They're powerful in changing how we look at life, and I owe a personal debt to Scarlett O'Hara that I cannot even begin to put a price on. This is what enables me to look past her warts. She pulled me up and out of the ashes. *Gone with the Wind* was the world where I escaped from my wounded, shattered self. My healing place. Beginning in ninth grade, I read Margaret Mitchell's masterpiece over and over, until Scarlett's wisdom took root inside me like a mighty oak that wouldn't blow over in a storm. My fragile psyche was healed, or at least, patched enough so I could continue to live.

As I witnessed Scarlett's devil-may-care self, she gave me a new sense of what I could be, how I could deal with the harsh realities of this life. To put it simply, I won back my life by my obsessive identification with Scarlett O'Hara. Now I model my responses to you, my loyal followers, on what I gleaned, am still gleaning, from this brave, ambitious woman and this brilliant work of art. Yes, the book is highly controversial, not exactly politically correct, and Scarlett is immoral in a zillion ways, and I detest how she puts on superior airs when it comes to black people. But let it be known that I am going to continue to love her, to let her work through me despite her warts!

There's so much more I could've said, but I've heard the human brain has a focusing ability of seven minutes. Speaking of that fact, I bought some sweet Carolina barbecue sauce and I'm about to talk myself into jumping up and cooking a half-dozen frozen corndogs. I force myself to stay in my chair and read responses. There are many, in the hundreds, which are only a sentence or less, stuff I can see at a glance is happy and complimentary and not going to require much more than a "Thanks!" from me. It's fun reading "Wow, that is some powerful good stuff! An insightful post, Scarlett!" and "I entirely loved this!" and "Brilliantly written!" and "I totally agree!"

There are also several dozen long expositions, but positive nonetheless, ones I know I'll have to read through several times before I'm ready to respond. I allow warm fuzzies to effervesce through me for a second.

I've done this long enough to practically feel the nasty ones before I even look at them. It's like the words are alive, the letters shooting hot darts at me. I read the first one, gulp, and hug myself. It says, "I hope you get run down by a taxicab like Margaret Mitchell did. She deserved it and you do, too, for propagating this type of trash."

The next one's not physically violent, but hurts all the same. "Of course it's not politically correct, you moron! It's not even historically correct! Margaret Mitchell is a partisan to the nth degree. This is not an impartial book, and the way she defends the Old South, the Confederacy, is despicable! I'm glad Sherman burned Atlanta, and *Gone with the Wind* ought to be burned as well. It ought to be banned!" The final one I can handle for the moment says, "Whoa! I usually ignore trashy posts, but my best friend sent me a link to this rubbish on *Scarlett Says,* and I just can't rest until I tell you that the themes and most of the characters in *Gone with the Wind* are truly evil. You ought to be ashamed of yourself. You need to go straight to your nearest bookstore and buy a copy of Harriet Beecher Stowe's *Uncle Tom's Cabin*! But I bet you won't. I bet you're a secret member of the KKK. I bet you're making up that part about having a black friend to ease your conscience."

I start to sweat. My entire body goes rigid as a bow's string. I get up, go open the freezer and lean in, stand there lifting my hair before I pull out a package of Gorton's Beer Battered Fish Fillets and spread them on a cookie sheet. I need brain food, and fish is brain food. While they're baking, I mix up four heaping spoons of mayonnaise with sweet pickle relish and lemon juice to make tartar sauce. That done, I stare out the window at dusk falling onto the boxwoods, imagine myself writing a retort to all the hate mail, including the fact that *Gone with the Wind* still sells 250,000 copies per year, adding to the thirty million sold since 1936. But I know it won't change anyone's mind.

I reach out and touch a tiny leaf on the African violet from Olie. It sits on my windowsill. I think about how I have not one but *two* black friends if you count Olie. The soil feels dry and I cup a palmful of water from the sink and give it a drink.

There's still thirteen minutes to go on my fish, so I read the bag, which says they're made with real draft beer for a hearty pub taste, and each serving has 120 milligrams of EPA and DHA Omega-3 fatty acids. Isn't that supposed to be good for you? Turning it over I find there are five servings at 230 calories each, but 1,150 is really not all that much, and from the looks of things I'll probably be up all night, and a body definitely needs more calories awake than asleep.

The second I pull them out of the oven, the grease hissing and crackling, Dandelion sprints over. I look down. I'm still surprised that such a loud meow can come from such a tiny creature.

"All right, all right," I say. "Calm yourself. I'll share." How much can a four-pound ball of fluff eat anyway?

Turns out they can eat a lot. I can't help laughing as Dandelion scarfs down an entire filet and pooches out her little belly in a misshapen way. It feels good to laugh. I finish, take our plate to the sink, and start running water. All of a sudden I hear Siggy's voice like he's standing right beside me. "A soft answer turneth away wrath, but grievous words stir up anger. Proverbs 15:1," he says. This is one of his favorites. I have it memorized because he quotes it to himself whenever Philip Giffin talks to him in a certain demeaning voice.

I don't think Siggy's proverb is wise in this case. I don't even know if there is a soft answer to the hateful things I just read. Anyway, it doesn't do any good to respond to hate mail because it's like what you learn as a child—if you do respond, you're only giving them what they want. Just ignore them. These online bullies want me to reply because it gives them power in their imagined relationship with me. Most of the time they'll just go away if you starve them for attention. The culture of Internet anonymity makes people feel free to lose their rage in words they'd never say if they had to say it in person.

It's still a bad feeling to know there are people out there who're having mean thoughts about me. I feel my heart racing, and after I finish cleaning up, I shake a few Tums into my mouth, pour a glass of Fresca, and sit back down at my keyboard. With a trembling hand I scroll down along more responses, wincing at one that says, "The publication of this book has shaped the South in some very heinous ways. Words are powerful, and this vigorous defense of the Confederacy according to the warped gospel of Margaret Mitchell has hurt many! Still hurts many. You ought to be ashamed of yourself for propagating a warped gospel such as this." I'm stunned at a comment that says, "Shame on you! God don't like ugly, and you have modeled yourself after an ugly person. Scarlett O'Hara is evil and selfish!"

I feel like someone is slapping me as I read, "Honestly, Scarlett, I've enjoyed reading your weekly blog ever since day one, even if I don't always agree with your posts, but this is just crazy talk. You've gone too far, and I'm not following you anymore. I'm sure there are many others who will unfollow you now, too."

After I sit there, open-mouthed for a long minute, I drain my Fresca and reread several agreeable responses. There is nothing in this world more satisfying than reading something like "Thanks for a fabulous post, Scarlett! You're absolutely right!" and "That was pure poetry." And "I especially agree with your points here, Scarlett. Thank you." Before I can stop myself, I'm reading Charles's first comment, and I have to admit, his words feel like a warm ray of sun shining down on my shoulders after an awful storm.

> My feisty Scarlett. You've outdone yourself! Honestly, I got chills reading this! Your thoughts and emotions are as familiar to me as breathing in regard to being lonesome and wounded in high school. I remember the day watching *Star Trek* saved my life! Now it's reruns of *Glee* and *Friday Night Lights* that I lose myself in. *Gone with the Wind* is indeed some powerful reading. I adore your gumption to both betray and defend this work of art, this Pulitzer Prize–winning work of art, I might add, and I look forward to the next pearl of wisdom that drips from your lips. Humbled in your presence, Your adoring Charles in Manhattan ☺.

Possessed with the warmth of his adulation, I read his second comment.

> My feisty Scarlett. When will we get to meet in person? I'm begging you on bended knee to be with me! I'm coming down South to the great state of Georgia, to your city, Atlanta, on December 14, 2014, for the seventy-fifth anniversary celebration of that epic film, *Gone with the Wind*! I'm telling you now to give you plenty of advance notice—five months! But before we do meet, for honesty's sake, I feel I must mention one particular affectation of mine. Are you ready? It's—

I wrench my eyes from the screen. Okay, here it comes. He's going to tell me he's a pathological liar. Or he's got Asperger's syndrome, or he's legless. No, he's into young girls. Or boys. Of course, it doesn't matter. Well, they do matter, but not to people who are just acquaintances. "We're just acquaintances," I say, and I mean it. I really do. I return my eyes to Charles's words.

> —the cigar! Tobacco was hands-down the soldier's comforting vice, and I wish to honor this part of the experience, and thus, at each Civil War reenactment, each time I don the blue, which I plan to be in full uniform for the soiree, I smoke cigars by the dozens. Just want to be up front and honest! Your worshipful Charles in Manhattan ☺.

I know smoking's not good for you, but it's not like smoking has ever offended me. In fact, it smells kind of exciting whenever I get a whiff of it when I'm out. I read his next comment, "Please, won't you post your photograph? Here's my latest, wearing my dress blues! With ever-increasing adulation, Charles in Manhattan ☺."

There it is, a picture of him. I stare at his symmetrical and rugged features. I'd pictured some toad-man, the type who went through school with a goofy home-done haircut and a pathetic expression that just invited other kids to shun him. But Charles is surprisingly attractive in a young Robert Redford kind of way. Blue eyes that shine with pleasure, full lips in a fierce smile, shining locks of blond hair to his collar. I am shocked and excited and all aflutter, and for one unguarded flash, I wish I did look like Vivien Leigh so that I could actually meet this man in the flesh. So I could run and jump and throw my arms around his neck.

In a PS he's written his e-mail address.

My mind is doing some autonomous bargaining with me, a loud lawyer with absolutely no scruples saying, "Come on, Joan Meeler, send the man your real photo and tell him you'll see him when he comes to Atlanta."

"No, no, no, no," I chant softly to myself, while very quickly typing, "Charles, thank you so much for your most kind words! Regrettably, I am busy on December 14."

I jump up when I remember some barbecue-flavored Fritos and a container of pecan pralines in the pantry. After a nice snack, I sit back down and begin typing one response at the bottom of the last ugly comment.

> Okay, here's the thing, all you mean trolls! You're not going to upset me! *Gone with the Wind* is *fiction*! Don't read it if you don't agree with it or enjoy it. As I said in my blog, the beauty of fiction is that you can explore large dark themes like racism and slavery and war without anyone ever getting hurt for real! These nasty comments, this kind of anonymous online harassment just shows you're cowards! That's one thing Scarlett O'Hara is not! Anyway, not all Margaret Mitchell's characters' views reflect hers! She said she's more of a Melanie in her personality. I'm reading two biographies about Margaret Mitchell, and it helps that I like and trust the author of *Gone with the Wind*, because the more I like a writer, the more I appreciate his or her work. Plus, when her characters do bad things, they can LEARN from them. Of course Peggy creates "villains" and horrible situations, because that's what makes fiction interesting! If every author played it safe, let fear of what folks would say drive their creative process, let themselves only write what's so-called politically correct, just think what great works of art we'd be without! For crying out loud! And I honestly DO have a black friend. I have two! One says he is very against what he refers to as "censorious interference." He reads

this blog, and just so you know I'm not lying, his comments are under his initials, S.O.S.!

I'm exhausted when I crawl into bed, way too tired to open Bitsy's card. I feel a small pang of guilt over breaking my vow, but I'm just too shell shocked at present to handle any more trauma, and I'm 100 percent certain Bitsy's birthday wishes are laced with emotional landmines. There is only one thing to do. It's time to escape into another world.

Snuggling into my cotton sheets, I relax some and pick up *Gone with the Wind* from my nightstand. I'm at the start of chapter 17: It's a hot dry day in May 1864, and General Sherman has the Yankees in Georgia again. They're one hundred miles away from Atlanta, in Dalton, so no one is worried particularly, that is, until the wounded Confederates from Dalton start flooding in. An army of refugees, dead and dying, descends on Atlanta. Grudgingly, Scarlett nurses them. After watching too many amputations where the chloroform is absent and the opium is a rare, precious thing, she pulls off her apron and sneaks away. Soon Rhett Butler's carriage pulls up next to her, and I'm caught up in the story like it's my first time as I read, "She watched the swell of his powerful shoulders against the cloth with a fascination that was disturbing, a little frightening."

Disturbing, frightening—this is so descriptive of how I feel about Charles that I gasp! Oh, how did I ever let it come to this? I worked so hard at building my happy solitary existence, and I didn't ask for these tingly feelings. And why does everyone assume a person is incomplete if they're not paired up with someone? It's my life and I'm at the helm, and I say what makes me complete. I slam the book shut, suddenly realizing what I've got to do.

"Thanks, Peggy," I say as I climb out of bed, "for putting it into words." At my desk I sit fuming. It was stupid to even let any notion of a relationship into my brain. I didn't realize how deeply I could fall into something, and I got carried away by the sheer momentum of the back-and-forth banter. It's been sweet, it's been fun, but it's time to cut off all correspondence with Charles. To quit Charles cold turkey! Siggy doesn't know what in the world he's talking about with all this "We're born to belong" and "Humans want to be connected to other people" and "We've got to have close personal relationships while we're on this planet."

One thing I know for sure is I definitely do not want the presence of another person in my bed at night, ever. I'm a light sleeper as it is, and even if he didn't snore or talk in his sleep, I'd wake up the second he turned over. And I cannot deal with disrupted sleep. I have got to have my seven-and-a-half hours of uninterrupted sleep, or I cannot function.

I type a Dear John note to Charles's private e-mail address, send it, and sit there with my hands curled into fists, my forehead all tense, thinking, *Late at night like this is when I'm going to miss him the most, when the ache will be the worst. The void I'll have to work to fill. I don't yet know what I'll sub in, but I do know it'll fade eventually, the memory and thus the yearning to have an online exchange with Charles in Manhattan.*

A few minutes later I hear the tiny bell on Dandelion's collar tinkling. I go and scoop her up and out of her box, and ask, "You hungry for a little midnight snack?" Well, a 2:47 a.m. snack. I go to the kitchen and open the refrigerator to get the half-and-half. I pour some into a cereal bowl for her, and then I get the half-eaten Oreo cheesecake ice cream out of the freezer for me. She laps her cream, looking at me with such love, while I finish off the ice cream. "Partners in crime," I say to her, smiling and ruffling the extra-soft fluff at her neck.

When I climb back in bed, she springs up and tiptoes along my side. When she gets to my neck, she puts the top of her silky head under my chin and nudges, purring and pressing insistently. I snuggle up to her silky presence. Soon she's asleep, and I don't want to disturb her, so I lie motionless, wide awake, blinking out into the dark, thinking that purring is such a lovely thing. Why can't humans purr?

8

"Miss Joan, you look about as sad as a hound fresh out of bones," Siegfried says. "Pure T hangdog. What's your problem, ain't had your required dose of caffeine yet this morning?"

I keep typing the memo for John Burke. Despite the fact that it's an inferno outside, I've had way more than my usual amount of coffee, and since I'm running on just a bit over three hours of sleep, I'm feeling even more unstable than usual. My hands are shaky, and it feels like I've got a dozen mad bumblebees in my stomach. I've got to finish this memo and update Giffin & Burke's website before I can even think about opening my secret file drawer and diving into the bag of Hostess powdered mini donettes that will be some small comfort.

"You ignoring me?"

I am, but I shake my head minimally.

Siegfried sidles close to my desk, and his looming presence forces me to look up into his eyes. "It's a Friday, girl. Now, you *know* that's a good day. Usually you're walking on air on a Friday. What's ailin' you? You feeling sick?" He nods at the jumbo container of Tums on my desk. "What can I do to turn your frown upside down?"

Siggy's wearing a big, honest, helpful smile. What alarms me is that his skin, the whites of his eyes have a much yellower tint than usual. Don't worry. I'm fine," I hear myself say. "Just a little bit of acid reflux."

"Come on," he says. "I wasn't born yesterday. I'm gonna tell you something you can take to the bank. 'A merry heart doeth good like a medicine: but a broken spirit drieth the bones.' Proverbs chapter 17, verse 22.'"

"Siegfried, my bones are *fine*."

"Figure of speech. Means if you go 'round sad and dejected all the time, frettin' and hangdog like you are, it'll ruin your health. A positive attitude is a healthy attitude. Now, tell me what's going on."

"I'm just tired," I say, closing my eyes and slumping a bit more for added effect.

"Tell me what's troubling you, 'cause 'A friend loveth at all times, and a brother is born for adversity,' Proverbs 17:17."

"Cut it out, Siegfried! I told you, I'm just *tired*."

"Look up here at me."

Reluctantly I do.

"Miss Joan, there's a reason you didn't sleep good last night, and most likely it's a mental reason. I know when I can't sleep, it's usually things going on in my head I can't make peace with. As you know, the brain's connected to the body in a powerful way."

I sit there a second, consumed with the need to pop a donette into my mouth. But I take a deep breath and say, "All right. I finally opened Bitsy's birthday card this morning." I feel the emotions surge through me again as I see the loopy lines of her script in my mind's eye.

"She got another one of those 'hunks' for you?" Siggy laughs, high and delighted. I wish I'd never told him what Bitsy calls the eligible bachelors she continually seeks out for me.

"Well"—I suck in a deep breath—"she did mention a hunk." *Or two*, I think as I reach down and pull open my secret file drawer and slide my hand into the donettes and grab a silky circle. My fingers hover in midair next to my thigh as I wait for Siegfried to leave. It hurts me to feel the powdered sugar drifting like snow to the marble floor.

"She just does it 'cause she loves you."

I make a sound of disgust deep in my throat. Turns out her gift this year was a thick stack of certificates—everything from an herbal wrap and a massage to a hair-color, cut and style, a manicure and pedicure, a wax job, a facial, a makeover, a membership to a gym, and five hundred dollars at her favorite little exclusive Buckhead boutique where I'm sure her favorite little exclusive sales girl has explicit instructions on suggesting slimming black clothes for me. I daydreamed about putting them in a deep glass mixing bowl, dribbling Wesson oil all over them, throwing in a lit match and watching them burn to a fine gray powder. But in the end, I burned only the card. I decided to put the gift certificates aside for an anonymous donation later in the fall to the annual auction for Scottish Rite Children's Hospital.

"It's true. She wants you to be happy. Folks show their love in many ways, and I expect your mama's working so hard to hook you up 'cause she wants you to have someone to have and to hold when she's gone from this earth."

I frown hard at Siegfried, hoping my eyes are shooting daggers. Will he never give up? What I want, need at this moment is for him to be gone and for me to shove this donette into my mouth. He doesn't know Elizabeth Hargrove Meeler. If there's anything she wants, it's for her own self. So she can feel like her offspring is not some pariah, some social outcast.

Bitsy's card was the oversized kind, and she filled an entire panel with a note about how nice clothes, impeccable grooming, and posture (specifically how the way we carry our body shows how we have or don't have self-confidence) are more important than things like bone structure and the size of your feet when you're older, as in "in your 30s" and out in the dating arena. Her final paragraph seemed bolder, blacker, like she was pressing down really hard with her Montblanc: *There's no reason in this world you couldn't attract a mate, Joan Marie! A healthy thirty-year-old woman with no ex and no children from a prior marriage, a woman who is a lifelong member of the Piedmont Driving Club, you could have a whole repertoire of eager hunks if you wanted! One for every day of the week! Love, Bitsy.*

Siegfried won't leave, and finally I have to pop the donette into my mouth, feeling the fine powdered dust of sugar melt on my tongue. My teeth ache, hurting so beautifully. I swallow without chewing, blink away the tears that come from gagging a bit, lift the white bag with the pretty red heart in the logo up just high enough so Siggy can see it. "Want one?" I choke out when I'm finally able.

"Believe I will," he says, leaning in and discreetly plucking a donette out with his slim fingers.

I watch him eat it gingerly, in three separate bites.

"Another?" I offer.

"Naw. That's good. Thank you. I'll leave you be now. But before I go, I need to give you some advice. 'Despise not thy mother when she is old,' Proverbs 23:22.'"

I'm coming perilously close to a meltdown. "Would you *please* cut it out with the Bible verses, Siegfried?"

"It's only 'cause she cares about you. I understand, 'cause your mama and me, we are on the same wavelength. I don't want one of my favorite people on this planet to be missing out on some of the greatest blessings in life either."

"I'm not missing out on anything!"

"Tell me why you stopped answering that poor lovesick puppy named Charles? Every time I get on *Scarlett Says*, he's begging you to send your picture, to meet him at some battle reenactment.

Sounds to me like he's smitten with somebody. You ain't busy on December 14."

I grit my teeth. I don't like Siggy's smug face. "Yes, I am! You don't know!" This past month has been infuriating, trying to get me and Charles back to just friends. But he didn't get the hint, and so I'm back to just ignoring his pleas and sending the Dear John letter. I miss our friendly banter, but after a dozen back-and-forth exchanges, I know it's no longer even a possibility. It's like his ardor grew even more after my Dear John note, and sometimes I feel like I am standing on this precarious ledge, teetering dangerously over a rocky hollow.

I do admit I feel something when I think about him. So I guess I'm not immune to crushes or fantasies. But, the thing is, I satisfy those needs through means other than face-to-face interactions with members of my species. All I have to do is go look at my bookshelf and gaze at all the books I haven't even read yet. Besides, I know there are millions more out there in the world! I'm happy, maybe even ecstatic, that I was able to get out when I did, that I didn't break down and profess anything in a weak moment. Things could be much worse.

"Aww now, Miss Joan," Siegfried's voice is loud. "I'm sorry. You know I'm a firm believer that virtual reality don't hold a candle to real life. To me, your social networking is antisocial. I believe you need to give Charles a chance. Give love a chance."

I lower my voice so it's barely audible, nod toward John Burke's office door, and say, "Hush!"

"I believe Mr. Burke is preoccupied." Siegfried raises his eyebrows meaningfully.

He's right. Meghan the college intern is in there and the door's closed. I was jealous of Meghan's gorgeous heart-shaped face, her silky blonde hair like a sheet, and her size-four self perched up on stylish pumps, until Siggy started calling her "Gold Ring" after the proverb that says, "As a jewel of gold in a swine's snout, so is a fair woman which is without discretion." I asked him what she wasn't discreet about, and he wouldn't answer.

"Why won't you send poor Charles a photograph?"

Is Siegfried serious? A laugh bursts out of me.

"If it's 'cause you're worrying about your looks, and the only way *I* know this is on account of how you constantly put yourself down, I have to say I think you're more beautiful than a dozen roses. But even if I didn't, you got to realize that happiness is the best cosmetic."

I sit there a second, try not to feel the tiniest shred of hope, then hear myself ask, "Is that a proverb?"

"No. But it's true. At lunch, let me snap your picture with my cell phone and you can send it along and Charles will fall down dead with your beauty." Siegfried tilts his head back and looks hard at me through those little glasses. "Anyway, here is a proverb that just slipped into my mind: 'Favour is deceitful, and beauty is vain: but a woman that feareth the Lord, she shall be praised.' Proverbs 31:30."

I laugh again. "Let's be realistic here, Siggy."

"You keep on ignoring the man, and he just might unfollow you. Then we'll see how you're gonna feel."

My stomach tightens at the ugly word *unfollow* because I've spent the last month grieving over this very thing. Over each and every one of those who have unfollowed *Scarlett Says*. Four hundred and thirty-two unfollowed me after I posted "The Dark Side of Scarlett O'Hara and *Gone with the Wind*." But just as quickly, I encourage myself with the fact that, despite this, my followers are up over seven thousand.

"I know somebody who won't ever unfollow you." Siegfried's voice is soothing.

"I know, Siggy. You're a good man, and I'm very thankful."

"Ain't me I'm talking about. I could be gone from this earth tomorrow. Any one of us could. I'm talking about the Lord. He won't ever take His eye off you, Miss Joan. Won't unfriend you either. No matter what you've said and done, or didn't do and say, or gonna say and do in the future."

I click onto Giffin & Burke's site, move my mouse to the August calendar and pretend to work, though my brain won't engage with Siegfried still standing there. All it does is make loud gibberish.

"Let me tell you a story, Miss Joan."

I sigh.

"I heard two ladies talking at the CVS when I was getting Olie's prescription, and one said to the other that she had unfriended another lady that plays tennis with them. Her companion looked shocked, and she said, 'Seriously?' and the other lady said, 'Mm-hmm. She messed up bad when she didn't invite me to her Derby party. Oh, she said she forgot and asked me to please forgive her, but our friendship is over! Kaput! I have removed her name from my list of friends on Facebook. You should, too.' That other lady said, 'Yes, I'll unfriend her too.'"

I swallow, say nothing.

Siegfried shakes his head. "I thought it was sad the way they tossed their friend aside with a couple of taps on a keyboard. We all mess up sometimes, and we need our friends to be understanding. None of us is perfect."

I nod. "Yeah."

"Unlike people, Miss Joan, you hook up with God, and He won't ever unfollow you. He won't unfriend you when you mess up. God promises to love unconditionally. This is His guarantee; 'Surely I am with you always, to the very end of the age.'"

I don't let myself say what I'd like to, that he's starting to get on my nerves with this God talk. I want to be considerate to the man, but I'm beginning to feel like a scratched record album. "Let's be realistic, Siegfried."

"I am being realistic! Charles in Manhattan asks you at least a dozen times to send him a picture, to come to his reenactments, and meet him face to face. How much more real you need?"

I want to scream so hard my eyeballs will bulge, yell at Siegfried to hush up. I've spent a lot of mental energy squelching thoughts of seeing Charles in the flesh. I mean, that's not even a possibility for a person like me. There's no use even *imagining* it. "Do you mind?" I snap, "I've got work to do!" The irritation in my voice is really coming through.

"All I know is he sounds like a really great guy." Siegfried shoves his hands in his pockets. "Going to Washington, DC, and participating in that commemoration they're doing."

I have to admit I am impressed with that. But I did, am doing my part every time I include links in my blog to the special events and exhibitions DC is doing to mark the one hundred fiftieth anniversary of the Civil War. I'm helping, too, but I don't argue.

After a few seconds, Siegfried says, "Yes, sounds like a real fine person to me. A fine man, sure enough."

I smash another donette into my mouth, click around mindlessly on my keyboard, which is covered with a fine dusting of powdered sugar.

"'Fore I go," Siggy says, "I got to know if you've got your blog figured out for this week."

Sometimes I despise the fact that Siegfried knows I'm hostess of *Scarlett Says*. Oh, how did this happen? How is it that a hermit such as myself, a person who works so hard to remain isolated, has to answer to this man who believes he has some superior other-worldly wisdom? Who doesn't even have an inkling from whence I've come? Has to answer to him about the very private sanctuary that I've spent massive amounts of blood, sweat, and tears creating.

I plunge my hand into the donettes again. After I swallow two more, I say in a quiet voice, "I do."

"That a fact?"

"Yeah." In fact, I have it mostly written and I feel pretty good about this weekend's topic. It's on that delicious contradiction that's become an age-old paradigm of women's views of men: Ashley versus Rhett. I've intentionally been doing a string of uncontroversial ones such as "The Number One Question Fans Asked Margaret Mitchell" and "From 'Fiddle dee dee' to 'Frankly, my dear, I don't give a damn'—Famous Quotes from *Gone with the Wind*." And I'm hoping this one will spark some great comments but won't get people so worked up that they decide to unfollow me.

"Well, what is it? Maybe I can give you some help."

I sit there, looking at Siggy, debating, and then his brown eyes are twinkling at me in that sweet, honest way he has, and so I tell him, "I'm discussing Scarlett's inner conflict. How she wants the solid comfort of Ashley Wilkes, but the real love of her life is the roguish Rhett Butler. She feels passion for Rhett."

He nods slowly, rolls his lips in, thinking. Then he says, "Well, I don't want to upset the apple cart, but it seems ironic that a person like you is writing about something like this. Seems to me like it would require experience with *real* life if you're gonna engage your readers. To write about passion, yearning, don't you need to taste it yourself?"

I sigh, flop back against my desk chair.

"What?"

"Just . . . can't you just lay off about that? Please?"

"Aww, I'm sorry." He puts his fingers on my wrist, gently.

At noon, I sit in the breakroom, my nose in *Road to Tara: The Life of Margaret Mitchell*. Lunch is a Double Whopper from Burger King I picked up in the drive-thru on my way home from work last night and reheated in the office microwave, along with a can of dill pickle–flavored Pringles, a twenty-ounce Mountain Dew, and a sleeve of imitation pecan sandies. I don't think obsession is too strong a word for what I'm feeling about studying Margaret Mitchell's life. I finished *Southern Daughter* five days after it arrived on my doorstep, and then I felt the need to dip back into *Gone with the Wind*, got to the end of that, and just started this one Wednesday evening. Already I'm near the end, right at the part where Margaret Mitchell has become an overnight celebrity.

I can literally feel poor Peggy's angst when fame is thrust upon her as *Gone with the Wind* generates hysterical fervor. I hear her phone ringing incessantly, her doorbell chiming so frequently her ears ring. I see the mailbox spilling over with fan letters, see telegrams appearing constantly, begging for interviews, speeches. Peggy knows she's famous, a literary celebrity, and as such is expected to give speeches, make comments, and appear in public. She feels besieged and she cannot handle the pressure. The poor woman can't even go out of her house without being instantly recognized. She wants to hide. Vows she'll never write another book. For self-comfort, she tells herself the public acclaim will surely subside, the hysteria will definitely die down, and when it doesn't, she feels brutally victimized. She begins to suffer extreme anxiety.

I'm hanging on every word as I read, "Part of her unpreparedness for the book's success was due to her lack of self-confidence."

Well, well. Peggy Mitchell is a woman after my own heart! A recluse with a fear of the public eye. Extreme anxiety and a lack of self-confidence. I feel for her, wish I could somehow slip into this biography (my empathy, my fervor to offer comfort is real though I realize Peggy is dead) and reassure her as I wonder how it would feel to write a book like that, one that "dramatically altered the pattern of my life."

At five o'clock, I shut down the computer, and still in my chair, I roll over to gather my handbag, my book and my favorite coffee mug, which I take home and wash each evening. I feel a shadow fall over me and look up. It's Gold Ring, standing there with her bronzed and bejeweled arms crossed over her chest, silky blonde hair cascading over one shoulder, frosted pink lips frowning.

I am just on the cusp of the weekend, *my* time, that rejuvenating, restoring two days I need desperately after five days of being "on" at Giffin & Burke. My plan is to head straight home. Well, actually it's the long way home so I can avoid Dr. Cynthia LaForgue's Veterinary office.

I feel my palms grow clammy. I despise the fact that I'm overly anxious around Meghan. At first I thought it was because I'm so not a party girl like she appears to be, but then I realized the reason is because she wears the continual sneer of one of those girls who ran with the elite clique in high school, that strata who looked down on all beneath them in the social structure. Plus she calls me "the receptionist" in a real snotty tone, like she doesn't know my name, though it's engraved in a gold bar above the title Administrative Assistant on my desk.

My heart is thudding, but I smile pleasantly as I stand up and meaningfully rummage around for my keys in my handbag. "May I help you, Meghan?" I say.

She's a whole head taller than me, and she looks down into my face, tosses her silken sheaf of hair behind her, sucks in, thrusts her firm little boobs out and exaggeratedly flares her nostrils to show her fear that she might dare touch me as she slides between me and my desk. She sits down in my chair and turns my computer back on. She clears her throat, says, "Give me the password already."

Very slowly I look down at Gold Ring's dark roots, my brain attempting to register the fact that this chick is sitting at *my* computer and telling me to give her *my* password. Unprepared at this invasion of my privacy, I nearly scream out, *You can't use my computer!* Even on my sick days, which I've only had two of in the whole time I've been employed at Giffin & Burke, my computer is sacred, off-limits.

"John told me I could use this computer for my journalism assignment."

She calls Mr. Burke *John?* My heart is bamming like sneakers in a dryer. I hold my hands together so she won't see them shaking. Oh, I really, really wish I could say something sarcastic, like *They actually let girls like you into college?* But, even if I could, I'm an employee here and I don't own this computer, and she's my boss's intern. Plus, if I protest too loudly, I'll look suspicious. I'm nervous about what could happen if she clicks on that icon on my desktop that's my direct link to *Scarlett Says*. It's purposefully labeled "Office Supplies List," but Meghan's just the type of girl who'd snoop.

"What's wrong with your laptop?" I ask in a tone so sweet it turns my stomach.

She raises her hands in a "beats me" gesture and a cloud of Chanel perfume rises toward the fluorescent light. "I dropped it and now it's having issues."

I make a commiserate sound, nod like this is a common thing for me, too, and like a kind teacher, lean over her chair, *my* chair, and instead of telling her my password, I type it in, and say, "There you go!" I even smile at her, let her know I am willing to be her friend as I settle on one of the low stools we keep against the side of my reception desk for clients to rest on.

In fact, my evening plans have instantly changed. I will remain here until Gold Ring is finished. I pluck one of the Giffin & Burke nail files from the glass fish bowl and go to work on my thumb. I wonder if I should try to make conversation with Gold Ring. I decide not to. It might slow her down, and I really need to get home to feed Dandelion.

Not a minute later, she squeals, "Ewww!" so loud and high-pitched that I flinch. I look at her horrified face.

"This keyboard is sticky and greasy and disgusting!" She lifts it, flips it over, jiggles it a bit and we watch all sorts of crumbs and sediment drift down on the desk—powdered sugar like snow, gnarled orangey cheese niblets from Cheetos, sandy crumbs from what I'm guessing were the pecan sandies. It feels surreal. People don't do stuff like this, I think. Does Gold Ring think I don't have feelings?

All of a sudden, she says, "You're disgusting," as she releases my keyboard over open air, holds her hands up, fingers splayed out wide like someone's pointing a gun at her.

There's a painful silence as the keyboard dangles, swinging back and forth like a hypnotist's medallion. I hug myself, wanting to crawl beneath the credenza and disappear into my armadillo pose. But I am paralyzed. I am not able even to breathe. *What should I do? I don't know what I should do. I don't know what to do, and my neck is tight.*

I'm still in shock mode when Siegfried walks through the lobby, whistling and jingling keys and swinging the small blue Igloo cooler that is his lunchbox. He sees me with my mouth open and takes a detour over to the reception desk.

"What's going on here, ladies?" he asks, looking from my face to the dangling keyboard.

Before I can get a word out, Meghan turns to look up at him. "John ought to fire this nasty person, because not only is she bad for Giffin & Burke's *image*," the irony of this makes her cackle, "she's totally ruining the equipment!"

I sit breathing now, but very slowly, so I won't scream like a lunatic.

"I mean it, Mr. Janitor. I watch this fat cow continuously stuffing her face while she works, and this keyboard is so disgusting I feel like puking! I need to go sanitize my hands!" Her eyes are wide with outrage.

Siggy tilts his head, takes a long look at Meghan with his eyes squinting. I can see a vein in his neck pulsing. "Young lady?" he says through his straight white teeth. "You ought to be ashamed of yourself. I know you're young, and maybe you ain't been to the school of hard knocks yet, and maybe you think the world is yours on a silver platter. But I want you to listen up and listen good. Everything we get on this planet is a pure–T gift. You ain't some superior being, and the world don't owe you nothin'! Just cause you're younger and skinnier than someone don't make you better. You need to learn some respect. Don't you doubt it for a moment, we are all God's children. Your mama didn't teach you that you don't treat nobody like a dog?"

It feels like a miracle has happened when I notice Meghan is blushing.

But Siggy doesn't release her yet. He tells her, "Here's something you need to tattoo on your brain, young lady. You ought to write this out by hand one hundred times. 'The merciful man doeth good to his own soul: but he that is cruel troubleth his own flesh.' Proverbs 11, verse 17. And here's another one, 'A high look, and a proud heart, and the plowing of the wicked, is sin.' Proverbs 21:4.'"

He's on a roll. "And here you go, in Proverbs 6, verses 16 through 19, it talks about seven things the Lord hates, and I want you to know that number one is 'A proud look.'"

Meghan stutters a few unintelligible sounds, staring at Siggy with wide eyes.

"I got another good idea," he continues. "If Miss Joan's computer grosses you out so much, they got plenty of computers the public can use at the downtown Atlanta library."

When Meghan is gone, I see his long slim fingers lifting my keyboard to its rightful place. He walks over to the custodial closet and gets out a little whisk broom with a dustpan attached to it. As he's sweeping up the crumbs, I tell him, "You don't need to do that, Siggy."

"I know," he says. "I want to."

I swallow, stand there as he returns the broom and comes back to collect his things. The words "Thank you" come up out of the depths of my being.

"You welcome, Miss Joan." He turns to me and puts a hand on my shoulder. "I hope you have yourself a beautiful weekend."

I notice Siggy has very pronounced bags under his eyes. His body has the exhausted look of someone battling physical pain. I'm thinking his skin definitely does look yellower, and so do the whites of his eyes. Even I can see that the sickle cell is overtaking him. Should I call Olie? Has he been drinking enough water? Worry hits me like a wave.

Somehow I manage to collect my things, stumble out of Giffin & Burke and down the steps and across Peachtree Street to the parking lot where my safe welcoming little Toyota sits. Though it's way over a hundred degrees inside, I climb in and close the door behind me and sit shaking and hugging myself for a good two minutes before I'm calm enough to crank up, lower the windows, and blast the AC. Very, very rarely, and this is one of those times, do I let myself even fantasize about quitting my job and moving in with Bitsy. I picture my old bedroom with the zebra-striped beanbag chair and the stacks of books knee-high in every corner, the Nickelback and Foo Fighters posters on the ceiling above my bed, where my eyes rested on all those lonely Friday and Saturday nights while everyone else was out partying. Just as quick, I shake that thought. It would be far worse to live with Bitsy than battle my social anxiety. Anyway, I bet she's had her "interiors man," as she calls him, purge all traces of my bourgeois existence. Plus, now I have Dandelion, and there's no way Bitsy would allow her.

If there's anything good about taking the long way home, it's that I pass Krispy Kreme Doughnuts on Ponce De Leon Avenue. My policy is that if the neon Hot Doughnuts Now sign is flashing in the window like it is now, it's my sign to go through the drive-thru for a dozen.

The AC is blasting my sweaty hair nice and cold, and when the cashier hands the warm box of doughnuts to me, they smell so good, I decide it's worth it to ruin my appetite, and by the time I'm at my apartment, I've gobbled down five.

I can hear Dandelion's excited meow as I'm putting my key into the lock. As I'm walking through the den into my bedroom to put some things away, she winds herself around my ankles so crazily, I'm afraid I'll trip. "Sit!" I command the gray ball of fluff, but she doesn't obey.

When I'm in my playclothes, I grab my mail, go in the kitchen, feed the cat, and pour myself a tall glass of cold milk and sit at the table. Dandelion leaps to my lap, nudges my arm, so I'll let her lap from my glass. Sometimes I do, but not today. I've been working on teaching her to sit, and I use milk to train her. I command her to "Sit!" and I don't give her the milk until she does. So far, and it's been two weeks, she's been successful four times out of about fifty. But I know she's not deaf or stupid, and things take time, so I'm not discouraged.

A few minutes pass, and I give her a bowl of milk anyway and fix myself a nice salad with mixed field greens, cucumbers, tomatoes, and a lite bleu cheese dressing to counteract the doughnuts. I eat it standing at the counter, thinking about calling Olie.

If she'd just allow me to tell her real quick about how depleted Siggy looked today, and then hang up, I might. But the thing is, on Wednesdays when she calls me, it turns into an hour conversation, me saying about one word to every hundred of hers, and usually just an "Mm-hmm" and a "Yes, ma'am." She goes on and on about her own medical issues and what the doctor said about Siegfried on his last visit, which frankly scares the wits out of me, and about how her ladies' circle at church has knitted him a prayer shawl, praying over each click of the needle and about how she puts it over him when he gets home at night, as he's sitting in the La-Z-Boy to elevate his legs. Once she told me about how sickle cell can delay puberty in teens and that Siggy still had a high falsetto voice in eleventh grade and the kids called him Sisfried and she had to go down to the school and "straighten some chirren out," as she put it.

I have to pick an opportune moment to hang up on Olie. I try and do it right in the middle of one of my own sentences, and that way she doesn't think I'm hanging up on her. I told her the second Wednesday she called, after we'd been talking—well, after I'd been listening, I should say—for two hours that I have a bad line here. And I had to hang up on her right in the middle of my words to prove it.

I decide I won't call her tonight. Maybe on Sunday afternoon. Friday night is *my* time, and I need it very, very bad tonight. I'm feeling so jangled that the sound of ice cubes dropping inside the freezer make me jump.

Every Friday evening at eight I microwave my Orville Redenbacher's Movie Theater Butter Popcorn, get my jumbo box of Milk Duds from the pantry, and settle in to the saggy corner of the sofa to watch *Gone with the Wind*. You'd think I'd get bored of it since I've watched it every week since I was sixteen. You'd think I'd fail to get a thrill each time I watch Scarlett notice Rhett for the first time, as she says to a friend, "Who's that? He looks as if he knows what I look like without my shimmy," or as Prissy declares, "I don't know nuthin' 'bout birthin' no babies," or when Scarlett is in the carriage with Rhett while Atlanta burns and he tells her, "Take a good look, my dear. It's a historical moment. You can tell your grandchildren how you watched the Old South disappear."

One scene that never fails to send somewhat uncomfortable achy-good feelings throughout me is when Rhett declares to Scarlett, "No, I don't think I will kiss you. Although you need kissing badly. That's what's wrong with you. You should be kissed, and often, by some-one who knows how." When that scene appears, I wouldn't notice a tornado if it came through the room. But the scene I live to see, my healing balm, what has reassured and restored me countless times, is right after Scarlett has killed the Yankee soldier who invades her beautiful Tara. She stands on the stairway and says in a rather matter-of-fact tone, "Well I guess I've done murder. I won't think about this now. I'll think about it tomorrow." That particular assessment, her decision to move on without looking her act in the eye, is what makes me know I can continue life on this planet, in this body. There was that time I didn't think this act of living might be possible. The night I took a bottle of Bitsy's extra-strength painkillers along with a mug of Jack Daniels into the guest room.

The running time of my cassette is just shy of four hours, if you include the overture and the credits. I never fast-forward, because listening to the theme from Tara is like a religious rite for me. It's midnight when I scoop a sleeping Dandelion from my lap, rise, and stretch before I eject the tape to slide it reverently back into its case. I am so deeply tired, I decide I'll skip brushing my teeth even though popcorn husks are wedged up in my gums. I just want to go curl up in bed with Dandelion and read *Gone with the Wind* until I drift off.

I take my bowl to the sink, say goodnight to my African violet, and then, who knows why, I pause at my desk, my finger just tingling to turn on the computer. I stand quietly for a while, thinking how I definitely don't want to wake up tired tomorrow on my day to blog, how I'm exhausted down to my bones from the stress of the work week and particularly Gold Ring's rudeness, and then, for some reason, I sit down anyway. I'm just going to look real quick, only glance at the number of followers, not even scroll down to responses, then I'll hop up and get to bed.

Well, well. Here we are and isn't this a nice thing to see right before bed? More than eight thousand people are following me. I smile as I think how great that's going to feel. Tomorrow's post about Rhett versus Ashley is sure to stir up tons of passionate responses, and hence, additional followers.

Siggy doesn't know what he's talking about. It's not ironic for me to write about passion. Maybe I haven't experienced physical love in the flesh, but I do know Scarlett O'Hara inside and out. Her yearnings became mine many, many times as I crawled between the covers of *Gone with the Wind* to live in that fictive world. Siggy will see his mistake when he reads my blog.

"Dandy! Come here, sweetie," I call, standing a bit unsteadily as I feel for my slipper beneath the desk with my right foot. And then, to my utter astonishment, I fall gracelessly backward into my chair, whamming my spine on the back, hard. Tears well up, I see stars, and I have to sit a minute, nursing the pain. After a spell, I reach a hand back and touch my back, checking for a welt. "I'm okay," I say, and start to get up, but then decide I better make sure.

A few minutes pass, and to my absolute horror my hands have somehow betrayed me and clicked to my responses. There's one from Charles. In fact, there are quite a number of them. That's no surprise. Though I haven't responded to him in seventeen days, he keeps on. He's certainly a loyal, or is that stubborn, follower.

But wait. I squint my tired eyes and lean closer. Is that someone replying to him? Yes, it is!

"Dear Charles," Nancy in Tennessee writes. "Thank you for posting all the links to the Civil War to Civil Rights events in Washington, DC. I can see you're a man with a heart. Plus, and this is so cool, you said your birthday's on June 9, 1989, and that's mine, too! Surely this means we're soul mates."

An odd little pang makes my heart clench at the thought of someone else having these intimate conversations with Charles. Also, I did not know he was only twenty-five. I just assumed he was my age, or older. If I ever went after a man, and I say *ever*, which I won't, I'd go for one who's a lot older than me. Finally, my back stops hurting enough to stand up. Dandelion appears at my ankles, winding and petting herself. She rubs her cheek one last time, looks up at me like *It's time for bed.*

Now I feel bad. She's just a little ball of fluff dependent on me, and she lives for this most delicious part of the day, and I've made her wait too long. "Come on up here and snuggle with Mama. We'll just read ourselves to sleep. Yes, we will," I say, climbing in bed and patting the mattress. *I don't care if Nancy and Charles do get together,* I think, pulling the cool percale sheet up to our necks. My back still hurts, and it takes a while to find a good reading position. *Why should I care? I don't care! You know what? It's actually a good thing. Maybe Nancy will distract him and he'll stop asking for my picture, stop asking me to get together with him. Won't that be a relief? Yes, it sure will.*

An hour later, Dandelion is sound asleep and I'm still reading, wide awake and caught up in Scarlett's emotions as I read about Rhett and Scarlett's passionate kiss.

"Whoa, now," I say, closing the novel. "That's enough." I place it on my bedside table, turn out the lamp, and lie there, trying to wipe my mind clean enough to fall asleep. But I can't. I know it's because words are powerful and it's from reading such a scene, but still, I'm horrified. *There's no way in the world I'm going, even incognito, to the seventy-fifth anniversary of the movie in December!* I'd been thinking for a crazed few days that maybe, just maybe, I might be able to control my social anxiety enough to go to downtown Atlanta and just watch the festivities in the name of research for *Scarlett Says.* But now I know I cannot do this. I know instinctively that I cannot rise above and conquer my anxiety.

9

On Sunday, the day I swore to myself to call Olie about Siggy's turn toward yellow, I sit in the kitchen at 7:00 a.m., drinking coffee and eating a pan full of warm Pillsbury sweet rolls covered with grainy orange icing that is absolutely delectable when paired with the soft dough that I intentionally underbake. Dandelion doesn't seem interested. She sniffs them, backs away, and curls up on the table to watch me. She looks adorable.

It's a perfect summer day outside. Nothing but blue skies stretching into the distance. I see a squirrel running along a pine limb, stopping, starting, stopping, its tail twitching in excited little jerks. I wonder if Dandelion ever longs to go outside and be in nature. "You want to go outside and chase a squirrel?" I say, pointing at the window, but she only stares at me. Oh, well. She wouldn't know what to do out there in the wide, wild world. Probably get smushed on Ponce de Leon Avenue. The thought of this makes my eyes fill, and I instinctively reach out and grab Dandelion and squeeze her a little too tight. She squirms and I let her go, thinking, *She's good. She's safe! She's inside and she's safe.*

I run my finger around the perimeter of the sweet roll pan to sweep up the last bit of orange icing and lick it clean and feeling downright calm and content, nurse my coffee. Not a whole lot I have to do today. It's luxurious to know my post on *Scarlett Says* for the week is done. It literally poured off my fingertips yesterday morning. And it's stunning, if I do say so myself.

At nine o'clock, I find myself seated at my desk, staring at the computer screen with my mouth open. I'm up to 9,472 followers and more pages of responses than I can count! "Ashley or Rhett— Peggy Mitchell's Paradigm of Women's Views About Men" is gilded. Turns out, people—men and women—are intensely interested in that old debate spawned by *Gone with the Wind*. Nobody is neutral. But it appears that all the arguments are fun in a good way.

I literally climbed into Scarlett as I wrote about her intense inner conflict, those seemingly contradictory sides of herself that make her so compelling. Hers is a delicious contradiction. And the thing is, her inner conflict is never resolved. In fact, the number one question fans asked of Peggy Mitchell after *Gone with the Wind*'s release was, "Did Scarlett ever get Rhett back?" Even Peggy didn't know. "I ended the book where it ended," she'd reply.

At different times in my life, I've rooted for both. When I was sixteen, the very first time I fell into Peggy's masterpiece, I was all for Rhett Butler. That roguish sexy scoundrel excited me no end. Scarlett would long for the subdued aristocratic and artsy Ashley Wilkes, and I would want to scream! I wanted to reason with her, "But, Rhett Butler's the one who makes your blood boil!" I remember girls at Pace Academy asking each other that very question as they walked down the hall, arguing back and forth.

"I despise so-called *gentle*men like Ashley," wrote one new male follower. "Nothing but a pansy!"

"Well, I think sensitive men are such good husband material," replied Novene from Georgia. "No matter what anybody says, sexual attraction fades, and a man like Rhett would probably be off making eyes at the first big bosom he sees."

"Men controlled by their passions like Rhett are just not trust-worthy," wrote Mary in California. "I'd much rather marry an Ashley than a cynical old playboy like Rhett.

"No matter what girls say, in the long run, they'd much rather have a man like Ashley Wilkes. He's elegant, and he loves literature, and art, the finer things in life."

"Wanda in Rhode Island wrote, "Rhett's nothing but a black-hearted scoundrel."

"He's not!" countered Wilhelmina in Ohio. "He's masculine! He sets Scarlett's heart ablaze, and who can put a price on that? Give me the fire!"

From there, followers argued that Rhett was immoral, unscru-pulous, self-centered, and disloyal to the South. They claimed Ashley was helpless when it came to real work, that he was too refined to be of any use to a woman, and that he could never have satisfied the passionate Scarlett O'Hara.

As usual, I slipped in a portion from the actual novel, and this time it was from chapter 47, right after Scarlett has learned she caused the death of Frank, her second husband. Rhett is asking her hand in marriage, and Scarlett tells him no, she doesn't want to marry anybody. Rhett responds, "You aren't telling me the real reason. What is it?"

Scarlett's thoughts turn to Ashley—the real reason she would not marry again. "Every part of her almost everything she had ever done, striven after, attained, belonged to Ashley, were done because she loved him. Ashley and Tara, she belonged to them."

Rhett interrupts Scarlett's thoughts with a forceful kiss.

"And before a swimming giddiness spun her round and round, she knew that she was kissing him back."

From there, Scarlett is done for. Physically, at least. She calls it a "rush of tingling confusion." I spy a rather long comment from Siggy. I'm a bit reluctant to read it after what he said about irony, but I take a deep breath and jump in.

Miss Scarlett, this is some powerful reading! Honestly, you amaze me. You definitely had a tug-o-war going on inside over Ashley and Rhett. But did that make it right to steal your sister Suellen's beau? To lie to Frank and tell him she was gonna marry someone else? But I got to hand it to you, in chapter 47 of *Gone with the Wind*, you did confess to Rhett, "I killed him." I like it when your conscience got the best of you and you was scared you'd die and go to hell. Proverbs 9:10 says, "The fear of the Lord is the beginning of wisdom." And I feel it is my duty to remind you that in Proverbs 6 it says there are seven things the Lord hates, and one of them is a lying tongue. Your loyal follower, S.O.S.

I shake my head in wonder. My fingers automatically fly to the keyboard, ready to type out, "Thanks for your comment, S.O.S., but let's try and be realistic here—" when all of a sudden I see Siggy at Giffin & Burke as he was on Friday. In my mind's eye, which eclipses my physical eyes, I see his soulful eyes, those chocolate brown discs surrounded by yellow. I see the yellowish tone to his beautiful mahogany skin as he kneels down to sweep up the crumbs that rained from my keyboard. He looks at me, smiles, and says, "You're welcome, Miss Joan. I hope you have yourself a beautiful weekend."

I type one word, "Thanks."

Before this moment, if you'd asked me if I'd ever attend a black church, or any church for that matter, I'd have laughed in your face. Just the thought of this is the epitome of scary for a person with social anxiety. But now I can think of nothing else except how I need to see what makes Siggy tick.

My fingers type in Google, then hesitate. What did he say his church is called? He sure talks about it enough. I ought to remember. Caramel Mountain or something? I picture liquid caramel

133

cascading down from a volcano's summit. That's not it. It's . . . it's Mount Caramel, no, Mount Carmel! Mount Carmel Baptist.

When I enter this, I find there are Mount Carmel Baptists everywhere, from Arkansas to South Carolina. I click on the one in southwest Atlanta on Campbellton Road and up pops a sophisticated website. At the top is an animated band of blue, with white cottony clouds and the words *Saving Souls* in a fancy script, moving behind a logo of praying hands. A good-looking black man identified as Reverend Timothy Flemming Sr. fills the rest of the home page.

I can tell he's charismatic just by looking at his posture and his face. His cheeks shine like he's made out of wax. And this is interesting, but not surprising—he's also a musician, a performer. I click on a link that showcases ten of his CDs: from *Old Time Camp Tunes*, in which he's wearing a flannel shirt and overalls, to one called *Got the Devil Under My Feet*," where he's in a suit, one wing-tipped foot planted on a prostrate devil.

Next I click on Church Tour, and I'm transported on a virtual visit to the sanctuary, gazing upon rows of gleaming wooden pews, then up toward the pulpit and the choir loft, where my eyes zero in on the sun shining through a round stained glass window. It's pretty impressive, but I'm disappointed that there's no congregation in the shots. I guess I expected to see Siggy's skinny self sitting among a sanctuary full of worshipers. The mission statement of Mount Carmel declares that they're an "evangelistic ministry dedicated to reaching people and changing lives with the Gospel of Jesus Christ." It further affirms, "Our vision is world evangelism, and our desire is to see God bless you in every way."

Beside this is a place you can click on to enter your prayer requests. When I click on Services, I take a deep breath. There sure is a lot going on at this place! But the one that makes my eyeballs spin is the Third Sunday Anointing Healing Service at 8:00 p.m. Healing? Does this mean healing as in curing-physical-afflictions-and-diseases healing? Or is it more like emotional healing of the mind? I've glimpsed televangelists laying on hands while I'm flipping channels, but I've never stayed with them long enough to see if the lame walk or the blind see. Curious, I click on it, and a banner with a Bible verse pops up: "Is any sick among you? Let him call for the elders of the church; and let them pray over him, anointing him with oil in the name of the Lord: And the prayer of faith shall save the sick, and the Lord shall raise him up," James 5:14-15.

Now, why, if Siggy believes in this Scripture stuff, doesn't he just go to one of these healing services and let the elders pray and anoint him? In fact, I'm *stunned* at the man's inconsistency. How can he just pick and choose what he believes to be true? If part is true for him, then all is true. The truth, the whole truth, and nothing but the truth. Surely he's heard this saying. The common senseness of my realization slays me. I'm going to talk to him about this picking and choosing he's doing. It's all or none.

Then I think, *Maybe Siggy only clings to the proverbs.* I Google "Proverb about healing" and up pops Proverbs 4:20-22: "My son, attend to my words; incline thine ear unto my sayings. Let them not depart from thine eyes; keep them in the midst of thine heart. For they are life unto those that find them, and health to all their flesh." I turn my printer on, print out the verse, fold the page in half, thinking, *As soon as I find a good moment, I'm giving this to Siggy. He'll see his error in black and white.*

I return to the Mount Carmel website, and it strikes me as odd that on Friday nights, of all nights, there's a Bible study from 7:30 to 9:00. Maybe it's a bunch of old people who have no social life or wounded singles out looking for love in a place that's not a bar. There are two Sunday morning services: 7:30 and 10:30. I check my watch, 9:22 a.m., and then try to recall which service it is Siggy would be most likely to attend. He's a pretty early a.m. kind of guy, but there's nothing to do but give it a shot.

I go to the bedroom and pull on a skirt with an elastic waist and a roomy peasant blouse, stick my feet in some low-heeled work pumps, then head to the bathroom to brush my hair back into a ponytail and rustle around in the drawer for my one and only tube of lipstick—Mohave mauve. I'm loathe to leave my kitty on a weekend, but I pour some extra half-and-half into Dandelion's bowl and say, "Mama will be home before you know it, sweetie."

Two minutes later, I'm sitting in the parking lot, feeling miraculously composed as I crank up and determine the best route to Campbellton Road. Happily, Sunday morning traffic is not bad. I drive along, turning onto Freedom Parkway and wondering who has entered my body and rendered me capable of doing this thing out of my normal routine. The more speed my little Toyota picks up, the more calm I seem to be. Then I think, if I can do this so easily, what's to stop me from going to downtown Atlanta for the seventy-fifth anniversary celebration of *Gone with the Wind*? I get a sense of happiness mixed with pain that I've gotten used to whenever I think of Charles. Nope, I cannot see him in the flesh, I quickly decide. It would be going backwards in progress. Then I think, Nancy in Tennessee might decide to go! But then I mentally note that Nancy in Tennessee is not feisty. She has no thoughts of her own, just parrots Charles and says, "Oh, Charles, you're so wonderful, talking about these 'From Civil War to Civil Rights' things going on in DC." I, however, challenge him. I say, well, I *used* to say, "Charles, why do you feel the need to reenact battles?" and things of that nature.

You can sure tell it's August down South. On the roadsides the weeds have that parched brown look, and the boughs on the pines are a droopy yellow green, everything weary looking. But then I see a Back to School billboard for Walmart, and I know fall will be here before we know it. Even though cooler temperatures are such a relief, I've always hated fall. Bitsy would get in a frenzy, an absolute obsession with preparing me for that all-important first day of school. She obsessed for weeks on buying me just the right designer wardrobe from Neiman Marcus and Nordstrom, and of course, an assortment of coordinated Manolos for my feet. She never let me forget she had to buy things in the "chubby girl" departments. She never tired of being disappointed that I was not involved in all the "right clubs." Conversations with her friends about what the popular girls were all doing sent her into a whirlwind of despair.

I turn on the radio to drown out the thoughts in my head. But as I merge onto I-75, a sign reads Montgomery, and that makes me think of Birmingham, where Siggy grew up, and then I can't help but wonder what it was like being raised by Olie. I contrast my mother's thin, stylish, sophisticated figure, her tinkling cocktail-party laugh, with Olie's soft, rounded pillowy self, her unselfconscious deep chortle that doesn't make me recoil whenever I hear it. I compare the way Olie makes jokes about her size, saying, "I like to refer to myself as super-sized. Super sounds a lot better than jumbo, don't you think?" and my mother's blasé-voiced false humility, "Oh, it's just awful having a medical condition like this overactive thyroid of mine. Simply exhausting when you're always trying to gain weight."

A car horn blares at me, and I realize I've strayed out of my lane. This scares me enough to freeze all thoughts for a bit, and soon I merge onto Langford Parkway. I press the accelerator and take the Campbellton Road exit. The website said Mount Carmel Baptist Church is 1.1 miles from here.

The parking lot is full. I ride around and around and finally find a space, pull in, and just sit there. I didn't see Siggy's emerald green Buick LeSabre. My dash clock reads 10:28. One thing I can say for sure is that black folks sure dress up for church, way better than boring whites. The ladies have on the most colorful hats, and the men are sleekly outfitted in nice suits and ties and polished shoes. I look down at my potato-colored peasant top and my skirt with a grease stain on the front, my stubbly calves, and my clunky sandals, and I feel anxiety rise in me like a wave. My heart starts knocking in my chest. I look down and I'm not surprised to see my hands clenching the steering wheel so hard my knuckles are white. I sit up straight, unclench my hands, breathe in and out deeply several times, and say so loudly it makes my ears buzz and my throat hurt, "I want to go home!"

I feel a shadow come between me and the sun over my left shoulder. Hear knuckles rapping on the window. A muffled male voice says, "You all right in there, ma'am?"

I open my eyes, turn my head slowly to look out at a handsome black face with a tidy Fu Manchu mustache. He's staring at me wide eyed. I manage a nod and then he smiles a beautiful smile with the straightest, whitest teeth I've ever seen and opens my door, stepping back like I'm royalty. "I'm Darryl Lattimore," he says in a buttery tone. "Welcome to Mount Carmel."

"Uh, thanks." I'm feeling overly conscious of my lumpy body and my plain clothes. He's dressed in a very nice fitted gray suit, starched white shirt, and a maroon tie. I spot a clump of shiny cards that say Mount Carmel Baptist across the top jutting up from his lapel pocket. An usher? Darryl steps up beside me, offers his arm.

I'm paralyzed. *Have I ever been escorted by a man? Let's see. Nope, this has never happened to me before in my entire life.* I remember dreaming, as a very young girl, of the day I would marry, how my father would escort me down the aisle to a fanfare of trumpets like I'd seen in a Cinderella cartoon. That dream curled up its toes and died when I was in the ninth grade. I never even got asked to a high-school prom. I never wanted to get asked.

Darryl dips his head slightly as he lifts those beautiful black eyebrows, and somehow I observe myself inserting my big arm through the lean and elegantly clad crook of his elbow. Awkwardly I put one foot, then the other, out on the blacktop and allow him to heft me out. I feel the heat rise up to envelop us, and I'm terrified

I'll sweat on this good-looking man before we even make it to the door of the church.

"This your first time to worship with us?"

"Uh, yes. Yes, it is."

"We're glad to have you. If you'll fill this out, we can keep in touch." Darryl pulls one of the cards from his pocket and hands it to me.

I smile, say nothing, and try to pant silently as I struggle to keep up with his purposeful gait across the parking lot. I hope he doesn't feel my arm quaking in his or see the sweat beads I know are congregating on my forehead. *Oh, why in the world did I do this?* I moan inwardly. *Siggy's probably not even here.* Side by side, we step into a blast of cold air in the lobby. It is nice. Plush carpeting, fancy tables and lamps, floral arrangements that are out-of-this-world pretty. The air smells like flowers mixed with candles. There's a hushed feeling and no people in the lobby. I can hear organ music, and Darryl escorts me right up to wide open double doors, where I stop, plant my feet. The sanctuary is packed, and I scan it quickly, don't see Siggy's distinct head. I want nothing more than to turn and walk back out that door. But my legs won't move. I'm helpless.

Darryl tugs me forward a bit, whispers so intimately in my ear I jump. "I see a seat over there to the left, near the window."

I get weak in the knees like I'm about to melt. But I shake my head.

"You don't want to sit over there?"

"No," I whisper.

"How about up front?" he asks, so close I feel the hair at my ear rustle. This sends shivers all the way to my feet.

"Oh, no." I breathe, "Not up there."

He chuckles softly. "The choir loft, then?"

"Um . . . uh . . . I'm looking for somebody. Somebody I know so I can sit with him."

"Who might that be?"

I'm looking at how weird my big toes are. There are wiry hairs on the toe knuckles. I hope with all my heart that Darryl doesn't see them. "Siegfried Obadiah Smith," I mumble.

"Oh! Brother Smith. Let me see if I can find him." Darryl steps forward, still holding my arm in his as he scans the sanctuary. At last I hear him inhale sharply, say, "There he is!"

Suddenly, we're parading down the aisle and I feel hundreds of eyes focusing on me. I'm very conscious of my whiteness, like a being that something has sucked all the pigment out of. My clothes are too plain. I clutch Darryl's arm even tighter.

He comes to a stop, makes a gesture to some folks at the end of the pew that I must be allowed to sidle by them. He releases me, gives me a gentle shove to show I'm to move along. I feel so helpless until my eyes find Siggy's profile way down the row, his half-lens reading glasses at the end of his nose. I move awkwardly along, aware of my bigness, my heart knocking in my chest. *If I were to die,* I think, *which I just might, at least it would be in a church. Maybe they could just lay me out, say a few words over me, and that would be that.*

At last Siggy turns his head, and when he sees me he gets this look like he's either seen God or the devil, then just as quick composes himself and beckons to me. There's a lady, a stout lady, sitting beside Siggy, wearing a lavish burgundy hat that covers the side of her face. He motions her to scoot over to make a space between them, and finally, finally I get there and sag down onto the pew, panting and sweating.

The woman turns to smile at me, mouths "Welcome," and it's Olie's broad, dark face, with those big luminous pearl earrings at either side! I don't know why it didn't occur to me she would be here, but seeing her makes me think of sickle-cell anemia, which I'm not in the mood for. Anyway, we're going to have to pretend like we've never met, or Siggy will know she told. I'll still call her tonight to discuss his yellowness. Or, I think, I could just scribble a note on an offering envelope, slip it to her and be done with it. Except, with him on one side, that'll be difficult.

The organ music stops, and Reverend Timothy Flemming strides up to the pulpit. "Let us bow our heads," he commands, "lift our prayers." He's even more handsome and charismatic than he was online. As he prays a long melted honey prayer, I take the opportunity to settle in, glance around. Today Oletha Evonne Lattimore is the height of fashion, wearing a lemon-green silk jacket and matching skirt, with an ivory blouse straining across her gigantic bosom. The colors are beautiful against her skin, and I wonder if she sewed the exquisite suit herself. Her hands are beautiful, too, a work of art. Nails a perfect pearlescent pink and just the right length, filed to nice ovals. I count four gold rings on her fingers folded on top of a white leather Bible. Siegfried wasn't kidding! That thing is swollen with slips of paper and slim red silk bookmarks with little gold crosses dangling at the tips. Also I see that the corners of the leather are worn, the pages dog eared. Much more so than my precious copy of *Gone with the Wind*.

It never ceases to amaze me what you can find on the Internet. I think about something I looked up last night. There are 419,218 words in *Gone with the Wind*, and almost double that, 823,156 words, in the King James translation of the Bible. It said that a typical novel is 80,000 words in length, so that means *Gone with the Wind* is equal to five and a quarter typical novels. I couldn't help looking up stats on Judith Krantz's *Scruples*, and it turns out Mother's favorite book is not typical. It's more than 200,000 words, and one review on Google called it the "money/sex/power" novel. For my twenty-first birthday, Mother gave me a brand new copy of *Scruples*. "It's time you read this, Joan Marie," she said when I'd pulled off the wrapping paper. "You're a grown woman now, and it's important you learn how to go about getting what you want in this world. I'm serious. You've become a hermit. An overweight hermit who wears the oddest collection of clothes. And you need to smile sometimes. If you keep your face in that grim expression, you're going to have a permanent wrinkle between your eyes. Men don't like women who are grim. But the good news is that it doesn't have to be this way! The time has come for you to reach for the stars: Joan Marie, you can do this, you can—"

Her lips continued to move, but the screaming in my head was so loud I couldn't hear another word of what she was saying. *A pathetic hermit?* I wanted to scream. *Well, you might not be a hermit, Bitsy, but you're pathetic too! Shopping till you drop, as you put it, and chasing after "hunks" who are twenty years younger than you!* But, of course, I didn't say this. And, for some strange reason I didn't throw her gift away. I've never cracked the spine, however, and I take pleasure imagining her seeing me right now. She'd have a fit. A genuine hissy fit.

I hear the reverend's words crescendo up to ". . . these things we pray, in your son Jesus's name, amen!" followed by a chorus of amens from the congregation. There's a rustle of purple silk choir robes as a flock of people arise from the loft behind the pulpit to sing "Amazing Grace."

I've never heard such glorious harmony in my entire life. It's so beautiful I could easily melt into tears, and it's made all the worse from sitting in a sanctuary filled with blacks and having recently watched a Bill Moyers special about a penitent slave owner named John Newton. Eventually, he became an abolitionist, and he wrote "Amazing Grace," and it's said that the melody originated from the tune of a song slaves sang. My stomach tightens at the memory of how my heroine, Scarlett treated blacks. My only saving grace is that the person who helped me get beyond that hangup is black and is sitting right beside me. I wonder how many others here at Mount Carmel are as generous minded and gracious as Siggy. I don't have many black followers. Off hand I can only recall about a dozen black faces out of 9,472. I wonder if he's told Olie about me and

Scarlett Says. Of course not. If there's anything Siggy is, it's honest and he said he's never told a soul.

He looks over at me, smiles and nods. It's not going to be easy to reveal my fears about his health to Olie. There's another hymn called "We Are Marching in the Light of God" that the congregation is to sing, and since I cannot sing, I whisper, "Ladies' room," to Siggy, and sidle out.

The ladies' room is beautiful. Elegant wallpaper and a veined marble floor and fresh flowers. There's a Chippendale-style chair in one corner beside a table with a box of tissues and a glass bowl full of rose petals. I gather a handful of paper towels to use as stationery and sit here, wondering what to say as I dig in my purse for a pen. It's going to be hard to put this in words, and my hands are shaking like I've got the palsy. Quickly I scribble two copies that read, "Siegfried Obadiah Smith is looking worse from the sickle cell—please pray harder for healing." I fold them both into tiny rectangles. One's to sneak to Olie, and one's to pop into the ornate box labeled Prayer Requests I saw in the lobby. It can't hurt.

I don't see Darryl anywhere, so after I deliver my prayer request, I slink back down the center aisle, sidle along the knees of worshipers and settle back in between Siggy and Olie. There's a palpable feeling of expectancy. Just as I entered the sanctuary, the Reverend said, "Let me tell you a story that will illustrate in living color just how powerful words are." Even I am holding my breath until he says, "Okay. It was a fancy-schmancy dinner party, designed to impress the neighbors. Wanting to make them admire her even more, Miz Scofield turns to her six-year-old. 'Timothy,' she says to him, 'please say grace over our meal.' He shakes his head, whispers, 'No, please, Mama, I don't know what to say.' She leans down and says into his little ear, 'Honey, you just say what you heard your Mama saying at lunchtime today.' 'Okay,' he says, nodding, bowing his head, holding his little hands together beneath his chin and

JULIE L. CANNON

praying sincerely, 'Oh, good Lord, why in the the world did I invite all these stupid people to dinner tonight! Amen.'"

Scattered laughter.

"Funny, isn't it? But"—Reverend Flemming strides along the raised platform, shaking his head—"it is to show you that words, what you say, can *hurt*. We house power in our tongues, brothers and sisters."

All of a sudden I feel like someone has grabbed me by the shoulders and is shaking me. My armpits are sending raging torrents down my sides. The gathered waistband of my skirt is sodden.

"Yessss," he draws out the *s* interminably. "Once words come out of your mouth, they can't be taken back. You can't say, 'Oops, would you please void that last thing I said? Just cancel it, and let's act like it was never said!' Uh-uh. Words are permanent! And they can cut like a knife. Leave a wound. A bleeding wound. You cannot go and retrieve those words. It's not possible. Words, once they come out, take on a life of their own."

He waves his hand. "Listen to what it says in James 3:5, 'Even so the tongue is a little member, and boasteth great things. Behold, how great a matter a little fire kindleth!'"

He gets a loud scattering of "Amen, Reverend!" and "You right, brother!" I am rigid as a two by four, my heart racing and my breath unable to reach my lungs. This man is speaking the absolute truth. This is exactly what happened in ninth grade! Those words, they came alive. How could I not have known this? Now comes an awful remembrance of looking in the mirror at myself that year: false eyelashes, bleached blonde hair, and so much rouge I looked horrible. I hold my sweaty palm to my mouth and listen as the reverend continues.

"Mm-hmm. Words can bless or curse, hurt or help, empty or encourage, bruise or better another person. Yessss, words can be a sword or a solace. You know what solace means?"

144

Nods all around me, but he defines it anyway. "Webster's says 'Solace means to comfort in sorrow, distress, or misfortune. A source of consolation, cheer.' Often when I'm writing my sermons, I struggle to find just the right word. Webster's can help, but I keep a thesaurus on my desk. It groups words of similar meaning together and helps me find just the word I need to convey my thoughts. Sometimes, people, we face struggles in our *lives*. When this happens, we find ourselves looking for just what we need to do, to say. What is our resource when that happens? God's Word. The Bible will guide us with wisdom. The more familiar we are with our Bible"—he pauses and from the corner of my eye I see Olie pat her Bible—"the more quickly we can find those words that will inspire us and others with God's love. Words that instruct us on the right path to take. Whether in word or deed.

"Listen, people. Our faith in God can make a difference in us and it the lives of others. If it doesn't, why are we wasting our time here? Can you answer that?

"The book of Proverbs is full of wisdom. True wisdom that offers us peace, freedom, joy. And let me tell you, King Solomon has a lot to say about *words*."

Here it is! Here's where old Siggy gets his fixation on King Solomon and the Proverbs! I sit up straighter, compose myself as best as I can.

"We're going to concentrate on chapter four, verses 20 to 24; 'My son, attend to my words; incline thine ear unto my sayings. Let them not depart from thine eyes; keep them in the midst of thine heart. For they are life unto those that find them, and health to all their flesh. Keep thy heart with all diligence; for out of it are the issues of life. Put away from thee a froward mouth, and perverse lips put far from thee.'"

I watch as Reverend Flemming goes down the steps to our level, striding along, nodding with his hands clasped behind his back. At last he pauses, looks up and out at us.

"Perverse lips. There are plenty of perverse lips talking on the TV, on the radio, coming out of our mouths. Out of *Christian's* mouths, too, lest you get all proud and puffed up. The word perverse means something that has turned away from what's good or right. It's become corrupt. Proverbs 15, verse 4, tells us this, "A wholesome tongue is a tree of life: but perverseness therein is a breach in the spirit." You hear that? You know what that means. It means a perverse tongue breaks the spirit. *Breaks* the spirit! Let me add this bit of wisdom, 'Whoso keepeth his mouth and his tongue keepeth his soul from troubles.' Proverbs 21:23."

For the next ten minutes the reverend expounds on perverse and froward words, throwing in Siggy's favorite proverb, about "Pleasant words are like a honeycomb, sweetness to the soul and health to the bones." I unfold and refold the bulletin Darryl slid into my hand as he released me. It says Order of Worship inside, and I see we're due for another hymn after the sermon. Looks like I missed the offertory and the doxology while I was in the ladies' room.

At last, the reverend changes gears in his tone. "Our heart's condition is evidenced by the words coming off our tongue. Let me ask each of you to pose a question to yourself. Are you speaking sweet or sour words? Words of faith or fear? I want you to look in your own heart with honesty."

Olie fidgets in her seat, and I wonder if maybe she's feeling uncomfortable, too. I recall bits of our last conversation, well, her monologue, if I want to be specific. "Siegfried's my only kin, you know, Joan. And as I've said, sickle cell is a evil, evil disease. I'm just trying to save money to take him to the Mayo clinic. I'm hoping to keep him alive until I've saved up five thousand dollars to get him to the Mayo Clinic. I know in my heart they can help my nephew. But sometimes it seems impossible on my earnings."

Aren't those words of fear? Of course they are! Olie's afraid Siggy will perish before she does. Next time I talk to her, I'm going to ask her why she doesn't carry him to the healing service. Why she doesn't speak those healing honeycomb words. Then I realize I could never be that confrontational with the bulwark sitting beside me. Anyway, I understand totally that the woman has fears over losing Siggy. I do, too.

I start tearing my bulletin into strips, quietly, thinking that Olie's not even Siggy's real mother, but she is a *real* one, nothing like what Bitsy is to me. With her skinny self clad in the latest tight designer miniskirt, pounds of gold draped on her wrists and her neck, her fixation on goings on at the Capital City Country Club. I wish I had someone like Olie. I wonder how different my life would be if I'd had a nurturing mother like Olie.

Two blogs ago, Charles commented that his mother, too, was only concerned about herself. He said that from the day he turned nine, she left him alone on Friday and Saturday nights to go out and party, often not returning home until the next morning. I loathe the way the human brain works! Now I cannot suppress an image of Charles in that blue uniform with the gold buttons. I see the hurt in those gorgeous eyes.

I pinch myself, focus on the ring on Olie's index finger. I count the blue stones, and there are four. I spell f-o-u-r over and over, then backwards. Finally the reverend is done, leading another prayer. Siggy's eyes are closed, and I ease my hand into the pocket of my skirt for the note. Real fast I slip it over to Olie, nudge her wrist with it. Her eyes flicker open, she sees it, nods, tucks it inside her Bible. She sidles over toward me a couple of inches, and I swear I can feel a current of love from her plump self. If it's not love, it's genuine acceptance.

We all stand up to sing a hymn called "Lift High the Cross." My heart's a jackhammer, and I shoulder my purse so I can scoot out quick before Siggy can introduce me to anybody. Siggy has a beautiful voice—mellow, soulful, and deep—so I just move my lips and listen to him. As soon as the reverend dismisses us, I'm out of here. We finish singing and the reverend pronounces some sort of benediction, and the split second he's done, I squeeze past Siggy, stepping sideways, getting free. I'm almost out, almost to the aisle, where I'll jog to the parking lot before anybody can thwart me, and I'm feeling pretty good, feeling accomplished, until one split-second later, I trip gracelessly over my own clodhopping feet. I land on all fours, striking my head and my left elbow on the pew. My purse goes flying two pews up as I spontaneously holler "Ouch!" and right away scramble to get up on my feet. I rub my head, my elbow. Nothing's terribly hurt except my pride. I'll just gather my purse and be gone.

But no luck. It's like a living nightmare as a dozen faces in differing shades of brown bend and hover, clouds of colognes and perfumes almost visible. I recognize Siggy's shiny black wing tips and his blinding white socks, and my eyes travel up his black suit pants, his jacket. The expression on his face is that of a wild man. "You all right, Miss Joan? Let me see your pupils."

"I'm fine!" I protest, closing my eyes.

"Well, praise Jesus. But you still need to sit down since you struck your head."

"Siegfried, you know this woman?" I hear Olie's voice, and I smell her magnolia mixed with essence of orange perfume. She deserves an Academy Award for Best Actress! Even I believe her question is sincere.

"Mm-hmm. Sure do. This is Miss Joan Meeler, administrative assistant at Giffin & Burke." I feel his long, dry fingers reach for my hand. "Miss Joan, I want you to meet Oletha Evonne Lattimore, my auntie."

For a moment, I'm unsure whether I can pull my part of this off. But I open my eyes and look up into her concerned face. Her hat is framed by overhead lights and it's like a halo. "Uh . . . hello," I say in my meekest voice. "Nice to meet you, Oletha."

She nods. "Are you all right?"

"I'm fine," I lie, struggling to my feet. Actually, now my head does hurt and I feel like I'm about to pass out. I can hardly get a breath to flow down my constricted windpipe, and sweat is pouring down my spine. I'm going to vomit on this nice carpet if I don't get out into the fresh air soon. Away from all these strangers. I hear faint murmurs of "She really ought to sit down a spell" and "Have brother so-and-so take a look at her."

The sky overhead and the asphalt beneath is my saving grace. It's really too hot to hardly move, but I race-walk all the way to my beautiful Toyota. Nobody else has made it to their car yet, and I crank, shove it in reverse, mash the accelerator down, and scratch out in reverse. I fly down Campbellton Road, Mount Carmel in my rearview mirror.

"Virtual reality is all I need!" I yell, swallowing a burning rush of acid. I open my mouth to let the AC cool my throat, go down into my raw insides. What came over me? Why did I even think that was a good idea? I suppose I should be grateful things weren't worse than they were. At least I'm safe now, and I did figure Siggy out a little bit, also crossed off letting Olie know about my concerns. That'll save me a lot of stress this evening.

I'm starving, and when I spy a Krystal right off Campbellton Road, my mouth waters so bad I pull into the drive-thru. Smelling the grease and onions fills me with anticipation. I order a number 3 combo: five Cheese Krystals, a side of Chili Cheese Fries and a medium sweet tea. I add a couple of apple turnovers.

Most of the time I try to wait to eat till I get home, but after my recent trauma I need it bad. I forgo the ketchup to make eating safer. Zipping along, stuffing my face, I realize I've missed my turn, going the wrong way. *I can make a U-turn*, I think. But even after three miles I can't find a place to do this safely. Now I have no idea where I am. I suppose I should stop and ask how to get to Virginia Highlands, but in spite of my great desire to be home, I cannot bring myself to face another stranger. I'll eventually get home, I reassure myself. I've got a half tank of gas.

Twenty-five minutes later I'm on Peachtree Street in downtown Atlanta. Somehow, like a homing pigeon, I've ended up right in front of Giffin & Burke. *Well, at least I know the way home from here,* I think, relief flooding me. I'm zipping along, sipping my tea and singing to John Denver's "Annie's Song" on an oldies station, when all of a sudden, I feel my mouth drop open. Out the window I see Dr. Cynthia LaForgue's veterinary practice. In a comatose state I note there's a new sign out front. In big red letters, it says NOW OPEN SUNDAYS. A silver Mercedes is parked out front.

Why did I follow Cynthia around like a puppy? Why did I think she was even worth the time of day? I've never liked loudmouth show-offs. What in this world made me bleach my hair, pad my bra, put on fake lashes? Where did that come from?

If I thought I was experiencing anxiety at church, it's now a panic attack that is a thousand times worse. This is undiluted terror, a meltdown of my very core. My face is on fire, and I have a sudden urge to hurl my Krystal burgers. I pull over, trembling head to foot, sweat pouring off my temples as I projectile vomit it all into the floorboard of the passenger side. I idle there as I try to catch my breath, blotting my chin on my shoulder and thinking of Cynthia's words, *our* words! They say time can play tricks on a memory, make people forget things they knew, and I wish I could forget some things. Reverend Flemming is right. Words can come alive and kill. I can still see every detail of Lydia Lydelle's backside as she stands at the lavatory that day. I heave again even though there's nothing left in me.

10

Dandelion is waiting at the door when I get home. I flop down beside her on the inside doormat and hold her to me so hard she lets out a pathetic little "Rowrrr?" I set her on the floor and she heads to the kitchen. I feel guilty already from leaving her on a weekend day, and I decide I won't make her sit before I pour her cream. I've been working extra hard with her on this, and she's sat on command once, I think, when I opened a can of tuna. She still loves the top shelf of the bookcase best of all, but she sleeps in the bed with me every night. We're pretty close. In tune, you might say. Now she's standing in the kitchen at her bowl, looking at me as if she can see the guilt I feel.

"Is your tummy growling, Dandy?" I hear myself say in baby talk as I heft myself up off the floor. I still cannot believe I do this, but it happens without my intention. Dandelion has birthed this tenderness in me that I've never experienced before. I mentioned it to Siggy last week, and he just nodded and said, "Women got natural, God-given inclinations to nurture things." I waited for a proverb about a barren womb or something, but he didn't add anything.

In the refrigerator is an uncut Publix key lime pie, but I can't eat. My stomach still feels wretched, and I'm bleary-eyed from a pulverizing headache. I had stopped at a car wash to clean out the vomit from the car, and I wound up just throwing the mat away. But the smell still added reams to the headache. I need a bath.

I pour cream in Dandelion's bowl, and from the corner of my eye, I see the base of my landline phone blinking. I know it's not the smartest thing to do in my present state, but I make my way across the kitchen to touch the button and listen to my messages.

There are three. The first one says, "Hi, Joan Marie, it's Bitsy," followed by her lilting, cocktail-party laugh, then, "Oh, I really crack myself up sometimes! Like you wouldn't recognize my voice! But I wanted to tell you that there's a fashion show luncheon at the Capitol City Club next Saturday, from 11:00 till 2:00, and I've made us—" I stop the message and erase her, mid-sentence. Next is Siggy, saying, "Miss Joan! It's 12:45, and we're leaving Mount Carmel, and first I want to say it was an honor to have you worship with us today. Second, Olie's worried about your head, and she says if we don't hear from you by 1:30, we're coming by your house." Quickly I dig my cell phone from my pocket, flip it open to check the time. It changes to 1:25 p.m. right as the next message comes on. I scroll through my on-screen phone book for Siggy's number, but cannot focus for the sudden pains in my stomach that come as a result of the new message. It's a girl's shrill laughter. Just lots and lots of laughter. I listen hard. There's no happiness, no lightness of heart in her laughing. It's mean. A mix of meanness and fury that I hear. I stand, stunned, gripping my cell phone, telling myself surely it's a wrong number, until finally my brain engages, and I get the brilliant realization that I can click stop, then erase, on this, too.

Quickly, I dial Siggy and tell him thanks for the concern, but I'm fine, that I've never felt better in my life, and I'll see him tomorrow at Giffin & Burke. They must be riding in the car because I hear their back-and-forth discussion about what I've said mixed with staticky gospel music coming from a radio. I hang up and go sit at my desk. Dandelion hops up in my lap and nestles into a warm furry ball. In my chest is the steady tick of relief that I'm home safe, that I've been spared a visit from Siegfried and Olie, and I can be blissfully alone for the rest of the day. I don't have to let myself think of Siggy or Olie or Bitsy or Cynthia LaForgue, or the mean laughter message. I won't even think of it tomorrow.

All of a sudden, it dawns on me that in the space of just a few weeks, I've been dragged unwillingly into so many relationships! Siegfried's constant pushing has layered on my past therapy. But I can't!

I can't.

I'm not going to allow any of this. I am a strong Southern woman, I've got gumption, like Scarlett, and nobody can make me care!

Not even my flesh and blood. I'm increasingly certain, as I sit and stroke my kitty, that the only way Bitsy and I could have managed to be close is if we'd held each other and wept together way back then at that awful time. It's too late now. If she'd been able to summon up some sort of sympathy, empathy, some gesture of caring that I was hurting so badly, things could be different. But she was, is, so self-composed and self-absorbed and influenced by "what the members of the club will think," there was nothing for me to do but latch onto Mrs. Darnell and Scarlett.

Bitsy had always abandoned me. Why should now be different? I had a mother who didn't seem to be able to hear me, who connected with me only on her terms, in her own manipulative way. I never felt safe, accepted, or loved. I rest my hand on Dandelion's side and feel that reassuring purr coming from deep inside her, recalling last Sunday when Bitsy came by and I had scooped up Dandelion before I answered the door.

I don't know what she was expecting, but Bitsy had stood there in silence for a moment, then gesturing with her forehead, she stepped back and said in a shrill voice, "You've still got that rodent?!" turned, and sped off on her Manolo Blahniks. Happily, I got to skip the usual lecture from her on how a woman can't catch a hunk without attractive clothes, a pleasant facial expression, and good posture. She called fifteen minutes later, and I let the answering machine pick up. "Joan Marie? I know you're there. I came by to tell you that I bought us a spot at the fashionable Crest Lawn Memorial Park. It's a two-grave plot, located in the Garden of Faith, one of the highest elevations in Atlanta, overlooking the skyline. These spaces can be for cremated remains or for a regular casket burial. Well, toodle-oo. And please get rid of that rat!"

I had just blinked at the phone. I cannot imagine, even as a pile of ashes or a collection of bones, to lie down in a cemetery beside Bitsy and feel her disapproval throughout eternity. What kind of person cares if where they're buried is fashionable?

My disdain and fury at Bitsy continued to echo, now making it hard to concentrate on much else. I spend a while just sitting there, stroking Dandy, suddenly reliving that awful Friday afternoon when the principal announced Lydia Lydelle's death over the intercom.

Say something, I begged silently that evening when Bitsy had come into my bedroom after I threw my prized lava lamp so hard it smashed on the bathroom tiles. *Say, "What's wrong, sweetheart?" Say that you're sorry I'm hurting, that everything's gonna be all right. Say that you've had to face tough things in your past and you made it through and you'll help me. Hug me, at least.*

Instead, Bitsy walked into my bathroom, toed a piece of glass out of her way, leaned into the mirror, turning her head this way and that to examine her skin. "Just go," I said, flopping down onto my comforter, cold and damp with tears, covering my head with a pillow. "Leave me alone. Please."

What had I been thinking, I asked myself over and over all that long weekend. Cynthia was a mean, shallow girl, not the kind of person I ever wanted to be. I'd been stupid. When I finally saw myself in the mirror, it wasn't the cleavage enhanced by a pushup bra or the platinum-blonde hair or the spidery false eyelashes that startled me so much as my eyes. They were knowing eyes. The remorse I felt that day was intense, and as time passed, as my anguish burned down to less hellish proportions, I found a certain numbing in Scarlett's story, in her attitude of "fiddle dee dee."

I jerked myself back to the present. Speaking of gumption, I've got to close certain thoughts down now! By an act of will, I take a deep breath and focus on ideas I've been having for my next blog entry. Coming up with a new blog involves a state of concentration that's sheer oblivion. It takes me right out of myself, and this marvelous hedonistic feeling is why I love, love, love being a hermit! Why I'm more than a bit grumpy when I have to deal with the unreasonable expectations of people.

When I'm writing *Scarlett Says*, I'm the queen of things in my head. I feel excitement build in my chest, spread down my arms to my hands, then to my fingertips as I start my computer, open a brand new document. I can't wait to play around with my idea, a theme of *Gone with the Wind* I found on the Internet called "Self-Reliance as the Key to Success." I found it on a scholarly site, in a list, sandwiched between "The Permanence of the Land" and "The Real Cost of War." I didn't read any of the commentaries below the long list of themes. I'm positive I can do this topic justice without anyone else's input. In fact, I've got the opening paragraph already written in my head.

I was born in 1984 in Atlanta, Georgia, the only child of parents who were both forty-one. My father was well established in his law career, and there was never any material want. My mother was a wife and a volunteer. They were very social, with a close-knit group of country club friends they'd partied with for years, and I don't think they knew what to do with

a child. I played by myself a lot. My parents enter-
tained at our house often and I remember what a
desolate feeling it was to be sitting in my bedroom
listening to the adults party.

Self-reliant, I learned to close my eyes and tell
myself stories when I was lonely or bored, which
was often. After I learned to read, reading became
my sanctuary. I could escape from everything that
was painful in my life, and I could be anyone I
wanted to be in whatever book I was reading. I have
to say it went along well with my natural tendencies,
for I'm a very solitary type of person. I recognize
the satisfactions of a more socially enmeshed existence than I cultivate, but I can go for days without hearing another human voice and never even
notice. I grew up believing that the greatest privilege was to be left alone and have all the time I
wanted to read. Books are wonderful companions,
the truest of friends. Unlike people, they're there
whenever you need them. They don't criticize you,
ignore you, or stab you in the back. Some books
I've read so many times that they're falling apart
are: *Misty of Chincoteague* by Marguerite Henry,
The Secret Garden by Frances Hodgson Burnett,
My Friend Flicka by Mary O'Hara, *A Tree Grows in
Brooklyn* by Betty Smith.

But my favorite will always be *Gone with the Wind* by
Margaret Mitchell. It makes me smile just to think
of that book, about the intense experience when I
discovered it. More vivid than real life, it will forever
be a part of me. I know *Gone with the Wind* is fiction. Partisan fiction at that! The gospel according
to Margaret Mitchell and the Confederate States.
Some even call it "a bitter lamentation for those

who lost the war" or "an anthem of defiance for those disconsolate with loss." But I owe a personal debt to this novel! Scarlett O'Hara saved me! I met Scarlett when I was in ninth grade. I learned so much from her. She inspired me with her headstrong, stubborn, and gutsy personality. I caught her fire for thinking of things "tomorrow" and for thumbing my nose at propriety. She gave me gumption, the courage to say no to the pressure of certain people. She's the perfect example of how self-reliance can be a key to success. I'm a firm believer in self-reliance. As I said, I've felt ignored most all my life and had to rely on myself since childhood. I owe my greatest achievements to the fact that I'm very much at ease being alone. Being self-reliant is a good disposition to have. I've even come to understand that Scarlett's coquetry was a form of self-reliance. Though I've never really been very fond of the "Southern Belle Syndrome," I can understand that for Scarlett it was a strong survival tool. She had to play games in order to get what she needed. It was a simple economic necessity. It served her well to flutter her lashes and to flirt over a fan. It literally kept a roof over her head.

But that said, no matter how much I love Scarlett and being a Southerner (except for being outside on those sticky hot days of high summer), what we were about during the Civil War (um, make that the War Between the States) was wrong! We lost the war and we deserved to lose it, because admit it or not, we were party to a very grave moral and social wrong: slavery.

All of a sudden, I blink. "Wait a doggone minute here, Joanie," I warn, highlighting that last paragraph and deleting it with the click of my mouse. "You sure don't need to get into any more controversial territory right now."

I wouldn't say I'm scared. I'm more than happy to take the risk if it'll change the world, but I'm just not in the mood at the moment to tackle issues that'll raise up any more virtual enemies.

It's time to stop. Dwell on the ending later. I needed to get some rest.

But first, a bath.

⁓

It's a quarter till eight, and Siegfried's waiting at my desk. I can see on his face that he has something for me this morning. I can also see it's not the usual paper bag with a warm apple fritter that he brings on Mondays. I set down a steaming triple-shot cappuccino from Starbucks, my prize for getting out of bed, dressing in business-woman clothes and showing up at Giffin & Burke when it's the last thing in the world I want to do. I don't want to insult Siegfried, but I'm desperate to gulp the three bitter shots that are the perfect balance to the sweetness sitting atop in a thin foamy layer of golden brown cream.

"Well, look what the cat drug in." He chuckles.

"Morning, Siegfried," I say, trying not to be too obvious about checking his color. Yes, the yellow undertones are still there, maybe even a bit worse, and something very unusual for Siggy—his face is so swollen you can't even make out his cheekbones which usually put me in mind of Abe Lincoln.

"Good morning to you," he says.

I settle my things in their places and turn on my computer, still standing because it seems rude to sit down with Siegfried waiting on tiptoe. I sigh a little because I'm exhausted. I've got way too much on my mind, and mentally I will him to go.

"So," he says in the gentlest voice, "how's your head?"

"Just great!" I say, forcing a huge smile. Feeling desperate, I glance around to see if he's set the apple fritter bag anywhere. I don't see one, and to be honest, I'm kind of upset. The apple fritters he brings on Monday mornings are so full of greasy goodness that the brown paper bag is almost sheer. They've got bits of tender, tart apples and crunchy cinnamon-sugar granules in pockets of the gooiest dough you can imagine. Now I'll have to make do with some Hostess powdered donuts out of the machine in the break room, and they're generally kind of dry, disappointing. But I will not complain to Siggy. I dig around in my drawer for two pens and set these out next to my keyboard, take a long drink of my espresso.

"She's cracking the whip."

"Huh?" I blink at Siggy, who has his arms crossed. I notice a long, slick piece of paper sticking out between his thumb and forefinger.

"Olie."

I'm a little afraid to, but I ask, "What do you mean?"

"Oh, she's on a health kick." He clears his throat, notches his voice up an octave or two. "'Siegfried Obadiah Smith, you don't need to be eating no fried food! You ought to know at your age you s'pose to eat healthy! Don't you go by that donut shop and clog up your arteries this morning. I done told you 'bout ten thousand times, you need to put *good* stuff inside! Sit down, boy. I made you some oatmeal.'"

I look down at my low-heeled navy pumps, off-brand Target specials that make Bitsy cringe almost as much as my size-14 skirt. "I'm sorry she's bossing you around like that," I hear my own voice say. I don't know where those words came from, don't know if I actually mean them or not, because I'm really disappointed about not getting my apple fritter, and plus, Olie does know a thing or two about sickle-cell anemia and what's good for her nephew.

It's not a very peaceful feeling being in the middle.

Siegfried says nothing for a bit, and I wonder if he knows that she told me. But why should I worry about that? I'm merely an innocent bystander. I stand there, looking at his face for a while, and then I sit down, take a gulp of espresso.

"It's fine. She's just taking care of me, the natural thing for a woman to do." He looks piercingly at me through those half-lens reading glasses on the end of his nose. "Just the natural caretaker instinct that's programmed into her. Women feel the need to take care of others, and that's just the way it is. I don't care what anybody says, virtual care don't count."

I sigh and tap the keys that get me to Giffin & Burke's site.

He touches my shoulder, gently. "Brought you a little souvenir. Something you can use to mark your page in *Gone with the Wind*." He hands me a slick bookmark, with a side view of some black hands, palms together in classic prayer, the tips of the index fingers touching startlingly red lips, and words beneath the image, printed in a fancy font: "There is gold, and a multitude of rubies: but the lips of knowledge are a precious jewel. Proverbs 20:15." On the back it says, "Mount Carmel Baptist Church—Atlanta, Georgia."

I sit there a second, feeling even more disappointment I try not to show. "Thanks," I say, tuck it in my purse, trying in vain to remember where I put the piece of paper I printed out with the healing proverb on it.

Siegfried clears his throat. "Those are words of wisdom, sure enough, Miss Joan." He stands there a while until I nod, start to click around on the keyboard like I've got something important to handle. I can't even start to function until I get my thoughts from last night sorted out.

The doors open, and Gold Ring sashays in wearing a lime green minidress and carrying an enormous black leather handbag. She tosses her shiny sheaf of hair, and it looks like it's shooting sparks. "Morning, Miss Meghan," Siggy says. She looks over toward the reception area and narrows her eyes at him, meets my gaze for a millisecond, then yanks her chin up and away. But I saw it, the contempt on her face. I hate that I'm wearing a gray blouse that enhances my undereye bags, and that my hair's lank because I was too tired to wash it. Also, I hate, hate, *hate* the fact that I'm relieved that I'm not eating at the moment.

Siegfried goes to the janitorial closet, and Meghan uses a key to let herself into John Burke's office, and not until several quiet minutes later do I allow my mind to return to last night. I'd planned my therapy. *Scarlett Says* was *supposed* to be a nice way to wind down into a heavenly state for a night filled with deep, sweet sleep. After a bath with lilac-scented bubbles, I fixed a little snack of a dozen Ritz crackers with pepper jack cheese melted on top and sat down at my desk full of warm anticipation. Dandelion came and curled in my lap. I ate with one hand, stroked her soft fur with the other until I felt her purring contentedly. I was feeling pretty good, ready to sink down into the warmth of my followers' words.

First I skimmed the sidebar and I was at 9,927 followers. What once seemed virtually unattainable, reaching ten thousand followers, no longer did. All these people wanted to see what I had to say. Me.

"Looks like I'm pretty successful now, huh?" I whispered down to the sleeping Dandelion. "Crowds are surging to hear me. Virtual crowds, but masses of people nonetheless!"

I even had this fleeting thought that I was on a roll and the more success I could achieve, the more the haunting memory of that shame would fade, and that eventually it would be way away somewhere, so far and so harmless, it was like it didn't even exist.

I just sat there looking down at Dandelion's sweet face for a while, letting the good feelings flow like a cool breeze on hot skin. Moving my eyes back to the screen, I began scrolling slowly down the pages of new responses. Still not a soul who was neutral on the grand old debate over Ashley versus Rhett, but it was all good-natured arguments.

I laughed aloud as I read a back-and-forth between two sisters. One, Belinda, kept saying that sexual excitement waned over time, and a woman was much better off in the long run with a man who was a gentleman, someone she could trust with her heart. One who wouldn't be ogling every woman who came along.

"Well, I know what I know!" her sister Wanda would reply. "If there ain't no physical passion, then there ain't nothing! ZERO! ZIP! ZILCH! I don't care what old Margaret Mitchell says, I know in my heart Scarlett would never have been satisfied with Ashley!"

I got the feeling that Wanda was a lot younger than Belinda. Remembering my early teenage crushes on the really popular boys, the so-called bad boys, and my longings to fit in, I was not surprised at her obsession with the Rhett Butler type. Even after graduation, the girls in my class remained fixated on the arrogant demigods who played football and other sports. I prided myself on how I'd matured way past those other girls, vowing I'd never foolishly fall for the cocky athlete just because he drove a Beamer and could party all night. Not that I got the opportunity, but I knew if I did, I'd only fall for the genuinely nice guy.

So I felt I understood both their arguments, even though I'd never had a relationship. I didn't let myself step into their argument, just enjoyed eavesdropping. I read on and on, satisfied in a maternal kind of way, loving when I read things like, "Great post, Scarlett! Subjects like the ones you address usually aren't applicable to me and my tastes, but this one is different! I never met anybody with your perspective. Probably saved me from a thousand hells."

And another one, "That was pure poetry, Scarlett, especially that last paragraph about all that inner conflict you were having. People aren't cut and dried. We all have contradictory sides sometimes. That's human. I'm just sad that your inner conflict never got settled. I mean, if either Rhett or Ashley had died, it would have made it easy, wouldn't it? Or if maybe one of them had, like, hit you or something, then maybe you could've chosen one and never looked back. You could have been happy."

I had to pause, rub my eyes and release a yawn. I checked my watch, a quarter after midnight, time for just a few more glowing responses.

"Dear, dear Scarlett," wrote Laycee from Mississippi,

> these emotions of yours are familiar to me. Beautiful and cautionary at the same time. Let me tell you about my marriage at sixteen. Okay, I remember literally melting at the sight of Jimmy Jernigan. I mean it, he was a wild boy, and I was a useless puddle of hormones every time I took in his finely sculpted biceps. Young enough to believe it would last forever and stupid enough to believe that that's what you look for in a relationship. I thought lust equaled love. Jimmy was eighteen, and I begged Mama till she let us get married. A few months into the marriage we couldn't pay the rent, we were living in our car, cooking on a grill made out of a window screen sitting up on cinder blocks over charcoal. I was still young enough to believe that was exciting, that it was romantic to eat beneath the moonlight no matter what. I thought it was daring the way Jimmy could steal chickens. I didn't yet know about Jimmy's girlfriends or his children or his police record. All I knew was I wanted to lie down beside him every night. Not till he left me when I was twenty-four did I get my first taste of power, the power I had within me to change my conditions to a better life, and now, at thirty, I look back and it shocks me, because I realize just how immature and scared to death he really was. I'm married to an Ashley type now, and I couldn't be happier.

I shook my head and took a deep breath before I could read the next comment. "Brava, Scarlett!" wrote Taylor from Texas. "You did a wonderful job with that old paradigm! Now, here's another great idea for your blog." I pulled my eyes away from the screen quick. I don't like to take suggestions from my followers. Too many cooks spoil the broth. If there's something I mean to do in *Scarlett Says*, it's to let my readers know all the wisdom I've discovered in *Gone with the Wind*, to help them see what has helped *me* make it in this world. I surprise myself sometimes by being so good at giving advice. But here's the thing—it's as much for me as it is for them, my loyal followers. I get lost in the worlds I create with my words. My blog confirms, validates me.

But, because Taylor's got such a kind face, I read his suggestion.

> Here's what puzzles me, Scarlett: Margaret Mitchell claims her characters are completely from her imagination. But her great-granddaddy was Irish and owned a plantation in Georgia. Margaret was just eighteen when her fiancé was killed during World War I, and he was a wealthy New York soldier. Not long after that, Margaret's mother died from influenza, and Margaret came home from college the day after her death! Remember Scarlett coming home to Tara only to discover her mother had just died from an illness? Now, here's the kicker—four years later Margaret married "Red" Upshaw. They were married only four months when he left Atlanta and never returned. Now, I ask you, is all this merely coincidence?

I stared at a water stain in the shape of Texas on the ceiling, thinking about the biographies on Margaret Mitchell. Peggy Mitchell had annulled her marriage to Red and remarried within a year. Her second husband, John Marsh, seemed a much milder sort. Maybe more in the line of Ashley Wilkes? As though sensing my deliberation, Dandelion roused herself, stretched, arched her back, rubbed her cheek against my wrist, and released a little "Meow."

"What do think, sweetie?" I asked. "Maybe I should write about that and call it something like . . . Characters Completely Created from Her Imagination"? I sat scratching Dandelion's ears, thinking and reading comments until 2:00 a.m. when I could hardly keep my eyes open. I decided it was time to get up, brush my teeth and go to bed. I assumed I was home free as I began scrolling down to the bottom to type my customary "Thanks for all the great comments, everyone!" I just knew I'd leave my desk with the good feelings gathered around me like a soft quilt. But by the time I'd passed a half-dozen comments from Charles, somehow I'd managed to register the fact that he was really excited because Nancy from Tennessee had told him she was now subscribing to something called *Arma Virumque Cano*.

I looked away from my computer screen, knowing I ought to just ignore all that. But why would he care? What was *Arma Virumque Cano*? Probably the name of some boring academic journal. I shouldn't have, but I Googled it, and found that in addition to being a Latin phrase meaning "I sing of arms and a man," it was the name of a newsletter by and for Civil War reenactors. I returned to my blog and read the whole back-and-forth between Charles and Nancy. It dawned on me that she was getting into the Civil War reenactment stuff. "I am most thoroughly impressed, Nancy from Tennessee. You're a woman after my own heart," Charles said to her after one of her gushings.

I sat there in disbelief. *What a crock!* Couldn't he see right through her? That she didn't really give a rat's butt about the "considerable range and accuracy of the Springfield Rifle-Musket," or the fact that most soldiers carried a sewing kit, called a "housewife"? The only arms she cared about were his wrapped around her, and she was no more a war-loving history buff than I was! It was just sucking up. Tawdry behavior!

I closed my eyes, rubbed my forehead, another sentence from Nancy seared on my brain: "Now, Charles, Scarlett may loathe the blue uniform and those gold buttons of the Yankee officer, but to me it means justice and freedom!"

Almost as bad as her annoying habit of continually harping on "Civil War to Civil Rights"! Saying every other blog how she was saving her pennies because she'd love nothing more than to visit Washington and attend some of the "festivities," or even worse, when she'd go on and on about attending a reenactment, so she could see the "boys in blue" in battle.

I swallowed the rough boulder in my throat. Charles said I was the only one who gets him! And plenty of times, I'd taken his words to bed with me, held them as I fell asleep.

"Dandelion," I said, "she's faker than a two-dollar bill." I stared at the small headshot of Nancy from Tennessee that accompanied her comments. Her tower of pitch-black hair molded with some styling product, her drawn-on long, skinny black eyebrows on her chalk-white face. I looked hard into her eyes, bright and spidery with her intentions, her thin lips a slash of garish coral-colored lipstick. There was nothing honest in her image! And skinny as a bean pole. The kind of skinny that's mean. Like Cynthia LaForgue mean.

"I wish she'd just go away!" I said to Dandelion, so loud that she flinched. "Not because Charles likes her! I just don't like the fact that she's not being honest. She's a poseur, trying to impress him."

I sat there a long while, staring at the screen. Nancy was one of those followers I wish had never wandered into my virtual fold. I couldn't care less if she were after Charles. Anyway, it was silly to even think of the two of them like that, because he'd never be involved with her in any romantic way. She wasn't the "generous" type he liked. In fact, I was actually glad she was distracting him from pestering me. But I did not need any poseurs on my mailing list for *Scarlett Says*.

With a heavy heart, I shut down my computer and went to the bathroom to brush my teeth. When I finally fell asleep, I had nightmare after nightmare until morning came.

—∞∞∞—

At lunchtime, I'm dragging so bad, I decide to have coffee and my usual twenty-ounce Mountain Dew. I set my lunch on one of the tables in the breakroom and fill my coffee mug, leaving an inch for cream. I set my cup on the counter so I can reach in to the back of the top shelf of the Giffin & Burke refrigerator for my own personal half-and-half. But the carton feels strange today. There's something crinkly on it. I pull it out and see a piece of notebook paper taped to it. Someone has written in sloppy letters with a red marker: *This is the last thing your ugly fat self needs.* I stand there, frozen, then my neck and face get hot, and my heart starts racing so bad I have to go sit in a chair at the table in the corner. A little rivulet of a tear leaks from my left eye like warm oil as I stuff the note into my pocket. I yearn to curl up in my armadillo pose and rock myself.

I feel a presence, look up, and see Siggy standing over me. "Are you . . . is there something I can do for you, Miss Joan?" He's got a rag and some kind of spray cleaner in his hand.

"No," I manage.

He sits down in the chair across from mine, but I really need privacy right now, so I fold my arms on the table and lower my forehead to rest on my wrist. It's quiet except for the low hum of the refrigerator, but I can feel Siegfried's presence like the loud wail of an air siren. I watch my knees for the longest time, and finally I lift my head to check my watch, thinking I better go on and eat and get back to my desk. I mess up and make eye contact with Siegfried and he smiles so tenderly and says, "You left your coffee on the counter. Want me to bring it to you?" And that's when I see the yellow tint in the whites of his eyes, and despite my better thinking, spill the whole story.

"I am ugly, aren't I?" I sniffle.

He looks at me, stricken, and doesn't say anything for the longest time. After a while he takes in a deep breath, shakes his head. "Don't you ever let me hear you say that again. You are beautiful." He reaches over, takes my hand and rubs his thumb across my knuckles. "I think we know who's behind the meanness. Don't have to be a detective to figure it out."

"Yeah," I say.

"I'm gonna give you some words of wisdom."

I nod, because I know I have no choice.

Siggy gives me a long, steady look. "'The discretion of a man deferreth his anger; and it is his glory to pass over a transgression.' Proverbs 19, verse 11."

I sigh. "Don't worry. I'm planning to just ignore everything. Eventually she'll stop if I don't react. Anyway, she's only a six-month intern, and I can handle anything for six months." These words surprise me. I don't really know if I could endure six months of this torture.

Siggy hesitates, and I think that we're done with the wisdom from Siegfried Says for now, but he begins shaking his head in this meaningful way. "I ain't about to let one of my favorite peoples be a doormat. I ain't talkin' bitterness, repaying evil with evil, but I'm gonna aks the Lord to deliver you."

I stare at him as he closes his eyes, bows his head and mumbles something. Then he looks up and says, "'Say not thou, I will recompense evil; but wait on the Lord, and he shall save thee.' Proverbs 20:22. Don't you worry. The Lord will take care of Gold Ring."

I'm stunned. I have never heard Siggy this up in arms about anything: slavery, illness, prejudice.

He goes to the counter, pours half-and-half into my coffee, and brings it to me, then sits down across from me again. After what I think of as a "meaningful moment of quietness," he says, " 'Rejoice not when thine enemy falleth, and let not thine heart be glad when he stumbleth.' Proverbs 24:17."

I swallow, say nothing, squirm on my seat a little. I don't know that I even *want* the Lord to pour out his wrath on Gold Ring. She's young, and you never know what's going on in a person to make them act a certain way. You never know if they're just having a bad day, say PMSing or battling a migraine, or if they're not really thinking about what they're doing or if they're just at that age where they're selfishly preoccupied. I can vouch for that.

"I know exactly what you need." Siggy nods. "You need to go to answer Charles in Manhattan."

I laugh. I'm not going to even consider the idea of getting our relationship going again, much less attending the seventy-fifth anniversary of *Gone with the Wind* when he's in town. "You're crazy, Siggy."

"No I ain't!" He slaps his thigh. "He's smitten with you, and you're smitten with him."

"I'm not! Anyway, my weekends are sacred. I write my blog, and I hang out with my baby."

"Say what?" His gray eyebrows fly up at the same time his mouth drops open.

"Dandelion."

"You serious?"

"I'm serious. When you first gave her to me, I wasn't exactly thrilled. Actually, I couldn't stand the sight or sound of her for the first three weeks. I was scared of her. I kept her in that pasteboard box. But now I'm totally in love with her! She's my world, Siggy! I'm teaching her to sit, and on the weekends she needs me." I close my eyes remembering how it feels to pull Dandelion against me as I write my blog. She's so warm, and her fur smells like sun-warmed cotton.

"Let me get this straight. You're teaching a *cat* to sit, and you can't leave home because of a *cat*?"

"That's right."

"Miss Joan, a *cat* can't carry on a conversation. That faculty is uniquely human. I believe you are yearning for a connection with a man. That's just reality."

My face gets hot. "I'm not! Virtual reality is ENOUGH!"

"Enough what?"

"Enough social interaction. I don't have any 3-D human friends. I don't want any."

"I'm your 3-D friend." His eyes start to well up with tears. "I've told you, Miss Joan, all this computer interacting stuff, it's the *anti*social network. Charles in Manhattan is a good guy. He's got a good heart, always talking about from Civil War to Civil Rights. That proves something, don't it?" Siegfried's voice rises urgently. He leans forward, the fluorescent lights overhead making his gray afro glow. "He's passionate about the right things. Plus, he's passionate about *you*!"

I guffaw at this. "*Look* at me, Siggy. I'm a socially backward loser."

Siggy shakes his head at me, but I'm not budging. No matter how stubborn he is. I know the truth.

"I think you're beautiful, Miss Joan. All right? You need to say that over and over to yourself until you believe it. Say, 'I am beautiful. I am beautiful.' There's power in words. I ain't talking no 'blab it and grab it' or 'name it and claim it' kind of thing, because it's the truth. And even better than beauty, you've got the best heart, the way you're always helping folks get their lives straightened out. What you up to now? You hit five thousand yet?"

I nod nonchalantly, but inside I'm Snoopy dancing. I'm up to almost ten thousand.

"If Charles meets you in the flesh, he'll fall for you even harder."

I smile. "You know, Siggy, I'm truly content the way I am. I got my blog, my cat. I got my books and a copy of the greatest movie of all time. I'm a happy island."

Siggy frowns. "'No man is an island,' John Donne."

"I am! I love being alone!" I sigh, then add, "Anyway, he's only twenty-five. And I don't want to be one of those leathery old cougars." I have a fleeting thought of Nancy from Tennessee, continually harping on "Civil War to Civil Rights."

Siggy throws back his head and laughs so hard, I think he'll never stop. Finally he collects himself. "Miss Joan, women live longer than men, so the age difference would probably even you out. Second of all, here's your chance to turn the *anti*social networking into the social network. I still can't figure out what it is that makes you want to crawl off in a hole and be by yourself all the time."

I swallow hard. Everything inside me is already hurting so deeply. My voice trembles. "It's just the way I am. You know that." I drink a slug of cold coffee and slam it down so it sloshes on the table. "I mean, we're not all socialites. I'm just a solitary soul, dealing with a little social anxiety. Okay?"

"I know." Siegfried gets quiet, his face contorting like he's in deep thought. Finally it begins to smooth out, like he's figured something out. "What do you believe triggered your anxiety?"

I stand up. "Life . . . uh, life did!"

He gives me a long, steady look. "What part of life?"

"Um, oh, you know, probably high school. Kids that age are cruel with all their social cliques. I never fit into any of them, and I just decided I'd be free from all human relationships. It's very freeing, you know, because so much of a social life is exhausting, worrying about making a good impression, saying the right things . . ." I stand up and gather my lunch trash to throw it away.

"Seems to me something big, something specific happened. What was it, Miss Joan? Boyfriend do you wrong?"

I'm momentarily flattered to hear him even say the word boy-friend, but it isn't three seconds till my hands begin to twitch. "I've got to get back to my desk and do those reports for Mr. Giffin."

Siggy hops up, comes over, and stands not six inches from me. He smells good, ironed with starch or something. He's silent so long, I glance over at his face. His brow is furrowed. Finally he says, "Tell me. You can tell me."

I shake my head.

"C'mon. I'll help you." Siegfried's voice is soft and buttery.

I feel my mouth open, saying words I know he won't understand. But they come out anyway. "Mainly I remember the next morning. Hearing the principal come on the intercom, asking for a moment of silence. Saying that Lyd—" I feel like I'm about to pass out.

"Somebody died?"

"Yes." I can't seem to swallow. "And I . . . I just . . . I couldn't . . . I . . ."

"Oh, Miss Joan, your heart ain't at peace." Siegfried reaches out, holds my cheeks with his cool fingers. "Run to the strong tower of Jehovah Shalom. He's got the balm to bring peace to your mind."

"Huh?" My confusion eclipses my anxiety.

"Proverbs, chapter 18, verse 10. 'The name of the Lord is a strong tower; the righteous runneth into it, and is safe.' One of his names is Jehovah Shalom which means peace." Siggy smiles, and the brown parts of his eyes are so deep and honest and caring. "You got that, Miss Joan?"

I nod, but only to get him off my back. Then I feel terrible because Siggy deserves honesty back. Despite our differences in religion, or rather my want of any, he's still my best friend. "Um, strong tower, the name of the Lord," I say, and I can tell it makes Siggy very happy just for these words to spill out of me. I hope he's not going to launch into one of his long sermons, because I'm getting nervous about being gone from my desk so long.

"That's right. You know that Hebrew class I'm taking?"

I nod, stifle a sigh.

"Well, in Old Testament times, a name not only identify somebody, but it is their *identity*. The Lord's got more Hebrew names than I got fingers, and each name explains something about Him. God reveals Himself, His nature to us through His names. You need to run to Jehovah Shalom."

The look on my face must tell him I'm confused.

"Shalom means peace, the absence of strife. Jehovah Shalom means the Lord *is* Peace." I watch Siggy's Adam's apple go up, then down as he swallows long and hard. "Way we gain God's peace over our lives is by trusting Jesus, obeying His commands, which results in a wholeness in our relationship with God and with other peoples. I believe you need that peace, Miss Joan. It would allow you to be *free*. Talk to God. Talk it out with Him, and you'll hush those voices in your head that are making you scared. Won't have to hide from yourself no more."

It's so quiet I can hear Siggy breathing. *Am I willing to pay the high price he's asking?* I ask myself. Willing to enter the world of my nightmares, to exchange pieces of my life—painful memories—to get this freedom? Words are powerful. Words come alive. I know that now. And I definitely don't want to speak certain words out loud. I've made up my mind, and for a second I think I'm going to slide by the harrowing flashback to my "day of shame." A split second later, as I realize that I'm definitely not, an overwhelming wave of anxiety blocks out awareness of Siegfried's presence.

Cynthia LaForgue tapped ashes from her cigarette into the metal waste can in the girls' bathroom as I sat in worshipful obeisance at her other side. All six of us girls in the higher echelon were taking part in our morning ritual of nicotine and gossip. Well, it'd only been mine for a little over three weeks, twenty-three days since the day I was invited into the fold, accepted. But it had been just long enough that I was feeling a little superior, by virtue of being included in this inner circle of the popular girls. We were all wearing matching Gucci designer jeans, the double-G logo prominently embroidered on our back pockets. I've got on my false eyelashes, my Lancôme eyeshadow, sculpting contouring blush, and the day before I'd begged Bitsy to make me an appointment to get my hair cut and highlighted. Not that I'd actually had to beg. She was ecstatic. Literally walking on air as she drove to the salon, me talking about my new tier of friends. Bitsy made me feel like a princess that evening, gushing, "Oh, Joanie, how gorgeous you look! You know what? You've finally come into your own!" I'd never felt this much delight from my mother, and I remember relishing it like a piece of fine chocolate on my tongue that morning as the bell rang to signal homeroom. Cynthia rose, and the rest of us got to our feet, closing our eyes in obeisance as she sprayed a communal cloud of Joy perfume to mask the cigarette smell. Just before I walked into Mr. Gregg's classroom, the principal came on the intercom and asked us all to pause for a moment of silence. He'd just received word that Lydia Lydelle had taken her own life the night before. I remember everything grew unearthly quiet. I knew why. I began to scream. My bones dissolved and my legs couldn't hold me up. I dropped to the floor in the hallway . . .

I'm going to scream right now, I realize, have a full-blown panic attack if I cannot stop the action of this shameful memory. I concentrate on taking deep breaths, on swallowing the hysteria creeping up my throat, willing the scene to face with all my might. Finally, I drop back down into my chair, wrung out. Siggy's patting my back, hard. He looks exhausted, too, tries to smile. "Don't you worry, Miss Joan. Everything's gonna be all right."

11

I'm beat when I climb into my Toyota at the end of the work-day. Almost too tired to tick off my mental grocery list. Nonfood items—cat food, Tums, Mountain Dew twelve-pack, laundry deter-gent, and Miracle-Gro Liquid African Violet Plant Food. I imag-ine myself administering these drops that are "specially formulated with five essential micronutrients for the unique needs of African Violets" and my bedraggled plant perking up. Who knew such a specific product existed? I've only been aware of it since the day Olie brought Aretha Franklin to me. Recently I named her after the Queen of Soul, and in her honor I've been playing J93.3 FM, Atlanta's Liquid Soul Radio. I hope they sell the drops at Publix.

On Peachtree Street, I stop at a red light, rehearse my food items—peaches, baby cut carrots, Publix instant mashed potatoes, Totino's Pepperoni Pizza Rolls, Swanson Salisbury Steak fam-ily entree, Sister Schubert's Homemade Yeast Rolls, and a Publix Authentic New York Cheesecake. My preferred Publix is the one in northeast Atlanta, on Piedmont Road. I think it has the best bak-ery, not to mention the best selection of cheese. It's Bitsy's favorite, too, but I know she only goes in the midmorning, not in the rush hour when the bourgeois working class are clogging up the aisles.

Once again, Publix is uneventful, and gratefully I return to my car in the steamy parking lot, settle my half-dozen plastic bags of groceries on the backseat and think, *Thank goodness they had the Miracle Gro, and thank goodness for familiar routines*! What was I trying to prove, even *contemplating* going to the seventy-fifth anniversary in downtown Atlanta? Talk about anxiety. That would be pure misery for someone plagued with panic attacks.

I think about how my physical body almost betrayed me today. I'm going to have to be more cautious. I'm prepared to do whatever necessary to keep myself an island.

I regret listening to Siegfried in the break room, letting him find that vulnerable place in my armor. How like him to quote John Donne. I am too an island! My past and my future are cut off. Only the now remains. But this kind of existence is rich and pure and vivid. The immediacy of the here and now, what more could I want? The fact of the matter is that Siegfried needs to respect my solitude! He doesn't need to intrude on my shores. He can delude himself all he wants, but we're all islands in the end. Why hook up with other people when you end up alone in the end anyway?

I guess it's only a natural instinct for the majority of humans. I think about Bitsy's absolute terror when it comes to having a Friday or Saturday night without a social occasion to attend. Well, any day or night for that matter. For her it implies rejection and unpopularity. For her it's worse than death to be that proverbial wallflower. I could start feeling a little superior if I let myself. I don't fear solitude. For me, separated from my own species, I'm ecstatic. I'm fortunate that I can find happiness when I'm alone, that nothing feeds my soul so much as pouring myself into *Scarlett Says*.

I turn up the volume on the Rolling Stones "Brown Sugar" and on a whim turn into the McDonald's drive-thru. I need hot food, food that needs no preparation or cleanup so I can get right to my blog. I order a Big Mac, large fries, and two apple pies. Waiting on my food, I decide that the commemoration of the movie *Gone with the Wind*'s seventy-fifth anniversary is basically just a big excuse for Atlanta to dress up and party. I pull out into traffic, a warm bag on my lap smelling heavenly, and all of a sudden I think maybe I can go if I'm in costume! It wouldn't be scary if I was dressed up like Scarlett. I'd find a black wig with sausage curls, a green velvet hoop skirt, a coquettish hat, and some white gloves.

But not half a minute later my eye starts twitching and my heart starts racing, and I know I'm not even going to trust myself to go in a costume. There's nowhere that compares with my cozy little apartment, time with my precious Dandelion. I drive the Toyota through moderate traffic, turning onto Ponce de Leon Avenue.

When the familiar lines of my building come into sight, instead of the relief I was anticipating, I feel tense. It's hard to describe this foreboding. *What is it?* I turn off the radio in the middle of "Go Your Own Way" by Fleetwood Mac. I've already made up my mind I'm not going to the seventy-fifth anniversary soiree. *What could possibly be causing this awful feeling?* I wonder as I pull into my parking spot, cut the engine, and sit looking at the smooth trunk of the crepe myrtle tree in front of me.

I'm still searching my head when I spy a young blonde girl walking through the parking lot. It's not Meghan, but I suddenly realize why I'm feeling this apprehension. It's the possibility of more mean laughter phone messages just waiting for me when I come home from work. I'm sure it's Meghan. Who else could it be? But what can I do? I recall what Siggy said about waiting for the Lord to deliver me, how the Lord will take care of Gold Ring. I also remember how he said not to let my heart rejoice when the Lord's wrath comes on her, not to gloat when she falls. It seems like the thing to do is just to go on inside, erase all the messages real quick without listening to them.

I get my keys out of my purse and set them in my lap so I can nestle my empty coffee mug down in the McDonald's bag, put my purse over my head and across my shoulders, drape all the Publix bags on my wrists and carefully step out onto the pavement. I shuffle along slowly, right up against a line of car bumpers, feeling like an honest-to-goodness bag lady, glad my apartment isn't far.

I reach my door and maneuver the key into the lock. Oddly, I don't hear the excited meows of Dandelion coming from inside, who, with either some super sense of time or really keen ears, always knows when I'm home. Well, she'll be happy when she tries the new, pricey pouches of moist cat food I bought.

But Dandelion is not waiting on the indoor mat when I get the door open. "Kitty, kitty, kitty, kitty!" I trill loudly, the way I learned from Olie the day she was here. I walk toward the kitchen, feeling strange, because there's never been a time since I've let her run free that Dandelion wasn't twining around my ankles, looking expectantly up at me as I walked. I put all the bags on the counter and tiptoe through the apartment, first checking her favorite bookshelf, then the sofa, the ottoman, under the dust ruffle of my bed, and then a pile of old towels in the floor of the laundry room that I use for rags. I look in all the kitchen cabinets, the bathtub, a collection of old baskets in the pantry I know my baby wouldn't fit in. Underneath my desk I find the printout about the healing proverb I made for Siggy, and I fasten it to the refrigerator with a magnet from a personal injury lawyer. On a whim, I open the oven.

But my baby is nowhere in my apartment. I don't know what to do. I cannot understand how she got out, I'm always so careful as I leave. I turn in circles, feel a rush of panic that tightens every cell in my body, followed by a wash of absolute helplessness that makes my shaking legs collapse. Sitting on the carpet, I wrap my arms around my shins and sink my forehead on my knees in my armadillo pose. For the next fifteen minutes I just rock, brainless and numb.

When my faculties finally return, I go to the drawer where I keep the huge Atlanta phone book. I look up the number for the Atlanta Police Department. Should I call the police? I don't know. Maybe I should call those vans I see riding around that say Animal Control.

I sit down at my desk and swallow a tightening in my throat before I Google *What do you do when your cat goes missing?* crying a little while I scroll down through pages of choices. There are a lot of services that will help you locate a missing pet, but they all charge a fee, and I have no extra money. Ever since I passed twenty-five, I've been meaning to start squirreling away a bit of each paycheck from Giffin & Burke, desiring that feeling of security I'd have if the worst happened, if I needed to survive before Bitsy passed on.

Now the worst has happened and I'm penniless. How have I been so foolish? Living from day-to-day, moment-to-moment, just expecting my good fortune to continue?

After some deliberation, I click on *Three Musts When Your Cat Is Lost* and scribble down everything it says. First you're supposed to search high and low because scared cats tend to hide, so search under cars, in drain pipes, and on roofs. Second, you're to create a sign and tape it to telephone poles in a radius of three to five blocks. The perfect sign includes a large color photo and the words LOST CAT in big dark letters, and you should offer a reward clearly marked on the sign. What am I going to do? I decide I'll write $250 on the signs, and if somebody finds Dandelion, I'll postdate a check for after my next paycheck and just do without something, probably food. I almost panic again when I read the last item—check with animal shelters. Sadly, many pets are killed in traffic, so call local highway and animal control departments and ask if anyone has found a body that could be your pet. I sit staring at the words, my heart in my throat.

I don't think that would happen. I don't think that could happen. Dandelion's terrified of cars. I don't want that to happen. I latch onto one reader's comment that gives me hope. It says that given time most cats will find their way back home. I'm sure Dandelion will come home. How can she not?

For seven hours straight, I sit outside my door beside a bowl of the moist and meaty cat food. At first it smelled very fishy, but now the odor's died down or else I'm just used to it. Speaking of getting used to things, I'm looking out on the most serene vista of suburban life. Street lights glow faintly in the dark, a dog barks in the distance, traffic makes random sounds, a squirrel twitches along the limb of a nearby pine. These are life rhythms I never see in my trek from my apartment to my Toyota and back again. I eye the moon, almost full. Part of me, a big part, agrees with those people who say it's impossible that man has actually walked up there. That all that man-on-the-moon drama beginning with Apollo 11 back in 1969 was simply an elaborate hoax.

At this point in time I don't believe in much, and when I think of what a stalwart believer and evangelist Siegfried is, it hits a raw, jangling nerve in me. What had I been thinking, even considering running to some Jehovah Shalom? I'm certain Scarlett would laugh at the idea of faith in a God who cares. In fact, in chapter 19 of *Gone with the Wind* it's been months since Scarlett has even been to church. The exact words are, "For some time she had felt that God was not watching out for her, the Confederates or the South, in spite of the millions of prayers ascending to Him daily." I certainly agree.

At 4:00 a.m., there are no happy kitty feet pouncing on the stoop, no eager meow as Dandelion spies her food bowl. It's such a loud silence, this sound of disappearance. How can she not come back? I sit remembering a time when I was fixing a late night PB&J and somehow the twist tie from the bread dropped to the floor. Dandelion had a heyday. She jumped and twisted and batted that twist tie for a good fifteen minutes. And then she plopped onto her back in the den, legs spread apart and head lolled back in exhaustion, snoring the cutest, high-pitched snore. That was Before. Things were so good then. I can feel loneliness move over me like a cartoon cloud, dark and gloomy, rainlike tears pouring down.

With a heavy heart, I lug my chair back to the kitchen. I'm surprised at myself when I see my grocery bags still in a heap on the kitchen counter. I guess worrying about losing somebody tends to take your mind off some things. My hands shake as I lift a soppy mess of once-frozen cartons from the Publix bags. I don't know whether the Salisbury steak or the pizza rolls or the cheesecake are safe to eat, so I toss them out. I unwrap my Big Mac; it's cold and limp. Reheated in the microwave, it's passable, and the fries are merely a carrier for salt and ketchup anyway. I scarf them down and drink two Mountain Dews so I can stay awake.

The phone rings and I freeze. Who would be calling at 5:00 a.m.? I listen as my message informs whoever it is that I'm not home, then a pause, followed by an old white woman's strained voice saying, "Lincoln? You up with the chickens this morning like I am? Lincoln, this is Barbara Collins, calling to see if you're still going on the trip to the pumpkin patch with the Golden Oldies this morning. Listen, the van's leaving my house at eight sharp, and if you want to, come on over early and we'll have coffee."

Poor Barbara. Briefly I contemplate doing a search on my phone for recent callers, calling Barbara back, and telling her she left her message on the wrong number machine. What if Lincoln doesn't make it to the Golden Oldies trip? But then my brain goes crazy when I notice there are four messages on my answering machine. I also notice my hands are twisted together so hard it hurts. Should I break my rule and listen to them before I hit the erase button? Someone could have found Dandelion and gotten my number off her little collar. For three proofs of purchase and $5.95 shipping and handling, I got a metal disc about the size of a quarter with Dandelion's name and my landline number. When I fastened it on her collar, she pranced around the apartment like a queen.

I swallow away the tightening in my throat, reach my pointer finger toward the arrow on the phone base that's flashing, draw my hand back, then reach out again. Surely Gold Ring would have tired of the mean-laughter phone calls by now, particularly since I've been ignoring my messages, and her. I poke the button before I can stop myself.

First is a cheerful young girl for Pace Alumni, asking if I'd like to contribute to the yearly scholarship campaign. Now it's a man clearing his throat, saying, "This is Rodney Calhoun, and I'm running for . . ." I delete him, then listen to a representative from AT&T, asking if I want the new TV, Internet, and phone bundle for just $99. I think I might be home free as the final message clicks on. No such luck. I stand rigid, my arms wrapped around myself, listening to bone-chilling shrieks of mean laughing.

The inside of my apartment is now too big. I pace from room to room, end up at the freezer, extracting a nice, icy box of Klondike bars I carry back to the couch where I set up camp until they're all gone. I'm even glad for the distraction of a brain freeze.

The next Friday night, I sit alone at my computer desk, eating a bag of Funyuns and a box of Milk Duds, staring at the fact of more than ten thousand followers for *Scarlett Says*. I remember a time when this would have made me ecstatic. I don't know, I may feel some happiness. I read several pages of comments, answer a few rather half-heartedly, feel my stomach clench up a little when I see Nancy from Tennessee fawning all over a comment from Charles.

Oh, what am I going to do with this weekend ahead? Every night since Dandy's disappearance has been horrid. All I've done at home is eat, walk the neighborhood, and wait. But at least there was work. Now I have two whole days . . . I close my eyes, lean my head back, and sigh from someplace deep in my soul. I miss Dandelion so much. I miss the presence of my furry little kitty friend sitting in my lap while I write, snuggling in my bed at night. Even if she doesn't talk, if she only sits purring contentedly while I read or watch a movie, it's nice. It's lonely now and I need my kitty back. I've gotten no calls from the twenty-five LOST CAT posters I stapled to telephone poles up and down Ponce de Leon. Thankfully, Aretha's doing well. I moved her next to my desk. She's sitting on an upside-down recycling bin. I attribute her new vibrancy to the African violet drops, because there's no window for sunlight in here. Well, it could also be that she enjoys Atlanta's Liquid Soul Radio.

Work has become a relief. I am glad for the distraction and relieved that Siggy is there too. I've been being cautious about not eating in front of Gold Ring, and I keep my pint of half-and-half down inside a half-gallon carton of unsweetened low-calorie almond milk.

My plan has been to pour myself into the solace of words. I stare at the top sheet of a notepad where I scribble ideas. But I cannot get a single cohesive thought. My head feels like it's full of fluffy cotton. I have to concentrate really hard to even think what month it is. I wish I could just get somebody to tell me which idea to pick for this week's *Scarlett Says*.

Suddenly I know the answer. "You can stop wishing, Joan," I say as I pop a couple of chalky Tums into my mouth. I know the perfect bossy person. Siggy will be delighted to tell me which one would be best. I fish my cell phone from the pocket of my sweat pants to call him.

"You want me to come over right now?" Siggy's voice is beautiful.

"Yes," I say, squeezing the phone hard, staring at the stack of extra LOST CAT posters: Dandelion's lopsided and beautiful features, bright and alive, my carefully printed words and numbers. It occurs to me now that it doesn't say enough! It doesn't say, *Please find my beautiful fluffy friend. I'm so lonesome I could cry. I didn't know what I had till it was gone.*

I need something stronger than the Tums. Maybe Valium? I'm extremely close to a full-fledged panic attack and, if not that, one of those things they call a nervous breakdown.

"I'll be there in thirty minutes."

"Thank you, Siggy. Oh, thank you," I say and hang up. My eyes return to the computer screen, and I skim along, looking for Charles's latest signature smiley face. I zero in on it and it's another heart-stricken plea for me to join him when he's in Atlanta in December. "My feisty Scarlett," he writes,

> I'll be dressed in my Civil War Yankee finery and we can celebrate Margaret Mitchell's Story of the Old South on screen! The gallantry, the antebellum finery, no more than a dream remembered. I hear there are people working to re-create the scene of Atlanta in 1939! Imagine that: Clark Gable and Vivien Leigh and Olivia de Havilland! And let's not forget Butterfly McQueen and Hattie McDaniel, the beautiful and talented women who played Prissy and Mammy, my personal favorites!

I don't answer. Anyway, they probably don't even make antebellum hoop skirts in my size. I reach over and turn up the volume on Marvin Gaye. I go to the kitchen for another Mountain Dew, thinking how rich Marvin's voice is, how sensuous. *This soul music is powerful.* After Marvin is done, "Jungle Boogie" by Kool & the Gang comes on, and I close my eyes, let the music's throbbing beat take control of me. I've never danced in my life, and it feels good to let it all hang out! *I may have missed my calling,* I think as I shimmy to the left, shimmy to the right, grind and sway my hips. I laugh out loud at the absurd notion of myself as a dancer. So what if I don't know what I'm doing? I'm having a really good time! But, oh, when did I get so out of shape? I have to stop to catch my breath, hold the stitch in my side.

After "Jungle Boogie" ends, Aretha Franklin's "Respect" comes on and I go into the den to sit down and rest. "Hey, sister," I say softly, touching Aretha's velvety leaf, "they're playing your song." I think of how many times I've heard "Respect" but never really listened to the lyrics. I've lived my whole life deaf! There's so much to these words!

I begin to sing along when Aretha gets to the chorus. "R-E-S-P-E-C-T. Find out what it means to me." The doorbell sounds, and I brush the Funyun crumbs from my lap, go to look out the peephole. It's dear Siggy. I boogie a bit as I open the door, sing "Come right in, Siegfried Obadiah Smith. I'm so glad you're here!"

"Hey there, Miss Joan." His voice is wary, but he looks absolutely wonderful, all dressed up in his nice dark suit with the highwater trousers, white socks, and shiny black wing tips; what I privately refer to as his human-exclamation-point costume. He's holding a bouquet of yellow daisies. "These are for you."

"Thank you! They're lovely. I've been dancing," I add, giggling.

"I see that."

I'm wearing a floppy T-shirt and yoga pants because Dandelion's departure is making almost everything else feel like an instrument of torture. My hair's sweaty and stuck to my forehead. I take the flowers and head for the kitchen to get a jelly jar, fill it with water, settle them in, artfully I hope, and place it on my kitchen table. I have to admit, they're lovely. "Can I get you a drink, Sig?"

"Well, sure," he says, sitting down. "Thank you."

"My pleasure." My chest flushes warm. Because the truth is, it is a pleasure to serve this man. I think about Proverbs 11:17, one he's quoted to me so many times it's tattooed in my brain—"The merciful man doeth good to his own soul: but he that is cruel troubleth his own flesh." My soul *is* nourished, I decide as I pour a glass of sweet tea. Not that I'm into any of the Bible stuff at all. It's just common sense, a fact of life, like the so-called Golden Rule.

"You got an exciting weekend planned?" Siggy asks as I set a glass in front of him. Oh, I hope the Publix sweet tea is up to his standards! It's certainly not as good as Olie's. I think of the last time he was here, about how Bitsy came by and freaked out when she saw him lying on my couch. I kind of wish she'd come by now, because wouldn't it feel great to show her he's still my friend? *Racist*—what a dumb thing to be!

"Actually, yes! And the reason I called you to come over is I need your help in deciding this week's blog topic for *Scarlett Says.*"

I see one of his eyebrows go up, a slight smile cross his face, and then he says, "Well, in that case, we gonna have to call it *Siegfried Says.*"

I know he's joking. I go to my desk for the notepad. "Okay," I say, "here's the three I've narrowed it down to," and this becomes true as I say it. "Self-Reliance as the Key to Success—Part Two," "The Permanence of the Land," or "Religious Passages in *Gone with the Wind.*"

Siggy rubs his chin. I expect him to go with the last choice, so I'm surprised when he says firmly, "'Self-Reliance as the Key to Success—Part Two.' Your first post on this was a huge success."

"Thanks, Sig." In addition to all the scholarly things on the Internet about this particular theme, I've got enough personal examples to write a novel. I'll need to be careful, however, the way I phrase some of my stories. I want them sincere and helpful without being a tell-all sensational-type thing.

Siggy nods. I hope he doesn't decide we're done now. It feels so cozy to have him sitting here while Chuck Berry sings "Maybelline" softly in the background. "Can I get you something to eat?" I ask in what I hope is a casual, off-hand manner.

He smiles. "Well, I am partial to those little white donuts you used to bring to work, if you got any of those on hand."

"Sure." I hop up to get my bag of Hostess powdered sugar donettes from the kitchen, hopeful he won't get a conversation going about anything at Giffin & Burke. Gold Ring still eyes me with a haughty sneer every time she walks from the front door to John Burke's office or back, which is a lot. I don't think it's business they're discussing in there, but I don't say a word about this. I rack my brain for a new topic of conversation.

As though sensing my need, Siegfried says, "I must have seen half a dozen posters of Dandelion on the way here."

This is not what I had in mind. Grief and fear begin an ascent to hysteria from some place they've been hiding. I freeze, try to get a sufficient breath.

Finally Siegfried says, "A thousand dollars sure is a lot of money."

I nod, then say, "Well, it's funny, you know. Bitsy gave me a card full of gift cards for my birthday, and I cashed them in. Actually I sold them on the Internet, and I had just enough for the reward money. Can you believe lash extensions at the nicer salons go for five hundred bucks?"

He whistles.

I pick up a donette, smash it into my mouth, say around it, "That's just to show you what kinds of things are important to my mother."

Siggy's brown eyes look deep into me. "What's important to you, Miss Joan?"

I cross my arms tightly over my chest. I start to say something like inner beauty or helping the poor, and though I do believe those things are very important, much more so than fake eyelashes, Siggy would see right through me. "Right now, finding Dandelion. It just seems so empty here without her. I don't care if she can't talk to me, Siggy. She's my everything! The perfect companion."

Siegfried doesn't say anything for a bit, and I shift in my chair, my brain buzzing along. "I put up twenty-five posters, at eye level, and I've had thirteen people call, but none of them had Dandelion."

He chuckles. "I imagine you gonna get a lot more calls with a reward like that!"

One positive thing is, I no longer have any fear about listening to my phone messages, even when I get the mean laughter ones. I just punch the erase button and hardly feel a thing. I guess you get used to stuff. Three times I've called the local highway and animal control offices, and thankfully no bodies that could be my Dandelion's have turned up. I'm amazed, speechless, at how I have become bold as a mother bear for my precious kitty who's now been missing for what feels like an eternity. "Oh, you wouldn't *believe* it," I say, "the pictures of cats people are trying to claim is my baby. If I wanted, I could have this whole apartment *full* of kitties!" I stop, afraid I'm about to burst into tears.

"I expect you could." Siggy eyes are warm and fixed on me like I really matter to him. Like he cares about my hurt places. And then I start thinking about his disease. How he battles this hideous awful thing without ever complaining. I notice that the yellow tint in his eyes and skin is stronger than ever this evening, and a lump forms in my throat so I can't swallow. I have to look away and will the tears to absorb back into their ducts. Otis Redding is singing "Sittin' on the Dock of the Bay," and I concentrate on the lyrics. While I'm mentally singing along, I work at thinking up a new topic of conversation. One that makes me happy.

"Guess what, Siggy. I'm almost to twelve thousand followers!"

"I know you are. You're one influential lady. Reporters going to be frantic to find out who you are and how you get such a following."

I almost laugh out loud. "My goal is twenty-five thousand now."

"Sounds good."

"Guess what else. I decided when I get to twenty-five thousand, *that's* when I'm going on my rampage against slavery."

"Oh, Miss Joan," Siggy says, shaking his head. "I thought we discussed this. Margaret Mitchell was writing fiction. She was writing the way things were. It wasn't politically correct, I agree, but you know I'm against censorious interference. Speaking words of wisdom: let it be."

I glance toward the den, my desk. "I'm not talking about putting down *Gone with the Wind*, Siegfried. I just feel this obligation, this responsibility while I've got a big audience, to bring up the *topic*. For open and honest discussion. That's all. Nothing wrong with that." I sit at the edge of my chair, fold my arms across my chest. *Isn't this crazy? Me arguing with a black man about this?* I put my hands on my hips and say, "I hate thinking about something as evil as slavery! It makes me feel sick!"

"It's just that I care about you, Joan," Siggy says quietly. "Concerned over your safety. Folks get crazy over certain topics, and ain't no telling what some will do. I wouldn't want nothing to happen to my favorite person."

I look away, embarrassed as usual when he confesses things like this. I don't feel worthy of his admiration. After a bit Siggy says, "Can I ask you something?"

I start to shake my head, but say "Of course" and go to the sink to rinse my sticky fingers. I note how ironic it is that Stevie Wonder is singing "Uptight."

"Seems to me you're feeling restless. I know you're missing Dandelion, heartsick about your little kitty, but I'm talking about something more here. Something you're hungering for."

There's no way I'm going to talk about my longings for Charles. I dry my hands on the dish towel, take a deep breath, turn to Siggy, and smile like anything. "I'm fine. I feel good. Great. I know Dandelion will come back eventually."

"And if she don't?"

I stand there, wordless. I will not let my mind go there. I have to believe I'll see those sweet green eyes again, feel that satisfied purr across my chest. A long moment passes, and then Siegfried says, "Don't stick your head in the sand, Miss Joan. It's important to pay attention to restless feelings." He stands up, starts waving his long, thin hands in the air. "What are you hungering for that you don't have? What changes do you need to make in your life? Hmm?" He strides into the den and I follow along. "Twenty-five thousand?" he says, gesturing at my computer. "Fifty? You think that's going to make you happy? Fulfill you?"

"Siegfried! What could be better than doing my fellow humans good by—"

"Don't go gettin' your feathers all ruffled. I'm just askin'. Food for thought and all that." He sits down in my desk chair. "I know a book you can go to that's got the power. The power to meet all your needs."

I know he's referring to the Bible. He reaches out and takes my wrist gently. "When you draw strength from the Gospel, you can have everything that really matters in this life," he says. "Here's how to get what you need from the good book. Pay attention to the different ways you feel restless and ask yourself what you're pursuing that ain't satisfying you. Then, every time you identify the source of a restless feeling in your life, keep in mind it's a signal, a signal meant to direct you to your ultimate need: a relationship with the Lord."

I pull away from Siegfried, perch myself on the couch, and keep my mouth shut. I really hate how he starts preaching and getting in my business like this. Thankfully, he doesn't keep on, and we just sit there a spell, listening companionably to "We Are Family" by Sister Sledge, then "Ain't Too Proud To Beg" by the Temptations. Minutes tick by and I'm struck anew by how easy it is to lose myself in soul music. And I look over at Siggy and think about how much I love being with him. He's so cool. A great person to hang out with.

All of a sudden, Siggy sits up tall, his back ramrod straight. He's staring at Aretha. He reaches out a hand and touches the yellow and green paisley-patterned pot she lives in. Now he turns and looks at me, hard. "Where'd you get this flower?"

He's on to us. The reality of this rises like the sun at dawn as I see clearly that Siegfried knows exactly where Aretha came from. He knows I'm aware of his sickle-cell anemia. I can't find any words.

I'm mute with how double-dealing deceitful I feel. I look at him, with what I hope is a contrite expression, then manage, "I've been wanting to tell you. But I didn't know what to say. She called me and she made me promise not to tell you, to keep an eye on you at work so you won't get dehydrated or overdo it on the job. It's only because she loves you so much." I'm smiling, nodding hard, but that painful lump has returned to my throat, and I can't stop the tears. I want to hug him to me. I want him to say, *Oh, it ain't nothing, really, you know. Not that serious. I'm fine, honestly. Olie just gets all hysterical about stuff.*

"Hey," I say softly, remembering the proverb I printed out that's stuck to my refrigerator waiting for just the right moment. "I've got something you need to see." I practically gallop to the kitchen, sort of praying, with my eyes wide open, *If You really exist, God . . . If You really do stand behind Your Word, then . . . well, then, whoever You are, wherever You live, in hearts, in heaven, whatever, then make Siggy well. Amen, amen, and amen.*

I thrust the page in Siggy's hand. He perches those little reading glasses on the tip of his nose, raises his eyebrows and reads aloud, "'Proverbs 4:20-22: "My son, pay attention to what I say; turn your ear to my words. Do not let them out of your sight, keep them within your heart; for they are life to those who find them and health to one's whole body."

"See?" I say as if I've never believed anything so much as this. A long moment passes and Siggy leans back, stretches his long arm across the top of the couch, tilting his head in what I'd call a reflective pose.

"Well?" I say because I don't know what else to say. I don't know how to preach to a preacher.

"I know those verses like the back of my hand." Siegfried's voice is solemn.

"Then, why—"

"You think I never ask God why? You think I never been round and round with Him about things? But to answer your question, well, some questions there ain't no answer to, at least down here on this planet." He reaches for my hand and squeezes it. "But let me tell you a fact I do know. I am blessed!"

I sit down beside him, swipe my wet cheeks on my shoulders.

"I ain't kidding. I consider myself *blessed*. Now, I never would have chosen this path, and I got to admit something like the sickle cell could be depressing if I allowed it to be, but acknowledging it ever single morning before I even get out of bed, that is what helps me to focus on what's really important in life, what I want to accomplish in my allotted years."

"You're not mad?" This just kind of bursts out of me.

Siggy waves it away like a pesky mosquito and says, "This body's just my temporary home. The instant my heart stops, my spirit's gonna be flying out of here. I'll be set free."

"You don't feel cheated?"

"The life expectancy of a person with sickle cell is forty-five years, and here I am, already fifty-seven, so that's twelve bonus years beyond what I ought to have. I got no regrets."

I look at him, and though I'm not surprised, I am astonished. I've spent innumerable hours regretting just one particular thing I said that I wish I could un-say.

Siegfried chuckles at the expression on my face. "It ain't that I've never done nothing wrong! I've learned that to lead a good, satisfying, abundant, and joyful life, you ain't got to be perfect. When I look back at my mistakes, I can see some value even in the things I messed up on. If I let them, my unwise choices make me a stronger and wiser person." He smiles. "Now, there have been several, that while I was in the middle of them, I couldn't see how they'd *ever* have any redeeming value, but I got down the road a piece and it was like the light came on, and I said, 'Aha!' I knew exactly what they was meant for."

Siegfried sits quietly, looking at me all hunched over. Finally, he says, "I'm gonna be here a while yet. I can't leave this world in peace until . . . I get the peace I need in here." He taps his chest. "Still got some work left to do on this terrestrial ball. I got to help a certain somebody learn to live her life with no regrets."

I look away, kind of laugh because I'm feeling really uncomfortable.

"You'll see, Miss Joan. I pray that in time you'll find what you're longing for—peace and love that's written in the stars."

I eye Siggy as he begins to lip-synch along to James Brown's "I Feel Good." Could Siggy ever understand my day of shame? Could he ever wrap his mind around the fact that I have to pay my pound of flesh for what I did to Lydia Lydelle? If I believed him about this so-called work left to do, which I don't, I'd tell him all the details and ask him what he thinks it is I ought to do to get the peace and joy he mentioned.

Siggy rises to his feet, puts his hand on my shoulder. "Well, expect I better get home to Olie before she has a hissy fit."

I nod, get to my feet, and walk him to the door. "I'll see you Monday, then. Thanks for coming."

"You ain't got to thank me. It's my pleasure." He walks outside, down the steps, and into the night. I step out, too, close the door softly behind me, searching the darkness for a cat shape along the edges.

I clean up the kitchen to the beat of Wilson Pickett's "Mustang Sally," and then I sit down at my desk with a bag of Pepperidge Farm Mint Milanos to write "Self-Reliance as the Key to Success— Part Two."

I know part of the reason I'm feeling happy. "Well, it's out of the closet, Aretha," I say, laughing as I slide the pot a little closer, stroke her velvety leaf. "And don't it feel good!" She doesn't answer, of course, but it does seem like she's swaying a little to "Shining Star" by Earth, Wind & Fire. Clacking along on my keyboard in that old familiar way is nice. I check my followers and let out a somewhat crazy-sounding shout of "Oh yeah!" with a skyward punch when I see I'm up to 16,321. *This is the life,* I think, nibbling a Milano, reading a few comments: "Right on, Scarlett!" and "Thanks for the insight, girl!"

I begin this week's offering, type my lead-in sentence: *Despite her obvious flaws, Scarlett O'Hara is still the very definition of self-reliance.* No, that's not right. I delete it and try, *Some may call her feisty, willful, independent, or just plain selfish, but Scarlett O'Hara wrote the book on self-reliance.* No. How about this? *Through her feminist heroine, Scarlett O'Hara, Margaret Mitchell suggests that overcoming adversity sometimes requires a ruthless sense of self-reliance.*

These are all falling flat. What I want to do is give my followers some encouragement and practical applications for life today. I need a lead-in sentence that entices, grips. My thoughts zip to chapter 23 of *Gone with the Wind,* the textbook chapter as far as Scarlett and self-reliance. Scarlett is terrified when Rhett tells her he's going off with the army, leaving her. She pleads with him not to desert her, but he tells her, "Anyone as selfish and determined as you are is never helpless. God help the Yankees if they should get you."

There it is. That's my Scarlett wisdom for this entry, and now I need to come up with some insight from my own life. I close my eyes, ponder, and suddenly I'm a wounded high schooler again, walking comatose along the benches in the locker forum, leaving Mrs. Darnell's English class with her gift in my hand. Her words, "Honey, here's a female character who went through her own personal hells and survived with something called *gumption,*" are circling in my head as I ride the bus home to Brookhaven, scurry down the sidewalk, the driveway, and up the mountain of brick steps where a note from Bitsy on the little Queen Anne table right inside the front door informs me she's at the spa till seven. I grab a

Perrier from the refrigerator and climb the stairs to my room where I collapse into my beanbag chair and open *Gone with the Wind* with trembling fingers.

The novel consumes me from word one. I follow my heroine as she manages to overcome adversity through brute strength of will, surviving both the Civil War and Reconstruction unaided. She rebuilds Tara after the Yankee invasion. She relies on herself ALONE, teaches me that I really only can rely on myself. Now the headline makes itself known: *You Gotta Get Your Gumption On!* I type like a maniac for the next two hours, getting Scarlett's story and mine down, and then, for the cream on top, I attempt a few illustrations from the present day. I long to inspire my readers to live an abundant and powerful life. I feel fairly confident that I am as I tell them they must work on honing their personal strength, that they must rely on NO ONE but their own self.

I click POST and shut my computer down. Though I'm not tired at all, it's almost 3:00 a.m., so I brush my teeth and lie on my side in bed with the lamp on and *Gone with the Wind* open beside me. Out of a habit that's not fading I pat the bed, call, "Kitty, kitty kitty," as Dandelion's face floods my heart. I smile through tears thinking of her leaping up to snuggle in beside me for the night, her high-pitched snore and the way her paws move in her dreams. There's no question she's coming back. It's just a matter of when.

I relish the thought that the blog I just posted on *Scarlett Says* is going to be a smash hit. It's strong, beautifully written, and offers so much to the reader. I see myself sitting down at my computer in the morning, the tally of my followers over 18,000. Siggy doesn't know what he's talking about, this praying he's doing that I'll find what I'm longing for. No, he sure doesn't. Because, at the heart of things, I'm content. My blog is enough. Maybe I should want more. But the simple fact is, I don't. Maybe it's not what everybody wants, maybe it's not the absolute, perfect life and all that, but I love writing my blogs, answering my followers, thinking about how I can make this world a better place to live. Wishful thinking, I know, but a girl can dream.

And a girl SHOULD dream. I should sleep. I know I should. But I can't. I try not to check to see if anyone's read the blog yet. Surely out of all those followers, someone's awake at this hour.

Maybe even Charles.

Three-thirty comes and goes. I miss Dandelion. Finally, at four, I get out of bed and check the blog. And grin.

I have responses. Several, and when I scroll down to those responses and see the praises, read about the aha moments, then I *know* it'll be *enough* for me. What's the harm in a virtual life? What is Siggy's deal, constantly calling it the antisocial network? I interact with people.

I shut down the computer. Maybe now I can sleep. I sigh, contentedly, as I open the cover of *Gone with the Wind*, flip to the dog-eared page marking my spot at chapter 54. I literally crawl into the words and I am Scarlett as she paces her bedroom, disgusted and humbled by Melanie's blind trust, pining for Ashley, then desperately needing a drink so she can fall asleep. She slips downstairs for some brandy, and encounters a very drunk Rhett. He's angry because Scarlett has been denying him the pleasures of her bed. He tells her he loves her, accuses her of lusting for Ashley and tells her he'd kill her if he thought it would take Ashley from her mind. After a long argument, Rhett suddenly seizes Scarlett and drags her upstairs, where he tears off her clothes and ravishes her body.

I'm getting a bit uncomfortable, so I slam the novel shut, turn out the lamp, and close my eyes. But I lie there bright-eyed and bushy-tailed at 5:00 a.m. I'm feeling something intensely physical that's hard to put into words. It's outside my rational brain's jurisdiction. Ten minutes pass as I concentrate on breathing deeply, steadily, trying to imagine peaceful images of ocean waves crashing on the beach. All of a sudden, I see Charles's face, those eyes. There he is in his blue Union suit.

One thing's for certain. I still can't sleep. I sit up in bed, admit to myself that something inside me has come to life and it's not going to let go. There's nothing for these mutinous impulses but to get out of bed and obey the voice. But . . . what? Answer Charles's responses to my last blog? Would that do?

I tiptoe to the den, sit down at my desk, and turn on my computer. I'm literally trembling as I go back through the archives of my past blogs to hunt down Charles's e-mail address. I find it, enter it into my address book, click on Compose, then quickly type, "Dear Charles. I am no longer able to resist your flattery, your overtures, your pleasing words. These feelings will not be denied, and the attraction I feel for you is powerful. On the other hand, the fear is powerful, too. This desire to keep unto myself no matter what. But, my love, this should not hinder an online relationship between us! I know that what has brought us this far is that respective social anxiety we feel. Charles, we're both social outcasts . . . both anxious in the 3-D world, and I've been lying in my bed, trying to think what it is we can do to quench our mutual desire. I must ask—is virtual love a possibility for you?"

I sign off with "Your feisty Scarlett," click send, and go into the kitchen, open the refrigerator, close it. Go to Dandelion's food bowl in the corner and utter a sort-of prayer that goes, "Please bring my baby kitty back home safe to me, please," then go unlock the door to lean out into the darkness for a good two minutes and listen as the crickets sing. I go back to my desk and turn on Atlanta's Liquid Soul. Ironically, Percy Sledge is crooning "When a Man Loves a Woman."

It's 5:20 a.m. No way Charles is awake this early. I pace around my apartment, nervous about what he's going to say. What if he says I have to meet him in the flesh? Well, I don't care what he says, virtual love will have to suffice. Despite our attraction, there are some personal codes I'll never violate. Charles will just have to understand. Maintaining my self-reliance is more important than face-to-face love.

At 5:29, I sit back down at my desk, shake a few Tums out of the container, chew them to a gummy chalk. The computer screen has gone blank with inactivity, and I just tap the mouse a little bit. Amazingly I see a response from Charles in my inbox.

I can only sit there, my heart beating like crazy, wondering how in heaven's name I, Joan Marie Meeler, have come to this moment. I have a sudden impulse to just hit delete and run while I still can. But I don't. I open that e-mail and I lean forward, press my hand to my heart, and read it in one big gulp.

> Oh, my feisty Scarlett! The only one who really gets me! I've been holding you close in my dreams so long, and when I saw this, at first I thought I was only dreaming! Yes, I'm game for "virtual love," as you call it. We'll just take things nice and slow. Perhaps, given time, you will decide to meet me in your hometown of Atlanta on December 14 for the seventy-fifth anniversary celebration of the premier of our favorite movie. As I said, we can meet in costume.

For the first time in my life, I know the power of the heart, the drawing love that's so strong it eclipses everything. There is nothing at this moment but me and my Charles.

12

After my exchange with Charles, I sleep soundly but briefly. By Saturday at noon, I'm still exhausted yet giddy with energy. Now I know where expressions such as "walking on air" and "the world turned upside down" come from. The headiness of first love is stupefying. How beautiful, how delectable my relationship with Charles! There are no others in the perfect unity of us. And, happily, we're free of ties or claims, unburdened by debts of the past or worries of the future. I'm walking around my apartment thinking about last night—this morning—and it just gets more beautiful and exquisite with every rehearsal.

Who knew mere words could do this? I especially like thinking about what Charles said, how I am the only one who really gets him. I went back through every single comment he's ever made on *Scarlett Says*, and I can tell he's not smitten over Nancy from Tennessee. I was stupid to even think he wanted her. I'm sure he knows how dried up and unfeisty she is just from looking at her face. He sure hasn't asked *her* to meet him at the seventy-fifth anniversary of the movie premier. And Tennessee's not exactly far from Atlanta. I rub my tired eyes and wander into the kitchen to think about fixing some lunch, well, it would actually be breakfast. Okay, brunch.

Strangely, I'm not hungry, and so I drink a can of Mountain Dew standing at the refrigerator, then go open the front door and step outside to call "Kitty, kitty, kitty" into the sunny day. Nothing but a couple of squirrels twitching about on the limbs of the nearest crepe myrtle. I can really feel fall moving in to Atlanta now that we're in October. I decide I'll go feed Aretha and check the responses to my post, though it's clearly too early for much.

Before I get the door closed, my phone starts ringing. It's Bitsy according to the caller ID, and oddly, without hardly a thought, any reluctance, I pick it up, press Talk, and hold it against my ear. "Hi, Bitsy." My voice sounds different, too.

"Joan Marie?"

"That's what you named me. How are you today?"

There's a long pause, during which I can hear my mother take in a breath, then gulp. "I'm fine, thank you," she announces brightly, and I can tell she's regathered herself. "How are you?"

"I'm good," I say. "In fact, I feel kind of . . . *ecstatic*!"

A beat, and then Bitsy says, "Well, great! I don't suppose you're up for dinner at the Sun Dial, are you? I'm craving Russell's ceviche and his vanilla bean crème brûlée, and I decided I would call my daughter and invite her to join me." She laughs her lilting cocktail-party laugh.

"Sure," I say, and Bitsy gets quiet for so long I wonder if she's passed out.

If I'm going out anywhere fancier than Burger King or Krystal, it's to Murphy's, in my own neighborhood, and that is a very rare occurrence. I've been to the Sun Dial on two occasions, both *before* the day of shame incident. Both were with Bitsy. One on the day of my thirteenth birthday, we went for lunch wearing what she calls "high-cotton," and we ate giant grilled portobellos and something for dessert called a gâteux. Bitsy was impressed and talked at length about the "presentation" of the food and the "elegant ambiance," which I did not appreciate and would have been much happier in my faded jeans eating a hot dog at the Varsity.

Then one evening, when I just turned fifteen and had my learner's permit, she took me along as the designated driver. I sat beside her sipping a ginger ale and watching her with a kind of horrified awe as she got sloshed on martinis in the rotating cocktail lounge. At 10:00 p.m. I took her elbow after she kept proclaiming loudly, "Would you just look at that magnificent Atlanta skyline!" I remember feeling like I was the adult and she was the child. I also remember promising myself "Never again."

Bitsy clears her throat. "So what time do you want me to come by for you?"

"Um . . ." I kind of wish I hadn't said yes. I would really like to stay home and watch *Gone with the Wind*, read, wait for Dandelion, and perhaps reconnect with Charles online.

"Joan Marie?" Bitsy's words are like little bitty arrows pinging my brain. "We need to firm up our plans. I've got a little present for you. Remind me to give it to you if I forget."

I hear myself saying "Wonderful," a word I rarely use. Then, "I'll just meet you there. At seven. I think I need to go now."

At 5:00 p.m. I go in the bathroom to examine my face, eye myself suspiciously. Same eyes. Nose still in the same place. Same shapeless, brown hair. I'm starting to feel a bit tense now that my mind has absorbed what I've agreed to. Well, I tell myself, won't old Siggy be proud of me. He's always telling me I need to offer the woman some grace. Then I decide it will be bearable only because I can tell him all about it on Monday morning. I go in my closet and stand, looking for something to wear that won't upset Bitsy too much and will be acceptable for the Sun Dial.

Closer to seven, I head for the restaurant, Atlanta's Liquid Soul drenching me with Fats Domino's "Blueberry Hill." I'm wearing a black sweater with Dolman sleeves, a swingy black calf-length skirt, black tights, and black pumps. Monochromatic is good for a slim-ming effect. I have my hair up in a French twist, and I'm wearing eyeshadow, blush, and jewelry all together for the first time in what seems like forever but was actually when I went to Mount Carmel.

As Fats sings about the thrill, I get it for the first time, that feeling that's been wafting around inside my consciousness since I wrote to Charles. The thrill of *us* fills the corners of my mind and moves into my chest, my stomach, my legs, as tingly as champagne. My entire body feels giddy. I feel pretty powerful, in control, as a matter of fact, and I entertain the very fleeting thought that if I can do this, drive to the Sun Dial to meet Bitsy, then maybe I *could* meet my sweetie in December. The Loew's Grand Theatre is what? Maybe a couple of miles down Peachtree Street from the Sun Dial, if even that.

The Sun Dial is considered the ultimate Atlanta experience for tourists and locals alike. It's a revolving restaurant sitting atop the Westin Peachtree Plaza hotel downtown, offering a 360-degree panorama of the magnifcent Atlanta skyline. I board the scenic glass elevator to ascend the hotel's seventy-three stories, the phrase *confident metropolitan woman* circling in my brain. Street lights and headlights and shop lights are bright points of light in this beautiful, busy city I see. I'm still not hungry, though I know Bitsy will ask for bread, then order appetizers before our entrees, and also dessert with coffee after.

It's seven sharp as I enter the Sun Dial, and I'm surprised Bitsy's not here yet. I ask the maître d' for a table for two far away from the bar. "Right this way," he says, and I'm shown to a table by an elegant white-coated host I think must be named Giovanni or Armand. He pulls the chair out for me, then returns to set two goblets of ice water with lemon slices in them on the thick white linen tablecloth and says, "Would madam care for a cocktail while she waits?"

"No, madam would not," I tell him. "Water's fine."

He raises one perfectly shaped eyebrow, gives me a tight-lipped smile as he snaps his order book closed. I can feel his disapproval as I slip my heels off and stretch my toes beneath the table. *I don't care*, I think, *Bitsy will make it up to him.* If I know my mother, she'll consult the wine list and pick by price.

With the buzz of "the thrill" still in my head, my sense of anxiety stands at bay, at a low hum, almost like white noise in the background. I have to keep my focus on Charles and the way I've been feeling all day. If I think too hard about the fact that I'm sitting in an Atlanta landmark, listening to elegant live jazz in the background, staring at a ridiculous seven-piece silverware setting, and holding a menu that weighs five pounds, the "white noise" will overwhelm. *Focus on Charles, Joan. On normal.* I lift the silver tongs from a plate of elegant butter sculptures and clack them open and shut soundlessly.

My ex-therapist would be proud.

At ten after seven my mother sweeps into the Sun Dial with all the panache of an actress. I can almost feel everyone holding their breaths, patrons and staff alike. I'm shocked because Bitsy is not her usual elegant, socialite self. She's wearing a metallic gold sweater dress, which clings to her tiny curves, and shiny black stiletto-heeled boots. Her hair is parted down the center, sleeker and longer and blonder than the last time I laid eyes on her. She's wearing dramatic black eyeliner and frosty pink lipstick that make her look like 1960s sex symbol Brigitte Bardot. All this is the antithesis of usual impeccable Buckhead socialite fall ensemble of a Chanel tweed suit and Jimmy Choo shoes, the iconic Hermes Birkin bag, and the elegant Cartier jewelry.

This is so . . . I don't know, so hip and trendy? My brain is attempting to register this change. Will her *insides* be different this evening, too?

"Hello, daughter," she says brightly, settling herself across from me. "Isn't it a beautiful evening to be out in Atlanta?" Her oversize Luis Vuitton handbag sprawls across the table like a lap dog.

"Sure," I say. "Hi, Bitsy. How are you?"

"I am fine," she says. "You certainly look good with a little makeup on, Joan Marie." Our waiter hovers anxiously at her side. "Oh, just bring me a martini," she tells him, waving her hand in a little dismissal motion in the air. "Extra dry, extra cold, three olives."

He turns again to me, and I shake my head. I know he thinks I am the sedate mother watching her daughter with silent admiration for the spontaneity of youth. I sip my goblet of water, untempted by the steaming basket of bread he left.

Bitsy looks at me, "You have no idea how I have longed for this moment, Joan Marie."

"What?"

"For my daughter to join me on a social occasion. Out in public. And look at you. You are a sight for these sore eyes."

I feel happy, a little embarrassed, and somewhat ashamed of my earlier thoughts. "Thank you," I say. We sit, me smiling and nodding, unsure.

"It's been, what? Over three months since I've seen you?" Bitsy continues. "And us not even ten minutes away from each other."

"Um, I guess," I mumble.

"Trust me. It's been three months, if not longer."

In the back of my mind I know this is true. And for some reason, the white noise is louder.

"I could fall over dead and you wouldn't even notice," Bitsy says, freshening her lipstick.

Fortunately the waiter returns with Bitsy's martini. "Would you care for a cocktail now?" he asks me.

I seldom drink, but this seems to call for something. "Yes, please. I'd like a glass of red wine." I smile tightly at my mother, then bury my face in the huge menu. What am I supposed to answer to something like that? Does she really think that? *Would* I notice if she fell over dead? Why are there so many choices on this menu? And then, running my eyes down the columns of salads and entrees, I think, *I'm not even hungry.*

"And for you, Madam?" the waiter asks, and I jump.

"I'll have the Caesar salad," I say.

"That's not enough!" Bitsy snaps. "Bring her what I'm having."

"So, that's two of our calico shrimp ceviche?" He beams, turning to her.

My body is as tense as a two by four. I clear my throat. "No! I want the Caesar salad, like I said."

He glides away and Bitsy pokes out her frosted bottom lip. "Sorry. Guess I was just picturing a nice, long six-course dinner with my baby girl."

I soften. Her motives aren't bad. "Okay, when he comes back, tell him I'll have the pan-seared trout."

Lobster crepes show up, and before I can respond, Bitsy digs in. I sigh and rest my chin on my palms. I didn't even hear her order appetizers. That's when her comment about "six-course meal" sinks in. She ordered when I was lost in the menu. No wonder my salad surprised the server.

"Delicious," she says. "This is certainly the way to outsmart my overactive thyroid. Oh, yes," she says, lifting her martini in a toast-like gesture. "It really is."

I lift my wine, try to relax my lips, which have been pressed together in a grimace that I'm sure takes more energy than a smile. I realize I'm more than a little tense. Bitsy's trying to be pleasant, there's no doubt about that. Soon the waiter comes with two bowls of steaming carrot soup. I can smell the orange and tarragon wafting up. I lean forward and take a spoonful.

"Good, hmm?" Bitsy says.

"Yes. It is."

Bitsy sips her martini, which I notice is down to a quarter of its original volume. "Do you have anything new going on in your life?"

My heart thumps as I try to think of some mutually safe topic. "Well," I begin, taking a deep breath, "I'm thinking of buying a little window greenhouse I saw in a Pottery Barn catalog. Growing some herbs."

She nods, twirls her long strand of shiny black beads. "That's nice. I've always envied people with a green thumb."

I think of Aretha and smile. She's grown at least a half inch taller lately; her leaves and stem are greener than ever. I like the idea of Bitsy envying something about me. Besides her maid and her part-time cook, Bitsy has a gardener. I try to picture her doing anything that makes her sweat. I take another sip of my wine, blot my lips.

Our entrees arrive along with another martini for Bitsy, and I look at that trout lying there dead on the plate and think about how at one point he was swimming along and enjoying his life in some body of water. I can't eat him. Then just as quickly I realize it's not that I'm inclined toward a vegan lifestyle. I appreciate good fish, good meat. I love good food in all its forms. It's that I haven't been hungry since Charles and I connected this morning. I force myself to take a small bite and move more bites around on my plate inge-niously, sneaking a couple of chunks into my napkin. Bitsy devours her ceviche and two rolls slathered in butter, all by the elegant glow of the lovely ivory candles. She'll probably finish off the appetizers and have two desserts. She eats like this when she's drinking, then she'll spend two weeks starving and playing tennis.

I watch the white-coated waiter at a nearby table. He's reciting the ingredients of the soup du jour with an elegant and restrained condescension. I check out the four patrons seated at the table, their faces lifted to him, their eyebrows high as they hang on every syllable, as if this is of critical importance, as if this might be their last meal.

Our waiter glides up, and Bitsy orders dessert and coffee for the two of us. I hear the purring lilt of flirtation in her words that assures excellent service, though I'm fairly sure the man is gay. I don't even protest her ordering for me.

He returns, as I knew he would, in under two minutes with a carafe of steaming coffee and a tray holding two elegantly presented crème brûlées and two bone-thin china cups. Bitsy digs into hers, remarking that it's even better than the last time she indulged herself. I tell her I'm glad, that I'm just not hungry and she's welcome to mine. Immediately after I say this, Bitsy removes her reading glasses, leans in toward me and says, "I have to tell you, Joan Marie, there's something different about you tonight. Through the eyes. No! *In* the eyes! You're not in love, are you?" She looks so hopeful.

"What?" I say, smiling a stupid, fake smile.

"I said, are you in love?"

"No! Of course not!" Now I need to go home. In my inbox are many comments. And I need to see if I have a call from someone who's found my Dandelion. There are lots of things I need to do at home. A long list. In the background, the white noise of my anxiety is suddenly bordering on a low roar.

"Oh!" Bitsy squeals. "I almost forgot, I brought you something." She hefts her enormous handbag back up onto the table, and with a ceremonial hesitation, a meaningful look into my eyes, she unzips the gold zipper. From its depths she extracts a flowered vinyl makeup pouch I recognize from the Estee Lauder ads in the Sunday section of the *Atlanta Journal* and places it on the table. There's also a Kindle and an iPhone and iPad, which she very carefully sets at a safe distance from her forest of beverages, and then she roots around, and with another louder squeal, pulls something out, and hugs it to her chest before presenting it to me. It's a fat, pulpy paperback.

"You've got to read this, Joan Marie!"

I stare at the book—*Scruples Two* by Judith Krantz.

"Now, Judith knows something about life," Bitsy says, nodding vigorously. "Did you know her first book, her first *Scruples* came out in 1978, the year she turned fifty?" She doesn't wait for my response. "Well, anyhow, then she wrote *Princess Daisy* and several more books, and this second *Scruples* didn't come out till 1992. That would make her sixty-four, right?" This time she looks hard at me until I nod.

"Well, I Googled her and it said over eighty million copies of her books are in print in over fifty languages. You cannot argue with that."

I sit back in my chair, shove *Scruples Two* into my purse, and say, "Remarkable."

She takes a gulp of her latest martini. "Yes, it is remarkable. You want to know more about this remarkable woman? I'll tell you more. She went to Wellesley College, and her dormmates called her 'Torchy.' Do you know why, Joan Marie?"

"Um, she smoked a lot?"

"No! They called Judith 'Torchy' because she held the dorm dating record! She was the only one to have thirteen consecutive dates with thirteen different men!" Bitsy sits, tugs at her earring, and looks at me, so long and penetrating I feel like a specimen on a microscope slide. Finally she clears her throat. "I want you to think about this, Joan Marie." She's wide-eyed and serious. "You need to . . . Well, I don't think you even *try*. You don't send out the vibes to show you're available. There are tons of hunks, *unclaimed* hunks, out there. You've just got to be alert to them and work it! You keep yourself hidden away too much. You keep yourself stuck in that drab little apartment. You need to get out there! I know one thing. I read the online dating ads constantly, and there are so many unclaimed hunks in Atlanta alone you'd never be able to date them all if you lived to be a hundred." She nods, slowly, sagely.

I sit, blinking. I don't know what I'm supposed to say. Looks like I'm in for an evening of the usual Bitsy, admonishing me on how to attract hunks. So I do what I have to. I fix my face in what I hope is an expression of considerate listening, close my ears from the inside, and bury myself in my own completely unrelated thoughts. I think about Siggy singing along with James Brown to "I Feel Good," and then I think about how, as I left my apartment to come here, there were a few stinky Xs missing from the food bowl outside my door. I'm fairly sure squirrels don't eat catfood. I'm waiting for Bitsy to get all this out of her system, and then I'll excuse myself.

After about ten minutes, I see her expression has changed, and I decide she must be on to a new topic. I conclude it's safe to unstop my ears. Immediately, I hear her soft, surprisingly undrunken voice saying, "How's your job going?"

I rarely discuss Giffin & Burke with Bitsy. It's almost up there with beauty and fashion and hunks, but she's sitting there, waiting expectantly, and before I can stop myself, I say uncomfortably, "I'm a little scared. But you don't need to worry."

Recently I heard rumbles of budget cuts and downsizing coming from Philip Giffin. I'd wondered what I'd do if my job were cut or my pay slashed. Also, the rent at my apartment had gone up seventy-five dollars a month, and my meager salary was already stretched to the limit. I couldn't afford to stay there if my pay were any lower.

Bitsy blinks. A look of horror washes across her face. "What do you mean, you're scared? You could lose your job?"

I shrug. "Maybe."

"You have no significant other to share the expenses of living with!" She reaches a bejeweled hand across the table to touch my forearm, and I flinch. "You could move in with me. Mi casa es su casa."

"No!" I glance down at my watch. I need to go. My stomach tightens.

"Why not?" my mother asks in a subdued voice. She's smiling pitifully, like she's just been told she has an interminable disease. "Tell me, please, Joan Marie. What is it you can't stand about me?"

Silence. "Um," I say and swallow hard, start to say I'm not the Brookhaven type, then change it to, "I just like to have my own things around me. You know, my own style? Plus, I've got a cat now, you know."

That ought to do it, I think as I sip my wine, still my first glass, mostly full.

"Well," Bitsy says at last, twisting her linen napkin into a coil like a snake. "I could handle a cat . . . if it just stayed in your room."

I gasp. Again, I'm at a loss for words until I think of the perfect reason this would not work. "She'd pee on your hardwood floor, claw the Oriental carpet, shred your drapes, and scratch the fine antiques."

"Nonsense!" Bitsy makes one hand flop forward to show how preposterous this thought is. "Anyway, your old room's exactly the way it was when you left home! From that tacky beanbag chair to the lime green wall-to-wall carpeting. I didn't change that awful black lacquered furniture you had to have, and I left the rock-and-roll posters. Johnny begs and begs, saying, 'This is so gauche! A travesty!' but I tell him, 'No, this is the way my baby girl left it, and this is the way it stays. Just close the door if you can't handle it.'"

I actually gasp, picturing the unbelievable scene Bitsy just described: her standing in the doorway to my old bedroom, arguing with Johnny Jarrelle, her forty-ish designer, a bossy man-child with a triangular goatee and fierce eyes that make me think of Errol Flynn. I realize my mouth is hanging open because Bitsy very pointedly opens and then closes her own mouth.

"I just want you to know it's there if you need a place, Joan Marie."

I can only nod, and suddenly another scene comes rushing in— the day I curled up into my very first armadillo pose in that very beanbag, rocking, careening internally. It was my first panic attack of many to come. The first visitation of absolute, unadulterated terror. In my anguish I craved for Bitsy to crouch down and say, "Joan Marie, are you okay?" but she chatted vacuously about getting together with her girlfriends while checking her face in my bathroom mirror. I cannot stop the next part of this memory either. I'm powerless as sprouts of shame and self-disgust push up in the soil of my consciousness. Those sprouts that live only slightly beneath my consciousness. And I know it's useless for me to even think I could live there with Bitsy, that I could kill the memory that would come every time I walked by that zebra-striped beanbag. That is where I would always think about that time I'd been responsible for something that had altered the world in an irreparable way. Where I would suffer from the knowledge that I had snuffed out an innocent soul.

I sit there, wide-eyed, dumb, until it comes to me in a blinding flash that this is the perfect moment in time for me to possibly put a little bit about that awful time to rest. At least air some of my fury at Bitsy, allow her a rebuttal of sorts while she's in this motherly mode. I decide I'll channel Scarlett's gumption, her boldness, and confront Bitsy.

"Bitsy?" I say. "Can I ask you something?"

"Of course!" She answers, that vacant brightness in her voice.

The moment feels surreal to me as I begin. "Do you remember when I was a freshman at Pace, and it was late September and a classmate passed away?"

She shudders and says, "Oh, Joan. There were several of your classmates that died in that awful car crash on Interstate 75 that rainy Friday night."

The anxiety is rising in my throat. I don't want to say it, but I do. "No, I don't mean them. That's sad, but I'm talking about Lydia Lydelle. She took her own life."

Bitsy makes a sound like "Hmm" in her throat and rolls her eyeballs upward, thinking. Finally she cocks her head, says, "Are you talking about that poor plump girl with the bad skin?"

I grit my teeth. How like her to focus on someone's *appearance*. "Yeah," I say, looking at Bitsy's perfectly made-up face, her painstakingly straightened hair. "She was a nice person. A beautiful person."

Our waiter hovers, turned toward Bitsy, waiting on her slightest command.

"We're good here," I say, banishing him. "All we need is the check."

Bitsy makes a gasp. "Oh, my lands! I haven't thought about that pitiful child in *ages*!" She sips her coffee, shakes her head. "I remember you had a fit for me to take you to her memorial service. Awfullest thing I ever had to do in my life!"

I stare at Bitsy. Remember how it was like moving heaven and earth to get her to agree to drive me to a Pentecostal Holiness church in Tallapoosa, Georgia. I remember how dead I felt standing outside in the cemetery as they shoveled dirt onto Lydia Lydelle's casket, her mother bent double, weeping.

"What?" Bitsy says. "It was absolutely tragic. None of the other cute girls from Pace were there. It was just a bunch of fat women in cheap polyester from that holy roller church. I don't know how Lydia Lydelle even *got in* to Pace."

I don't answer. I'm seeing red. My mouth won't form the words to inform my mother that Lydia had won a scholarship for doing so well in science in middle school. She'd blown away all competition at some nationwide science fair with some experiment on molecular biology. She was a brilliant person who probably would have found a cure for cancer had she lived.

"Well, it's true, Joan Marie. I'm sure even you wondered about that. The poor girl was so . . . so country. Unsophisticated and dumpy and . . ." Bitsy waves her hand, sips her martini, then her water, then her coffee. I marvel she hasn't been to the ladies' room once in the whole two hours we've been here. "You know she'd have been happier in a public high school in south Atlanta with her own kind."

"I don't know that!" I bark. "How would you know?" I feel a lot of fury toward Bitsy right now.

She looks at me, holding very still. "Everybody needs peers, Joan Marie. You know that child was miserable with nobody like her there. No wonder she took her own life." Bitsy shakes her head slowly, her earrings reflecting the candlelight. "It's so sad. It's why I paid that cute little cheerleader, Cynthia LaForgue, to take you under her wing. I wanted you to fit in, Joan Marie. Have some peers."

I cannot breathe. My heart is somersaulting, and my ears are roaring. I wouldn't be surprised if I had a heart attack right here. "You *paid* Cynthia LaForgue to be my friend?" I shriek, my voice shaking. Open-mouthed, I sit staring at Bitsy, who simply nods, using her bejeweled hands to pat the air softly, telling me to keep it down, we're in public. Inside it feels like a knife is being inserted in my pelvis, then turning, twisting, gouging deeper.

"I ended a life because of you and your shallow, evil ways! That is *unforgiveable*!" Hot tears dribble into my mouth. The trout fights the carrot soup in my stomach. I'm going to vomit, and I jump up, my napkin falling in my wake as I rush to the elegant ladies' room.

After my stomach is empty, I shuffle to the sink and pat my damp forehead with a towel and slump against the wall of the ladies' room. I'm teetering at the edge of a genuine meltdown as I look back over the crazy patchwork quilt of my life, the years stitched with deception and lies. I rehearse what I'll say to Bitsy. *You betrayed me! I can think of nothing crueler to do to one's child. Popularity is a god to you, and you ruined my life!*

I brace myself when I hear Bitsy's voice come in before her. "Joan Marie? I'm sorry. Don't be mad at me. I didn't know it would make you so mad. I had no idea. Forgive me?" She places a hand on my shoulder. I see she's holding her martini in the other hand. "To err is human, to forgive divine. Haven't you ever heard that? Now can we please drop this? I want to focus on happier things."

I shrug away from her hand, run out of the bathroom, by our table to grab my purse and then to the scenic glass elevator, where it seems to take about five hours to descend the seventy-three stories. I run to my Toyota, yank the door open, and dive inside. I don't care if I get a speeding ticket because I'm getting myself home fast.

I shoot a glance at the kitty food bowl as I let myself into my apartment. I fantasized briefly on the trip home that some sovereign power would get Dandelion home tonight to offset the emotional damage I just sustained. But no such luck.

I want comfort, to be wanted. I sit down, kick off the uncomfortable pumps, let my hair loose and shake a few Tums down my throat. And I click *Scarlett Says* to life.

Well, here's something—my followers have crossed over the twenty thousand mark. Apparently "Self-Reliance as the Key to Success—Part Two" has struck a chord with many. Bitsy fades from my head as I scan the pages of responses and see a string of positive affirmations. I wait in vain to feel that all-encompassing effervescent euphoric buzz of gratification. I'm so close to my goal . . . but there's only a dead space in my chest. I drop my head because it's heavy. A tear escapes, and I feel as though some already-dangling stitch that held my heart up has been snipped. I'm really not in the mood to weep right now. I so much do not want to collapse into a blubbering heap, but it seems I have no choice in the matter. Blinded by pesky tears, I reach out to turn on Atlanta's Liquid Soul. Wilson Pickett is singing "Mustang Sally."

Within a couple of stanzas, I'm better. The music allows me to arrest—if only for a few minutes—the pain and despair of my life, gives me a chance to connect with an inner self that's powerful. The lyrics carry me away to some other place where a flat-footed woman named Sally has been running all over the town. "You better slow your mustang down," Wilson warns her, and I snuffle up the last of my crying. The music strengthens me, and I mentalty declare, *For all intents and purposes, Elizabeth Hargrove Meeler is dead to me. I am an orphan.* I know these are not good thoughts and that if I confessed them to Siggy, he'd have a fit.

I glance over at my purse where I chunked it just inside the door. *Scruples Two* is lurking like a snake inside. I know what I must do. Down on all fours I go, crawling across the carpet like a baby, my knees getting momentarily stymied by the fabric of my skirt. I pause and pull the skirt up and through my thighs, tuck it into the waistband at my back so it's like a big diaper. I hear a very angry voice inside me saying, *Be sure to rip off the cover. That's what they do with those cheap mass market romances in the grocery store anyway . . .* half a minute later, I'm sitting Indian style beside my purse, reaching in, expecting the book to singe my fingers as I pull it out. Somehow I look down as I'm ripping the cover off, and I see the words *For my beloved daughter, Joan. Love, Mother* inscribed in Bitsy's distinct script. First, I'm just stunned. I didn't expect it to be personalized at all, and if she did write anything, I would imagine *Truly, Bitsy,* or *Best, Elizabeth Hargrove Meeler.*

"Pure lies, pure hogwash!" I screech so loud I see stars. "You cannot win me back with seven words! You're no mother, and you don't have the foggiest notion about how to love anyone! I am *not* your beloved daughter!" *Okay,* I thought. *That'll show her.*

Then why, I wondered as I stomped the defaced book down into the garbage, *do I feel so bad?*

I stomp my way back over to my desk, sit down, nudge the mouse, stare at the screen, at the beautiful responses of my loyal followers. I don't need her. I don't need a mother. I feel 20,000-plus pairs of warm arms reaching out to embrace me and my words.

"Fiddle-dee-dee to this emotional tripe!" I say. "There's no way I'll ever reconnect with that shrew! She deserves to be ignored! She has cut the cord!" I feel a surge of happiness, power.

I sit on the red sofa, feeling fine and strong, waiting for the VHS of *Gone with the Wind* to roll through the credits, tapping my foot to "Tara's Theme." I'm transported for a beautiful 238 minutes whereupon, at 3:00 a.m., I rise, stretch, and turn off the VCR and the television.

Before I leave the den I pause at my desk to see if I've got a new e-mail from Charles. I don't, and before I shut everything down, I click on *Scarlett Says* to see if I've gotten anymore followers. No additions since last time I checked, but there are several more comments. One is a lengthy note from Barry Freeman in Minnesota with the first sentence in all caps—"PERSONAL STRENGTH CAN LEAD TO LOSS!" I'm stung by the words, but it doesn't keep me from continuing to read.

> Scarlett, you're so wrong. You say that in chapter 23 of *Gone with the Wind*, which you claim is the 'textbook chapter' as far as Scarlett and her so-called successful self-reliance goes, that "Scarlett O'Hara swore to herself that she would never rely on Rhett Butler again." BUT, let me refer you to chapter 54 of our hallowed volume. Here is where Rhett tells Scarlett he is sorry for her, sorry to see her throwing away happiness with both hands. He says, "We could have been perfectly happy if you had ever given us half a chance, for we are so much alike. We are both scoundrels, Scarlett, and nothing is beyond us when we want something. We could have been happy, for I loved you and I know you, Scarlett, down to your bones . . ."

I wrench my eyes away, look at Aretha, at her cheerful purple-blue bloom. It's not that my followers never argue; in fact, I like a good confrontation, but there's something different, personal about this one. I hate it. I have to read the rest of what Barry wrote:

> Now, allow me to put you in mind of the very last pages of Peggy Mitchell's masterpiece, her resolution, we should call it. Where Scarlett is begging Rhett not to leave her. She pleads, "Oh, my darling, if you go, what shall I do?" Rhett shrugs, tells her, "My dear, I don't give a damn." I think you'll agree with me, Scarlett, that though in some situations, self-reliance can be the key to success, in this one, and in many others in our lives, personal strength can lead to loss. I'd hoped that you'd be more insightful, this is not what I expect from you. Think again, Scarlett. You owe it to your loyal readers to present us with truth.

I'm stunned by the lenthy rebuttal. The worst thing is, Barry could be right. Scarlett did do herself out of happiness. I sit a minute, my hands holding each other hard, staring at the computer screen, when all of a sudden a message from Charles in Manhattan pops up in my private e-mail account.

"My feisty Scarlett," he begins, and I drink in the beautiful smiley face.

> I am a man of principles. I cannot in good conscience defy my own sense of what is right. I will not besmirch, soil your reputation, or dishonor you with some cheap, tawdry affair. I am a man of committment.

I stop breathing before I read on.

> And so I'd like to make an honest woman of you. I think that we should make our relationship official

217

and marry. Therefore, I am asking for your hand. Will
you, my feisty Scarlett, the only one on this planet
who understands me, take me to be your lawfully
wedded husband?

Beside this proposal there is a link to a site called virtualvow.com.
I sit still as stone. *Is this real?* I pinch myself hard, hear myself gasp, say
"Ouch!" Yes, it's real. I sit a long time, listening to the humming of
the refrigerator, the soft sounds of passing traffic on Ponce de Leon
Avenue, trying to absorb this. I think of Charles's profile picture, his
noble and beautiful and valiant features beneath that Union soldier
hat. His shining hair. His piercing blue eyes. He is a good man.

Finally, I click on the link. At the top of the page is written *Free
Online Weddings! We provide free online/virtual proposal, engagement, wedding, and divorce services. What better way to show your
love than through a virtual wedding ceremony! You can send your
proposal, invite your friends, enjoy a classy interactive wedding ceremony, and have your "married status" available to show to everyone. We cover it all! We handle all the same services and features that
you'd have in a full legal marriage. Print a frameable certificate.*

I let out a long, deep breath and imagine the 20,000-plus followers of *Scarlett Says* witnessing our union. Nancy from Tennessee
has a thin-lipped frown on her skinny, over-powdered face. After
this mental scene fades, I click on Virtual Vow wedding chapel,
and then on Wedding Archives. Under Recent Ceremonies, I read
a transcript of the first one. The traditional wedding vows are alter-
nated between Bride and Groom, then finalized by the pair saying
in union, "Through Jesus Christ our Lord. Amen."

In a zombie-like state, I brush my teeth and go into the bedroom. I arrange my sheets and my fleece blanket, open *Gone with
the Wind* and set it along the edge of the mattress, step out of my
slippers, and prepare to nestle in, but then, just like that, every
shred of desire for my regular routine drains out of the soles of my
feet. Charles has asked me to marry him! Okay, so it's not a legally

binding union, but getting married—even "virtual" married—has never been my intention, even in my wildest dreams. Not that I really let myself have a lot of wild dreams.

I suddenly wonder if I ought to drop to my knees here at the edge of my bed and pray. The thought has been hovering at the back of my mind, a lurking need to find out if there is some higher power with a higher wisdom who cares about humans. Someone I can talk to about hard decisions in life. I shake my head, say aloud, "Nah. If there were some giant up there in the sky, he wouldn't wake up for something like this. He'd yawn, say 'leave me alone if it's not about starving children in Africa or a forty-year drought. Don't you remember what I said? "God helps those who help themselves." ' "

It's a cliché, and I have a feeling that's not really in the Bible. But I believe it's true. It has to be true.

13

I got the answer to both your dilemmas, Miss Joan," Siggy says, pausing the push broom in front of my desk. "The answer that comes from the Word, that is sharper than any double-edged sword." He pulls a rag from his pocket to wipe away a smudge on the fishbowl that holds the Giffin & Burke nail files.

It's Wednesday afternoon, one hour before closing time.

Siegfried's been dwelling on my dilemmas, as he calls them, since I spilled them out. I held both of them in for a long time, but they finally bubbled out. I'd kept putting Charles off about the proposal, but he was insisting that we make a commitment. All of it was making me out of sorts, and Siggy always notices. He keeps asking me why I look so distracted and downtrodden. The fact is, he doesn't look so good himself. His skin tone is much yellower, and I don't really want to acknowledge it, but he's begun limping, wincing when he thinks no one is looking. I want to deflect the concern back on him, but he isn't having it. He has told me a hundred times, "It grieves my heart to see you moping."

I'm a bit reluctant to hear Siggy's solutions, solutions I know are primarily "Thus sayeth Solomon in the Proverbs."

"Okay, let me hear them," I consent at last.

"This ain't from the Proverbs," he announces, in his tone of "I know what you're thinking."

I feel my brow furrow.

His eyes twinkle as he says, "Miss Joan, you're human. You done met a man you're attracted to. We all got needs," Siegfried adds cheerfully. "I vote you marry Charles."

"Well, it's nice to know I've got your vote," I say in a clipped voice, thinking: *I'm not telling him it's a virtual proposal for a virtual marriage that's not even legal because he'd drop dead right here on the office floor. If I hear him say one more time that my Internet relationships are really antisocial, I'll scream.*

Not legal. But to me it's a commitment. The kind I think Charles would honor. And it would stop a thousand questions from running through my head. A thousand doubts.

"Humans got fundamental needs, and one is close-up, personal relationships," Siegfried says, reading my thoughts. "We're born to belong. We need strong, affectionate bonds with other peoples to be happy." He raises his eyebrows meaningfully. "I don't want to see you throw away your chance at happiness with both hands, Miss Joan."

"You stole that line from the blog!"

Siegfried grins, just keeps looking hard at me.

I sighed and motioned for him to sit down. I relayed the entire conversation from my night out with Bitsy, plus all about how I taunted Lydia Lydelle for the pure joy of feeling superior, of thinking I belonged in that despicable group led by Cynthia LaForgue. I try for the millionth time to understand why I looked up to Cynthia. I used to think it was about teenage friendship, joining forces for the joyous sake of being companions, some kind of teenage-girl-soulmates-because-we-clicked kind of thing. But I know now that's hogwash, that I know Bitsy paid Cynthia to be my friend.

Now that I know Cynthia's motivation, I have a deep need to know what this thing was that caused *me* to hook up with her and feel superior to Lydia Lydelle. I want to gauge the intensity, the validity of my feelings as Lydia Lydelle had come lumbering into the girls' bathroom wearing that cheap, cheap K-mart sweatsuit. She always looked as if she knew things the rest of us didn't, as if she had secret hardships she had to bear.

Lydia seemed more in tune with real-world kinds of issues, not the superficial things most teen girls looked up to. I remember thinking when I first saw Lydia that we might have things in common, that I could perhaps be her friend. Then when Cynthia started paying attention to me, that all fell by the wayside. I felt some sort of high-and-mighty thing. I felt superior that morning. Now thoughts of what I said just make me feel small and empty.

"Why, Siggy?" I ask. "Why did I follow Cynthia LaForgue?"

He takes a deep breath. " 'The full soul loatheth an honeycomb; but to the hungry soul every bitter thing is sweet.' Proverbs 27:7."

I try not to scream. "Please spare me the riddles. Just tell it to me straight."

"Okay, it's like this. Know how when you're full, stuffed, nothing really tastes good? You can take it or leave it?"

"I guess."

"And when you're hungry, I mean really starving, almost anything tastes delicious? Best thing you ever ate?"

"Uh . . . sure." What in the world is he leading up to? He pauses so long, I look over at John Burke's office where Gold Ring disappeared into more than an hour ago. I wonder what they do in there. I have an idea, because she doesn't always come out looking as polished and put together as when she went in.

Finally, Siggy clears his throat. "Okay, see, you were starving for a friend. For someone to like you. And when Miss Cheerleader, popularity queen, started paying attention to you, you were so hungry, vulnerable, you hooked up with her without hardly a thought."

Tiny bubbles of discovery go off in my brain. He could be right! I hold my hand to my mouth and feel ever so slightly better. I look at Siggy awhile, thinking how it feels so nice to hear something I like for a change. I have a quicksilver daydream of going home with him at five, sitting at the supper table with him and Olie, and then going into what I'm sure is a cozy den with an afghan on the couch, potted plants dripping from side tables, while we watch the evening news on TV, talking about mundane things like the weather and what's on sale at the grocery this week. For some reason I get a little dewey eyed at this mental image, but Siggy doesn't seem to notice. Embarrassed, I start clicking mindlessly on my keyboard, say, "Okay, well thanks, Siggy," and he limps off, heading toward the break room.

Shortly Gold Ring emerges from John Burke's office. Her hair's all messed up again, her top twisted like she pulled it on too quickly, and her face looks like a cat who's just swallowed a mouse. She sashays up to my desk. "I need you to type a letter to these people," she commands, handing me a slip of paper with the name and address of the Tokyo Health Spa on Larkspur Terrace in Decatur. "Give them our history, our rates, and tell them I'd like to call on them next week." She double snaps her fingers and, with hardly a beat, adds, "I want this out pronto!"

I cringe a little bit, but not the way I used to. I almost wish I had a big bag of powdered donettes sitting on my lap, some smelly Doritos at my elbow. I would stuff my face right in front of her, letting crumbs dribble into the keyboard. But I've stopped snacking at my desk. Not because of this girl's disdain, but because I just don't feel the urges anymore. I kind of miss the stealth of slipping my hand down to my secret snack drawer, of the comfort of a sneaky treat, but it's fading as this has been going on for almost a month now, this loss of appetite. I'm losing weight, and my clothes are starting to get loose. Maybe between being in love and walking the streets in hopes of finding Dandelion. . . .

"Meghan," I lean forward, say her name in a whisper. "Did you know your top's on inside out?"

"What?" She scurries off to the bathroom.

I toss the scrap of paper in my inbox, my shame transformed into satisfaction that sits in my lap like a happy cat.

⸎

So we did it. Saturday, October 25, at 3:00 p.m., I sit at my desk, waiting for my frameable marriage certificate to print out, to "officially" say I'm now Mrs. Charles Gruber. Unconsciously this morning, I dressed in a white blouse, a white skirt, and fleecey white footie socks, and I'm sipping a Fresca that's kind of like champagne. I lift up the warm sheet of paper from the printer's tray. The words are solid, black, in a lovely font, with a beautiful border. I'll buy a gold frame next time I'm in the Dollar Tree and hang it above my computer.

Virtual Vow was right. At noon, Eastern time, we had a classy interactive wedding ceremony with some of our closest virtual friends. Nancy from Tennessee never responded, but 15,476 of my followers on *Scarlett Says* did, and one was S.O.S. from Atlanta. Of course, I was scared he was going to have a fit about the fact that it was to be a virtual ceremony, but that just shows you never really know somebody, because Siggy sent his virtual blessings and said he wouldn't miss it for the world. I imagined Siggy sitting on the front row, beaming like the father of the bride.

What I didn't expect was how nice it feels to be committed. When I said, "I do," vowing to stand beside my husband through richer and poorer, in sickness and in health, it was like something came alive inside of me, some ferocious loyalty not unlike what Scarlett feels for her family's land in *Gone with the Wind*. Only this is laced with tenderness.

I'm startled by how dedicated I feel to a man I've never met, as if I'd take on the world to defend him. And us.

Right after our ceremony, I went to the bedroom and dumped the tangle of items in my jewelry box on the bed and rooted around for a pair of rings as close to an engagement and wedding ring as possible. I slipped them on my left hand and stared for a good ten minutes before I rose to continue pacing, waiting to have a private conversation with Charles after our guests have left.

"I'm here, my beloved bride, my feisty Scarlett," Charles begins. "Or, may I call you Joanie now?" I did divulge my given name to Charles Alexander Gruber but asked that he not share it with anyone.

We open up to each other, our most dearly held dreams, our past, our hopes. We make promises I know we both will keep. Now there's this connection, like a wire cable stretching from Atlanta to Manhattan.

I shut my computer down at 11:00 p.m., go stare at myself in the bathroom mirror and see a woman transformed. It has only been a few weeks since I struggled to meet Siegfried at the Varsity. Who knew that the love of a friend, a cat, and a man I've never met would change my world, more than any therapy ever could.

"Morning, Miss Joan," Siggy says, rising with a grunt from one of the fancy Queen Anne chairs in the lobby of Giffin & Burke and shuffling over to pull my desk chair out for me. He's definitely in more pain these days. I like to tell myself it's just the cold virus that's been traveling around the office for the past month. *He's going to be fine. He'll shake it soon just like the rest of us.*

I've been living in euphoria for the past three weeks, and I'm protective of it. I want to stay in this constant state of anticipation for my nightly meetings with Charles. He's become the focus of my life, and I can't believe how close we've become.

I've dropped pounds because I rarely eat, having discovered I can exist on much less, calorie wise, and that I'd much rather spend time chatting online with Charles than take the trouble to fix, buy, eat, and clean up food. When I do eat, it's things like bananas or some oatmeal bars I found on sale at Publix. I feel good about all the money I'm saving from not buying frozen dinners or fast food.

"Good morning to you, too, Siegfried. And thanks," I say, before clicking my computer on. I like the way my wedding rings sparkle as my fingers tap the keys. Today I'm preparing lots of things for an out-of-town conference almost everyone in the office is going to, even Gold Ring. Shortly after the incident with the blouse, Mr. Burke asked me not to discuss office business with his wife anymore. Not that I ever did. But there's also been no more talk of cutbacks.

Now I've been told not to let John Burke's wife know who's going to the conference. It's in Dallas, Texas, and so from this coming Thursday till next Tuesday, Siggy and I will be the ones "holding down the fort" here in Atlanta.

I print, then file an itinerary, noting that Siggy has polished the floor beneath my desk to a high shine. It smells cleanly of Pine-Sol. He's back in the reception area, and I allow myself to really look at him. There's a terrible weariness to him, and for a split second, I feel outraged at Olie. How could she let him leave the house like this!

"Let me get you a Coke," I say, scurrying to the break room with my purse. When I get back I sit beside him on the other Queen Anne chair.

"Drink this." I hand him the ice-cold can.

"Thanks. You're an angel." He sips the Coke. "So," he says, "how the newlyweds?"

A long moment passes as I try to come up with the right words. I fail, but manage, "We're happy." I cannot stop the silly grin that floods my face.

Siggy chuckles. "I guess you are," he says. And then abruptly, "Why won't you say you'll meet your beloved at the anniversary celebration in December? He asks you every single day, and you keep saying you're busy. You two are man and wife now, but it's just online. Not legal. You need to seal the deal. In the flesh, you know? That's important to men."

"Siegfried," I warn, rising to go back to my desk.

"Now, now. Don't have to get all defensive on me," he calls. "Charles seems to have his heart set on it."

Thankfully Siggy doesn't follow me. I sit in my chair and try to concentrate on nothing but the e-mails in the Giffin & Burke inbox.

At noon Siegfried leaves to walk down Peachtree Street to get soul food at Gladys Knight and Ron Winan's Chicken and Waffles. I dial Olie's number. I clutch my can of Fresca in one hand, the receiver in the other, and brace myself.

"Hello, Olie, it's Joan."

"Joan!" she shouts, clearly surprised as we only talk on Sunday evenings, and that, when she calls me. "My boy okay?"

"Yes, yes," I say. "I just need to ask you . . . Siegfried seems . . ." I sigh. "Here's the thing. I'm worried about him."

I want Olie to say it's ridiculous to worry. Olie does not say this. She tells me she's scared because Siggy's crises are getting more frequent and much worse. He lives with contant pain in his chest, abdomen, joints, and bones. Plus, his leg ulcers are infected. He's on meds for the pain and the infection but may need to be hospitalized. "As you know, Joan, pneumonia is the risky thing. Just pray it don't turn into pneumonia. Pray I get me some money to get him to the Mayo Clinic."

"Um," I murmur. My mind has gone utterly blank. I'm an imbecile.

"I'm so glad you there for him," Olie says. "I know I can count on you to be his guardian angel at Giffin & Burke."

"But . . ." I don't think of myself as an angel. A devil is more like it.

"Now, just be sure he drinks enough, and keep him from stress. Stress the worst thing. Doctor say do all you can to reduce the stress in Siegfried's life. Sickle-cell crises can occur as a result of stress. Keep my boy hydrated and calm, Miss Joan," Olie admonishes as she does at the end of every conversation.

"I will," I say. "Bye, Olie."

"Bye, hon. You a good woman."

I feel helpless as I listen to the dial tone buzz in my ear. This was not what I wanted to hear.

That evening I eat a small bag of cashews and some grapes while sitting at my computer. It's still two hours until my time with Charles, and I scroll down the responses to *Scarlett Says*. I'm up to 34,344 followers. I imagine myself punching a fist up in the air, yelling out, "Whoo-hoo!" and then, what? Will I just relax and blog without constantly watching the tally of subscribers? I've been striving toward this for two years and four months now. It was to be the golden ticket, the silver trophy that made everything right. I was desperate, so desperate to reach fifty thousand, and soon I'll actually be there. Will it be what I dreamed?

I will not think about the future now, I decide, scrolling on down, absentmindedly skimming responses. My hand freezes on the mouse when I see a smiley face beside a message from Charles in Manhattan. "My beloved Scarlett, please say you'll join me on December 14."

I grit my teeth, swallow, and shake my head hard. "It is enough!" I shout so loud that I imagine Aretha flinching. Virtual reality *must* be enough. It's one thing to be online husband and wife and quite another to meet in person and find out that mysterious chemical bonding, that irrational yearning, might or might not be there. *What if he met me and we didn't click in 3-D? What if he didn't find the in-person me as witty and sharp and feisty as the online me?*

Worse yet, what if my panic attacks flare up? I haven't had as much a problem going out in public since my "marriage." *What if . . .*

Plus, since October first, I've lost seventeen pounds. When people see me who haven't seen me in a while, they say, "Wow! Don't you look good!" But here's the thing—my beloved likes his women "generous." Does that mean a twelve or a twenty? Butterflies begin to circle in my stomach, and sweat beads pop up on my forehead. Thank goodness I know the remedy for this now! My hand reaches out to turn on Atlanta's Liquid Soul. Earth, Wind & Fire are singing "Let's Groove," and as I boogie in my chair, my stomach calms.

I decide I'll write my husband a letter, to his private e-mail, of course, tell him I cannot handle a 3-D event. "Dear Charles," I tap hard on the keyboard. "I don't mean to keep putting you off, but the truth is, I'm not sure how to be together in the real world. I don't have the strength to be feisty in 3-D. I don't have the constitution for the bravado and the trust that's required. I guess you could say I'm kind of preoccupied with some things from my old life."

The sharp click of each letter forms a word, a sentence, putting my chaotic thoughts down in black and white. This is powerful and satisfying and I continue. "I just can't see me having the kind of relationship people have when they're carefree, when they're so happy and oblivious and carried away by their passion that they can go on a date and not even notice the cold, cruel world."

I finish with slow, deliberate strokes. "I hope you'll understand and not love me less, nor leave me. I remain, your beloved wife and feisty Scarlett." I read it through once more and quickly hit Delete before I have a chance to change my mind and send it.

Now I have no idea what to do.

———

On Thursday at lunch I sit with Siggy in the breakroom. He opens a lettuce-green Tupperware rectangle with dividers that just screams out "Olie!". He nibbles at his tuna sandwich, pushes his carrot sticks around, sips his tea. He spent the morning wearing a fedora hat he found in John Burke's office, walking around, cleaning and saying, "Sure is nice to be the president of the company, even if it is only for three days" and "I vote we give the staff a raise and a two-hour lunch." I'd see him wincing every now and again, pausing to rub his legs. I work at being a pleasant coworker who says upbeat things and offers him water every so often.

I can see it written all over his face, how bad he feels right now. He's more swollen, more yellow than I've ever known him to be. I fork up a bite of my salad, eat that, then take a handful of grapes from a sandwich bag and pop them in my mouth. Noticing he is not really eating his lunch, I slide my granola bar across the table and say, "You'll love this. Oats and cinnamon."

"Ain't you sweet," he says. "Thank you, Miss Joan." Then he looks hard into my face and says, "What's wrong?"

"I don't know. Nothing. Just thinking over some things. But isn't it fun having the office to ourselves! No Gold Ring, no bosses. Yeah, I'm happy. Happier than I've ever been in my entire life."

"What you thinking over?"

"I don't know. Everything."

He sits back, looks at me. "Marriage?"

"Well, yes, some. Bit it's more than that. I keep wondering if I ought to . . . tell him about something in my past."

"You mean spill your guts type of thing?"

I nod, watch Siggy take a bite of the granola bar. His eyes are so kind. Wise. "Do you think husbands and wives ought to tell each other everything?"

"Hard for me to say, 'less I know what you referring to. I do believe in that 'honesty is the best policy' and all that. Don't you?"

"Um, yeah . . . maybe, actually, I don't know. This whole thing's so new to me. I've never had a romantic relationship before. I don't think you have to tell each other every little thing from before you met." It isn't a question, but he answers.

"You don't think?" Siggy says softly, tilting his head back and looking at me for a long time through those half-lens reading glasses. He lowers his chin, gives the ice cubes in his tea a swirl, watching them meditatively.

I say nothing, wait for what I know is coming.

He clears his throat. "In Proverbs 9:5-6, Wisdom says, 'Come, eat of my bread, and drink of the wine which I have mingled. Forsake the foolish, and live; and go in the way of understanding.'"

What in the world is that supposed to mean? How does it relate to what I'm talking about? I want to blow it off, but at the same time I like that it seems to have sort of rejuvenated old Siggy. Plus, I sure don't want to stress him out. So I simply say, "That's nice."

"Yeah, you right about that." He crunches another bite of granola, swallows it, smiles. "Ain't nothing to compare with Wisdom. Peoples need Wisdom. 'He that walketh with wise men shall be wise: but a companion of fools shall be destroyed.' Proverbs 13, verse 20. And 'The law of the wise is a fountain of life, to depart from the snares of death.' Proverbs 13:14. And 'So shall the knowledge of wisdom be unto thy soul: when thou hast found it, then there shall be a reward, and thy expectation shall not be cut off.' Proverbs 24:14." He pauses, shakes his head. "A lot of people don't know true wisdom is theirs for the taking. Think it's all a bunch of pie in the sky."

I don't answer. This thought has occurred to me on many occasions.

He looks at my bowl. "You done?"

"Yes."

Siggy rises, takes our things and dumps the leftovers into the trash, stacks the dishes in the sink and runs water over them and begins to wash. I sit and watch him, his gentle movements, his humble attitude. I wish I could go stand right up beside Siggy, lay my head on his skinny shoulder and ask, *How are you feeling?* But I don't.

I sit at my desk for the rest of the afternoon, answering the phone, answering e-mails and updating the Giffin & Burke website. I write a short description of the Texas conference and post it on the company's Facebook page with a picture of everybody on the shuttle bus heading to the airport. I open the day's mail when it comes at 4:00 p.m. and enter the bills on the online payment calendar. I order some more cleaning products and make sure our pest control appointment is set for next Monday. It's pretty quiet, most of our clients know the office is virtually closed, and every time Siggy goes by I smile and nod at him, lift my Fresca up in a toast that says, *It's you and me against the world.*

About 4:30 p.m., it is deader than a swimming pool in December, and I am so bored I'm fighting to stay awake. I've done everything there is to do. I've even caught up with the comments from my followers on *Scarlett Says*.

Siggy straightens up the front office. *His gait is shuffling, uneven*, I think, watching him as he aligns the magazines and polishes the glass-topped side tables. I think about his mini-sermon on wisdom. It's not like I've never heard those verses before, but now I feel curiosity mixed with my usual exasperation. Despite his death sentence, Siggy has an obvious contentment about him. I wonder if it's because of this so-called future filled with hope he was talks about? Who wouldn't want a future filled with hope, and obviously, I don't want to suffer any more harm.

At a quarter till, just when I think time can't pass any slower, the front door flies open, and Eulalie Burke bursts in like a horse running from a fire. When I look across the foyer at her standing there, turning her head left, then right, her Cleopatra hair swinging and her dark eyes wide open, the irises like two lasers, I freeze. Eulalie oozes fury, stomping and punching at the air.

Eulalie Burke doesn't often come to Giffin & Burke. I've seen her maybe four times in all the time I've worked here. She has a really high-powered lawyer job and supposedly earns twice what John Burke does. In her tailored cream suit and pumps, she is the walking illustration of a take-charge career woman. She spies me and stomps over.

"That little—she went to Texas, didn't she!" Eulalie slaps her bejeweled hands down on my desk. I jump a little. For one crazy moment I think she's going to slap me too. I look over to Siggy who raises his eyebrows.

"I saw the picture on Facebook," she spits. "Saw her all cozied up next to John on the shuttle bus."

I sit there too shocked to answer. My knees feel weird. I can't meet her eyes. What if I get fired for posting that picture? I honestly wasn't thinking. I consider this and say, "Are you sure she wasn't just all happy and excited to be going? You know, an ambitious intern who's really eager to learn the business?"

I can't believe I'm defending a girl who tortures me. A girl who snubs me and makes fun of my wardrobe. It took me two solid weeks to get over the note she stuck on my half-and-half. I think of all the mean laughter phone calls, how arrogantly Gold Ring struts across the office on her three-inch heels, tossing her sheaf of hair as she turns her face away from me.

Eulalie just laughs. "I'm going to tell you something you can take to the bank. Meghan Gallagher is not an ambitious intern! She's a self-centered, two-bit, conniving tramp! I've never, ever, not even in the movies, seen the same kind of a heartless, soulless woman who has no shame! John can act like he's just some caring fatherly figure for this girl half his age. So what if she lost both parents in a plane crash when she was two? So what if she's been physically and sexually abused by her adoptive family? Does that give her the right to do whatever the devil she pleases, ruining other peoples' lives?"

Eulalie Burke leans toward me. "She's a liar and a cheat and a thief, and I'll tell you what this picture on Facebook means! It means John lied when he told me Meghan wasn't going. He swore on the Holy Bible she wasn't going. What this means is"—Eulalie begins to stride back and forth, waving her hands—"there'll be no more, 'Honey, it's a pure innocent relationship. Eulie, doll, I'm just helping this poor abused, parentless girl find her way in the job market.' No! In fact, there'll be no more anything! John Burke is out the door when he gets home from Texas!" She smiles, puts her hands on her hips and shouts to the ceiling, "This equals divorce!"

Laughing uncontrollably, Eulalie Burke charges out as fast as she came in.

I sit rapt until Siggy comments. "That shore was something."

"Yeah," I sigh. "It was all my dumb fault. I wasn't thinking when I posted that photograph. Mr. Burke is going to fire me."

"Naw. I imagine he's gonna fire Gold Ring's pretty little behind, and then he's gonna get down on his knees and beg Eulalie to keep him."

I hear some being inside me cheering when Siggy mentions Meghan getting fired. I collapse onto my desk laughing.

" 'Rejoice not when thine enemy falleth, and let not thine heart be glad when he stumbleth.' Proverbs 24:17." Siggy's voice threads into my ears. It's sobering. But part of me sure does want to rejoice. How can a person not be glad when her enemy meets trouble? Am I expected to be some iron woman with no emotions?

"What if I can't help it?" I ask, watching his face.

"You can be bigger than that, Miss Joan. Takes the help of a higher power, takes wisdom of a higher level, but you can do it."

I'm not bigger than that. In fact, I'm miniscule. I feel smaller than a gnat. I look down at my keyboard. "I guess I'll never become a good and noble and saintly person who doesn't wish ill on her enemies," I confess. "But I did feel a little sorry for Meghan when I heard about her parents and the abuse."

"See?" Siggy observes. "You gettin' there. Ain't none of us born that way. God has to work at changing our hearts. What Olie use to tell me when I'd get to fussin' about the way some people act, she'd say, 'Siegfried, remember what Mr. Atticus Finch said in *To Kill a Mockingbird*. "You never really understand a person until you climb into his skin and walk around in it." ' "

I nod. I've read *To Kill a Mockingbird* a dozen times, and Atticus Finch is one of my heroes. I completely agree with his theory, but I wonder, even if you *understand* a person, does that count as compassion if you're still a little bit happy when she gets her comeuppance? I reflect very briefly on Bitsy's occasional, mostly-when-she's-well-lit references to her unhappy homelife as a child.

Siggy holds my gaze for a moment. "They's a reason God calls his people sheep. Sometimes they act real ba-a-a-a-a-d." He chuckles. "Can I tell you a story about two scoundrels in the Bible? Men that God had to work hard on, changing what was in they hearts."

"I guess so," I say, sighing and deflating as I do.

Siggy clears his throat. "This story is from Genesis. Jacob was a scoundrel with a capital *S*. He tricked his brother Esau out of his birthright. Deceived him. On the run after that. By and by, Jacob needed to travel through the land where Esau settled, and he figured his brother was gonna pour out the wrath he deserved. But God had been at work changing Esau's heart. In fact, God been at work inside Jacob, too. The Lord had changed Jacob's character little by little through the struggles Jacob and his family faced."

Siggy rises painfully, shuffles over, and puts his warm palm on my forearm. His face is radiant as he continues. "We all go through struggles, Miss Joan. Things that may break our will, or maybe our physical body. May break our hearts. But they make us better people if we let them. God wasn't through with Jacob even after that story I just told you. He wanted to make Jacob into an even better man, so one day God initiated a wrestling match that went on from dusk till dawn. Jacob was stubborn. He wouldn't give up. So the

Lord had to 'break' him. Broke Jacob's hip so that he walked with a limp for the rest of his life. God renamed him Israel, means 'he struggles with God.'" Siggy mops his brow with a hanky. "We all wander, Miss Joan, we all struggle with God, and we're all wounded some how or another. The trick is keeping in mind that God is a good shepherd, and don't get bitter and turn away. You got to keep following Him, even when you don't understand His method."

There's a long silence, and we both sit there, me not totally convinced. "Aren't there any proverbs about somebody getting their comeuppance?" I ask after a bit. I'm referring to what Gold Ring did to me, but evidently Siggy thinks I mean John Burke.

"Oh, yes," Siggy says, a tiny smile playing on his lips. "If Mr. Burke wants to run around cheatin' on his wife, lyin' to her, he's gonna be sorry, because, 'He that covereth his sins shall not prosper: but whoso confesseth and forsaketh them shall have mercy.' Proverbs 28, verse 13."

I don't like hearing this proverb. It makes me want to cry when I think about what I did to Lydia Lydelle. I'm bombarded with two emotions: the first is total conviction, the urge that I need to confess what happened. The second is this overwhelming sense of relief. *Finally . . . the chance to get all this stuff from my day of shame out of me, to tell someone who seems eager to hear it and to help me. Someone who won't judge me.*

I work up my nerve. "Um, Siggy, I have something to tell you."

"Yes?" His warm dark eyes meet mine, but I'm stricken mute as I feel my heart racing, sweat popping out in my armpits. My stomach starts churning, and I'm on the verge of hyperventilation. It's the worst panic attack I remember. I'm ready to die until Siggy clasps both my hands. Finally, miraculously, some of his strength enters me so that I'm able to breathe again.

"I killed Lydia." Tears run down my cheeks, snot runs into my mouth, but he just nods, waiting. It takes several uneasy minutes for me to gather it all together, but looking into Siggy's eyes, I release the facts. I'd already told him about the humiliation of finding out Bitsy had paid Cynthia, and that I'd become too much like her. Now was the time to say the rest.

"So, Lydia was putting on makeup in the girls' bathroom when we were in ninth grade, and Cynthia laughs and says, 'Don't bother, Lydia. Won't make any difference to a fat, ugly heifer like you,' and I laugh, too, and say, 'Yeah. Cynthia's right. It's just a waste of time. Nothing will help your lard butt. You're hopeless,' and the girls in our clique cheered me on, but that night Lydia hanged herself. And that's why God would never want me. I'm a murderer."

Siggy doesn't respond at first, then he just wraps his arms around me. "Joan, honey, God will always love you. No matter what."

I sobbed until his shirt was soaked. *No*, I thought, *He can't.*

Saturday night I'm lying in bed trying to read *Gone with the Wind*. I can't focus because my mind keeps going to scenes at the office. It was a pretty low-key day on Friday, especially if you compare it to Thursday. We didn't hear a word from the staff in Texas, or from Eulalie Burke. Siggy seemed more energetic than usual, and I came home, had my chat with my beloved, and today my blog, "Scarlett—The Strongest Female Figure in Literature," flew off my fingertips like magic.

But at 4:00 a.m., I still can't read or sleep, so I grab a can of Fresca and turn on the television. I flip around the channels, watch infomercials and bits of reruns. Tears keep coming and it's annoying. I have nothing to be upset about. Close to 6:00 a.m., I click off the television, grab the afghan from the back of the couch, wrap up in it and lie back to stare up at the ceiling. Now my tears feel like they're more from pure exhaustion than anything. *At least I have no commitments for Sunday*, I think, finally drifting off into a fitful sleep.

14

It's a quarter past two by the wall clock when a faint scratching sound pulls me from my slumber, makes my skin tighten. I feel for my cell phone in the pocket of my sweats. My brain is blurry, but it doesn't take much to dial 911. They'll get here pretty quick, especially on a Sunday afternoon when streets are fairly traffic free. I put one foot on the floor, open my phone, and have my index finger poised on the 9, mentally rehearsing my street address for when the operator picks up, when the noise gets more frantic. I freeze, swallow. I'm not sure, but did I hear some kind of anguished cry coming from outside the door?

Maybe it's not an intruder! Someone needs help! I tiptoe over to the door, clutching my sweatshirt at the neck, and peep through the peephole. I can't see anyone. I imagine them crumpled at the doormat. I call through the crack, "Who's there?"

The scratching gets even more frantic.

"Who is it?" I say, loudly. "State your name and I'll help you!"

It grows quiet. It definitely is an intruder. I imagine grisly scenes from TV shows. If this is my end, it's sad that I met it right before I began writing my pieces about racism. I look around my apartment, at my desk and my beautiful marriage certificate, at all the books on my bookshelf. Who'll get them? Oddly, there's a twist in my gut that I never answered Bitsy's constant questions about burial plots. Never got my affairs in order.

I lean my head against the door jamb, tighten my grip on my cell phone, close my eyes and wait. A second later I hear a strained faint "Mew." In my foggy state, it takes a minute to hit me, a minute before I thrill to the familiarity of this voice. I yank open the door and a blast of cool air whooshes in. A tiny furry figure stares up at me, hollow-eyed and pathetic. I fall down laughing hysterically, and for the next ten minutes, I lie there, cradling the fluff-covered bones of my baby. Dandelion looks like a drowned rat. I'm shocked to see her after this long. Even more shocked that she's so skinny, practically a skeleton, and there are open sores all around her tiny neck. "You're beautiful," I tell her over and over. Finally I get up and carry her over to the bag of stinky Xs in the pantry. I pour a few into my palm and cup it beneath her mouth. But she will not eat. There's no half-and-half, and I use my free hand to mix some non-dairy powdered creamer with warm water in a saucer. Dandelion won't touch that either. I carry her to the couch and hold her to my chest, rocking back and forth. Her breathing is very shallow and her eyes are rheumy looking. Her eyes and nose are running, like she has a kitty cold from being outside in the weather. She looks like she's in pain, and it hurts that she can't talk to me.

A cold prickle creeps up my spine: she's come home to die. My knowing is sudden, irrefutable. "I need to get you to a vet quick," I whisper. But it's Sunday. Who's open on Sunday? A mental image of the sign reading "Cynthia LaForgue, DVM, Open Sundays" flashes through my head.

My heart is thudding like tennis balls in a dryer as I put on shoes and grab my keys, keeping my eye on Dandelion nestled in the crook of the couch. I think for a second I've lost my mind, but I seem to have no control over the fact that my shaking legs are walking me to the bathroom. I grab a towel and carefully roll Dandelion in it and walk out the door with her, leaving my apartment wide open.

I've definitely lost my mind, I think as I speed down Ponce de Leon Avenue with Dandelion wrapped like a burrito in my lap. *Do I really want to go and look Cynthia LaForgue in the eye? Do I want to pull this thread? To unravel that whole ugly incident? If I discover any more heinous details about my past, I'll be even more neurotic, and I have enough irreparable issues to deal with. Plus, if I do this, it's like spitting on Lydia Lydelle's grave . . .*

I grip the steering wheel, about to do a U-turn, while asking myself a question I already know the answer to: "What would Scarlett do?" I glance down at the tiny face, the translucent eyelids, the frazzled whiskers, and press the accelerator. Waiting for the light at the intersection of Peachtree Road, I start to hyperventilate. I can't shut my eyes, but I inhale through my nose deeply, then exhale in a loud *whoosh*! I reprimand myself, *Oh, for heaven's sake, Joan, you can't pass out now! You gotta get your gumption!*

I press the accelerator for the green light. My hands are still shaking, but now it's more from anger at Cynthia LaForgue than nerves. Yes, it's definitely fury, starting somewhere in my chest and radiating out through my arms so I feel like Superwoman, a woman so strong, on a mission so important, I could literally rip the cables from the poles along the side of the road.

"I'm sorry, Lydia," I shout, "but I've got to save my baby!" I'm terrified and at the same time furious and replete with determination. I zoom through a green light on Peachtree Street, going a lot faster than the forty-five-mile-per-hour speed limit. I turn onto Juniper Street and soon I see the sign for Dr. Cynthia LaForgue, DVM, but I don't let my mind travel anywhere except the matter at hand. I screech to a stop, cradle my baby, jump out, and run to the glass door. A bell tied to the handle jingles and sets off a cacophony of dog barking from down the hall. There's no one at the front counter, and I hitch my handbag higher on my shoulder and yell out "Emergency!" At the same time a muffled voice calls from down the hall, "Be there in a sec!"

I stand, swaying side to side, rocking Dandelion as I glance around at posters advertising heartworm pills and flea treatments. Behind where the cash register sits is a framed diploma next to a photograph of a golden retriever with very kind, wise eyes.

A tall athletic blonde-haired woman in a white coat comes striding toward us with her arms extended. "Who've we got here?" It's Cynthia's unmistakeable voice.

"Dandelion." I place her in Cynthia's arms without hesitation, adding, "she's been missing for a long time, and she just came home, and . . . I thought she was going . . . I thought she might . . ." before I melt into tears.

Cynthia nods, peeling back the towel, running her fingers all over my kitty, murmuring, "It's okay, sweetie. I'll take care of you. Bless your little heart." I follow them down the hall to an examining room where Cynthia places Dandelion on a silver table, rustles around in a plastic tub of instruments.

I stand as she examines my baby, chin on my chest, sort of praying to something or someone that my baby will be fine. Cynthia LaForgue has on expensive white clogs. I glance up and note that there's no wedding ring beneath her thin blue examining gloves. She couldn't be single, I think, not a girl like her. Probably doctors don't wear rings because of sanitation or something. Her long blond hair is in a ponytail clipped to the back of her head. She's got firm, flawless skin, perfect white teeth. She hasn't aged a day.

"Upsy daisy," she sings, putting one hand beneath Dandelion's belly and gently lifting my baby to her feet, keeping her hand there. I can see the concern on Cynthia's face as Dandelion lists to one side, collapses to the table. She touches Dandelion's ear to peer inside with a little light and Dandelion flinches. "Sore to the touch," Cynthia says, and without looking up, asks, "did you notice how she tilted her head when I stood her up? May be some type of

241

inner ear infection going on in addition to the ear mites I saw. Have you noticed any diarrhea or vomiting?"

"No," I say so softly. "But she just did come home right before we came here."

"She's in rough shape. It's incredibly lucky you found her when you did. I doubt if she'd have survived much longer. I'm going to do a fecal, test for FELV/FIV to see what her status is there. We'll also test her for leukemia, check for intestinal parasites. I can tell just by looking at her that she's dehydrated and malnourished." Cynthia strokes Dandelion's cheek. "I've got some special food here I'll give her to get her strength back. But I'd strongly recommend further testing."

"Yes," I say, even though I have nothing but eleven dollars and some change in my purse. But there is the reward money.

Cynthia scribbles something on a pad. "I deal with a lot of ear issues, but it would be a good idea to have her seen by a vet who specializes in neurology. What Dandelion's dealing with may be a combination of ear and neuro issues."

"Yes! Definitely. Can you recommend a cat neurologist?"

"I'll call Dr. Jacobs. I went to vet school with Mark. He's the best in his field, and normally he's off on Sundays, but I'll beg him to see her today. That said, however, I want you to prepare yourself for the worst. This little lady has some hard things she's dealing with. She may pull through. I hope so. I believe in miracles. But I want you to be prepared, just in case."

I can't answer. My brain chants, *Oh no, oh no, oh no. I'm not ready to consider a world without my Dandelion.* It's one thing for her to be missing. Then there's hope. It's another to consider . . . My knee bones dissolve, and I slide to the floor dramatically.

I'm surprised at how quick Cynthia is kneeling beside me, patting my hand and saying, "It's okay. We're going to do all we can." I only nod, my mind quickly retracing all my steps of the day, the way someone does when they've had a car wreck. But I end up knowing

I did all I could, quick as I could, and I'd do it all again the exact same way. Just like I know I'll sell my soul to pay for all this medical stuff. I suck in a breath, whisper, "How much will everything cost?"

Cynthia looks intently at my face, opens her mouth to speak, but before any words come out, I see the sudden shock of recognition. "Joan Marie Meeler from Pace Academy?" she says, those perfectly plucked eyebrows flying up. "It's you, isn't it? I *know* it's you! Wow! You haven't changed a bit!" I don't really like hearing this, but she goes on. "A real blast from the past! How are you, girl?" This last part comes out like a squeal, and Cynthia opens her arms and leans in toward me like she expects we'll embrace.

I just stare mutely at her modelesque beauty, until finally she lets her arms drop back to her sides, stands up, and returns to her patient, murmuring softly, "Easy, now, Miss Dandelion. This'll make you feel much better, I promise."

I manage to remind myself what I'm doing here, ask softly, "So you remember Pace Academy too?"

"Sure do." She smiles over at me, shakes an imaginary pom-pom. "Rah rah rah. Sis boom bah! Go Knights!" Cynthia shakes her head, still smiling. "Boy, that seems like a million years ago. Remember Coach Baird? Also taught American History? That big meathead who kept getting the American Revolution and the Civil War mixed up? Somehow he got it stuck in his brain that Robert E. Lee had signed the Declaration of Independence and Benjamin Franklin was a Confederate General." She laughs, shakes her head. "We had that class together, and I was so glad I sat beside you because you were the smartest one in our whole class! You should've been the teacher, Joan, because you always scored perfect on those standardized tests Coach Baird passed out. You know, the ones he'd have flunked if he had to take them? I knew you were going to graduate and show us all up."

I blink, feel my cheeks get hot. I haven't thought about Coach Baird since . . . well, since high school.

"So, what are you doing these days?" Cynthia asks.

I watch her, scribbling more things down on a clipboard that says FRONTLINE Plus on the clip. I suddenly wish I could say I host a blog called *Scarlett Says* with forty thousand followers that helps people deal with troubling issues in their personal lives and in society at large. I wish I could let her know somehow that I haven't wasted my life. "I'm an administrative assistant at a marketing firm," I mumble.

"That's nice," she replies, running her fingers along Dandelion's tummy. "Are you married?"

"Yes!" I laugh, hold up my left hand.

"Beautiful rings," she says, and I like hearing wistfulness in her voice. "I never did do that. Guess I'm just married to my work. But I really love helping helpless animals," she looks over at me. "It's my calling. I do it because our world's a much better place, a brighter place, because of pets, and keeping pets healthy and happy helps keep people healthy and happy." She looks at me and I don't know what to say.

"Great," I say at last. "Speaking of that, how much is it going to, uh . . ." I'm sure feline neurologists and all those tests won't come cheap, and I need some time to think of where I can get that kind of money. I mean, I *will* come up with it, somehow or other. It's just that it probably won't be today.

"Listen," Cynthia says, and I fancy she's considering my scuffed, faded Nikes, my unprofessionally cut hair, "we'll work something out. I'm thinking this kitty is going to take a couple of weeks to fully recover, and it'll be my pleasure to be the one who holds her paw through it all." She smiles, and her eyes are bright and sincere with her offer. Her posture is a confident pillar that rebuffs any protests on my part. I'm humbled, and I want to say thank you because I truly am, but at the same time I'm acutely aware that there's still that ugly, painful memory teasing at the periphery of my thoughts. There is blood, the innocent blood of Lydia Lydelle crying out for resolution.

I clear my throat, stand up, allow the fury to build. "Hold on a minute, Cynthia. We've got something to discuss here first."

Her eyes widen. "Okay."

"I know my mother . . . I know Bitsy paid you to hang out with me in ninth grade."

"Yes, I remember," Cynthia says, but I can't tell if she really does.

"First of all," I say, feeling tears slide into the corners of my mouth, "I can't believe she would do that, and second, I can't believe I thought you actually wanted to be my friend. I followed you around like some pathetic twit! I thought you were a goddess. I thought you had some sort of superior wisdom. But you were mean."

Cynthia has her hands clasped together before her, listening intently. "I was awful, wasn't I? Thought I was the center of the universe. I hate even thinking about how I—"

I cut her off. "Yeah." My hands are shaking as I remember every detail of that day. "We were in the girls bathroom in ninth grade and Lydia Lydelle was looking at herself in the mirror, putting on makeup, and you basically said she was fat and ugly and not to bother. And I agreed with you because I wanted you to like me!" A sour bile rises in my throat.

Cynthia just stands there, and I'm thinking how can she be so unaffected by this? Then it hits me that she doesn't even remember it! It was just an ordinary day for her. I spew out what I've been holding in for fifteen years. "That night Lydia hanged herself! We murdered her. That's what we did!"

"Oh, Joan," Cynthia murmurs. "Don't blame us for Lydia's death."

This chick is not connecting the dots. She's not getting it. I look Cynthia in the eye. "I do blame us! I blame us for crushing poor Lydia with our evil words. But you're more to blame for her death than I am because you started it! I was only your stupid follower, and that because Bitsy paid you! You shouldn't have said those evil things to poor Lydia Lydelle. Don't you even feel GUILTY about what we did to her?!"

Cynthia flinches slightly, stands there looking at me. Finally she says, "I was wrong, mean. I accept that. But why should I feel guilty about Lydia's death?"

"Don't you think stabbing poor Lydia with our words had a little something to do with her killing herself?"

"Seriously?"

"Yes! Seriously! If the Queen Bee were to pronounce you an ugly, fat misfit, don't you don't think that would depress you? A fifteen-year-old girl? The height of vulnerability?" I stand there, hands on my hips, open-mouthed. "We *crushed* Lydia, and it was no different from being there in her garage that night, tightening the rope around her neck and kicking the chair out from under her!"

Cynthia looks down at Dandelion, strokes the soft fur at her neck. "Well, that was awful of me and I'm sorry. I was mean."

"Yes! You got a lot of pleasure cutting people down. You used to make me feel smaller than an ant. An inferior flea! And when you started being so buddy-buddy with me, inviting me to sit with you at lunch and hang out with you and the cheerleaders in the bathroom, I thought I was something! I wanted to be exactly like you. I was evil and hurt poor Lydia!" As I'm saying this, it feels terrible, painful, yet it also feels clean, like alcohol poured on a cut.

Dandelion lets out a feeble meow, and Cynthia pivots, bends over her, murmuring, "Easy now, sweetie. Easy." She turns back, looks at me for a long moment, and says, "I want to assure you, Joan, I'm no longer that person. I hope you'll forgive me, and I hope you'll believe me when I tell you you're putting too much on what we said. That's not why Lydia hanged herself."

My jaw trembles. "What makes you think you know why Lydia killed herself?"

"Look, Joan, I know you don't think much of me, but this is the honest-to-goodness truth. My father was the psychiatrist they assigned to Lydia's mother. He'd worked with her for years before Lydia's death. Mrs. Lydelle had ODD, which is Oppositional Defiant Disorder, a pretty common problem in families of lower socioeconomic status. Depression goes hand-in-hand in people with ODD, and Mrs. Lydelle's depression made her physically and emotionally unavailable to her daughter. Apparently Lydia's suicide was an attempt to get attention from her unresponsive mother." She looks at me, her eyes imploring. "Mrs. Lydelle brought the suicide note Lydia left to one of her sessions with my father. I'm not divulging anything private because it was a matter of public record! I can't believe you didn't hear about it . . . well, actually maybe I can. All this didn't come to light till six months after Lydia died. Lydia's note said that she'd caught her mother and several different men in bed together and was thoroughly disgusted. She said in the note that maybe now that she was dead, her mother would pay some attention to her. I'm not lying, Joan. It's all on public record." Cynthia has been speaking so quietly that I've been leaning close to hear, and now I take a few steps backward.

"Joan?" I hear her calling my name softly, but I can't answer until Dandelion makes a feeble cry. I almost forgot what I was doing here! I go to my kitty and kiss her furry cheek.

"Why don't you fill out the forms there," Cynthia nods at another clipboard with a pen attached, "and we'll get this little sweetie all checked in. Did you bring her immunization records?"

I shake my head.

Cynthia looks at me with compassion. "No worries. Be sure you leave your phone number on the form, and I'll be in touch."

Everything's exactly as it was in my apartment when I get home after three hours away. I close the door, put my purse away, and sit down at my desk.

After everything warms up, I type in Google.com, and my fingers mysteriously take on a life of their own, clicking on keys that spell the words Death of Lydia Lydelle, 1999, Atlanta, Georgia. In seconds, several pages of links appear. I stare at the screen as I scroll down, mesmerized by how many articles and discussion forums my classmate generated.

I go back to the top and click on them one by one, reading every single solitary word. Matthew LaForgue's name appears in many, and there's a close-up photograph of Lydia, her mother, and a photocopy of Lydia's suicide note in at least a half dozen. By the time I've reached midway, I have the note printed on my brain like a tattoo. I hear Cynthia's voice imploring me, "It wasn't our meanness that killed her." Now I know that's true. It's right here in black-and-white print in an article from the *Atlanta Journal & Constitution*, from Lydia's own pen.

I literally feel the guilt sliding off me, a terrible burden lifting and leaving an odd sense of absolution. I feel lighter, but at the same time abashed, since my error colored much of my life, my thoughts of other people. I sent out a ton of undeserved fury and hate.

What do I do now? What does all this mean? My whole intent with *Scarlett Says* is to be a healing force. I look at my hands, jump up from my desk, and circle the perimeter of my apartment. My whole entire past is changing because one fact changed, a detail that came to light altering everything. It's such an important detail, so critical, and my whole cache of stories are no more than lies now. I need to go back and recast certain memories.

I walk, and as I do I also travel back to ninth grade at Pace Academy, something inside me changing the camera lens through which I view that scene. Tuesday morning in the locker room, five minutes left till the bell for homeroom rings. Cynthia calls her posse for a quick nicotine fix in the girls' bathroom. She has on her Calvin Klein jeans, her body-hugging aqua top. Her long blonde hair is straight, and she wears silver hoop earrings. I'm wearing a Mexican tunic over my designer jeans, a colorful and fashionable top that hides the jelly roll at my waist. I smell the Pine-Sol as we sit Indian style on the cool tile floor, making a ring. Susan Dickey, a junior, is at Cynthia's right, and I'm at her left, feeling especially honored to hold Cynthia's big leather shoulder bag in my lap. It's full of wonderful, intriguing things. I'm impressed at how Cynthia is not one bit fearful of the teachers or the principal finding us. She pulls out a package of Virginia Slims along with a hot-pink cigarette lighter.

Lydia walks in, uses the toilet, shuffles to the sink, washes her hands, then leans in to apply some Bonne Bell lip gloss. Cynthia blows a stream of smoke, passes the cigarette to Susan, then glances over her shoulder at Lydia, turns back to our circle and says, "Wonder why Lydia Lydelle even bothers? Won't make any difference to a fat, ugly heifer like her." But it isn't loud. It's so low even I have to lean in to hear it, and plus another girl beside Lydia has got the water in the sink gushing. I remember how I felt bad about doing this, but still, I laughed, nodded, leaned in conspiratorially and whispered, "Yeah, you're right Cynthia. Just a waste of time. Nothing'll help her lard butt." The girls all snickered softly, and I basked in their acceptance, the exclusiveness of our group as we sat, sucking in nicotine. I look hard at Lydia's back in this scene, but there's really no sign she heard our mean exchange. She blots her freshly glossed lips on a paper towel, balls it up, tosses it into the trash can next to the door, and leaves just as the first bell rings. Maybe she did hear, but her brain was too full of fury and pain at her mother for our comments to hurt.

Now my mind returns to today, and I see Cynthia LaForgue bent over Dandelion, ministering to my baby, and it is those healing hands, her generous offer that make me think there might be common ground for us. She loves to help people, too. Loves making part of this world a better place. If I'm fair, if I stop ascribing all this evil to her, maybe I can begin to know her, and we can even be friends.

I sag down onto my bed to acknowledge another memory I need to recast. A bit more reluctantly, I pull up a scene from the following day. It's late in the afternoon and I see myself curled in my bean-bag chair, my heart completely broken over hearing the news that Lydia hung herself. All I want is for Bitsy to hold me and tell me everything's going to be all right. But it seems all she cares about is making sure she looks good for seeing her girlfriends. What occurs to me now is that I never said a word to her as I lay curled in my spot. Bitsy couldn't read my mind, and anyway, Wednesday evenings were always when she met her girlfriends for dinner. Maybe Bitsy's seeming indifference was only because fifteen-year-old girls are notoriously moody. Sometimes they need to brood, cry alone. In fact, I'd often demanded my privacy back then.

If what Siggy says is true, and I certainly don't want to misjudge anyone else's motives, if it's true that Bitsy paid Cynthia to be my friend because she loves me and didn't want me to be alone, then she really was acting out of motherly love and concern. It seems the very least I ought to do is go to her and tell her I don't hate her, that I forgive her for going behind my unpopular back and hiring someone to be my friend. I can't blame Bitsy for ruining my life anymore.

I walk to the kitchen, peer out the window over the sink at the pearly pink sky of dusk. There's a veil of low-lying clouds, their underbellies dusted with a very heaven-like gold. *If only I'd known*, I think, staring at the surreal clouds, *how would my life have gone*? What am I supposed to do with all this new knowledge?

I go to my desk and sit down, touch one of Aretha's velvety leaves, and very quietly begin to cry thinking of that day Olie brought Aretha to me, a thank-you gift for keeping a vigilant eye on

Siggy. I turn on Atlanta's Liquid Soul to elevate my spirits. Earth, Wind & Fire is singing "Got to Get You into My Life." *Is virtual enough?* some part of my brain asks. Should I meet Charles in 3-D? If I don't, will his ardour wane? I don't want my marriage to break apart. It would feel much worse than when I lost Dandelion. I click on my e-mail inbox, pull up Charles's latest request to meet him at the seventy-fifth anniversary gala for *Gone with the Wind*. I take in a huge breath, hit reply, and with strong, heartfelt keystrokes type, "My beloved Charles, my schedule has miraculously changed! I will meet you at the gala in December. But I've got to warn you, and I hope you won't think less of me—haha—but I'm not very 'generous' anymore. For various reasons, the pounds are sliding off, and I am starting to have cheekbones. Your feisty Scarlett."

⚬⚭⚬

It's Thursday, November 27, and I'm counting the days until I meet Charles in the flesh. Thank goodness the weather has changed. It's cooler and the trees are turning, except for our Georgia pines. That's outside. Inside me is this growing anticipation, along with the steady tick of my love for Charles, and this fluttering that feels like, well, what can I call it except giddiness? I've been submerging myself in preparations. I have a checklist of things to do in preparation: pedicure, manicure (both self-administered), bleaching the hair above my lip, waxing, finding a dress and shoes. Oddly, I wouldn't mind having those gift certificates from Bitsy back for the haircut, color, and style. But I will never resent having spent most of it on Dandelion's recovery.

Speaking of Bitsy, this is the first year in time out of mind that she didn't invite me to go with her to some Thanksgiving cocktail party at one of her single girlfriends' homes in Buckhead or Ansley Park or Brookhaven. "Joan Marie," Bitsy said in a breathless voice when she called three days ago, "I've decided to go on a spiritual wilderness retreat in the north Georgia mountains. It's at a wellness center on the Nottely River." My mother is not one who likes being away from her creature comforts, and even to hear her say the word *spiritual* was shocking. We've transitioned into a sort of cease-fire, a reasonable relationship, primarily by phone, but I did go in person to Bitsy's house when I told her the true story of Lydia Lydelle.

It's hard to put into words what I felt when I ventured upstairs and found my old bedroom untouched. Like a shrine, it seemed. I cried when I slumped down into the beanbag chair, staring at the Nickelback poster, whispering, "I'm sorry I blamed you. For anything."

She was silent so long I thought maybe she was mad at me. But then I noticed there were tears in Bitsy's eyes, and she said, "I had no idea you were hurting, Joan Marie. I just thought you were ill. That's why I pushed the therapist on you. Will you forgive me?"

I nodded, got up from the beanbag, and we managed an awkward hug. I was overly conscious of my drab, baggy clothes and the fact that she didn't chastise me for them. But what was really surprising is Bitsy didn't even mention my weight loss. After a long moment, I showed Bitsy my wedding rings and told her about Charles, and then she took my hand and her tears actually splashed on the rings.

At the moment, I've got Dandelion in my lap and I'm tickling her neck with my left hand, eating a Lean Cuisine, and answering my followers with the right. Turkey medallions are floating in a nice mushroom-flavored broth, and there's cornbread dressing with celery and onions and some cinnamon apples. Every so often, I feed my baby little nibbles of the turkey. Her ribs are still pretty sharp and there are patches where her fur is still sparse, but overall she's good. When I went to get her, Cynthia said Dandelion had used up about six of her nine lives and to make sure I keep her from going outside.

On that following Monday, I walked into Giffin & Burke all full of expectancy and excitement about telling Siggy how great Dandelion was doing. I had seven photos of her on my cell phone to show him. By quarter after nine, he still wasn't there. *He might be coming in late*, I told myself. I sat at my desk, staring at the front doors.

By noon, he still hadn't arrived. I decide to call Olie, and when I hear her voice, I know something isn't good. "Hello, Miss Joan. I'm sorry. I meant to call you last night, but things around here got busy."

"Is Siegfried there? Is he on his way to work?"

"He's here, child, but naw, he ain't gonna be at work today."

A feeling of dread swamped me. "What . . . what's wrong?"

"Well, he sound a little congested this morning, so I'm gonna keep him here, keep him still. Might carry him to the doctor if he don't get to feeling any better. When he coughs, it sounds wet, and I just pray it ain't fluid in his lungs."

I swallowed the lump in my throat. "Me too. Tell him I miss him. And also, tell him Gold Ring got fired."

"What?"

"He'll understand," I reassure Olie.

"All right, honey. I better go now and see about my boy."

I hang up, angrily swiping at the tears on my cheeks. Siggy does make it to work on Tuesday, but it is after ten. When I ask him how he feels, he says, "Finer than frog hair," but I can see on his face he is in pain. He humps over like an old man.

He sits with me at lunch, while I eat my yogurt parfait. Since my sizes keep changing, I'd bought a black knit dress off the rack at Target, and I am wearing it today, along with some dangly silver earrings and ankle boots with a bit of a heel.

"Look at you," Siggy says, slapping the tabletop. "Done turned into a fashion model."

I protest. "No." But the truth is that I feel almost pretty. I look in the mirror at my face sometimes and think, *It's a fine face. A face a man could love.*

"Yes, you are," Siegfried says. "Way prettier than Gold Ring with all her designer clothes and fancy hair products and makeup. That's for sure. She was missing a heart, like the tin woodman in *The Wizard of Oz.*"

"Well," I say, "she's had a lot of trials to bear. I almost felt sorry for her when Eulalie Burke slapped her."

"Mm-hmm," he says. "That was something. I still don't know how Mrs. Burke kept all that rage quiet, just lurking like a spider when the airport shuttle delivered everybody."

It was a violent scene I'll never forget. When they'd returned that Tuesday morning, Eulalie Burke was here, sitting in her husband's office like a statue. Around 11:00 a.m, I heard Philip Giffin's distinct voice as he pushed open the doors. "Home sweet home! Everybody take a minute and put your things down, and let's meet for fifteen minutes in the conference room, then we all get the rest of the day off." He didn't get ten feet inside before Eulalie Burke strode out of John Burke's office like a general.

"So, your little tramp didn't go, hm, John? Would you like me to file for divorce right now or after I kill you? Right now, I think I could kill you with these two hands." She held up her hands, balled into fists, expensive bracelets jangling at the wrists. John Burke backed away, shielding Meghan with his arm, and then Eulalie turned and ran back into his office and reemerged with a ceramic panther I recognized from his bookshelf. Screaming loud as a banshee and tossing that shiny Cleopatra hair, she hurled it at the couple. There's a gouge in the wall near the reception area where the panther hit, so deep you can hide a penny in it. Meghan didn't utter a word through all of this. She didn't even whimper as Eulalie walked up and repeatedly slapped her face, both sides, saying, "You ungrateful little tramp. I welcomed you into my home, treated you like a daughter, and this is how you repay me?"

As all this was happening, my main feeling was pity and concern. Pity for the girl whose face was almost white with fear, and concern for a marriage I really knew nothing about. Late that night, after the fact, I acknowledged to myself that I did not rejoice as my enemy fell.

It was surprising, a satisfying hope that my core is steadily growing more compassionate.

15

In the wee hours of the Friday after Thanksgiving, I'm jolted awake by the phone on my bedside table. It's Olie, telling me Siggy's in the critical care unit of Piedmont Hospital. "He been asking for you, Miss Joan."

Shaking all over, I dress in the dark, and when I arrive at the hospital, Olie is sitting in the waiting room, her hands resting on a gigantic black patent leather handbag on her lap. I lean down, hug her neck, and say, "Thanks for calling me. Is he okay?"

She shakes her head, closes her eyes. Tears are in her voice, "Naw. He ain't okay. Doctor say he got pneumonia."

My stomach is in knots. "Can I see him?"

"In a bit. They doing something with him right now."

I sit down beside Olie. I'm surprised to see she's wearing blue terrycloth bedroom slippers and a faded, wrinkled house dress that snaps up the front. Her hair is flat on one side. "How long have you been here?" I ask after a bit.

"Since about midnight."

I nod, my throat aching. There are magazines on fishing and cars and beauty and homemaking, but I'm in no state to read. Olie picks up a green Gideon's Bible from the table beside her, but she doesn't open it. Just holds it on top of that handbag.

"Do you need anything from the vending machines? Coffee? A soda?" I ask her.

"Naw. Thank you, though."

I take Olie's right hand and smile over at her. "So. You got here at midnight?"

She looks in my direction, smiles halfheartedly and makes a noise in her throat like, "Mm-hmm."

It's odd to be this near Olie and not be hearing a stream of words from her. I don't know anything to say, and I sit quietly, watching the steady stream of nurses and patients and families. There's one very old man, sitting alone with his face in his hands, his shoulders shuddering every now and again, and a Hispanic woman with two toddlers, passing out juice boxes and Goldfish crackers and coloring books, telling them, "Hush now. Hush now."

I'm full of wonder about how many different lives there are in this world and the different calamities that can strike at any moment. My heart starts knocking around in my chest, and I decide to turn my thoughts to unemotional matters. Giffin & Burke is closed tomorrow, well, today. I look at the clock on the wall above the check-in desk: 5:00 a.m. I was planning to go to PetSmart and buy more kitty litter and then stop at Lowe's to look at their plants. Thought I'd write my blog today, a day early, and have Saturday free to do more preparations for the seventy-fifth anniversary. Things like cleaning my apartment, hunting up recipes on the Internet, and shopping for the ingredients for two of Charles's favorite dishes: spinach manicotti and banana pudding. Since I don't cook, this is akin to learning a foreign language, and I'm determined to show him what a good homemaker I can be.

I jerk back to the present, settle in better, and decide I'll just switch gears if it turns out Siggy has to be here for a day or so. I'll just push my plans back, as they say. At seven I go to the ladies' room, get two cups of coffee—black for me, black with sugar for Olie—and return. With a fairly steady hand, I give Olie hers and she says, "Thank you, child. The nurse say we gon' get to see him in about fifteen minutes."

I see she's been stockpiling Kleenex from a box on the coffee table, folding them in a tidy stack and pressing them into a pouch on the side of her handbag. Daylight is filtering in from a window near the door. It looks like today's going to be sunny. I clear my throat, say, "Know that African violet you gave me?"

Olie nods.

"Well, I just want to tell you that she, um, *it* is beautiful! So green and happy. I never had a plant before, and I wish you could see her."

Olie takes my hand now, looks tenderly at me. "I'm glad, Miss Joan." She sighs, and I can feel her hand relaxing into mine.

I don't know what to say next, so I say, "I'm sorry Siggy's sick."

"You call him Siggy?" Her gray eyebrows shoot up.

I laugh. "Yeah. I call him Siggy. In my thoughts he's Siggy, too."

"Oh, I think that is a nice name." She chuckles, soft and low. Then she reaches up and fluffs her hair on the flat side. Digs in her handbag and puts on some lipstick the color of gardenias. We sit quietly awhile, waiting. Finally an orderly comes toward us, hands clasped in front of him, nodding, and without a word the two of us stand and gather our things.

"There she is, Miss America." Siggy's voice, faint and hoarse, meets me as I stand on the threshold of his dim room, looking across its short length at him lying in bed. "You a sight for sore eyes, Miss Joan."

I smile, my throat aching, say, "You are, too."

He's tethered by a myriad of wires, his chest elevated. I don't know what to do, but he nods his head slightly at the green chair beside his bed until I tiptoe in. "Make yourself at home," he says when I'm near his head.

Olie's standing at his feet, her hands holding what I think has to be his toes through the sheet and thin blanket. "I'm good," I say. "Let Olie have the chair."

"No, no. I been sitting long enough. I *need* to stand up." She nods at me. "You take it."

I can see there's no arguing, and I sink down, place one hand on the cool silver side rail of Siggy's bed. With a grunt, he lifts his long, skinny hand and rests it on top of mine, the skin so transparent I can see veins running like rivers through it. "I sure am sorry to ruin your holiday weekend," he says after a bit.

"It doesn't matter. I don't care."

He hesitates, then says, "I wanted you to come so I could say good-bye in person."

Olie pivots on her heel. "I need to visit the ladies' room. Be back in a bit."

When she's gone, I stupidly ask, "Where are you going?"

"Going home."

"Oh, I see. I bet Olie's glad. Will you be back at work on Monday?"

"Miss Joan, I ain't talking about Cascade Heights. I'm talking about heaven. I expect I'll be dead before Monday." Siggy doesn't say this in a self-pitying or fearful way, but as a matter of fact. He's smiling, and his voice sounds as if he's about to burst into song at any moment.

"I don't want you to die," is the best I can wrench out, and it hangs inadequate in the space between us. I shake my head in disbelief. I need to kill his awful words, so I add, "You don't know. You're not God."

Siggy presses gently on my hand and waits till I'm looking directly into his eyes to say, "You right. I'm not God. But some things a person just knows. My work on earth is done now. Gonna go hang with the Father and the Son."

We stare at each other for a long moment, and then I tell him again, "I don't want you to die! I hate that you're sick! I hate God for making you sick!" Inside my brain I am cussing up a blue streak at God as I move closer, put my hand on Siggy's narrow shoulder, press gently.

"I'm gonna tell you something, Miss Joan," he sings in rich syllables. "It's all right. In fact, I'm happy, 'cause where I'm going it's way more beautiful than the best day here. Though I be walking through the valley of the shadow of death, I ain't scared because I'm gonna keep going, and the Good Shepherd's rod and staff, they comfort me."

Reflexively, I tuck this statement away, to think about later. I'm pretty sure it's from a Bible verse and therefore suspect as far as real-life application, but looking into Siggy's eyes, I know he's speaking the truth, as far as not being scared. There's a peace evident there, a view into a world beyond that has absolutely no fear in it.

I have a respect for his upbeat attitude, but still, I'm outraged. "You can call God a 'good shepherd' all you want!" I blurt. "But it doesn't change the fact that you're dying and I don't want you to! What am I supposed to do? I want your honest answer, Siegfried Obadiah Smith! Not some pretty little verse from Proverbs."

Siggy lies there quietly, looking at me from the sides of his eyes. Finally he says, "We live in a fallen world, a imperfect world, and lots of things about this so-called human condition a mystery. Sickness and disease and trials and turmoil, guess it's just the way things is down here in an imperfect world. Answer be ours down the road a piece when we get to Glory. We gonna have, how do you say it? Unveiled eyes."

I sit there, staring at a little plastic cup with blue pills in it perched on a silver tray that swings over from one of those mechanical arms like you see in dental chairs. I clear my throat. "I'm up to 46,732 followers, Siggy." Soon as I say this, it's killing me to realize it'll be one less when my dear friend is gone. There are so many things I'm going to mind about a life without him.

Almost immediately, Siggy raises himself a good inch, winces slightly, and says, "You go, girl! I'm proud of you!"

"Even though it's the *anti*social network?" I can't resist teasing him.

"Even so." His eyes are twinkling as he says, "Didn't you tell me you gonna meet your other half next month?"

"Yes, I did."

"You not pulling my leg, now, are you? You gonna meet Charles in the flesh?"

"I honestly am."

"Oh, if there's any regrets to leaving now, it's I wish I could be there to see you two lay eyes on each other for the first time."

I swallow, say nothing.

"Know what?" Siggy says after a while, looking over at me, "You're a whole different person than the Joan Meeler I met the day she applied for a job at Giffin & Burke. Not just the outsides I'm talking about, either. You got confidence now."

"Thanks."

"You are gonna love getting out of your cocoon. The world is a rich place, Miss Joan. Rich with beauty and peoples and experiences and . . . love."

My cheeks heat up, and I look down at the faded denim over my thighs. I don't know what to respond to this, because truth be told, I am a little nervous about the physical aspect of meeting Charles. I haven't totally thought that part through, but I guess I'll have to eventually, unless I decide to just let nature take its course. Last week I studied the scene in *Gone with the Wind* where Rhett ravishes Scarlett. I watched it on film, and then I read it, thinking, *I'll absorb some of Scarlett's gumption for my foray into this world.*

Finally Siggy says, "I know you gonna have the time of your life at that big party in downtown Atlanta!"

"Okay." I don't know what else to say.

Olie enters the small room, and her eyes sweep over us like spotlights. I smile, nod almost imperceptibly as I rise from the chair and beckon for her to have a seat. This time she doesn't refuse, she settles her ample hips on the Naugahyde and rests her handbag on her lap. I see the green Gideon's Bible tucked inside. She pulls it out, and very slowly thumbs through the pages. When she stops, she reads, "'But I would not have you to be ignorant, brethren, concerning them which are asleep, that ye sorrow not, even as others which have no hope.' First Thessalonians 4, verse 13." She closes the Bible, looks at me. "That's from a letter Paul wrote to the Thessalonians. Asleep means dead."

"Amen. I'm going home now," Siggy says, and it's like he's looking right past Olie, past me, talking to something or someone only he could see.

I tiptoe over and kiss him softly on the cheek and whisper, "I love you, Siggy. Go in peace." Less than a minute later, his long, thin body relaxed. It was like somebody had removed the main pole of his tent and it had billowed to the ground.

"Ohhhh, Miss Joan, he's . . ." Olie moans from the chair, shaking her head.

"I know," I whisper.

It's not long until the doctor comes and then the nurse, who remove the wires and tubes that tethered Siggy to this earthly existence. Olie's beautiful face is glistening with tears. She's strutting back and forth in the tiny room now, murmuring under her breath, "Jesus, you got to come help me hold all this pain. Take it, my Jesus. Take it, I'm asking. I can't hold this pain no more. It is too big for me." She's waving her hands around like Jesus can see her. "Come on, now. I am waiting."

Respect for her sorrow in this strange time keeps me from hugging her, so I stand against the cool wall. "I'm so sorry, Olie. I loved him, too," I offer when she's quiet. It hangs inadequate in the space between us. I don't know how long I stand there, it feels like an eternity.

"Is there anything I can do for you, Olie?" I ask finally. "I can get you some tea. Something to eat. Do you want me to stay here with you? I'm happy to stay as long as you want, or I can go in the waiting room and let you be alone with Siggy."

I hear her saying something, sounds like maybe it's, "Pray for me, child," but I'm mortified at my inadequacies. I creep out and go to the hospital chapel so I can be in a quiet place. I'm beside myself with my own grief, with empathy for Olie. "Oh, God," I begin, "if You're real, please take care of Olie. Comfort her."

The knot in my stomach feels monumental, and it seems crazy, but even as I cry, I feel happy, thankful. I know I had a priceless gift in knowing Siggy, however long or short it had been. I recall what he said about how if I embraced the true wisdom, it would give me peace, freedom. How if I followed God, He'd never unfollow me. Kneeling down, inside one transparent moment, I whisper, "I want to be Your follower, Lord." I step out of this temporal world, outside the fury and the disappointments, the anger and the guilt, and I rise weightless. Peace radiates through the top of my head down to the soles of my tingling feet, an otherworldly current reassuring me that death was Siggy's passage to a place where he's free from the grip of pain, of suffering. His earthly tent can no longer be buffeted by the storms here.

When I walk into my apartment at 5:00 p.m, I'm exhausted but still wrapped in this otherworldly presence, this peace that passes understanding Siggy loved talking about. Dandelion is wild with hunger, meowing and rubbing my ankles with her head furiously. "Hey, sweet girl," I croon as I pour stinky Xs into her bowl, then sit on the floor of the laundry nook to watch her eat. The phone rings, and I get to my feet quickly to answer. It's Bitsy.

"Joan Marie?" she says, and I can tell by the question in her tone that she wants to get together.

"How are you?" I say.

"Okay." Now comes what I call a pregnant pause.

"Bitsy?"

"How are you?" she says in the tiniest voice I've ever heard come out of her mouth.

"Not too great."

"I'm sorry your friend died."

"Who told you?" I'm holding the phone so tight I'm shaking.

"Oletha Yvonne Lattimore called me. She told me that Mr. Smith passed away."

"Yes."

"I'll come over and sit with you if you'd like."

"No, I'm good!" I say too quickly.

"But I know it's a hard time for you."

My face gets hot, and I feel my heart speed up. "Yeah. Okay, it would be nice to see you. But I thought you were out of town."

She hesitated. "I got back this afternoon."

I hang up and lean against the sink, stare out the window, and silently pray for help to be a better daughter than I was. It sure won't be easy, this path I'm taking, because part of me still pities Bitsy and her mentality, but I also know that forgiveness is strong, resilient, like stretchy strands of a spider's web, weaving around us and holding us together.

The next morning, I fix breakfast for me and Dandelion. As I eat my oatmeal, I cry a little for Siggy, but probably mostly it's for me being without him now, then I smile some, remembering eating the takeout sushi that Bitsy brought for supper last night, watching the movie *Julie & Julia* with her and Dandelion later.

I clean up the kitchen and sit down at my desk, feeling so full of energy I can hardly be still. Is it fate that when I turn on Atlanta's Liquid Soul, James Brown, the king of soul, is singing "I Feel Good"? The trumpets are going wild, a sax pipes in, and I start shaking my booty so much that Dandelion hops off my lap, eyes me warily from the corner. But I'm too antsy to be still. I'm dying to get going on my new life, and at the same time, a little afraid this high feeling won't continue.

But my future's got to be brighter than my past. I suck in a deep breath and vow that I'll travel forward with faith, trusting that a new way will create itself as I venture forth. With this thought in mind, I turn on my computer, wait on it to warm up, then skim the latest responses from my followers, noting which ones I'll need to answer. I decide I'll tend to them later. Right now it says I'm up to 48,995 followers, and I feel compelled to go ahead and post my blog on *Scarlett Says*.

The words flow like hot syrup.

> Most of you know that I've been inspired mightily by Scarlett's indomitable spirit in both the novel and the film *Gone with the Wind*. I mean, how can this story not inspire you? I'm betting most every woman wants to be a little bit like Scarlett O'Hara: flirtatious, beautiful, popular. All of us, male or female, want to believe that tomorrow it will all be better. We want to be like Scarlett—a survivor who overcomes plenty of obstacles. Now, I also acknowledge that many of you have expressed discomfort with the fact that both the book and the movie *Gone with the Wind* feature some superior attitudes toward African American characters like Mammy. I will admit, for the umpteenth time over the years of writing this blog, that I don't care for

this either! I despise our country's legacy of slavery. But issues like race are complicated, and so is this movie's legacy.

Can we just agree together to acknowledge that Margaret Mitchell's masterpiece, *Gone with the Wind*, whether film or novel, is a great artistic achievement? And if we allow this, let us agree that it can also be used as a jumping off point to discuss and educate about race and slavery?

I want to remind you that *Gone with the Wind* tells the story of the Civil War (some may prefer to refer to it as the War Between the States) and the era of Reconstruction from a white Southern point of view. Not all white Southerners thought and acted like these fictional characters, but I think we all agree at this point in our mental evolution that some attitudes during that period of our history were definitely a sin, and I am glad society has evolved to the point where we realize we are all created equal in God's sight. What I will say about that in regard to the movie is that the actual making of the film *Gone with the Wind* helped break down a racial barrier. Hattie McDaniel, the wonderful actress who played Mammy in *Gone with the Wind,* was the first African American to be nominated for, and to win, an Academy Award! Born to former SLAVES, Hattie continued to open doors that had previously been closed to African American performers!

That's right, my friends, because of her portrayal of Mammy, Hattie McDaniel won Best Supporting Actress in 1939! Whatever your thoughts, positive or negative, about that aspect of Margaret Mitchell's masterpiece, you've got to admit the movie made from her novel was a step in moving us forward.

My African American friend Siggy, Siegfried Obadiah Smith—you know him as a follower by the name of S.O.S.—said to me on his deathbed, "I know you gonna have the time of your life at that ball!"

What he was talking about is the fact that I am heading to downtown Atlanta next month, mid-December, for the festivities celebrating the seventy-fifth anniversary of the film *Gone with the Wind*. There are scads of events, from a re-premier at the the historic Fox Theatre to a benefit gala at the elegant Georgian Terrace Hotel to some activities on Peachtree Street at the Margaret Mitchell House and festivities in Clayton County. Plus, there are goings-on at a museum in Marietta, Georgia, that is devoted to the book and the movie. So, here's to Siggy, "Let's celebrate!"

16

When evening comes, I crash. My head is throbbing, and I'm so tired I collapse onto the couch at 7:00 p.m. My limbs feel like they're made of lead as I stare at the gray silent eye that is the TV set. Another gray silent eye looking at me is the laptop. I just spent three hours at it, answering my followers' comments, and I wonder if I can summon the energy to turn it back on for my nightly time with Charles at 8:00 p.m. This is highly unusual. Generally, the anticipation gets me so wound up I can hardly stand it. Usually, I'm counting the minutes till we're together.

Last night Charles told me he's been crossing off the days till our rendezvous. *I cannot get these days to pass quickly enough, my love! I am so eager to be with you!* he wrote.

But now I feel like the days have flown by way too quickly. I need more time to ready myself. In addition to the events at the Fox Theatre and the Georgian Terrace Hotel, Charles said he wants to visit Oakland Cemetery, the final resting place of nearly seven thousand Civil War soldiers and our dear Margaret Mitchell. In fact, he wrote, "I'd like our first kiss to take place on Peggy Mitchell's grave by candlelight."

Something about this disturbs me, and I was hoping Oakland Cemetery would be closed after dark. But I checked their website, and it says they're open 365 days a year from 8:00 a.m. to 8:00 p.m. It gets dark by 6:30 in December. The thought of this latest request is unsettling, to be sure, but just the thought of us together for real still makes my stomach jump. I can't stop worrying about if we'll click in the flesh, if there isn't that spark. Will we tremble as our fingers, our lips touch?

I know I can study, work to channel more of Scarlett's gumption by watching and reading *Gone with the Wind*, but as I lie here thinking of all the complexities of human relationships, a gnawing little knot of anxiety grows in the core of my heart. What if Charles doesn't like the way I smell? What if my voice annoys him? What if I'm not what he's imagined.

I hear Siggy's words, "I want you to have somebody to be with in your old age, Miss Joan. I ain't talking about the antisocial network neither," and I feel my eyes start to fill. I shake my head, hard. I've got to get up from here and *do* something.

Ugh! I wrinkle my nose. Dandelion's litter box smells way too pungent. It's past due for a scooping. I head for the laundry nook, calling Dandelion as I do. She's always fascinated by this task, and she sits nearby, watching intently and waiting until I'm done. I reach down to scratch behind her sweet ears. Then it occurs to me that Aretha hasn't had her African Violet Plant Food drops in weeks. As I'm administering those, suddenly I realize I need to hunt up a recipe and bake something for Olie, carry it over to her house with a sympathy card.

On Friday, December 12, I ask for the day off from work to finish my elaborate preparations. Olie gave me the secret family recipe for her luscious pound cake, and I bought everything so

I can bake it tonight. I've got to go back to Vintage by Judith, a store in Marietta, to pick up the antebellum dresses I ordered and then had to have altered. I swallowed my pride and took out a five-thousand-dollar loan from Bitsy to get me and my apartment ready for Charles's visit, and I ended up spending a third of that on three absolutely gorgeous dresses.

The first one is similar to the dress Scarlett wore to the barbecue: an off-the-shoulder green floral print, highlighted by ribbons, trim on the shoulder, ruffles, and a really wide satin belt. The weather hasn't been very cold, mid 60s at the lowest, and if we do some of the activities in the middle of a sunny day, it could work. I gave in to temptation and bought a southern belle bonnet with a tie to go with that dress. Second is a burgundy silk gown with three bands of wide, black lace in rows above the hem. It has long fitted sleeves and comes with a white blouse beneath, a cameo broach to wear at my neck. I added white gloves and a ten-inch folding fan. But the final one is my favorite. It's a replica of Scarlett's green velvet drapery dress, what I think of as *the symbol* of her fierce determination. It comes with a velvet hat that has a feather and cord tassels and a matching velvet handbag.

For my hair, I'm going to pull it back in a bun and wear this black crocheted thing over it, but leave corkscrew curls in front of each ear. I'm going to do a hair trial run and put on the green dress and black satin slippers, some dangly jade earrings and parade around my apartment. I'm going to work on copying Vivien Leigh's feminine demeanor. I bought a full-length mirror at Target, and I plan to stand in front of it and say "Fiddle-dee-dee!" and "I'll think about it tomorrow!"

I'll never achieve Scarlett's seventeen-inch waist size, but finally, for the first time in memory, I fit into a single digit size. All three of my Scarlett dresses are size eight. This is a huge personal victory, because even when I was a teenager, I wore a size twelve. Vintage by Judith has corsets, too, and they come with attached flexible steel

bands to make your skirt stand out like a bell. When I was trying the corset contraption on, I held on to a pole near the dressing
room and imagined the sales girl was Mammy behind me, pulling and tugging and admonishing me. I went to Bitsy's salon and
got highlights put into my mousy hair. When the stylist finished, I
looked in the three-way mirror and was shocked to see one of those
women who looks like she really takes pains with her appearance.

I didn't know if Charles would appreciate my ancient Toyota.
I thought about renting a limo, but instead I ended up driving to
Whispering Pine Road in Winder, Georgia, to a business called
Back When Carriage Rides. They lease carriages for romantic out-
ings, and the one I chose is white with a burgundy interior. For
passengers there are twin rear seats facing one another, and it comes
with a driver who sits higher. The top of the carriage can be up or
folded back, weather dependent. The website said it's safe for traffic, day or night, that the horses are experienced in dealing with
busy streets. My main concern is how difficult it will be to hop up
in there with a hoop skirt on.

I'm feeling fidgety on the afternoon of December 13. I take several hours and re-read every single exchange between Charles and
me. It seems very possible that we will love each other forever, but
what if I'm a flop at real-life kissing? Don't most girls practice kissing at slumber parties in their early teen years? Don't they giggle as
they discuss techniques with peers, then take turns demonstrating
on pillows, on their own forearms? I missed all that. Instead, I head
for the instructional guide that got me through the uncertain spots
before.

Opening *Gone with the Wind* to the place that inspired what
I've heard referred to as the "best movie kiss of all time," I place
it on the kitchen counter. I imagine Vivien Leigh studying the

script for the movie and decide it'll be easier in costume. I go to my bedroom and climb into the corset, the green floral gown, and my dainty slippers. I work painstakingly to sweep my hair up into something reminiscent of Scarlett's.

I tiptoe back to the kitchen, grab a Fresca from the refrigerator and sip it as I pour over the lines of type like a dying woman searching for instructions on how to breathe. I decide I need to backtrack a bit to set the scene for the coming kiss, so I go to the previous scene where Rhett is telling Scarlett he's leaving to join the Confederate army. She's shocked, stunned, breathless. "Rhett, you are joking!" I read aloud, and at the same time I say my first line, I work up tears of fright to splash on my forearm the way Margaret Mitchell wrote it.

As the words come out, I find myself naturally climbing into character, into this delicate balance of femininity and feistiness that I know will make me irresistible to Charles. I decide I'm going to practice it till I own it. I twirl a bit, rustle my hoop skirt, acutely aware that a different person has emerged. "This is your real life, Joan Marie Meeler," I say, my eyes full of tears. I won't mess up with this 3-D love thing.

It's December 14, and I'm standing in the lobby of the Georgian Terrace Hotel at 1:45 p.m. The Georgian is on Peachtree Street in midtown Atlanta, right across from the Fox Theatre. Charles and I plan to have a late lunch here, then visit Oakland Cemetery for our you-know-what, and from there, return to Peachtree Street, to the Fox Theatre for the re-premier of the movie *Gone with the Wind*.

I'm already feeling fidgety, and when my cell phone rings, I jump. I manage to fish it out of my tiny velvet evening bag. A text from Charles says he's right on schedule. That means I've got fifteen minutes, and to keep my nerves at bay I visit one of the Georgian's three ballrooms. The warm hues, the points of light refracted off crystals in chandeliers dripping from the high, ornate ceiling give a timeless feeling, and I linger somewhat peacefully.

At 1:59, as I'm walking into the lobby, I feel my jaw drop open. A stunning man is stepping through the front door, dressed in a dark blue Union uniform with four brass buttons glinting in the light. On his head is a forage cap of stiff wool with what looks like a round circle perched over a leather visor. Our eyes meet, he smiles, and when he's five feet from me, he stops and bows dramatically. I'm the embodiment of the word agog as I stare at that familiar yet not familiar face. All my carefully rehearsed greetings fly out of my brain.

"Charles in Manhattan! I am delight—" I have to take a deep breath, try again. "I'm so happy to finally meet you." I stand there, hoping I sound more confident than I feel.

Charles nods, extends his gloved hand to my gloved hand in an elegant gesture. "The feeling is mutual, my feisty Scarlett. I must say you are more beautiful in person than I even imagined." I feel his hand clasp mine, warmth from his flesh seeping through the thin fabric layers. Something like an electrical zing almost makes me gasp aloud. I'm amazed I don't see some blue arc stretching between us. I stand there, blinking, thinking, *If this is how it is now, it's going to be really crazy when we touch skin-to-skin.*

I manage a "Thank you," and we embrace lightly, his wool collar scratching my neck. Disappointingly no skin touches in this contact either, and I'm a little dazed as he says, "Mademoiselle?" extends his arm, gesturing palm up toward the Livingston Restaurant & Bar just off the lobby. When we reach the doorway, Charles steps aside and allows me to enter first.

A maître d' leads us to a secluded table where Charles removes his hat, clasps it before him, waiting till I'm seated before he seats himself. This man's got excellent manners, and I can't get over how handsome he is in person. His teeth are white and straight, his body lean and taut. Also, I could've worn heels because he's at least half a foot taller than me.

Our waiter appears in an instant and I sit there blinking as Charles turns to me. "What will you have, mademoiselle?"

My nervousness sits on my tongue. "Uh . . . I'll have whatever you're having!" I say, and Charles orders from the Theatre Menu: two French Fennel Soups with brioche croutons and gruyere cheese and two chopped vegetable salads with sweet onion dressing. The server brings a basket of warm, crusty bread and two iced teas with lemon wedges. Charles and I remove our gloves while staring at each other, smiling.

He butters his bread, and I take a deep breath to make small talk as we wait for our entrees to arrive. "How was your flight from Manhattan?"

"Good, good. Uneventful, which is good in my book!" He laughs, and I decide he's got a really nice laugh.

I talk about how Giffin & Burke is so close to the Georgian Terrace, we could walk there in ten minutes, watching him as he chews his bread, mesmerized by his nice, thick eyebrows, his Roman nose, and those aquamarine eyes.

The bread is delicious, crusty and chewy, but I have no appetite, and I take small nibbles. We don't say anything for several minutes. I don't know whether to bring up his Civil War reenactment hobby or *Scarlett Says*, and so I just sip my tea thinking about our online conversations, wondering if we'll soon be doing that same spontaneous banter in person.

Charles stirs his tea with a fork. "Can I tell you a couple of secret fears I had about meeting you in person?" he asks, a smile playing on his lips.

I nod, feeling an anxious flutter in my stomach beneath my too-tight corset.

"First, I was terrified that you wouldn't kiss me if I didn't give up my smelly cigars."

I blink at this man. "But you love your cigars!" I'd already told myself if I didn't care if he tasted like a chimney.

Charles wrinkles his brow. "That's true. But I can't think of anything worse than you not wanting to kiss me."

I watch him, dumbfounded that he would do this for me. Before I can think of any words, he laces his fingers together, plants his hands on the edge of the table and leans forward.

"What I was scared about," he says in this solemn voice, "is your dialect." He laughs, shakes his head. "I was worried you were going to have one of those annoying nasal Southern twangs that would get under my skin. You know?"

"Um—I guess—" I make a nervous little laugh.

"Well, I've got to tell you that I adore your drawl! I could listen to you all day long and never get tired of it."

He has no idea how relieved I am to hear this. "Thank you, Charles in—" I feel suddenly awkward. Obviously, I can't go around calling him "Charles in Manhattan" the way I do in my thoughts. His full name is Charles Alexander Gruber, so I ask, "What do you want me to call you?" wondering if perhaps growing up he was called Chuck or some other nickname.

"I'd be pleased if you would call me Chas." The *s* in Chas he pronounces like a *z*, so I repeat it softly, "Chaz."

He must think my screen name is awkward, too, because he tilts his head, and asks, "Would you rather I call you my feisty Scarlett or would you prefer Beloved? Or how about Joan Marie?"

"Um, Joan is all right," I tell him. "But please don't call me Joan Marie."

Our soups and salads arrive. "So," he says, dipping some crust in his soup bowl and looking meaningfully at me, "Do you realize how amazing it is that two people like us have come out of our cocoons? How we're 'out there in the real world' like this?"

Charles's question takes me by surprise, rattling me a little with its directness. I feel my face getting hot, but I manage, "Yes. We're really overcoming. It's amazing."

"Yeah!" He nods vigorously. "Especially when you consider the things we've both been through in our lives! I think the costume helps me. Well, I know it does!" He laughs some more and snaps the suspenders holding up his trousers. "But, costume or no costume, you're the one who inspired me, Joan. I thought I could just stay the way I was forever! Doing my occasional battle reenactment and loving you online, long distance. I'd never wanted to 'get out there' and be with any woman in real time. Know what I mean? And then, all of a sudden I meet you, this beautiful woman, this feisty smart woman who grabs me by the heart, and suddenly, I can't not go be with her! I guess there are some things. . . ." He puts down his fork, leans back. "I never thought I'd have to do this, Joan, follow this longing, this urgent *need*. I never thought I'd be compelled to fly down to Atlanta, Georgia, just to be with some woman. Be with you in the flesh. Have a real relationship, you know? A physical encounter?"

I'm mute for a minute, and then I just sort of blurt out, "Yeah, I know! The heart wants what it wants, and it won't shut up! Humans were made for close physical relationships."

Suddenly Charles tosses his napkin onto the table. His eyes have this spark to them as he clears his throat, says, "Joan? I vote we skip dessert and go on to Oakland Cemetery. There's something I've been waiting to do. and I'm not feeling very patient. Do you concur?"

I've never experienced such a tangible *physical awareness* of someone before. The electric tingle of our gloved hands touching was unnerving enough, but there's this physical magnetism radiating from Charles that I cannot resist. "Let's go," I say without hesitation.

It's a bit after four o'clock when we walk out of the Georgian Terrace. The sky has turned overcast, and a strong wind has kicked up. A plump uniformed chauffeur named Spence who works for Back When Carriage Rides is waiting. He opens the door to our carriage. "Would madam like the top up or down?"

"Down, please," I say, even though I'm shivering. I want Charles to see my beautiful city all dressed up for the holidays. Spence takes my elbow and hoists me up into the carriage, doesn't even grunt with the effort, which I think is very gentlemanly. Charles hops in and settles beside me on the bench. I notice his leather shoes, called brogans I think, that lace up over his ankles. A haversack for rations and a canteen are draped across his shoulder. There's a black knit shawl type of thing folded on the seat beside me, and I shake this out, drape it over our laps as the horses clip-clop from the curb into the traffic of Peachtree Street.

The horses are brown, but their manes and tails are this wonderful dark gray, almost black color, and they've got blinders on the sides of their eyes. Too bad, I think, because beautiful Christmas decorations and lights are everywhere in downtown Atlanta. Red, green and gold lights are wound round the utility poles and there's a huge wreath on the front of the Fox Theater. Cheerful poinsettias line the walkway of the entrance. Traffic's heavy, but relatively sedate, folks out shopping for Christmas and joy riding. Organ music is coming from somewhere, strains of *jolly old Saint Nicholas, lean your ear this way,* lending an anticipatory, festive spirit to things.

"So," Charles says after a bit. "You ever been to Oakland Cemetery?"

"No. I've read a lot about it online, though."

"Well, nothing substitutes for that real 3-D experience, now, does it?" His eyes are smiling. "I'm really looking forward to seeing the place." His gloved hand snakes out from under the shawl and touches my gloved wrist. An involuntary shiver runs up my spine.

I'm visualizing us at Margaret Mitchell's grave, locked in a steamy embrace like Scarlett and Rhett.

My tongue is tied and Charles is quiet as we jounce along, jingle bells on the horses' harness making a nice sound as the carriage moves. It isn't fifteen minutes until we're pulling up to the gates of Oakland. Spence stops the horses, hops out, and comes around to hold his hands up to lift me down.

I stand on the ground, blinking, feeling a little surreal as I gaze at the walls and the impressive gate. The date 1896 is engraved on the keystone of the gates' highest arch, though I have read that the original six acres was established in 1850. Charles is beside me now, offering his arm, looking at my face. There's no way he could miss the hot blush I feel blooming in my cheeks. *Please Lord,* I'm praying. *Let me get this right.*

I hook my arm through Charles's, and with my heart hammering, we walk into Oakland. The first thing I notice is a mausoleum with a life-size statue of a man on top. "That's Jasper Newton Smith," I say as we stand just inside.

"Striking figure," Charles whispers in a reverent tone. It's getting dusky, and headstones in the distance look like gray teeth. I think about how there are seventy thousand people interred at Oakland. We don't say anything for a minute, and then I take a deep breath, ask, "Do you want to go to Margaret Mitchell's grave?"

Charles's eyes are big. "I want to visit the military section."

I nod, smile like this is fine. Like I'm not aching to kiss this man right now. I know the way from a map on Oakland's website. I lead him toward where Civil War soldiers are laid to rest. It's a forty-eight-acre cemetery, and we pass a fountain where water spouts, and small irregularities in the flow are like music. Oaks and magnolias dot the dusky landscape, and I notice how Charles is taking all this in. I feel my skin prickle when we reach the edge of where the soldiers lie. I hesitate, and Charles stops beside me. He gasps as he looks at the ocean of identical stones, lined up perfectly. I look at his face, wonder if he's thinking about his reenactments.

At last he glances over at me, says "Shall we?" in a reverent tone. We walk along somberly past the gravesites until several minutes later when Charles suddenly stops. "Look, Joan," he nods at an inscription, "this soldier died when he was only eighteen."

"This one was in his early twenties," I say, pointing at a headstone adjacent to the one Charles is referring to.

He glances over, and I notice his eyes are narrowed. "Saw a general back there. He was only twenty-five when he died!" Charles stops in his tracks, pulls his hand from mine to slap his thigh as he releases a great whoosh of air. "I've never felt the reality of war like I do now!" His words are so loud I cringe.

"Don't you hate thinking of all the lives lost, Joan? Of widows grieving and children without fathers, of sons who never made it home?" Charles turns to me, his face pink with fury.

I am frozen. I can only nod. I know something sadder that I'm not going to say. I can't. I can't start crying now.

I glance over at the anguished face of a lion on a marble monument. It's the Lion of the Confederacy that guards a field of unknown Confederate and Union dead. I've read that out of the 6,900 burials here, three thousand are unknown. I feel my eyes start to fill, and I try to distract my thoughts so I don't melt into a pile of tears. I move up beside Charles and take his hand. "Come with me," I say, hardly believing my boldness.

He walks beside me in the direction of the African American section. Five minutes later, we're standing and staring out at close to twelve thousand grave sites. I take a deep breath. "You know what?"

"What?" Charles says, turning slightly toward me while still keeping his eyes on the cemetery.

"When you said you wanted to come here, and I did all that research, it said that Oakland was not always welcoming to black Atlantans. When Margaret Mitchell was buried here in 1949, it was segregated. It was segregated until 1963, even though many of the African Americans buried here helped create the foundation for what the city is today. In fact, this section is a testament to the period of history during which segregation was at its height."

Charles looks sharply at me, and says, "You're not surprised by that, are you?"

"No. I . . . I'm not surprised. I'm just . . . sad. You know my dear friend Siggy passed away recently."

"Yes. Is he buried here?"

"No. But when I was at his church's graveyard for his burial, I got so sad thinking about how the Oakland website said that the black section lacks a great deal of headstones, monuments, grave markers in general because in the past many of their grave markers were made of wood, and they've decomposed over the years. A lot of the people buried here in the black section are unknown. I mean, I know it's modernized and all now, striving for social equality and all the good stuff, but still, it just . . ." Words fail me. I think of blacks picking cotton, polishing the boots of their white owners, mammies tightening corsets, feeding white babies.

"Yeah. That's rough," Charles says, his head bowed.

For a long while we don't talk. I long to put my head on Siggy's shoulder, hear him reciting a proverb, asking me why I look so hangdog. All of a sudden, I think about a story I read on Oakland's website. I perk up. "Come over here," I say, and we walk over to the one and only mausoleum in the black section. "Antoine Graves," it reads, "1862–1941." "I'll tell you a story about this man," I tell Charles.

"This feller looks important."

"Yeah, he is. He was a principal but he got fired, and when he died he was prominent Atlanta real estate."

Charles's eyes are big. He waits.

"Okay. He was the principal of the Gate City Colored Public School, and when Jefferson Davis died, his body passed by in front of the school on the way to Richmond, Virginia, for burial. They ordered the schools to close so everyone could attend the memorial parade. But Antoine Graves refused to do it. He refused to honor a man who fought for slavery. Mr. Graves was fired as a result." Inside I'm a cocktail of admiration and sadness and joy as I stand there quiet and still. It's gotten fairly dark now, and I can't see Charles's face anymore.

I hear him clear his throat. "Speak up for those who cannot speak for themselves, for the rights of all who are destitute." His voice slices through the dark like a two-edged sword.

"What did you just say?" I'm stunned by his words . . . *Speak up for those who cannot speak for themselves.* I know I've heard this, or some translation of this before.

"That's a proverb," Charles says simply. "Proverbs 31, verse 8."

I feel my body grow rigid, all my blood rushing to my head. When I don't answer, Charles touches my shoulder. "Are you okay?"

"It's . . . I'm all right. It's just that I think war and slavery are both despicable! Such loss. We've got to work for peace. For equality. Our world desperately needs peace. We need folks to reconcile, strivings and wars to cease. Love and respect. Peace on earth. Peace meaning where people love and respect each other and we are all equal. Peace in our hearts. Free from guilt, fear, anxiety."

Charles is quiet after my long diatribe, and I don't know what he's thinking.

"There's my feisty Scarlett," he says finally. He steps over to stand facing me, and this close, I can see the pride in his eyes.

I feel gumption taking me over. "In heaven there is no North or South, Union or Confederate," I declare loudly, and my voice sounds like it's in a movie. "There's no black or white either. We're all free. Do you believe, Charles? In eternal equality and bliss in heaven?"

He nods, and I can tell he really does believe. It's such an odd question, but maybe not if you're standing in a cemetery, among a bunch of tombstones and crosses. There's still a lot I've got to learn, want to learn, about this man I married. Not even counting his plea from several e-mails back that said he wants us to have a real wedding ceremony with a minister, in Manhattan, so his family can attend.

We stand there, listening to the sounds of the night, wind through the magnolia trees, traffic moving in the distance, a bird rustling in some leaves nearby. "Shall we visit Miss Peggy's grave now?" Charles's voice has a smile in it.

"Yes," I say, and we set out along a well-worn pathway that meanders across the gentle hills of the cemetery, my gloved hand in his. I look over at his handsome profile in the gray shadows. "I've heard it's modest," I warn as we pass a low stone wall.

I've seen photographs of my heroine's headstone a dozen times, online and in books, but still, when we reach the gravesite, and I can make out her name carved in stone, my heart stops at the realization that she's *here* in the red Georgia clay. Charles and I stand in the midst of all the imprints that man has made in the dusty soil. *Definitely unremarkable*, I think, staring at the long angular headstone, one side devoted to Margaret and the other to her husband, John Marsh, and in the center, a bit taller, a section that says in all caps, MARSH, with some type of stone urn on top.

On Margaret's side, it reads MARGARET MITCHELL and centered beneath that, MARSH, and below that, BORN ATLANTA, GA, then underneath that NOV. 8, 1900, and DIED ATLANTA, GA, and finally AUG. 16, 1949.

That was it. It strikes me as odd that it doesn't say something to the effect of *Here lies the author of the novel* Gone with the Wind. *Creator of the legendary Scarlett O'Hara.*

I'm feeling a little sad, thinking how Scarlett was almost completely fearless, but this woman who created her, who never wanted public acclaim, who ran from the public eye when her novel generated such hysterical fervor, is still besieged by fans. I'm startled when from the corner of my eye I see Charles kiss his palm, then walk along the edge of the gravesite to lean in and touch the marble headstone where the name Margaret is carved. He turns toward me. "She's the reason we found each other. She's the reason I'm a happy man."

I swallow, try to speak, cannot. Charles comes and kneels at my feet, removes his gloves, tucks them in his pocket and rustles around in the haversack. "Joan," he says, his blue eyes fixed on my face, "I know you've already got rings on your finger, but will you please accept this token of my love?"

He's holding a circle of gold with what looks like a ruby glinting in a classic solitary setting. After a long moment of looking into those eyes, my own fill with tears and I nod. Charles immediately tugs the glove off my left hand, slides the ring on my finger, then folds my hand between his large ones.

I am not prepared for our first real touch, and the electricity that surges from my hand to my head, down to my feet, then up again makes me gasp aloud. Instantly Charles pulls his hand away like he got scorched.

"Whoa," he says, then laughs, gets to his feet. He leans in so close the hairs all over my body stand alert. "You know what, my feisty Joan?" he says in a throaty voice. "You need kissing badly. That's what's wrong with you. You should be kissed and often. And by someone who knows how."

Without missing a beat, I say "Oh, and I suppose you think you're the proper person."

Charles is right on cue, too. "I might be, if the right moment ever came."

The most swooningly romantic lines I've ever heard or read or imagined just got even more so. A shiver runs up my corseted spine, and I have to look away from his gorgeous face for a split second so I won't die on the spot. I'm dying to make this man my husband, and when his warm lips meet mine, my heart beats crazily, my head swoons, and I melt. Charles kisses me for an eternity, and oh, it's powerful. I cannot imagine how he learned to kiss like this. I'm feeling a little desperate, then Charles pulls away a centimeter and whispers, "I love you. Every day."

"Me too," I say, my hoop skirt billowing back behind me. With a sigh, Charles pulls away from me. I'm reluctant, too, to break this amazing connection.

There's a tenderness in Charles's voice when he asks, "Will you be my wife? Today *and* tomorrow?"

I nod. He takes my hand and leads me toward the gate.

We hope you enjoyed Julie L. Cannon's *Scarlett Says* and that you
will continue to read Abingdon Press Fiction Books.
Here's a sample from Julie L. Cannon's *Twang*.

1

Those first days in Nashville were happy. Happier than any I
could recall. It was no accident that I had Mac's cousin pull his
sputtering Vega to the curb on the corner of Music Circle East
and Division Street. The Best Western was in walking distance
of Music Row.

All my belongings were stuffed into two huggable paper
sacks, and when I marched down that strip of red carpeting
into a marble-floored lobby with a chandelier, I knew it was a
palace compared to that drafty cabin in Blue Ridge with peeling
wallpaper and warped floorboards. Room 316 had pretty gold
and maroon carpet, gold curtains at a window with an air
conditioning unit beneath it, two queen beds, and two glossy
wood tables—one in the corner with a lamp, an ice bucket,
and a coffeemaker and the other between the beds with a
phone, a clock, and a remote for the television. There was even
a little bitty refrigerator, a microwave, an ironing board, and an
iron. What else could a person need?

More curious about having my own indoor bathroom than
a television, I tiptoed in there first. Nothing had prepared me
for what met my eyes. Clean white tiles on the floor, a marbled
sink, a blow-dryer, a stack of sweet-smelling towels, and fancy

soap. The washrags were folded like fans, and there were free miniature bottles of shampoo and conditioner.

To say this felt like paradise would not be an exaggeration. Turning around and around until I got drunk with my good fortune, I collapsed and fell flat onto the closest bed, laughing like a maniac, some pathetic yokel finding out she'd won the lottery.

Although bone-tired on account of being so journey-proud that I hadn't been able to sleep a wink in forty-eight hours, I couldn't fathom closing my eyes. I hadn't eaten in as long either, except for some pork rinds and a Pepsi on the ride. But I was like someone possessed: hungry only for the feel of Nashville, thirsty only for the way she looked. I promised myself for the hundredth time I would not think about my mother and the fact I'd left no note. I told myself I'd eat some real food and get sleep later, after I'd explored my *new* mother. I took the elevator downstairs to find some maps.

At the front desk, a sign said the Best Western had free breakfast: sausage, biscuits and gravy, waffles, eggs, oatmeal, muffins, toast, bagels, yogurt, and fruit. The elation I felt at this was not small, and I couldn't help a happy little laugh.

A short, overweight man in a blue seersucker suit and bright orange tie bustled out of the room behind the front desk and said, "What can I do for you this evenin', missy?" He had a tall pink forehead like you'd expect on a bald man, but his hair— and I could tell it wasn't a toupee—was this lavish white cloud that put me in mind of an albino Elvis. I could see amusement in his startlingly blue eyes.

I didn't bother to mention I was twenty-two, hardly a missy, because he'd said it so kindly and I was used to being mistaken for a much younger girl. "I wanted to see if y'all had any maps and stuff about Nashville, please." I smiled back at him, noting the name engraved on his gold lapel bar: Roy Durden.

"We got maps coming out our ears! What other information you looking for?"

"Everything."

He nodded, turned, and stepped to a bookshelf along the back wall, squatting slowly, carefully, as I watched in utter fascination to see if he'd manage to get his enormous belly to fit down between his thighs. He unfastened the button on his suit coat and the hem brushed the sides of gigantic white buck shoes. Eventually, he rose with a loud grunt, carrying an armload of papers. "Alrighty," he said, spreading them on the counter like a card dealer in Vegas. "Let's see what we can do for you."

"Thanks." I reached for a glossy brochure that said *Tour the Ryman, Former Home of the Grand Ole Opry*. It was lavishly illustrated with pictures of artifacts from early Opry years and old-time country music stars like Minnie Pearl and Hank Williams. There was a headline that said you could cut your own CD at the Ryman's recording studio. Thanks to my high school music teacher Mr. Anglin, I had already accomplished that task.

"Snazzy, huh?" Roy was nodding. "Now, that there is one hallowed institution. Tennessee's sweet-sounding gift to the world. Place the tourists flock to." He was talking with his eyes closed and this rapturous expression on his face. "Up until '74, fans packed the pews of the Ryman every Friday and Saturday night. Folks loved that place so much that when the Opry moved to its current digs right near the Opryland Hotel, they cut out a six-foot circle from the stage and put it front and center at the new place. So the stars of the future can stand where the legends stood." Roy grew quiet for a worshipful moment.

"There's this one too," he said at last, pushing a slick brochure that read *The Country Music Hall of Fame & Museum* toward me.

Mac, my boss at McNair Orchards, used to say he could see my face in a display hanging in the Hall of Fame, right between Barbara Mandrell and Tammy Wynette. Mac got my head so full of stars, I could hardly think of much else except to get to Nashville to show the world my stuff. I stared at the photograph of a building that looked to be an architectural wonder in itself. One side was an RKO-style radio tower, while the main part had windows resembling a piano keyboard, and an end like a Cadillac tailfin. "That's nice," I offered.

"Yep, real nice," Roy said, his fingertips grazing more brochures reading Belle Meade Plantation, Margaritaville, General Jackson Showboat, Wildhorse Saloon, and The Parthenon. He lifted a map of Nashville. "Be helpful for you to know Second Avenue runs north, and Fourth Avenue runs south."

"I didn't bring a car."

"That a fact?" He looked hard at me. "Well, downtown and the Hall of Fame are in walking distance, but it's a ways to the Grand Ole Opry." Roy's index finger touched a spot on the map. "There's also a place called Riverfront Park you could walk to, but I got to warn you, missy, Nashville sits down in a bowl, between a couple lakes and rivers, so it feels like you're walking through hot soup in the summertime. Can be right intolerable." He swiped his florid face at the memory of heat as I flipped through the pages of a brochure, pausing every now and again to stare at a picture of a star singing on a stage, the crowd going wild. There was an energy in those photographs, a palpable current of voice and instrument and the sweet thunder of applause. For a long time I looked at a picture of Dolly Parton and Porter Wagoner, their faces suffused with a bright, joyous light.

"You like this one?" Roy asked, making me jump.

"Um, yeah."

"That was in '75, the night Dolly and Porter sang their last duet together. I was close enough to see Dolly's makeup." There were tears in Roy's eyes.

"Wow," I said.

"Wow is right."

"Can I have it? Can I have all these, please?" I tried not to look too eager, but every cell in my body wanted to scoop up the brochures, rush to my room to study them, to dream of climbing right into the beautiful photographs.

"Go ahead. You must be a first-time tourist."

I didn't think of myself as a tourist. I was there because of a promise I'd made, and the voices I'd heard over 103.9 FM back in Blue Ridge. Mountain Country Radio assured me that Nashville was the place for a person bitten by the singer/songwriter bug. "Um . . . I just like music."

"Wellllll, you come to the right place then. We got live music right here at the Best Western." Roy swept one arm out in a magnanimous gesture toward the other side of the lobby where I saw a doorway to what I'd figured was the dining area. A sign in the shape of a giant guitar pick said *Pick's*, and next to that was another that said *Great Drinks!*

"Y'all need anybody to sing at Pick's?"

"Naw. We got our bands booked a good ways in advance."

"Wonder where musicians who're looking for work hang out," I said in a casual voice, gathering the brochures.

"Nashville draws musicians like honey draws flies, and a body can't go ten yards without bumping into one of them looking for work. Tons of wannabes in here constantly, trying to make their way. Dreaming the dream."

From the tone of Roy's voice, I couldn't tell if he was trying to give me a warning or just stating facts. "Well, thank you," I said, turning to go.

"Wait. How long you plannin' to stay?"

Barring any unforeseen expenses, I knew about how far my much-fingered roll of $20 bills would go. The Manager's Special of $65 per night came out to two weeks for $910, leaving $90 for food and incidentals, and surely in that time I'd have some paid work singing. A recording contract if Mr. Anglin's prediction came true. Seeing his dear face in my mind's eye made a little guilty tremor race up my spine. I needed to get back to my room. "I paid for three nights up front," I said, turning to go again.

"Hey!" he called, spinning me on my heel to see those intense blue eyes looking at me. "You sing?"

I hesitated, then answered, "Yessir. Play *and* sing. Write all my own material."

"Well, well. What's your name, missy?"

"Jennifer Anne Clodfelter."

"Mighty big name for such a slip of a girl. Anybody ever tell you you're a dead ringer for Cher?"

I nodded. By twelve I was constantly compared to the dark, exotic celebrity when she was young, starring in the 1970's *Sonny & Cher Comedy Hour.* I was tall and willowy, and my straight blue-black hair fell to my waist. But, where Cher wasn't exactly well-endowed, I was ample in the bosom department. The other difference between me and Cher was that my eyes were green.

"So . . . . what style of music do you do, Jennifer Anne Clodfelter?"

I borrowed some confidence from Mac's words when he handed me my last paycheck. "I'm the next Patsy Cline."

"Alrighty." Roy chuckled. "Then let me guess. You do traditional? Or maybe early country?"

"Huh?"

"You said you're Patsy Cline. But, there's tons of styles. Got your Nashville sound and your country rock. Then there's rockabilly, bluegrass, honky-tonk, outlaw, and Bakersfield sound. Cowboy Western and Western swing. Oh!" he clucked his tongue. "About forgot Texas country style, and the new traditionalist, and can't leave out the contemporary sound, and of course, alternative. Though I don't cotton to alternative."

My heart started racing for fear my ignorance would show. "I'm the old kind of country."

"I see. So, you want to be a star?"

I saw mischief in those blue eyes, and I didn't know how to answer this question either. At last, I nodded.

That's when he began regarding me with amused pity. "If that's the case, you'll really want to be here a little longer. Actually," he paused and drew a long breath, "you'll want to be here nine years."

"Huh?"

Roy cleared his throat, and it seemed he stood on tiptoes because he rose up at least two inches. "Nashville may be the creative center of the universe if you're a singer and a songwriter—got all kinds of resources here for learning the industry, lots of places you can sing—but folks don't call her the nine-year town for nothing. They say it takes nine years to break into the scene, to become an overnight success. I've lived here all my life and I love her, but if you're looking to break into the music business, she can chew you up and spit you out like nobody's business."

I must've looked sad or confused because Roy's face softened, his voice grew smooth as silk, "You got people here?"

"I'm on my own." Four simple words—the truth of it stunned me.

"I got an extra room at my house."

"Um . . . thanks. No offense, but I'm fine on my own."

"Ain't trying to rain on your parade, but I've seen plenty have to wait tables or worse. Randy Travis was a cook and a dishwasher at the Nashville Palace before he could make it on his music. Seen a good number turn around and head home, too, tail tucked between their legs. You might need a place if—"

"I said I'm fine."

Roy rolled his lips inward, considering. "Independent type, hmm? Well, good luck. But don't worry if you change your mind." He drew in a long breath. "If you change your mind, you just come right on back and see Roy. I'm here most evenings after seven. I just figured if you're new around town, trying to make your way in the country music scene, it'd be good if you had somebody to fall back on."

Back in my room, I sat on the bed, Roy's words hanging over me like a dark cloud. *Chew you up and spit you out,* and *Folks don't call her the nine-year town for nothing.* Just like that, a dark cloud moved over me. This spirit of despair was something I often felt, and it had a Siamese twin who drove me to do really rash and stupid things. That was how I'd made my worst mistake to date, acting on blind impulse. And now impulses to bolt from Music City were gathering forces. I knew despair was the worst thing, the killer that blinded you to possibilities, and so I clenched my teeth, closed my eyes, and forced myself to go back all those years to a little scene that happened on the stretch of linoleum between the music room and the gym.

"Really, Jennifer, you have a gift you need to share with this world." It was between classes, and Mr. Anglin whispered in this intense voice, his small mouth barely moving against my ear. "Promise me you'll get these demos to Nashville." I recalled that his hands clenched into fists, even after I gave him my word that I'd do it. Mr. Anglin often reminded me he'd heard thousands of singers in his job of music teacher at the high school and choir director at the church, but I was the only one who'd ever moved him to tears. My songs and the way I sang them pierced his heart.

Speaking of hearts, Mr. Anglin had been well-loved, and his memorial service in April of my junior year had been a large affair involving the entire staff and a good number of the nine hundred students from Fannin County High, as well as a huge flock of people from the church. The odd thing was that Mr. Anglin's burial, prior to the service, was private. Mr. Anglin was a bachelor and had been an only child with no living parents, so there was no family to have requested this.

No family I could confess to . . .

After the service, when everyone was in the fellowship hall drinking coffee and eating cakes brought by dozens of church ladies, I walked out to the cemetery to see his stone. I put my hand over my heart and said, "I'm sorry. I had no idea you'd take it so hard. Please forgive me." I walked around Mr. Anglin's new home. He loved flowers, and toward the fringes of the graveyard, there was soft purple wisteria dripping from tree limbs. There were flowers near the graves, too, and I'm not talking about artificial arrangements poked down into stone vases. There were daffodils and dandelions in pretty shades of yellow, and a line of white irises. When a jot of blue caught my eye, right at the edge of where the dirt had been disturbed for Mr. Anglin's casket, I let out a little, "Hah!" and bent to pluck the tiny stem of a forget-me-not. I turned to Mr. Anglin's headstone again, and with tears in my eyes I said, "I won't forget you, ever. I promise I'll take the demos to Nashville." But even with this graveside declaration, I'd continued on the path of that heedless decision that put him there in the first place.

Here it was six years later, and I was only just beginning to honor my promise. I felt the slick brochures from Roy Durden and looked down at the bold words: The Country Music Hall of Fame & Museum. "I might be in the Hall of Fame one day," I said out loud, picturing myself with all those legends and pressing my free hand over my heart to feel a trembling hopefulness deep inside that moved outward making all of me shake. Then it was like I had this knowing, this sense that what I was imagining I could actually achieve. I hopped up, splashed cold water on my face, and took the elevator downstairs again.

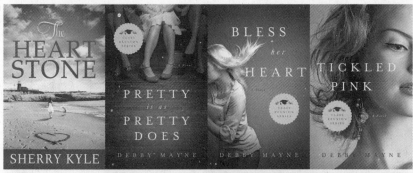
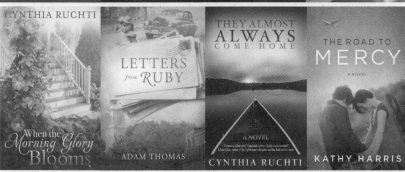